SCIENCE FICTION
IN THE TRADITION OF TOMORROW

Keith Roberts is one of the most exciting of the
writers responsible for science fiction's current
popularity. Since the publication of *PAVANE*—
his haunting chronicle of an alternate-England in
a modern Dark Age, where radio is a guild secret
and giant steam-lorries lumber across the
moors—he has been compared to Ursula Le Guin
and to Frank Herbert, author of *DUNE*, in his
power to weave the fabric of whole societies and
evoke the strangeness, wonder and depth that
marks science fiction at its greatest.

THE PASSING OF THE DRAGONS

THE SHORT FICTION OF KEITH ROBERTS

KEITH ROBERTS

A BERKLEY MEDALLION BOOK
published by
BERKLEY PUBLISHING CORPORATION

Berkley Publishing Corporation
200 Madison Avenue
New York, N.Y. 10016

SBN 425-03477-1

BERKLEY MEDALLION BOOKS are published by
Berkley Publishing Corporation
200 Madison Avenue
New York, N. Y. 10016

BERKLEY MEDALLION BOOK ® TM 757,375

Printed in the United States of America

Berkley Medallion Edition, APRIL, 1977

CONTENTS

THE PASSING OF THE DRAGONS

THE SHORT FICTION OF KEITH ROBERTS

The Deeps

It was bound to happen. For generations, the chain reaction of population explosion had been going on and on. While medical skill grew, while longevity increased nearly beyond belief, humankind everywhere bred and bred and bred. Houses, estates, factories to serve the vast new economies spread and sprawled, twitching out across good land and bad, climbing mountains, suffocating rivers. Town touched town, touched town; the pink octopus tentacles of houses grew and thickened as the machines graded and scraped and hammered. Green belts and parks vanished, fields were swallowed overnight. Here and there voices were raised; the voices of economists, scientists, philosophers, even at last theologians. But they were swamped in the great universal cry.

Give us room . . . The shout went up night and day from a hundred million throats, the slogan blared from loudspeakers, blazed from hoardings as political parties jockeyed for power. Increasingly, room was what they promised. Room for more houses, more estates, room to rear new families that cried in their turn for room and still more room . . .

All over the world countrysides vanished, eaten. Wars flared as nations bit at each other's borders, but still the Cities grew. The huge estates were searched, forced to yield their last acres, their secret gardens. And all for nothing, it seemed, because still the cry was heard for room. Skyscrapers soared, fifty stories, seventy, a hundred, and it was not enough. The Cities bulged outward, noisy with music and the sound of human life. A hundred yards thick they were and blaring with light, complex with stack on twinkling stack

1

of avenues. Raucous, Technicolored, sleepless. Everywhere, they reached the sea.

And they could not stop. The pressure, the need for room, pushed them out again. The houses sank like silver bells into blueness and quiet, and at last there was room enough.

● ● ●

Mary Franklin sat in the living area of her bungalow, knitting quiet for once in her lap, and tried to watch the telscreen at the other side of the room. Across her line of sight Jen passed scuttling, bare feet scuffing the carpet, the straps of her lung flapping round her shoulders. Across and back, then across again, frantic now, going to a party at the Belmonts on the other side of town, and late. Mary raised her eyes to heaven, represented temporarily by a curved steel shell. She concentrated on the screen where a demonstrator, in vivid colour, divulged to her audience the inner secrets of a variant of crawfish mayonnaise. Jen yelped something inaudible from the bedroom, thumped the wall. (Why . . . ?) She padded across again and back. Mary raised her voice suddenly.

'Jen . . . ?'

Thump. Mumble.

'*Jen!*'

'Mummy, I can't find my . . .' Indistinguishable.

'Jen, you're not to be late. No more than nine, understand?'

'Yes . . .'

'And for *land's* sake child, *put something on* . . .'

'Yes, Mummy . . .' That in a high voice, wearily. And almost instantly the roar of the sealock. Mary got up in quick rage, walked halfway to the radio gear, changed her mind, went back to her chair. Jen, she knew well enough, would conveniently have forgotten her phone-leads.

She kicked the channel switch irritably in passing; the picture on the wallscreen jumped and altered. The set began to disgorge a Western; Mary lay back, eyes nearly shut, half her mind in the ancient film and half on the blueness overhead. The endless blue.

Jen, defiantly bare, hung twenty feet above the hemispherical roof of her home. Bubbles from her breathing rose in a series of shimmering, dimly seen sickles to the Surface overhead. As always, the sea had made her forget her compulsion to hurry; she began to paddle slowly, feet in their long fins catching and driving back wedges of water. As she moved she looked below her, at the lines of domes with their neat, almost suburban gardens of waving weed. She saw the misty squares of their windows, the brighter greeny-blue globes of the streetlighting swung from thin wires above the ocean bed. Warnings were hung on long streamers of wires for swimmers; there were well-marked lanes, corresponding to the streets of the city complexes Jen barely remembered, but many people ignored them. And most of the children. Technically she was out of bounds now, gliding along like this only a few feet from Surface.

Visibility was good tonight; onshore winds could kick up a smother that lasted for days, but there had been nearly a week of calm. Jen could make out through the almost haze-free water the faint shimmer where the engineers, her father among them, were working on the new extension to the theatre and civic centre. When it was finished, the installation would be the pride of Settlement Eighty, the town its inhabitants called Oceanville. There were a dozen other Oceanvilles scattered up and down this one stretch of coast, hundreds possibly in all the seas of the world. She shivered slightly although the water was not cold.

Beyond the lights, beyond where the divers floated round the tall steel skeletons, were long sloping stretches where the town buildings petered out and the coral and sand of the inshore waters gave place to the silt of real ocean. There was a graveyard, tiny as yet, where a few bodies lay in their metal cans; beyond again, past grey dunes where the light faded imperceptibly to navy blue and black, were the Deeps. Above anything else Jen liked to go to the new buildings, sit on one of the girders, look down into the vagueness that was the proper sea, bottomless and immense. Just stare, and listen, and wait. She would go there tonight maybe, after the party.

She let herself relax, holding air in her lungs to increase buoyancy. Her body floated upward, legs and arms slack; Surface appeared above her, a faintly luminous upside-down plain. Points of light sparkled where the moon-track refracted into the depths. Jen wagged lazily with her flippers, once, twice; her body broke the Surface and she felt herself lifted by the slight action of the waves.

She looked round. The sea was flatly calm, dark at the horizon, glinting with bluish swirls of phosphorescence round her shoulders and neck. When she looked closely, she could see the organisms that made the light floating in it like grains of brightness. Way off was the orange cloud reflection over the land, where the universal Cities bawled and yammered. Jen lay still, supported by the water. Once she would have pulled her mask aside, breathed in the wet salt of ordinary air. Now she felt no desire to do so. She turned slowly, treading water, took a last look at the moon, and dived. Her heels stirred up a momentary flash of light. Once below she moved powerfully, stroking with her arms. She arrowed down to West Terrace where the Belmonts had their dome. The party would be in full swing already; she was missing good dancing time.

Hours later, Mary prodded one of her rare cigarettes from the wall dispenser. She frowned a little, drawing in smoke and letting it dribble from her nostrils. She lay back and watched the fumes being sucked toward the ceiling vent. The telscreen was off; the last badman had bitten the dust and she had grown tired of watching. The bungalow seemed very quiet; the buzz of the air conditioning plant sounded unusually loud, as did the recurring clink-thump of the refrigerator solenoids from the kitchen.

She stood uncertainly, fingered her throat, took a step, paused. She went to the alcove by the kitchen that housed the radio link and telephone. Beside the handset the dome metering equipment chuckled faintly. Inside the grey housings striped discs spun, needles wavered against their dials. Force of habit made her check the readings. All normal, of course . . . She touched the phone, pulled at her lip with her teeth, made herself take her hand away. A quarter of an hour, that was nothing. When she was dancing Jen forgot the time. They all did. She would be home in a few minutes, by nine-thirty at the latest. She knew exactly how long to outstay an order . . . Mary went back to the living area, turned the telscreen on, clicked the channel switch to five. While the set was warming she walked through to David's cubicle, peered in. He was asleep, hair tousled on the pillow.

Nine-fifty.

Mary got up again, walked to the window in the curved wall. She drew the curtains back, looked across the street at the neighbouring houses visible through the faint residual haze. A little fear stirred somewhere at the back of her mind, throbbed, stilled itself again. She wondered, fear of what? Accidents maybe; they happened, even in the best-run towns. Jack—but it wasn't that. She laughed at herself quietly, trying to shrug away her fit of nerves.

These late shifts of her husband's were a curse but there was no help for them; the new building was going ahead fast and as engineering controller for the sector Jack had to be almost constantly on site. She told herself, physically her husband was not far away. She could ring him if she had to. How far off was the new complex, a hundred and fifty yards, two hundred? No distance, by terrestrial standards . . . But here under the sea, just how far was a hundred yards? Could be a lifetime, or an epoch. She grimaced. That was what the fear was about, what the . . . throb . . . tried to tell her maybe. That under the sea, patterns and values could change ineradicably.

She sat down, crossed her knees, laid her head against the back of the chair. After a few moments she picked up the abandoned knitting and stared at it. She was making a sweater, though there was no point in the exercise. The domes were air-conditioned and sea temperature only varied a few degrees through the year; nobody needed sweaters down here and the yarn was expensive. It came from Surface and all Surface things were dear. But it was something to do, it kept her hands busy. Above all, it was a link with the past.

Ten o'clock.

The face of the clock was round and sea-blue, the hands plain white needles. They moved in one-minute jerks; Mary imagined that she could see the tiny quiver that preceded each jump. She stubbed out the cigarette. The party would be long finished now, the dancers dispersed.

Dancers? She shook her head. She could remember the dancing in the Cities, the pulsing rhythms, frenetic jerking. That pattern, like everything else, had changed. She remembered the first time she had heard what they called sea-jazz, the shock it had given her. Jen had a player in her bedroom, it wailed and bumped half the night, but the rhythms, the melodies, were like nothing she had ever heard landside. The music howled and dragged, the beats developed timings that defied notation, had in them something of the slow surge of the tides. It was music for swimming to.

The Belmonts had a dance floor but it was outside, in the sea. Airposts surrounded it, and speaker casings; round them the kids would swirl like pale flakes among the hordes of fish that always seemed to be attracted. 'But Mummy,' Jen would say if she protested. 'You just don't *gel*, you're not *wavy* . . .' It was all part of the new phraseology; the boy down the block, Kev Hartford wasn't it, he *gelled* for Jen, he was a *wave*; but the lad from the airplant, Cy Scheinger who had visited once or twice, was out of favour. He was *neapy*, a *scorp*. (Scorpion fish?) The sea, and thoughts of the sea, pervaded their whole lives now even to the language they spoke. Which was natural, and as it should be . . .

Why did we call her Jennifer? Why, of all the names we could have used? The Jennifer was a sea-thing, and accursed . . .

It was no use. Mary killed the sound from the screen, walked back to the phone, lifted the handset and dialled. She listened to the clicking of the exchange relays, the faint purr-purr at the other end of the line. An age, and the receiver was lifted.

'Ye-es?' The slight coo in the voice, unmistakable even through the surging distortion of the sea. The Belmonts were just a little conscious of their status; Alan Belmont was fisheries manager for the area. Mary licked her lips. 'Hello? Hello, Anne, this is Mary. Mary Franklin . . . What? Yes, fine thank you . . . Anne . . . is Jen still at your place by any chance? I told her nine, she's late, I wondered if . . .'

Anne Belmont sounded vaguely surprised. 'My dear, I shooed them off positively hours ago. Well, an hour . . . Hold the line . . .'

Unidentifiable human sounds. Someone calling faintly. The wash . . . crash . . . of the sea.

'Hello?'

'Yes . . .'

'Just before nine,' said the phone. 'We sent them all off, there's no one here now . . . You say she's not back?'

'No,' said Mary. 'No, she's not.' Her knuckles had whitened on the handset.

The phone clucked. 'My dear, they're all the same; ours are hopeless, time means *nothing*, absolutely *nothing* . . . But I'm quite *sure* you needn't worry, she'll be along any moment. Perhaps she's with that *Cy* boy, whatever his name is . . . yes . . .'

Ice along the spine, moving out like fingers that gripped and clutched. 'Thank you,' said Mary. 'No, no, of course not. Yes, I'll let you know . . . Yes, goodbye Anne . . .' She laid the handset on its cradle, stood looking at it, not knowing what to do. The sea pushed at the dome gently, slurringly.

A quarter after ten.

Mary stood very still in the middle of the living area, lips pursed. She had called the airworks; Cy was off duty, could not be traced. And two or three neighbours and friends. No Jen. She could not ring Jack at the construction office, not again. Down here you helped your husband, pulled your weight. You didn't run panicking at every little thing . . . The trembling had started, in her legs; she rubbed her thighs unconsciously through her dress. She touched the hair pinned into a chignon at the nape of her neck. In front of her, on the sill of the window, a plaster foal pranced, hooves outlined against greenness. The greenness was the sea.

Decision. She pulled at her hair, shook it free round her shoulders. She unsnapped the clasp at her neck, wriggled her dress up over her head. Beneath it she wore the conventional blue leotard of a married woman. She plucked automatically at the high line of the legs, kicked her sandals off, crossed to the equipment locker. She came back with her sea gear, lung, mask and flippers. She dressed quickly, fastening the broad straps round her waist and between her legs, the lighter shoulder harness that held the meter panel across her chest. Habit again made her check the dials, valve air, slap the red cancellator-tab on her shoulder. That was another safety factor; if for any reason air stopped flowing from the pack and that tab was not touched, a built-in radio beacon would arrow town guards down to the wearer.

She looked in at David again, satisfied herself he was still sleeping. She walked to the sealock, stopped on the way to see herself in the half-length mirror. She was heavier now, her hips had broadened and there were maybe faint worry lines round her mouth. But her hair was brown and soft; landside she would still be a desirable woman.

She looked round the dome slowly, seeming to see familiar things in a new light that was bright and strange. The bungalow was double-skinned, the inner ceiling finished in octagonal plates of white and pale blue plastic. The half-round shape, dictated by considerations of pressure, had the secondary advantage of enclosing the greatest possible volume of space; deep-pile carpets covered the floors, the furniture was low and streamlined, easy to live with. The telscreen was tucked neatly into an alcove; to each side of it were wall tanks with fish and anemones. Through a half-open door she could see the kitchen. It was miniaturised but well equipped, with plenty of stainless steel like the galley of a ship.

The whole bungalow was as safe as it was functional. In the unlikely event of a fracture in the pressure shell, the second skin would hold the sea while instantaneous warnings were flashed to a central exchange, ensuring help within minutes. Not that anything could or would go wrong of course, the whole system was too carefully worked out for that. People had been living undersea for years now, and fatalities were far fewer than on the overcrowded land.

Mary grimaced, stepped through into the lock and closed the inner hatch. The ceiling lamp came on; she pressed the filler control, heard the hiss as air was expelled through the outlet valves.

She squatted in rising water to work the straps of the flippers over her heels, straightened up. The coolness touched her hips; she pushed her hair back, spat in the mask and rinsed it, pressed the transparent visor onto her face. The plastic was self-adhesive, moulded to her skull contour; it fitted from forehead to chin. She palmed the earphones into place, reached under her arm for her mike leads, flicked the tags onto the magnetic contacts in her throat. The compartment filled, water rising greenly over her head. As the pressure equalised, the outer segment of wall slid aside automatically, letting in the hazy glow of the street lighting. Mary kicked away and floated up from the dome, sensing the old lift as the sea shucked off her weight. Her hair swirled across her eyes gracefully, like fronds of black fern.

She swam slowly across the town. To each side, lines of round-topped buildings marched out of the haze. Some of the houses were still new and bright with their coated steel skins, others had grown a rich waving cover of algae. In the main street the shop windows were brightly lit; the plate-glass ports displayed seafoods set on white dishes garnished with fronds of weed; there were aqualungs and radiophones, Surface ware of all sorts, clothes and books, records, dolls, toys. Here the ocean floor had been cleared to the rock that underlay the sand; overhead were slim arches to which were moored the sledges of out-of-towners, the fish herders and oceanographers whose work took them to lonely domes scattered over the bed of the sea. There were lights on the gantries; each globe hung glaring in greenness, surrounded by a flickering cloud of tiny fish like moths round a terrestrial lamp. Over everything was an air of peace, the dreamy peace of dusk on an ancient, unspoiled Earth.

There were few human swimmers about, but here and there, careering over the roofs of buildings, Mary caught sight of glistening shapes. Dolphins—they had been quick to discover the sea-floor communities and take advantage of them. Many families, in fact, kept one or more of them as semipermanent pets, became very attached to them. Other creatures occasionally troubled the townships—sharks, rays, the odd squid. But the repellants carried by the swimmers in their harness had been developed to a stage where there was little to fear. The town guards could be relied on to harpoon or shoo off any of the big fellows who hung around too close or too long, though in the main there was little to attract predators.

Disposal of garbage was rigidly controlled; locking offal into the sea was about the worst crime in the book, it could result in being sent landside. The 'monsters of the deep', in so far as they existed, tended to avoid the colonies. They disliked the brightness and noise, the bustle, the thud of many vibrations criss-crossing in the water. As Jack never tired of pointing out, life down here was as safe or safer than on land.

Mary doubled back, passing the king-size domes that held the town distillation plant. The per capita consumption of fresh water was fifty percent higher for Sea People than for Terrestrials. Frequent bathing was necessary to remove ingrained salt from the skin; supplying salt-free water was one of the biggest problems of the ocean-floor settlements. Beyond the distillery was the airworks. The electrolysers reached halfway to the Surface, each mass of tubes contained in an insulating shell of helium. The current for the oxygen separation came from strategically sited tidal generating stations up and down the coast. Many domes were already on tap from the plant; eventually they would all avail themselves of the new municipal service, though they would retain their own gear as a fail-safe in case of emergency.

Mary swam round the huge stacks, peering into locked shadows, calling softly through her mask. 'Jen . . . Jen . . .' The harness pack radiated the word into the water, farther than a human voice could reach in air, but there was no answer. She clung to a steel stay twenty feet above the seabed. Bubbles curled up from her in a shimmering stream as she tried to quiet her breathing. A group of children went by, out late and swimming fast; she heard their chattering, realised with a cold shock how similar it was to the noises of a fish herd in the hydrophones. She shivered. Thoughts like that had been plaguing her for months now, maybe years. She called urgently, but the child-shoal swerved aside, accelerating and vanishing in the gloom. There was quiet; beside her the great cans vibrated, the sensation more felt than heard. The stay seemed to buzz in her fingers.

She let go quickly, because electrolyser stacks cannot make any sound. She concentrated. That deep, thudding boom . . . Was it her heart, or just fear, or was there something . . . something else . . . No, it was gone. Slipped over the edge of perception, into silence. She started to swim again, thoughts churning confusedly. She remembered a conversation she had had with her husband weeks back. They had been lying abed after his shift had done; the house was silent, or as silent as it could get. Just the airplant, buzzing in the dark . . .

She had spoken to blackness. 'Jack,' she said, wondering at herself, 'the Deeps. Have you heard what they've been saying about them—that they talk?'

'I've heard a lot of rubbish.'

She said, 'They talk. That's what the kids say. Jen . . . she says she's heard it a . . . thing, I don't know what. A calling. Jack, be serious, listen to me . . .'

'I am serious,' he said. 'Completely. Mary, there's nothing in the Deeps except one hell of a lot of water, at one hell of a pressure. Oh, there could be a slip somewhere, volcanic activity maybe, a long way down, that would send up pressure waves, you might be able to feel them, but that's all. I'm an engineer, I've been working with the sea more years than I want to think about, now take my word, I *know*. This . . . thing, it's a fad with the kids. You get little gangs floating out there waiting for revelations, I've seen 'em. I don't know where it started but it's just a craze, it'll die off when something new comes along . . .'

She was quiet, thinking of all the towns stretching through the warm seas of the world, all along the Continental shelves. The domes were snug and secure, automated; nothing could go wrong. But what if . . . what if there was an enemy, something more insidious than pressure? Something in people, in me she told herself, or in Jen. Something working outward from the roots of the brain . . . She said abruptly, 'Jack, how can you be so damn sure you're always right?'

The bed creaked as he moved. 'You going Continental on me, Mary?'

She did not answer. His hand reached the contacts on her throat, stroked. 'You know what I told you. What we agreed when they put these in. Once down, always down.' He paused. Then, softly, 'What's for us on land?'

She lay remembering the lowness of the roofed City streets, the flaring miles of fluorescent strip, the crushing sense of overcontact. Hive phobia of a crowded planet.

He could play her mind, he always could. 'Listen,' he said. 'You can still hear it deep down. The roaring. Escalators, pedivators. Traffic. Dancehalls. Wallscreens all yelling, fighting one against another. Buy this. Buy that. Vote for freedom. Use our toothpaste. Don't copulate . . . Just remember it, Mary. Markets. Moviehouses. The whole heaped-up, tipped-up jumble we made for ourselves. Is that a thing to go back to? Take the kids to? Well is it?'

No answer. He carried on talking. The old vision. 'Down here we've got peace. We've got security. Well, as much security as people can find anywhere. And more important, we've got a democracy. A real practical working democracy, maybe for the first time ever. Down here your neighbour's house is always open because that's the way it has to be. We can't afford to fight each other, the sea takes care of that. And the sea's forever.

'So we've got unity, and drive. Right now maybe you reckon there's a lot of us but I say we're still villages, settlements. We're dependent on Surface, we still buy down supplies. But it won't always be like that. I can see whole nations and tribes of us scattered over the oceans, everywhere in the world. Right down into the Deeps. We'll be independent. We'll draw everything we need straight out of the sea: Gold, tin, lead, copper, uranium, you name it you'll find it's right here in the sea. Billions of tons of it, waiting to be used. In a small way we've started already. The land's old, burned out. Let the Continentals keep it . . .' He chuckled. 'Tell you what, we'll pop up one day, in a thousand years maybe, for a little trade. Find they've gone. All of them. Blown each other apart, starved, lit out for the planets, anywhere. We wouldn't know. If the whole world burned up, how should we tell? We shouldn't care . . .'

She was making patterns in blackness, drawing on the pillow with one finger. Biting her lip. He touched her hair; his hand found the pendant warmth of a breast and she moved irritably, twisting away from him. 'I was thinking,' she said, 'about the kids. All the kids we've got down here—'

'All the kids,' he said tiredly. 'Mary, all the kids have *changed*. Adapted to their surroundings, now that's the most natural thing. We'd be having to worry if it wasn't happening. This environment, after all it's alien. Outside racial experience. In a sense this life of ours is being lived on a new planet. We must expect new skills, new adaptations, and they'll show in the children quicker because the children have known nothing else. That's the way it has to be, that way's right. This has taken a long time coming out in you, Mary, can't you see what's happening?'

'I can,' she said bitterly. 'Can you?'

'Mary, listen here a minute . . .'

She felt that obscurely he was still hedging. His mind maybe would automatically reject anything that could not be measured and calibrated. She wanted to scream; the confidence, the know-how, suddenly it all seemed so much smugness. The sea was infinite, from it could come an infinity of fears. She said, 'We all . . . they say we all came from the sea. Well, couldn't we . . . regress, you know, sort of slip back . . .'

He clicked on the bedside light. 'Mary, do you have any clear idea what you're saying?'

She nodded vigorously, trying to make him understand. 'I thought it all through, Jack. I mean about birds losing their wings and seals—didn't seals go back into the sea, degenerate somehow? And now us, the children, they . . . swim like fish, more and more like fish . . .'

'But hell,' he said, 'Mary, do you know how *long* a thing like that takes? A biological degeneration? How many millions of . . . Oh look, Mary, look here. A million years. That's how long we've been around, give or take a few thousand. And that's nothing, nothing at all. It isn't . . . that.' He snapped his fingers. 'You're thinking on the fine scale, the historical scale. All that time, that million years, wasn't enough for us to lose our little toes. Look, the Earth's a day old. Took twenty-four hours to evolve, go through all the cycles of life and get to us. You know what we are, what all our history is? The last tick of the clock . . . That's how long evolution takes, it's a very big thing . . .'

But it was no use, she'd heard it all before. 'Maybe it won't be like that this time,' she said. 'We . . . evolved that quick, at the end. Maybe we'll go back now just as fast . . .'

'It isn't anything to do with it,' he said. 'Nothing at all.'

She said desperately, 'We were so smart, Jack, getting out like this, living in the sea. Making a new world. But maybe . . . couldn't that somehow be what the sea really wanted, all along? What we were *meant* to do? Oh, I know this sounds crazy but believe me when I see the kids . . . Jen slipped the other day, in the kitchen. When she tried to get up, I think she tried to turn like she was swimming—she forgot she was in air . . . And David, he swims just like a little shrimp . . . When I see things like that I think . . . Oh, I don't know what I think sometimes—maybe we're not . . . pioneers at all. This thing about the Deeps, they say they call, pull . . . Maybe we're just sort of being sucked back, that's where we belong . . .'

He was angry, finally. 'All right. So this craziness is all true. We've got a racial memory in our brains; in our nervous systems. We remember the beginnings of life all those years back, so many years we can't even count the thousands. Well then, we're home already, Mary. Right where we are, this is where life started. In the shallows, swilling in the sunlight. Not in the Deeps. It moved down there, same time some of it spread onto land. There's nothing can call us from there. We don't belong there, never did.'

She was quivering a little, looking at the pillow, seeing the texture of it. Every strand in the weave of the cloth. 'I wanted to stay human,' she said. 'That was all. Just to stay human, and the kids . . .'

He touched her. 'You're human,' he said. 'You're all right.'

She wouldn't look at him. 'I think,' she said, 'I think now . . . I'd take the Cities. Jack . . .'

He didn't answer, and she knew the expression on his face without looking. Something inside her seemed to twist and become cold. He would do anything for her maybe, except that. He would not go landside, not now. The empires, the herds and tribes of the sea, they were in his brain, they called too. The dream was too strong, he couldn't let it go.

He pushed the clothes back and swung his legs off the bed. She heard the little swish as he picked up a robe. 'Mary,' he said, 'why don't you get a little checkup? You're run down, it's my fault. I should have realised . . . Too much time on your own, you don't get about. Not any more. Maybe you should have a trip landside. Go and see your folks. Tell you what—I'll get a couple of days leave, we'll have a run up to Seventy-five, take the kids, how's that? They've got the new theatre up there, whole pile of junk. Sound okay?'

She didn't answer. 'I'll have a talk with Jen,' she said. 'I'll do it tomorrow. This is silliness, it can be stopped . . .' He walked out, turned on a light. Started tinkering in the kitchen. He brought her back coffee laced with rum. She pulled a bedjacket over her shoulders, sat drinking, hands gripped round the warmth of the cup. Feeling the trembling still deep in her body, hearing the buzz of the airplant, imagining the silly, silly meters checking and recording. Pressure, humidity, oxy-level, all the things that didn't matter. While Jack sat and watched her, smoked and smiled and did not understand . . .

Mary swam the length of the town again, moving slowly, watching to right and left the domes nestling in shadow, their windows like square bright eyes. The sea was darker now; in the real world above, the moon was setting. Surface was just visible as a greyish sheen; tall weed fronds were silhouetted against it, leaning majestically to the current like trees bowed by an endless wind. The tide was setting out, toward the Deeps.

After that talk with her husband, her restlessness had become worse. Quite suddenly it seemed the whole furnishing of the dome was oppressive, stultifying. The curtains had come down, the glinting blue fabric with its faint interlapping tidal patterns had been put away. Mary had hung new yellow cloth, sun-yellow, printed with designs of buds and flowering trees. She had banished the spiny amber-spotted shells and the urchin lamps, Jen's untidy collection of sea bed fossils, even the cushion covers on which she herself had once worked swirling Minoan patterns of weed and octopi. In their places were landside things, figurines of horses and kittens, panting china dogs. Creatures long vanished now but that reminded her of Earth and the way humans lived once on a time.

Every ornament, every yard of cloth, had had to be bought from Surface; the cost had been enormous but once started Mary had seemed unable to stop. Jack had raised his eyebrows but said nothing; Jen had protested more noisily.

Things had reached crisis pitch the day Mary found, in the wall tank in Jen's room, a piece of old human skull, coral-crusted, put there as a home for crabs. She had slapped her daughter for that, a thing she had never done before, and emptied tank and contents through the lock. Jen had fled squalling, into the sea, and not come home for hours. After that Mary spent a week scraping the whole top of the dome, polishing away the velvet coat of sea-growth till the plastic-covered panels gleamed like new; but it seemed the more she did, the more she tried to banish the presence of the sea from her home, the more the sea invaded. At night, lying quiet, she imagined she could feel the slow push of the wave force against the bungalow, tilting it this way and that, slow, slow, this way . . . then that . . .

She drove herself across to West Terrace, built slightly higher than the rest of town on a curving ridge of rock. Nearly to the Belmonts' dome and back, calling all the way. Jen was not in town; or if she was, she refused to answer. Mary's face was wet now inside the mask and her lungs were labouring. Thoughts tumbled in her mind. Nitrogen narcosis . . . no longer possible, the lungs delivered an oxy-helium mix. Oxygen intoxication then, the thing they used to call rapture of the depths; that could make you throw your mask off, breathe water and die. But it was nearly unheard of. Low down on Mary's back, and on Jen's, were other contacts. They led to cells deep in the body that metered the blood itself, tasting it for oxy-content. The lungs were self-compensating. Pack failure? Crazy, the gulp-bottle on Jen's belt would give her twenty minutes' breathing. And the beacon, there was the beacon. But beacons could go out . . .

Mary doubled, swerving under the rigging of the street lamps. Across to where she could see the divers working on the new building complex. The bodies hung round the curving ribs, tiny with distance, silver as fish under the glare of the lamps; below, the windows of the construction office just showed in the gloom. Soon she would call Jack, she would have to . . . She felt the fear again, like a coldness round her heart. There was only one place she had not been. She began to swim purposefully away from the town and its lights, towards the Deeps.

Just beyond the domes the sea bed fell away in a series of troughs, miles long and wide. Unseen, their contours could still appal the mind. This was the frontier, the last frontier maybe on the planet. She passed over the graveyard, trying not to see the frail crosses sticking up from the silt, name tags fluttering in the current like grey leaves. Out to where the last light faded, and beyond . . .

She was in a void, bottomless, pit-black. Above her a vagueness that was just one shade less dark than darkness itself. Not light; some trailing ghost maybe, that light had left behind it. Mary drove deeper, hopelessly, feeling pressure begin to squeeze her body like cold hands. She was panting, though there was no sound of it in her ears; her breathing alone could not activate the throat mike. She called again; her voice was a vibrating thread, nearly lost in immensity.

And there was something, a blemish in the gulf. Tiny, nearly invisible, its shape so vague it mocked the retinas. Mary swam, hair flowing; there was a longness, a paleness, like a body caught and floating on some denser stratum of the sea. Deep down, far below . . .

'*Jen!*'

Mary kicked out, desperate now, her movements losing smoothness and coordination. Fighting the pressure was like butting at a wall; she imagined her whole body shrinking, condensing, becoming tiny as a fish.

'JEN!'

She'd reached the thing, she was stretching for it with her hands, when it moved. Eeled away, rolled . . . She saw the bright cloud of breathing suddenly released, the fins threshing. Heard her daughter chuckling in her earphones.

Fear turned to anger. Mary arced in the water. 'Jen, get back this *instant* . . .' She grabbed again and the girl eluded her, quick as a fish. 'Mummy, *listen* . . .' The voice bubbled through the sea. 'It's loud tonight, *listen* . . .'

She listened, straining. Found herself not breathing. It was impossible; no outside sound could come through her blocked ears. Nonetheless, it came. There, and again . . . A thudding, but not a thudding. Some pressure, like a concussion against the brain. Immeasurably slow and powerful and somehow *ancient* . . . Pulsing with her heart, fading, swelling back to touch her body. Earthquake or volcano, she had no idea. Nor did she care. Somehow it was sufficient that the sensation, the not-sound, was there. This was something immemorial, eternal. The true, dark, jet-blue voice of the sea . . .

Woman and girl hung a little apart, bodies vaguely glowing motes against a hugeness of water. Mary felt she could lie all night, not speaking, just soaking in the strangeness that seemed to fill her by rich stages from feet to head. Hearing rhythms that were not rhythms, that blended and crossed, melding each into each like the sounds of the sea-jazz. Soothing, calming, somehow *warm* . . .

She could hear Jen calling but the voice was unimportant, remote. It was only when the girl swam to her, grabbed her shoulders and pointed at the gauges between her breasts that she withdrew from the half-trance. The thing below still called and thudded; Mary turned reluctantly, found Jen's hand in her own. She let herself float, Jen kicking slowly and laughing again delightedly, chuckling into her earphones. Their hair, swirling, touched and mingled;

Mary looked back and down and knew suddenly her inner battle was over.

The sound, the thing she had heard or felt, there was no fear in it. Just a promise, weird and huge. The Sea People would go on now, pushing their domes lower and lower into night, fighting pressure and cold until all the seas of all the world were truly full; and the future, whatever it might be, would care for itself. Maybe one day the technicians would make a miracle and then they would flood the domes and the sea would be theirs to breathe. She tried to imagine Jen with the bright feathers of gills floating from her neck. She tightened her grip on her daughter's hand and allowed herself to be towed, softly, through the darkness.

Therapy 2000

It was the earplugs that started the trouble. Or rather the absence of earplugs, the difficulties Travers encountered trying to purchase such an antique and potentially unsociable commodity. Although he had of course prepared a cover story; in fact he had four, each vaguely less credible than the last. But not even as a laboratory technician conducting experiments in a new and highly secret project concerned with sonic warfare was he successful. Earplugs were not to be had.

Once implanted though, the notion wouldn't leave him. He developed the reprehensible habit of stuffing his ears with assorted scraps of paper, tissue, anything that lay to hand. He considered the Sound-absorbing properties of a wide range of substances. Hot wax at one time seemed a possibility; but there was no way of controlling its runniness. Working on one's own perhaps, one's head turned thus, sideways on the table . . . His one experiment was a messy failure. Wax was definitely out; but other things, equally definitely, were in.

He became absentminded. His vagueness manifested itself in increasingly painful attempts to ram further objects into ears already stuffed to capacity. The trouble was of course, the whole trouble was, that nothing *lasted*. A few minutes, perhaps only seconds, of delirious numbness, the total lack of auditory sensation; then Sound would once more begin to seep and creep in at the edges, through the interstices of the wadding; and there were the devils again, albeit muted, hoofing and pounding inside his skull.

He developed a new theory, one that despite scientific implausibility he was unable to drive from his mind. In essence, it was that the plugs *soaked up* noise, became soggy with din and therefore permeable. His fresh preoccupation dictated rapid, frenetic changing of plugs and alternation of materials. Ceramics were in now, and well greased hand-carved wood. These latter masterpieces he lay regularly in the sink, ostensibly to drain.

This was Travers' life. At dawn, with the Dicky Dobson Rise and Glow Show, he obediently rose. Two hours later—two hours of Sporting Roundup, and the Humming Hillbillies, and Keeling Cocos Walker and his Set and the News in Brief and Howdy Again Folks and all the rest—the interlock tube disgorged him at his place of work, the forty-storey highrise topped, as a cake is topped with icing, by the two floors and mezzanine annex of Maschler-Crombie-Cohen Associates. There it was his pleasure to paste up an endless flow of newssheet small ads, juggling objects as disparate as hormone cream and harmonicas into proper relationships with the fat-face type, the bursting stars and dollar signs that since time immemorial had been deemed fitting to proclaim their excellence.

'Pasteup man'—the ad game, for decades now merely the poor relation of the PR industry and one of the more conservative of professions, still attached such antique labels to its minions. In fact Travers used a Grant and Digby, a bulky combination of epidiascope and dyeline printer that enabled images to be enlarged, reduced, squeezed, expanded and jazzed up at pleasure before being fixed by the simple pressure of a button. It was a nice machine; some illusion almost of privacy might be gained once Travers had involved himself in the intricacies of its various folding black plastic hoods. Though even there, of course, the office din penetrated. No video, naturally; but the wallspeakers belched forth, for the stipulated Union minimum of six and one-quarter hours a day, their repetitions interlaced with the irate shouts of the studio manager pursuing this or that vanished example of still life: and of course each artist had his own Mintran propped beside him so that at any one instant the total effect might be enriched by tinny renderings of subjects as far removed as Puccini and mid-twentieth-century Progressive Jazz.

At sixteen hundred hours Travers tubed homeward to begin his long evening of leisure. The tubecars were all fitted with Trivee now; he wondered how the youngsters had ever sustained their short journeys without it. He himself, he had decided, was no longer young. He could remember tubecars without Trivee, and many other things; after all he had given twelve years of his working life now to the Grant and Digby. Once indeed while shaving—the twenty-first century, in other respects the acme of technological perfection, had not as yet universally disposed of the human whisker—he discovered a single fairly long white hair. He told Deidre about it that night; but she merely laughed at him in the cool slow way she had, and told him how little age mattered to real men and women, and kissed him and ran away to throw a pebble in the sea.

This was Travers' life in the evenings. The tubecar dropped him again at the foot of his own Elbee. Then he would ride the elevator —they were talking about Trivee for elevators too now, he'd read—past floor after shouting floor to his own room on the forty-third. Though the phrase 'own room' struck him from time to time as curious. If by some mischance he happened to find himself one day not in Room 633 but in another of the eight hundred-odd cream-and-floral plastic boxes that comprised the Living Block, how, he wondered, would he divine that the cell was not his own, his private, personal and totally secure fragment of twenty-first century culture? From little marks perhaps, dents, scuffings on the walls where from time to time he had hurled objects in those fits of childish pique that seemed to be becoming more frequent with him. The missiles of course provoked no reaction; so Sound-soaked were the walls that one crash more or less had become as nothing between friends. So Travers' boots, the condiments from his meagre eats cupboard and occasionally Travers himself, were projected against yielding, translucent walls of rose-budded plastic behind which shadows that were human and shadows that were electronic bawled and strutted throughout the livelong day. And through all but a fragment of the livelong night.

But how precious that remaining fragment! Travers had long since counted the number and decided on the exact disposition of the Trivee sets within his immediate range of hearing. Basically, he was surrounded. Above and below, naturally; and on two sides. The third side of the room, the corridor partition, though by no means impervious, provided the nearest approach to a dead area. The fourth side was the party-wall of a toilet. There was no window. Rooms with windows were expensive; eighty dollars a week against the mere fifty Travers paid for his pad. Not that the absence of a view perturbed him unduly. He was, or had become, impervious to views. He had not, unfortunately, become impervious to Sound; an outside wall would have afforded him another slight zone of quiet, rendered less multidirectional the continuous assault on his senses.

                              *   *   *

Travers lived what amounted to his life in the three hours between the Wee Small Show (that came after the Late Show and the Late Late Show) and the dawn chorus of the inimitable Dicky Dobson. At one time, the gap in transmission had lasted four hours. Before that, four and a half. Travers had watched its remorseless closing with terror and dismay, rather as a primitive man might observe, frowning, the inexorable swallowing of the sun during an eclipse. Once indeed the gap had been reduced to a mere two hours; but (possibly for the first time) God had come to Travers' aid. Not admittedly in His own person but through the offices of Walk-In-Light, that immensely powerful body with cells in every country of the globe. Travers heard the announcement perforce, one evening; in accordance with the illimitable possibilities of mathematics, three neighbouring Trivees had at last become tuned to the same channel and the results penetrated the latest version of the Travers Sanity Protector with tolerable ease. The declaration was made by the Chairman of Walk-In-Light in person; at megadollar expense, he reported proudly, the Corporation had negotiated one hour's Silence per day, for meditation and for prayer. Presumably there was an outcry; but Walk-In-Light were rich, very rich indeed, and the ban had held. Travers, in gratitude and curiosity, had even sent for their pamphlet, *Salvation*; it came in a Manila-tinted plastic envelope on which a naked man and woman, both tastefully sexless, held up arms to an engulfing orange sun. Travers was intrigued; not so much, admittedly, by the prospect of Immortal Friendship as by the soundproofed Chapels of the order, where meditation time could be purchased on a ticket-and-rota basis. But enrollment and subscription fees were high, out of the question for Travers with his mere $200 a week, and he had had reluctantly to shelve the dream.

His other dream—the important dream—remained.

He called her Deidre. Or rather by mutual consent they had decided her name was Deidre. She laughing and golden, flicking her golden hair. She was his one vice, hope and recreation.

He didn't know, or couldn't remember, how Deidre had come into being. Born of childish fancies perhaps, those stories children tell themselves at night beneath the bedclothes; but Deidre was not a night-shape, a succubus. She was real and vivid, real as any woman, more real than some; she got the blues and headcolds and PMT and once she cut herself and bled, she'd have her quiet moods and reflective moods and there was one special kittenish mood where nothing he said was right and nothing he did was right and he'd get mad, knowing she didn't mean it but thinking she didn't realise how Time was slipping and fleeting. Then they'd fight or she'd just sit quiet and watch him, her face calm and frozen and in pain; and next day would be hell. Hell at the office, hell inside the projector where images of her swam bright and golden-brown and sea-blue, distracting spots before his eyes. Next day and next night, till the last Trivee flicked off and she'd come running to him, a little girl, out of cool dusk or dawn, and say how long it had been, how it had been so long. Then she'd tell him about her day and what she'd done, the clothes she'd made—she was brilliant at making things, clothes, homes, happiness, anything—and ask him how it had been, how things had gone with him. And it would come pouring out, the frustration, the hopelessness, the endless grey and bright-vivid din in the endless grey and bright-vivid city, the human hive of Nothingness. Then she'd hold him in her arms, head pushed hard against her breasts, and croon and laugh and make him forget and he'd lose himself in the warmness of her and sleep to wake, and sleep again.

That Deidre was real was his own private and carefully-considered conclusion. Somewhere, somehow, a spatial, a temporal link had gone bust, he'd come halfway across into another reality, the only reality that held any meaning for him. A time link, almost certainly; for the things Deidre showed, the places they roamed, couldn't exist. Not now, not any more.

Did she invent the places, to please him? He'd asked her often enough. But she only laughed then, invariably, and teased him, and wouldn't say. He'd thought for a time she was keeping something from him, some lonely secret that once unlocked might plunge them both back to the limbo of night and day. But there was nothing; she told him that once, honestly and simply, hands round his hands, blue eyes searching his, flicking forward and back in those little shifts and changes of direction that were so much a part of her. When she spoke like that, with calmness and assurance, there was no doubting her. In that voice, and with that manner, she had told him there was indeed a God.

Being real brought its drawbacks. For who could tell in what of a hundred, a thousand ways, Travers might harm his girl? Something done or said, unknowing, in the day, some curious link forged that

might . . . what? Destroy, poison somehow all that was lovely and
real? With the knowledge, Travers experienced a huge reaction.
For months afterwards, nothing was too good for Deidre. And
Deidre was so deliciously, so easily capable of being spoiled. For
this she took, accepted, with that same naïve—not naïve, that
wasn't the word, nor childish nor simple either—that same delight,
that revelling in things physical, that characterised all she did.
'Look after me,' she would say. 'Wrap me up. Make me feel all
warm and yummy.' These things he did, rejoicing yet still afraid;
that one day, one day . . .

'Tosh.'

Deidre was sitting on a beach. Her favourite beach. The curve of
sand, white where the sun had dried it, cream-brown where the
retreating tide uncovered it, stretched to a high hill, a green headland crowned by a clump of wind-swept trees. Beyond the headland
were others, pillars of rock that marched in stately progression,
sunlight misty on their faces, to the bright haze of the horizon.

'Boo,' said Deidre. Then once more taking his hands, 'Dear, *I
love you*. Can't you see—oh I can't explain, I'm no good with
words. But can't you see that's all that matters?'

He wouldn't answer, not then. He was wrapped in thought. Till
she scooped up sand to flick at him, and ran away, plunged into the
sea. And they came back, to the hut by the beach—it was the hut this
time, not the cottage. She had a cottage too with white walls soaked
in sunlight and hung with brass and copper pots and pans and a great
hearth with inglenooks and deep, deep creamy-white sheepskins for
rugs. They would pile the skins and make love on them, in the
dancing leaping shifting light of the flames. Afterwards was when
he could most look after her. Coffee simmered on the hearth; he
would take a cup to her and lift her, still wrapped in the fleeces, hold
her while she nuzzled and drank. And she would half wake up, or
barely wake up at all, lie tousled and golden and supple, the
flamelight on her face, eyes shut, making the warm-cat noises in her
throat, smiling maliciously to tease him; then want to go back to
bed, and do it again, and sleep, sleep wonderfully. And he would
brush her hair, long silky hair she'd grown for him, and she would
purr some more and call him childish names and coming from her
the brown warm syllables didn't sound wrong. Then at last they
would hurry and scramble, both afraid of Time, like kids caught at a
cookie-jar more than responsible, responding Adults; and she
would hold him again, briefly, and kiss him once more and—

How did she leave him?

He didn't know.

But the cream walls of the cubicle were alive with light, and beyond them the familiar hated voices hammered.

'Wakey-wakey, Rise and Glow; it's the Dicky Dobson Show . . .'

While Deidre faded, wraithlike and sad, into mists.

But the days; the long, pointless, Sound-filled days! The hours stretched it seemed interminably until he could call her again. Sleep, for Travers, was impossible against the din; and tranquillisers were equally denied him. Once, drugged, he had tried to summon Deidre and she could not or would not come; she had been just a darkness in the dark, a silhouette that cried and cried as a bird might cry, paled and thinned to vanish into another dawn. Hence, he had never touched the stuff again. Hence, the games with the plugs.

Deidre disapproved of them when he told her, bit her lip and frowned. She would not tell him why; he sensed the hurt and worry, and felt lost, and a whole irreplaceable hour passed before they were themselves again. After that he said nothing more to her. He had never, as far as he could remember, kept a secret from her before.

Three days later he found out, in part, why she had been concerned. He developed an abscess.

It was very painful. To be more precise, it was as if a small blazing sun had become locked irrevocably and agonisingly on to his jaw. Sleep with it was out of the question; though he sensed the hands of Deidre, the soul and life-force of Deidre, striving to reach him through the blanket of pain. He shouted and cried, banged his head, fainted perhaps; in the morning, at first light or before— before, even, the Dicky Dobson Show—he was forced to seek his doctor.

Four agonising hours before his appointment. He videoed his studio manager, who laughed at his face then asked if it would help if he cried and when Travers, wordless, shook his head, laughed a good bit more. By then Travers had become grotesque, the pus bursting and squeezing into new pockets, causing fresh inflammation. Though with the increased swelling the pain was mercifully eased. The spiritual pain was worse now; the knowledge of wrongness and stupidity, of having somehow, through what he had done, hurt Deidre. He needed urgently to see her, explain, hold her in his arms. But that was impossible. Instead, there was Doctor Rees.

The doctor was annoyed. With, Travers suspected, good reason.

For the Foreign Bodies Doctor Rees accused him of inserting into
his ears—some scraps and oddments were apparently retrieved—
were the primary cause of suffering; and Travers' suffering was the
primary cause of the doctor wasting his time. Travers was upset. He
liked Doctor Rees; or more exactly he tried to like him, conscien-
tiously and seriously. Yet it was difficult; for the doctor had a Trivee
clamped to his desk and while he worked and diagnosed Kandin-
sky—for the fifth time that week, Travers had counted—fought
again his classic fifteen rounds with Bleeding Billy Cheshire. Shafts
of colour played across the desk-top, and there was Sound. Travers
was developing, he decided, a retentive memory. He had the frantic
commentary by heart, nearly word for word; he found himself
correspondingly more ready to twitch at every Covering Up, every
barrage of Leftsandrightstothebody, every Scarlet Niagara.

But the doctor was talking.

He was a bland young man with a paunch. And unbelievably,
quite extraordinarily, spotty. Secretly, Travers blamed that on the
Trivee. It was another of his theories, equally unscientific; that
continued Sound, aimed largely at the head, must in time be
absorbed till the tissues, becoming as one might say waterlogged,
rejected each new assault of breves and semibreves, each shock-
wave of octaves and dissonances. Doctor Rees' face sweated
Sound, through the entire audio spectrum; forty hz to fifteen
thousand, with traces of twentieth harmonic discernible only by
oscilloscope. The Harmonic, or Unharmonic, Theory of Pus-
tules . . .

Travers really must pay attention. He was being sent to a Specialist, he understood, because this must stop. Yes, he nodded, yes; he
understood and did agree. They had dressed his face for him; it felt
clean and comfortable. He would do anything, anything at all; for
his own good, he appreciated that. Or there would be real trouble;
and Travers, unconsciously and a trifle mysteriously, would be in it.

He told Deidre, that night. She had half a hundred questions for
him; about the doctor, and what he had said and done, and the
Specialist Travers was to see. What sort of Specialist?

Travers blushed, feeling foolish. He had been too nervous to ask.

But he thought once more what he had thought many times
before, what a splendid nurse Deidre would have made. He saw her
in a cool ward, white and starched and tall, with a headdress like a
great crisp linen butterfly. He woke for once refreshed; and the
image sustained him through his hours at Maschler-Crombie.

In the evening though, there was trouble again.

He had wanted to call Deidre early. Really early, just for once. Because there was so much to say again, about his short, tumultuous day. He'd heard—just heard mind you, it was only in the wind— about a new position going at Maschler. An upstairs job. He'd asked his studio manager and Rawlinson hadn't refused, definitely hadn't refused. Hummed and hawed maybe and glared over his glasses tops and doubted this and doubted that, but he hadn't said no, not outright. There were fifty dollars a week in the change, the chance of an outside room. Travers felt nearly faint at the thought. An outside room, with all the privileges it entailed; a whole wall, one complete side of his existence, free from din! In his mind's eye he already saw the room, himself sitting at the window; a summer night maybe, with the millions on millions of winking jewel-lights that were the city shimmering and crawling, a living map spread out far below . . . After that the reality of Pad 633 was hard to take. Particularly now that he had been forbidden his secret vice. He sat and brooded in the brightness and yammering din, hands cupped to the sides of his head; lay down on his pallet, tossed, got up, made coffee, drank it, lay down again, sat. The hands of the wallclock crawled with impossible slowness, marking the seconds and minutes sullenly; as if even the clock wished to deprive him of that interlude of peace still so achingly far away.

Towards twenty hundred hours a curious mood took possession of him. For the first time, perhaps, in years, he found himself questioning why he, Travers, must be singled out for such bizarre misadventures. The affair of the plugs, for instance; thinking back, reconstructing his every action, he could find no flaw in logic, no point at which one might say 'Here, Travers went off the rails.' No, he had done what he had done out of a need; a quirk perhaps, but basic necessity to him as an individual. Then he took to wondering if there had ever been a time—in the Cambrian for instance, or the lazy, lagoon-haunted Devonian—when there had been Quiet. If there was in fact any place now (apart from those priceless Chapels that had made the fortunes of Walk-In-Light) where Quietness might be said, even briefly, to prevail. Certainly not in what remained of the countryside. He had scraped and saved years enough to buy his one brief vacation away from the city, but it had been pointless. Everywhere, every few yards it seemed, in those carefully-preserved fields, on fragments of beach, in the hills that at one point defined the city's limits, they had set up comfort posts; the tourists, wandering aimless and a little scared, clustered round them plugging in earphones, handsets, recharging the accumulators of Mintrans, drawing a precious ambrosia of Sound into their very souls. There had been nothing for him there. None of those empty beaches of his, or Deidre's dreams, no sighing of wind in grass, plash and chatter of waves and rock and sand . . .

He found himself, against his will and better judgment and much to his surprise, using his vidphone. The directory numbers flicked past green and vivid as he spun through the lists. He found what he was looking for, dialled Post Office, Central Tower, gulped twice and made his complaint as clearly and concisely as he could.

The gentleman who faced him from the small, fizzing screen was sympathetic. Yes, yes, excess of Sound, very regrettable; each citizen was of course strictly controlled, was given a decibel rating in exact accordance with his status; was Travers *sure* local db regulations were being abused?

Travers was sure.

Then, said his new friend and benefactor, action would be taken. Immediately. Central Engineers combed the city constantly in search of defaulters; a van was on call in the locality, was in fact already on the way. Not to worry, Mr. Travers; just sit tight, and wait for the light . . . With an impersonal, professional grin the complaints clerk erased himself.

I've done it now, thought Travers, with a mixture of terror and exultation. *Deidre, I've really done it now* . . .

But what if . . . suppose, hope against hope . . . suppose something was actually *done*? Travers imagined, or tried to imagine, Silence. Spreading like a balm, like the stately ripples on a pool, from his cubicle, through and across the building. He gave himself up to dreaming. He saw himself the patriarch, the archpriest, of a new faith. What if, from its tiny beginning, that faith was to continue to grow? Through the city, the country; leaping seas maybe, to span the world. The vision was giddying and immense. Silence; a new creed gathering hundreds, thousands, millions perhaps of converts. How large a box, he wondered, would be needed to ensure total Quiet? Walls a yard thick, a hundred yards, half a mile? Money would be no object. He saw the treelined roads that would radiate from the shrine, the traffic on them crawling and muted. He saw the place with inner vividness, the white square sun-drenched block of its walls. Inside, an eternity of Quiet. With Deidre . . .

The caller telltale above the door winked insistently, an angry red eye.

How long had he been engrossed? Minutes only; but even Sound had temporarily faded from him. He drifted to the door, dreamlike still in his new and temporary exaltation.

There were two engineers. And a vast amount of apparatus, meters, bowl-shaped direction finders, trolleys replete with controls and dials, a microphone on a collapsible stand, its head flattened and jointed like a shining chromium snake. They plugged in this and tested that, logged the time, reported back to headquarters, checked Travers' name and Identicode; consulted sheafs of tables and notes, produced from somewhere a huge plan of the Elbee—they were it seemed wonderfully well equipped—and at last were ready to begin.

Travers prayed, silently.

The microphone head turned questing, while the dial needles swung and quivered. Lights flashed off and on; Travers felt sweat break out on his forehead and beneath his arms.

The microphone was snuffling at the ceiling now.

'Negative,' said the Post Office man. 'Two point eight (something or others) inside max.'

They pointed the little machine at the floor.

'Negative there,' said the operator, recalibrating. 'Five off zero reading.'

But the screaming and yelling, the music, the rhythms that mixed and madly overlapped, the brilliant, endless din; this was *negative*? The microphone was deaf, or not adjusted. They were cheating him.

'Look, mister,' said the Post Office man. 'You got us on a kind of bum call here.'

'Wait a minute . . .'

Fresh hope.

The mike head was pointing at a corner of the floor. Almost, to Travers, it seemed to be quivering. As if scenting a victim.

'We've got a nine five over there,' said the operator. 'O.K., mister, you got a case.'

Direction-finders were put into operation. Dials consulted, the plan spread out on Travers' pallet.

'That's the guy,' said the Post Office man, pointing. 'Name of Lupcheck. That's an eighty dollar fine. O.K., Mr. Travers, thanks for calling us. Can't have people getting all upset by racket. Not good for the system.'

And with a final scurrying of leads and flexes, a vanishing of shining, incomprehensible objects into boxes, they were gone.

Travers wrung his hands.

Lupcheck . . . He knew Lupcheck, well enough. And Lupcheck knew Travers, their paths had crossed once before. Lupcheck drove a crane at the local hypermart; a bulky, bright blue affair that raced continuously, with pneumatic hissings and snorts, along the complication of rails suspended above the acre and a half of displayed wares. Grapefruit, canned goods, toilet packs and Min Trans, artificial flowers, eggboxes and cheese, each and every conceivable commodity was seized by Lupcheck from its warehouse rack, flung to its allotted place as the dumps dwindled under the feverish, picking hands of the Consumers. Often Travers had admired his dexterity with the crane; till one day some complicated event took place that left a Consumer buffeted and hatless and spilled banana clumps and tinned Sevilles and marmalade pots and cereals across the floor. The Consumer shouted something angrily at the roof, and was answered, and kept on shouting, till Lupcheck swung down— he had a little spidery unexpected ladder that extended from the side of the crane. Lupcheck was not tall; but he was very broad, and sported orange-grey hair that grew in erratic tufts across his wide skull and thick, reddish forearms. His fists were large, with knuckles that were seamed and cracked; one swipe from one fist and the Consumer's spectacles were terribly embedded in the side of his face, and blood was dripping and splashing in big round gobs on to the floor, and the Consumer was crying while Lupcheck climbed, still annoyed and grumbling, back to his machine. And Travers walked quickly to the exit, feeling ill and not wanting the things he had bought, wondering with a sort of sick amazement why he had never realised before the full destructive power of the ball of bone at the end of a human arm.

Travers was afraid of Lupcheck. Now he had cost him eighty dollars.

Some time after the decibel hunters had gone, one might or might not have detected a small reduction in the overall uproar from the Trivees. Travers passed a restless night, too miserable for sleep, unable to summon Deidre. As always, disbelief came with the cessation of the din. It was like trying to remember pain; it seemed inconceivable that the Elbee had not always been wrapped in a breathing quiet. Lights flicked off in the surrounding cubicles till Travers lay staring into velvet dark. In the dark, he cursed himself bitterly. What a little thing it seemed after all, this simple matter of Sound! For no reason at all, or hardly any reason, he had jeopardised the coming morning. And denied himself Deidre, and hurt her; he had no doubt of that. He composed himself for sleep with a species of desperation; but dawn inched up, and Dicky Dobson burst into his daily cacophony, while Travers still lay red-eyed and restless. Now, horrors yawned; for if he avoided Lupcheck, this was in any case the Day of the Specialist.

Lupcheck caught him in the elevator.

Travers thumbed the controls in panic but the other was too fast for him. He rammed a shoulder at the door as it was wheezing shut; the mechanism whistled peevishly, slid open and closed again with Lupcheck inside. The elevator started its smooth descent.

Lupcheck twisted his fingers in the front of Travers' clothing, lifted him to his toes and pushed him against the side of the car. Travers wheezed, staring into bulging pale-blue eyes. As had happened before, he felt curiously detached; a part of his brain realised that Lupcheck was genuinely angry and puzzled over it while his eyes recorded the coarse texture of the other's skin, the networks of tiny branching veins, the individual tousled hairs of the thick brows, some reddish, some white, some grey. A tiny muscle twitched at the corner of Lupcheck's mouth and Travers wondered for an instant of time whether the crane operator might not be as unhappy as he. Then the rage came, swimming and cold. It dictated that Travers should drive his knee into Lupcheck's groin, bring down a disabling fist on the junction between nose and eyes. What he had seen in the hypermart held him back. Lupcheck was invincible; there would be other blows, like the blows of a great salty hammer, too terrible to be borne; and things breaking inside Travers' mouth, he could see the blood already and feel the pain. So he hung limp while Lupcheck banged him at the side of the elevator again, and growled and promised and swore.

Whatever happened now Deidre would be angry. Angry at his cowardice, angry if he fought and was uselessly hurt. So Travers had to hear the things Lupcheck said, and make the undertakings Lupcheck required, and scuttle away, when Lupcheck finally released him, grateful and reprieved. The rage still seethed and boiled; it wouldn't leave him now, he knew, till Deidre had suffered for it. As ever, against his will. But suffer she must; if for no other reason, for the folly and incompetence of God.

The rage buoyed Travers on his way to Hospital Block. He had been there once before, years ago, and dimly remembered the way. He shoved along crowded underpasses echoing with the high-pitched clatter of Travellators, the heavier thunder of streetcars. Trivees, set here and there in walls and roofs, competed with the din. Interspersed with them were talking posters and advertisements, round the borders of which blue and pink and scarlet, white and yellow flame-shapes and tartan-patterns raced. Hospital Block was well signposted. It seemed to extend electronic nerve fibres into the underpasses; soon Travers found himself confronted by the conflicting possibilities of Path, Ear, Nose and Throat, Ophthalmic, Geriatric, Cancer and half a dozen more ominously labelled departments. The light-trails—follow the Red and Blue—also flashed, confusingly. He went wrong twice, backtracked, found his way eventually to a Travellator that wound smoothly up a steepening incline, deposited him in the reception area of the place.

This too he remembered. The endless concrete walls, the hard white glare of lighting from many troughs; and the din. Loudhailers, aimed in all directions, rasped strings of Identicode numbers, referring Outpatients to any of a score of gates and elevators. In line after line of frontless, unpainted cubicles, cases deemed unworthy of admission to the maze above were treated by frantically-rushing white-coated staff; beyond was Casualty Section, hectic with the influx of an entire city. Ambulances, delivered at intervals of seconds from a range of entry lifts, disgorged stretchers and walking injured; more staff, nurses and orderlies, swarmed round them. There was a constant clanging of alarm bells, a clash and rattle of trolleys. In one place Travers saw the wreckage of a vehicle, transported in the maw of a huge recovery truck, decanted with scant ceremony on to a sloping slipway. Men scuttled forward, one lugging the cylinders of an antique oxy-acetyline cutter. The victims would presumably be extracted on the spot, like fresh bright herrings from a can. Travers shuddered and turned away, presented his Identitag to the impersonal scrutiny of an Appointments Monitor. The machine blinked, ticked rapidly and rewarded him with a punched and coded card. He hurried on, jostled now, deciphering his instructions as he went.

Within the Block proper the din was if anything worse. There were wards, full of noise, bright-glimpsed as he hurried past; corridors echoing with the mechanical clatter of trolleys and utensils. He was harried and buffeted, directed from point to point. At length, high in the building, the wall codings began to make sense. He found his corridor, counted off doors, presented the card to a scanner and was mechanically admitted to a featureless, carpeted anteroom.

At least it was quieter here. A solitary Trivee played, its Sound muted. A receptionist—human at last—took over the direction of Travers' affairs. He was told to sit and wait, given a plastic-leaved magazine to thumb. He read, automatically, words that made no sense. And prayed for Deidre. At other times, other great crises in his life, the technique had worked. He closed his eyes, concentrated. Forced back the light that filtered through the lids, forced back the Sound.

'*Mr. Travers . . .*'

Travers looked up with a start at the testy repetition. Again, he was off on the wrong foot. Now he had annoyed the Specialist.

He was ushered to an inner office. Here, at last, was Quiet. A Quiet so intense the whick-whick, the slow whirr and rustle of the ceiling-mounted fan sounded loud. The Specialist consulted a plastic-covered folder of notes, frowned, clucked and shook his head. Then he steepled his fingers, regarding Travers morosely over their tips as he talked.

The great man made his points carefully, occasionally tapping the desk top for greater emphasis. First, Travers must realise the considerable problem he and others like him posed to a modern society; a society, the Specialist stressed, organised on sound historical principles for the greatest good of the greatest number of its members. He repeated, in effect, the admonitions of Doctor Rees; while Travers nodded dumbly, wishing to be no inconvenience. Only wanting, were the truth to be known, to escape once more into his desert of Sound.

But that, it seemed, was not to be. For the Specialist was still talking, questioning and probing now, insistently. The direction of the questioning was strange. Things from Travers' childhood, remote events to be dredged up and re-examined and puzzled over.

Travers answered the questions, reticent at first then more eager, till at last the whole grief came blubbering and boiling from him, the Need, the great Need of his soul, for Quiet. The notion of the Shrine.

Travers stopped, appalled. But the Specialist was beaming now, urging him to continue. The Specialist himself understood Travers' problem; he really understood. As for a solution; why, within this modern society, in this best of all possible worlds, anything could be achieved. And the Need was after all very simple to fulfill. The answer? No mile-thick pill-boxes, no apparatus, no romantic, unattainable dreams . . .

Travers blinked as the full beauty of the solution dawned on him. So simple, so sublimely simple, simple as Relativity, simple as all truly great and original ideas . . . It would mean of course the sacrifice of his new position, the end of the day-old dream of an outside room; but his mind glowed already with the other, greater possibilities. Happiness, total and complete; for him, and for Deidre. He saw himself already, breaking the wonderful news; of Time; Time unlimited. Time for them to be together. The world faded; he saw nothing but the bright and perfect future. He nodded, feverish, voiceless in his impatience, eager only to sign the forms the Specialist proffered him, and begin.

He was conducted to yet another room. Aseptic this time, white and gleaming. The nurse who readied him was brown-skinned and supple. Like Deidre, almost; with silky hair, a wave of it he was sure, hidden by her neat white cap. But she shoved and pushed at him indifferently, as if he were a carcass, a simple hunk of meat unworthy of human consideration. Her eyes, when they once met his, seemed full of a bored contempt; then he saw the Mintran speaker in her ear, the spidery flex running into the collar of her uniform, and was able to return the stare from the height of a loftier indifference.

The local took effect immediately, an icy numbness spreading from jaw to neck and temples. He was led to a chair that moulded itself to him as he sat, reclined and tilted at the touch of innumerable shining levers. A lamp was switched on, planet-bright and close; he felt the momentary pulse of heat from it on cheeks and nose before a cloth was laid neatly over his eyes. His head was turned; fingers probed his dead cheeks, dimpling.

The instruments made little sounds. Ringings, and clinks. Then closer squeaks and gratings, once a crunch; then nothing. Nothing at all.

The cloth was withdrawn; and Travers stared round dazed. The nightmare was ended; cleanly and neatly, in a mere instant of time. No more Dicky Dobson now, no more Rise and Glow; no more Travellators, no more Mintrans, no more traffic, no more people; nothing. So perfect was the technique, they had assured him, that his balance would be unimpaired; just a simple matter of excision, removal of tiny bones that worked in sequences of other tiny bones, alignments functioning with jewel-precision to transmit hell from the four quarters of the globe to the inside of his skull . . .

The faces were mouthing at him now. Nurse, anaesthetist, surgeon; praise or curses, congratulations or contempt. He smiled back, euphorically. He neither knew nor cared.

And there was the silent city, outside. The silent tubecars and the silent Travellators, the silent people and the silent vehicles. A million silent windows, eyes of cubicles that housed a million silent Trivees. Somewhere Lupcheck drove his silent crane, mimed his silent rage; poor stupid defeated Lupcheck, who now didn't matter at all.

Work was out of the question for today. Travers threaded his way home carefully, watchful for the dizziness they had warned him might possibly occur for a time. He elevated to his room, slid the silent doorpanel closed. Beyond the walls, as ever, electronic patterns danced. He smiled at them too, a smile of benediction.

He undressed slowly, now with all the Time in the world. The worry of the night, the strain of the day, had exhausted him. He curled up on the pallet, pulled the covers round himself and fell almost instantly asleep.

The beach flicked on. And there was Deidre running, running as she had never run before. He ran too, feeling his feet stumble in the sunwarmed sand, arms outstretched. He tried to hug her, but she pushed him away. He saw then, bewildered, the sheen of tears on chin and throat; and her eyes, the terrible accusation there. She fell to her knees, holding her throat and rocking with misery, asking again and again the same silent question, *why, why,* till understanding came at last.

Deidre was dumb.

Boulter's Canaries

I've known Alec Boulter for years. He's always been a damned clever chap. He keeps a rein on his imagination now though. Once he almost got too clever to live.

Boulter is an engineer by profession, but he can find his way about in electronics as well as anyone. He's a skilled turner and fitter and if I also mention that he writes and paints and has an interest in the occult you'll begin to see what a way-out character he is.

He's never made a great deal of money of course. This is the Age of Specialisation. The trend nowadays is for people to know more and more about less and less. There aren't any openings in commerce, or for that matter in science or the arts, for an unpredictable combination of mechanic and mystic. I sometimes feel Boulter should have been born back in the Renaissance. Da Vinci would probably have understood him.

At the time I'm thinking about he was taking an interest in amateur movies. I'd done a little work on it myself; nothing great, but better than the baby-on-the-lawn stuff you usually see. When Boulter started to dabble I sat back and waited for something remarkable. It was not long in coming.

He handicapped himself by choosing to work with sixteen millimetre stock. That isn't really an amateur gauge at all. Boulter wanted quality though, and in those days the standard of processing was a lot lower than it is now. If you'd told us for instance that medium-price equipment would ever give tolerable results from a striped eight-mil print we'd have laughed at you. But the cost of processing the wide-gauge stuff was high and it curtailed Boulter's activities more than somewhat.

He was never interested in plain movies. He shot sound right from the start. I remember the first recorder he ever owned used paper tape. Fantastic to think how primitive we were, and it was only a handful of years ago. He soon graduated and had one of the first Ferrograph decks to come out. Later he used an Emi, then a Ferrograph stereo. After that he built some machines of his own. For location work he rigged up a deck that would run from his station wagon. The results were first rate.

We travelled round a lot covering subjects that took his fancy. He tried all sorts of things from regattas to car auctions. He picked up a couple of awards at Edinburgh, but he was never really concerned with things like that. He went off on a new tack.

I went over to his place one day and found him with a collection of textbooks, some Ordnance Survey sheets and an A.A. guide. As soon as he saw me he said, 'Ever heard of Frey Abbey, Glyn?'

I nodded. 'Vaguely. Up north somewhere, isn't it?'

'Yes. I make it a hundred and twenty from us, give or take a few miles. What do you know about it?'

'Not much. Wasn't there some talk about poltergeist activity?'

He laughed. ' "Some talk" runs to about twelve volumes. By all accounts it's one of the most haunted spots in the country.'

I said, 'I'm not really with it. What if it is?'

He slapped the books decisively. 'It's interesting. I'm going there. Want a run up?'

'It's a bit of a distance. I'm easy though, I'll come if you like. What are you going to do up there?'

He said, 'Take pictures of ghosts.'

I laughed, then I saw he was serious. I said, 'How are you going to set about it?'

'I dunno. I expect something will suggest itself. Have a look at these.' He handed me some photographs.

I thumbed through them, I said, 'I don't suppose they're yours?'

'No, they belong to Kevin Hooker. You know, that chap at the film society. Thin, wears glasses. He was at Frey last week. Thought he'd try his hand.'

I said, 'Well, tell him before he tries it again, to get a new camera.'

He said, 'There's nothing wrong with his camera. It's a Rollei, and he can use it. These are control shots from the same neg. They're rather interesting. He took them in between the others; one shot of the ruins, then one a quarter of a mile away, then another of the ruins. And so on.'

I went through the prints again, more carefully. There was very little left of the Abbey. Just a few stones and some hillocks in a field. Boulter said, 'They dismantled the original building in the seventeenth century. I suppose they were tired of the manifestations. A very learned Prior tried his hand at exorcism. He was buried a week later. It's all in the book here. It isn't very pretty.'

I frowned. Each shot of the ruins bore queer blemishes. The black patches seemed to have no relation to the field of the camera. They looked as if they were poised here and there over the remains of the walls. Apart from the spots print quality was excellent and there was evidently nothing wrong with the check negatives at all. I said, 'Why did he do these other prints, Alec?'

'It's an old trick,' Boulter said. 'Nobody can take pictures at Frey. He knew about it. That's why he had a go.'

I said, 'You mean this has happened before?'

'Every time.'

I said, 'That's fantastic!'

'Yes, I know. That's why I'm going.'

I began to get interested. 'But you're doing movies. Has that been tried before?'

'Couldn't say. There's a first time for everything.'

We drove up the following weekend. On the way he expounded his theories. 'It's been said there's a poltergeist up there. I don't hold with that. The site has been deserted for centuries. It isn't in the nature of poltergeists to hang about after the humans have gone. If people knew more about them they wouldn't quote them so readily.'

'How can you tell what isn't in a deserted place?' I said. I was having some odd thoughts about things that are only there when you are not. Boulter snorted. 'To my way of thinking a poltergeist isn't a ghost at all. Not in the classic sense of the term. It's a sort of energy projection. In every well-documented haunting you'll find there's a child or an adolescent concerned somewhere. The thing follows them around from place to place. Eventually the manifestations just fade away. There's never any purposive quality about them. I don't think a poltergeist has an existence apart from the mind that creates it. They say it feeds, taps off energy. I don't go along with that. I think it's telekinesis tarted up with a new name.'

When he talks like that you believe him. I said, 'So what are these things at Frey?'

'Don't really know. My guess is Elementals.'

'What are they when they're at home?'

'Nobody can say. It's more a proposition than a definition. I suppose you could describe them as Nature Spirits. The psychical research folk pass them off by saying they're spirits that have never inhabited a human form. A sort of raw energy that has always existed.'

'Is that feasible?'

'You define feasibility and I'll answer you.'

I said, 'That puts me off somehow. I was hoping for a diabolic twist. You know, the House of the Lord being taken over by the Great Enemy.'

He smiled. 'Don't bring God into it, it makes things too complicated.'

We found the place without any trouble. We stopped in the nearby village, had a couple of drinks and a snack at the local pub and managed to fix up some accommodation for the night. Then we went up to the Abbey.

I was not over-impressed. There was very little to see. We walked along the old foundations and climbed a few of the grass-covered remnants of walls. We had brought no gear. Boulter planned to make an early start in the morning. We worked out the best site for the camera and paced the distance to where we could leave the van to make sure our recorder feed would reach. Then Alec took out his cigarettes and we lit up. I stood with my shoulders hunched against the evening wind. I said, 'The only trouble is we shall be shooting blind.'

'What?'

I said, 'We shan't know if we've got any woozlums until the stock comes back from processing.'

Boulter said, 'Eh? No, we shan't.' He seemed to be preoccupied. After a moment he said, 'You'd expect to hear something some-where, wouldn't you?'

'What sort of thing?'

He gestured vaguely at the hills, the darkening sky. 'I don't know. A lark. Some bird or other. There isn't a thing, Glyn. Hadn't you noticed?'

I had sensed something, or a lack of something. I listened carefully. Apart from our voices there was not the slightest sound. The wind moved against my face, but even that seemed to be silent. It was as if some deadening layer insulated the spot, cutting it off from the rest of the countryside. I looked round at the barren land, the moors rising behind us. Way off the lights of the village were beginning to twinkle. Boulter said, 'You'd expect a lark at least.'

'Too late in the year for them,' I said.

He shrugged. 'Maybe. Anyway, let's try something.' He turned and walked away. I followed and he waved me back. 'Stay there for a minute, Glyn.' He moved a few more paces then stopped and turned. He said, 'Does my voice sound all right?'

It certainly did not. I said, 'You're faint. Sounds as if you're talking through felt.'

He nodded as if the words merely confirmed his suspicions. He walked another ten yards and the effect was increased. It built up rapidly with distance. At fifty yards I could see his mouth moving and knew he was shouting but not a scratch of voice reached me. The place was as dead as an anechoic chamber. I made wash-out movements with my hands and pointed to the road. It was getting dark rapidly and I didn't fancy the spot after night had fallen. He joined me at the gate. 'That's the funniest damn thing,' he said, 'I bet if you charted the dB drop you'd end up with an exponential curve. Queerest acoustic I ever came across.'

I agreed that something was certainly odd. I hoped it was only the acoustic.

Next morning was fresh and blowy. We set up the camera on the spot we had chosen, a hummock of grass from which it could command most of the ruins. Then I brought the recorder from the van. I placed the mike a few feet from the camera and went back to check for wind noise. The deck speaker was dead. I tested the connections. They seemed perfectly all right. I called over to Boulter. Either the dead effect had lessened or the darkness of the previous night had made it seem worse than it was. I said, 'The recorder won't work, Alec. Can't quite see why.'

He came over with the look on his face that he reserves for special problems. He tinkered for a time, starting and stopping the motors.

They ran readily enough. Then he fetched his Avo from the car. He tested systematically, sat back and shook his head. 'It should be O.K., Glyn. Try it again.'

I turned up the audio gain to bring the windboom through the deck speaker. There was nothing doing. Boulter looked baffled. I'd never seen him licked before, and this was his own machine. Then he said, 'Fair enough, Glyn, take it back to the van, will you? Don't disconnect though. Just put it in the back. I want you to record "Mary had a little lamb." Over there somewhere.' He pointed towards the village.

I knew better than to argue. Boulter never does anything without a reason. I got the stuff back into the brake, turned round in the gateway and drove off. A quarter of a mile away the machine functioned perfectly. It gave me quite a shock. I started to experiment. I fixed the mike through the window, turned up the recording gain and drove back towards the ruins. At two hundred and fifty yards the windrush from the monitor faltered. At two hundred there was nothing. I repeated the test to make sure then went back and told Alec. He shrugged. 'That's it for the moment, then. We can't run a mike lead all that distance. We shall have to think of something else.'

I said, 'Do you think there's something we can record?'

He answered ambiguously. 'I know there's something we can't.'

He took a few shots of the ruins with me walking about demarcating the lines of the old walls. We left it at that until the afternoon, when we repeated the experiment. We drove back on Sunday after a last look round, and he dispatched the neg for processing as soon as he could.

The results were disappointing. There were some peculiarities; once the whole field fogged for no reason that we could discover and there were several patches where the focus seemed to have gone haywire. Most of the stuff, though, was quite normal. I shrugged. 'Well, at least we've exploded the myth. You can take pictures at Frey. I suppose that wraps it up.'

Boulter shook his head. 'You've forgotten the recorder that wouldn't record. There's something there all right, Glyn. I'm going up again next weekend. Give it another whirl.'

As it happened I couldn't go with him that time. He made two more pilgrimages on his own. He rang me about a month after our first trip. He sounded excited. He said, 'I've got something damn queer, Glyn; can you come round?'

I went over. He had converted his lounge into quite a reasonable viewing theatre, with projector and room lights controlled from a desk within arm's reach of one of the easy chairs. The mech was running when I walked in. He switched off immediately, unlaced and set it to rewind. He said, 'I'd like to go through this from the start. I think you'll find it's worth it.'

I noticed a bottle of Scotch and some glasses on the occasional table. I nodded at them. 'What are you celebrating?'

He said, 'Breakthrough. We'll have a drink first. I'd like to put you in the picture. What you see will mean more.' The leader started to flack-flack round on the top spool of the projector and he touched the console in front of him to stop the motor. I sat down. I said, 'What have you been playing with?'

He poured drinks. 'Filters,' he said. 'Cheers, by the way. All the best. I tried various stocks first. I was thinking about infrared or something like that. I used the filters as a last resort. The answer's easy, Glyn; polarisation.'

'What does that do?'

'Makes 'em visible. Well, it makes something visible anyhow. I don't quite know what. I just put a polaroid screen over the lens. I rather think it's more effective at some angles than others but I couldn't be sure. Anyway, it's pretty good.' He got up and relaced the projector than came round and started up. He said, 'See what you think.'

The room lights went out. On the screen appeared a clockface. It was mounted on a blackboard and underneath was a slip bearing the date. Boulter is nothing if not methodical. He said, 'I knew the filter worked because I'd tried it the week before. I used the clock because I had some idea of establishing a cycle of activity. As things turned out there was no real need for it. You'll see why. The camera was focused on the datum board right the way through. That's why the ruins are a bit off.'

The clock read eleven fifteen. A couple of minutes of film went through with nothing untoward, then Boulter touched my arm. He said, 'Look at that, then.'

In the field behind the clock a shape had appeared. It was totally lacking in definition. Its edges seemed to pulsate and waver. It looked exactly like positive fogging except that it moved slowly, creeping across the grass from the right hand to the centre of the screen. It paused at the bottom of one of the ruined walls. Boulter leaned forward slightly and I guessed something remarkable was coming. The shape stayed where it was for a moment, throbbing slightly; then it *climbed*. . . .

I said, 'Good God, Alec, it's—'

'Following the contour of that wall. Exactly. And if you can tell me any camera fault that would give an effect like that I'd be fascinated, if ungrateful.'

I shook my head. 'You're safe enough, Alec. This beats me.'

When the thing reached the top of the wall it was joined by a second appearance that also entered from the right. Woozlum number two moved a lot more rapidly and seemed to blend with the first. Then they separated and both left the support and floated towards the camera, expanding as they came into star or octopus shapes with wispy arms of blackish fog. I drew in my breath sharply and the screen went blank. Boulter laughed. 'At that point I stopped the test. I couldn't know what I was getting of course. That was a set five-minute run. I did two tests half an hour apart. Here's the second one now.'

This time only one of the shapes was visible. It seemed to be moving across the top of a wall. After a time it floated vertically off screen. The last two minutes of the film were uneventful. Boulter stopped the machine.

I said, 'Activity's pretty constant then. What the hell are these things, Alec?'

The room lights came on and I blinked. Boulter took out his cigarettes, lit one and threw me the packet. He said, 'They aren't physical in the sense that we understand it of course. We're not photographing anything there, just a hole into which the camera cannot see. Why it should affect film stock that way and not the human retina is anybody's guess. But as for activity, have a look at this.' He started up again.

This time the hands of the clock were moving visibly round the dial. I said, 'Stop action. What's the time lag?'

'Minute intervals between frames. The maximum I could get. I made up a unit for it. It seemed the best way to get a cross-section of a weekend at Frey.'

There was a lot of fast, dark movement all over the place. After a moment or two the picture faded out. That was nightfall of course; half a minute at this speed represented twelve hours of real time. In the darkness the things were still visible, surrounded by faint haloes that the daylight scenes had concealed. As far as I could see there was no cessation of activity. I said, 'Busy little chaps, aren't they?'

Boulter said, 'Yes, aren't they just? Sunday was even better. This is it coming up now.'

The first acceleration was to one frame per thirty seconds, the next to one frame per fifteen. At that speed the movements were most effective. The things seemed to dart and flit about, perching here and there to preen their vague outlines on the tops of the old walls. That was when I coined the phrase by which we came to know them. I said, 'Christ, they hop around like ruddy canaries.' Alec chuckled. 'They're a new breed. Boulter's canaries. Sounds good, doesn't it?'

The slow test continued. I watched it, fascinated, while Boulter explained his next steps. He had left the camera running while he tried a new experiment. He had set up the tapedeck again and fixed round it a frame of chicken wire which had been earthed to a perforated copper rod filled with brine. With the aid of the contraption he had managed to record a test tape. He stopped the projector, crossed to the deck in the corner of the room and started it up. His voice came through the playback scratchily, as if from a fifty-year-old recording. He said, 'I think that must have annoyed them.'

'Why?'

'I tried shooting again that evening. See what they did.'

He switched on the projector once more. The shapes appeared. This time they engaged in what seemed to be purposive movement. From the walls they launched themselves into the air and each one floated directly towards the camera, spreading into the tentaculate shape I had already seen. Up close each filled the field before fading behind or through the lens to make way for the next. After a time the screen went blank. Boulter switched off and the main lights came on. He said, 'Well, there you have it. How long they played goose and fox I don't know. I packed up and came home.'

We discussed the whole business far into the night. Boulter was keen on the theory of some localised electro-magnetic disturbance and outlined a few ideas for learning more about it. I wasn't so sure I wanted to know. I hadn't minded the things as they flitted about, but that progression of grabbing shapes was another matter altogether. There was too much deliberation in it. Boulter scoffed at the idea of danger. 'There can't be sentience in the way we understand it,' he explained. 'Any more than there can be a brain in the Northern Lights. The thing is, we can attract them. We should be able to go on from there without too much trouble.'

I shook my head. I'd been doing some reading of my own. 'The old abbot tried some independent research. He didn't live five days. And there was a monk too. He had himself locked in a haunted cell all night as an act of faith. He wore half an inch off his fingers scratching to get out. They found him stiff in the morning.'

'I think you're flapping a bit, Glyn,' Boulter said. 'I'm as ready as the next to admit the possibility of paranormal happenings, but in this case we're not dealing with anything as complex as that. After all we're getting the history of Frey at secondhand through a fog of ignorance and superstition. Any queer things can probably be attributed one per cent to the canaries and ninety-nine per cent to auto-suggestion, self-hypnosis, call it what you will. This is an electro-magnetic disturbance of some kind. The behaviour of the tape recorder proves it. It's localised and it has some damned interesting characteristics. For instance, this crawling up the stones. You can't rule out the possibility of a static effect there. If you saw a balloon roll up my arm and had no knowledge of electricity you'd take me for a magician.' He laughed. 'Old Ronnie—you know him, he gave that lecture at the club once—he was on the phone from the lab just before you came. I told him it was a new optical effect we were trying out. He offered me a hundred quid on the spot for the lens we were using.'

We arranged to go to Frey again during the coming weekend. I had a touching faith in Boulter's ability to assess the situation. If I'd had less faith then I'd have fewer grey hairs now. The matter stayed on my mind through the week. I suppose *Aves Boulterii* had taken a good hold on both of us.

This time we only set up the recorder. We ran some tests with the deck protected by its odd-looking cage, then Boulter fixed the mike in a parabolic reflector on a tripod. Why he does these things I can't say, but he seems to have a knack of divining the best approach to fundamental research. I watched the recording gain and he moved the prab slowly, scanning the grass area of the foundations. He'd taken the trouble to calibrate the mike support so he knew exactly where to aim. We had no luck with the first sweep and he went off and set up numbered posts at measured distances from the tripod. By sighting on these he could get an even better range. He explained he was trying to pick up at about four feet from the ground, the average of the apparent height of the canaries. He started to move the reflector bowl again. He said, 'I've even been wondering whether we've been getting real or virtual images. This should answer that at least.'

I was about to ask him how he could be sure the canaries emitted anything when the gain meter twitched. I caught his arm and he looked down. The prab was pointing at the highest of the walls, just where we'd seen most of the effects. I put the cans on but there was nothing to hear. The meter zeroed and I reached up and caught hold of the prab handgrip, wobbling the bowl to get back into focus. We held the emission for half a minute before it faded. Boulter resighted the prab on the base of the wall and we picked up something else immediately. I shoved the earphones back and said, 'What is it, Alec? I can't hear anything.'

Boulter frowned. He was trying to juggle the reflector and keep one eye on the recording meter. He said, 'Run tape, Glyn. Fifteen i.p.s. I think we shall need it. It can't be subsonic if you can follow it with a bowl as small as this. Must be high frequency. There's a devil of an amplitude though. Ouch, look at that needle kick. No wonder our ears got screwed up.'

We recorded for about ten minutes then we ran out of responses. I shut down and Boulter locked the prab and got out the cigarettes. I was none too happy. I said, 'I suppose we've annoyed the things again now.' I looked back at the ruins, brown in the sunlight. There was nothing to see. Boulter laughed. 'I shouldn't concern yourself too much. There isn't anything to worry about.'

There was a sharp clang and the tripod fell over on the grass. He moved faster than I'd ever seen him. I was sitting near the little knoll on which we'd first placed the camera and he flung himself flat beside me. He said, 'Get down, Glyn.'

'What the—?'

He shoved me in the chest and I got down anyway. He glared round. He said, 'Some bastard's taking pot shots at us.'

'What?'

He said, 'Look at that thing. If he'd hit the prab I should have been really pleased.' He pointed at the tripod and I saw a bright mark where something had glanced off the mounting just beneath the panning head. Below it on the wood was a long furrow. I stared incredulously. I said, 'Well, if that was a shot it came from straight above us.'

We both looked up; one of those stupid involuntary actions. The sky was empty of course. We stayed where we were. The tension

began to mount. After all, it was a queer situation. The two of us
lying there, the deserted moors round about the ruins, the bright car
in the distance; and an invisible marksman, apparently aerial,
waiting for another chance. After a while Boulter got up. He
frowned at me then walked away and stood looking round the
horizon with his hands on his hips. Then he called. His voice had the
faded quality we had noticed on that first evening. He said, 'Come
on, Glyn. You look a bit of a nit down there.'

I sat up carefully. 'And you'll look a bigger one if our sporting
friend has another go.'

He laughed, throwing his head back as if I'd made a huge joke.
He said, 'Nobody shoots at people on the open moor these days,
Glyn. This is the twentieth century.'

I picked up the tripod and fingered the mark on the wood. I still
had a nasty feeling that there was something at my back. 'Then what
made this?' I said.

He shrugged. 'It must have been a solitary hailstone.' And that
was as far as he would commit himself.

We packed up the gear soon afterwards. I for one had rather lost
heart in the project. We drove back to the village and had a meal.
Then, surprisingly, Boulter decided to move south that night. I
didn't argue with him. I'd seen enough of Frey for one week at least.

We got back in the small hours and I stayed overnight at Alec's
place. By the time I got down next morning he'd had breakfast and
was already tinkering about in the workshop. He had a variable-
speed deck there and it was on that we first heard the sounds.

I was still eating when he came and dragged me out to listen.
He'd worked out the frequency of the emissions; they ranged from
fifteen to twenty k/cs. He switched on and turned up the playback
gain. The wall speaker began to pipe. It was a queer sound,
undulating and quavery. It was like a choir of singers poking around
after top C and not quite getting there. Yet not human singers. It
upset me more than the visual record had done, but Alec was alight
with enthusiasm. He tried to talk me into going to Frey with him
again. He had some things he would like to try out.

I refused. My nerves were beginning to get ragged. I said, 'In any
case I'm tied up next weekend.'

He laughed. 'Who said anything about the weekend? I'm going
back tonight.'

I gave him a short run-down on my views about the proposition.
He tried to get me to change my mind, but he was talking to the Rock

of Gibraltar. I left him shortly afterwards still raving about his way-out ideas. Apparently he wanted to communicate with the canaries. He managed that of course though not quite in the way he had thought.

It was midweek when I heard from him. I thought his voice sounded strained on the telephone. He was rather mysterious, just asked me if I'd like to come round and see something remarkable. I said sure, whenever he liked. He said a curious thing before he rang off. 'Come when you're ready, Glyn; I don't think there's any risk.'

I put the phone down and stood looking at it. Risk? I didn't like the sound of that. What risk, and why tonight? I shrugged. Boulter was always devious and infrequently incomprehensible. I reached for my jacket.

I was standing by the door of my flat looking round before I turned off the light when there was a crash of glass from the bathroom. I hurried in thinking a cat or something had got through the window. There was nothing. At first I couldn't account for the noise, then I saw my shaving mirror was smashed. The fragments were scattered all over the place. None was larger than a pea. I picked one up and examined it, feeling at a loss. As I stood there the door of the wall cupboard opened and bottles and shaving brushes began to fly at my head. I backed out, slammed the door of the flat and hared to the car.

It was a bad night, cold and spitting with rain. I peered through the screen looking for Boulter's drive. I swung up to the house and turned off the engine. In that second there was a sharp 'ding' and the car rocked on its springs. I sat still and any hope I might have had left me. That had happened twice on the journey. Both times there had been a vehicle in front of me and I'd attributed it to a flung stone. I remembered the attack on the mike tripod at Frey. They'd got my number then, whatever 'they' were. Something told me Boulter was faring no better. I touched the doorhandle and it was yanked out of my hand as something threw the car door open. I ran for the house, hunching my shoulders against the rain.

Boulter let me in. He was smoking when he came to the door and I noticed he had not shaved. He wasted no time in preliminaries. He said, 'Dump your coat and come through, Glyn. This is worth seeing but I don't know how long we've got.' As I followed him down the hall I saw a ridge appear in the carpet. It ran rapidly away to the end of the corridor. He opened the door of the lounge and a directory flew from the phone table. He fielded it as it passed his head and slammed it back down. He said, 'Circus tricks. Don't let 'em throw you.' I followed him and he closed the door after me. Instantly a thunderous knocking began. I saw the door panels jump with the force of it. He yelled, 'Oh, shut up. I'm talking.' The noise subsided.

I sat down before I fell. I said, 'So we were attacked that day, weren't we?'

He looked up from lacing the projector. 'Only indirectly.'

'Then I've just been indirectly attacked again,' I said.

He looked incredulous. 'You?'

'Well, the car. It's got a damn great dent over the windscreen. And despite your well-known cynicism my flat has been taken over by a poltergeist. As I see, you've got one here as well.'

He said, 'It was only to be expected. There's no danger. You're better off here anyway; I'm insured.'

I wondered what he was talking about. Then I saw he had the camera and the mike set up facing the tall windows. I said, 'Alec, what the hell are you playing at?'

He finished with the projector, came round and stubbed his cigarette. He lit another and sat down. He said, 'No interruptions, Glyn. You can ask questions later. I want to fill in the background as quickly as I can. I went back to Frey last Sunday as I said I would. This film was shot on Monday. I only got the results tonight. I shall have to get you to help me run them.

'As I said, I wanted to set up a system of communication. I'd changed my ideas about nonsentience, by the way, after our last trip. I reasoned it thus. The canaries—I'll call them that for want of a better term—emit frequencies of up to twenty-thousand cycles. Not sound as we understand it, but it can be rendered as such. That's enough for present purposes. Also they seemed to be attracted by any electro-magnetic disturbance in their area. I decided to have a chat with them.'

'How in Hell?'

'Comparatively simple. I set up a signal generator. I shot twenty k/cs at them with a Morse key.'

I stared at him. I was beginning to see the reason for all the upset. I said, 'You prize bloody clown, you've finished the pair of us.'

He shook his head impatiently. 'I don't think so. As I was saying, I signalled to them. I sent arithmetic progressions first, one, two, three and so on, then some geometric sets, squares and cubes over short series of numbers.'

Despite my shock I was interested. 'How did you check results?'

He started the projector. I saw he had set up the datum board again, this time with a panel in which numbers could be shown. He said, 'This was before I signalled at all. As you can see one of the things is in field.'

The screen went blank and he shut down for a moment. He said, 'Can you handle the recorder, Glyn? I should wheel it across to the chair. Then you can see the screen.'

I did as he asked. When I was settled again with the deck at my elbow he said, 'O.K., switch on, will you? This is an edited transcript of course. I slowed the emissions as I did the first set, and re-recorded them.' In the speaker I heard his voice, overlaid with what we had come to know as Frey distortion. It said, 'Camera running. First series transmitted. Additive progression in ones.'

The embryonic voices began to pipe and flutter. The projector started up, showing the visual he had taken at the same time. The slowed sound bore no direct relation to the picture of course but the film confirmed what the track had already suggested. The things were present in great numbers. They seemed to be agitated and were drifting rapidly up and down the low hummocks of stone. I left the recorder running and Boulter switched the mech in and out to keep roughly in sync with the tracks. After each transmission from the generator he had started the recorder, changed the number on the datum board and filmed a set period of fifteen minutes in slow action. It became evident that the canaries had been greatly excited by the signals. Their movements became quicker and quicker and soon developed into that floating projection towards the source of their annoyance that we had seen before. This time the movement was too fast for the camera. Boulter reached back and slowed the projector. We watched the jellyfish shapes jerk towards us, hover and vanish. Boulter laughed. 'Not very pretty at close quarters, are they?' I shuddered and agreed.

He sat back. He said, 'By the time I reached the ninth test—that's it coming up now, stop a minute will you and I'll get back in sync—by the time I got to that, which was the end of the series, things had really hotted up.' He speeded the projector again, got the number nine on the screen and nodded to me to start up the sound. He said, 'This was the cubic progression. Bit of a bore; in case you hadn't worked it out it goes two, eight, five hundred and twelve.' His voice echoed him from the tapedeck. 'Ninth test, a cubic progression from two. Partially completed.' 'I stopped at about two hundred in the third figure. I had to; they knocked the generator about fifty feet. I took this immediately afterwards.'

The projector showed a flashing whirl of dark movement. The corresponding sound was eerie. It was as if hundreds of the things were present, piping and fluting for all they were worth. There was another noise as well, one that I hadn't heard before. It was much lower than the normal emission, sounding by comparison almost husky; a chittery, whirring sound with a gibbering quality to it that started my scalp prickling again. Boulter said, 'The canaries, very cross indeed.' The film record ended and he switched off the machine and brought the room lights up to a glow. I shut down the playback and was glad enough to do so. There was silence between us for a moment. I was still trying to digest what I'd seen and heard.

I said, 'That's it then, Alec. You've stirred a hornet's nest this time, no mistake. It was them that knocked the mike down that day. They did it to the signal generator on Monday.' My voice rose slightly. 'And better than that. They've followed you home. And all you had to do was ring me and they had me too. They've got the pair of us taped!'

He nodded sombrely. Something scratched at the door. I didn't feel like opening it. He said, 'Sorry about all this, Glyn. They do appear to have extended their operations. I should have listened to you earlier on.'

I got out a cigarette. I felt I needed it. The middle of the room was bright enough, but round the walls the shadows seemed to crawl together, thickening and darkening. I stared at the evidence of twentieth-century know-how: the tapedeck, the projector, the camera and mikestand. I felt I was in some sort of dream. But it was all true enough. I said hollowly, 'If ever men were haunted, we are.'

He was quiet for a space. Then he said, 'Yes, unfortunately that is true.'

I was dazed. I said, 'Well, what are you going to do, Alec? And furthermore, why the hell did you drag me over here? Or ring in the first place? It's your mess. You said on the phone there was no danger.—'

He said, 'Yes, I know what I told you, Glyn. I still believe that. In a way I have to. You must too.'

'But what are you going to do?'

He got up and bent over the tapedeck. He spun the reels forward then stopped and switched to playback. The speaker began to emit a steady, high-pitched note. He said, 'Four thousand cycles. At this speed they won't react.'

I experienced a sinking feeling. I said, 'Look, this isn't a suicide pact. What the hell?'

'They're angry, Glyn,' he said. 'They resent disturbance. Maybe they don't like the idea of anyone having any real understanding of them. But there's just one hope. That they're not mad with us. And to my way of thinking there's only one method of finding out. They've tracked something they resent to this room. We must find the depth and direction of that resentment. I've no doubt they could kill us if they wished. If they do, too bad. I don't think they will. If they spare us; well, we shall be able to sleep easy again. This is the only way.'

I reached out to grab his wrist, but I was too late. He had already taken the speed control up. The note rose, turned to a whisper and vanished into supersonics. I tried to reach the recorder and he pushed me away. I said, 'You're bloody mad.' I grappled with him and tripped. We both went sprawling. Then it happened.

The door and the windows resounded to a series of cracking blows. Then the latch burst and the door crashed open. The windows, frames and glass, exploded inwards in a shower of fragments. I saw the recorder jump in the air and poise impossibly on one corner, and as it hung there the deck dented in half a dozen places as if from the blows of huge, invisible beaks. I just had time to see the camera toppling and the bowl of the prab flying towards me, then there was a flash and an electric fizzing and the lights went out. I lay in the darkness with a crashing and snapping going on round me as if a pack of gorillas was loose in the room, taking it apart. The air seemed thick and pressure waves like those from explosions pushed at my eardrums. I heard Boulter's voice saying faintly, 'Don't move. Don't try to stand, don't go for the door. Don't get in their way.' I did as I was told. I don't think I could have moved far anyway. I was paralysed with fright.

The destruction seemed to go on for an hour though it was probably over in five minutes. Then the noise began to die down. My eyes had got accustomed to the darkness and I saw the curtains flow out over the ruined windows, jumping and flicking as a host of invisible somethings shouldered them aside. Silence fell, and the drapes stopped moving. Boulter stood up. I saw him silhouetted against the light from the windows. He said calmly. 'Well, that's that. Somewhere I should have some fusewire. . . .'

Later, after we had cleared up the mess of glass and dural that had been a tapedeck, a camera and a microphone, he condescended to explain why we were still alive.

'I had it more or less worked out after that incident with the prab. These things are sentient, and they're damned easily aggravated. But they've got their limitations. I suppose any intelligence must have with the exception of the Prime Mover itself. For instance, they could have stopped operations a lot more easily by going for us that morning. We were standing there, we were easy meat. But somehow they couldn't accept our brand of radiation as a motivating agent. They simply flew at the thing they could detect. In that case the mike. Later, the signal generator. Now of course they've cleared the lot. Pity about that, there was some good equipment there. But it was machines, Glyn; machines every time. In all the centuries they've lived, and nobody will ever tell their age, they've never come to terms with the human brain. Maybe they did at one time, and they've forgotten. I just don't know.

'I don't know if they understand progressions either, or if their reaction was simply to sonar emission. It's a pity; I'd like to know more but I don't fancy setting up the gear again, even if I could afford it. Next time they might twig us . . .'

I must say that was one sentiment with which I could most heartily agree.

As far as I was concerned that was the end of the matter. I've never gone back to Frey, and don't intend to. I would be safe enough of course as long as I did nothing but sit and look. But I know what's there, you see. I just don't fancy the idea any more.

As far as I know Boulter forgot the whole thing within a week. He likes to move on and try out new ideas. A short time ago he heard about the startling experiments with laser light emissions that are being done in the States, and right now he's trying to think up a substitute for synthetic ruby so that he can build a gun of his own. I'm all for it; after what he played with at Frey Abbey, death-rays seem positively homely.

Synth

The apartment was small, as all twenty-second-century apartments had perforce to be, and looked out from its fifty-storey height over the panorama of roofs and canyons that was the latter-day London. On one near roof a spark of colour lodged against a grey mansard showed where a solitary sunbather took advantage of the lull between dawn and First Shift; the rest of the buildings were deserted, stark and detailed in the still light. The geometric wilderness stretched to horizon haze; Earth once had many things to show more fair.

The windows of the flatlet boasted movable frames, a rare anachronism these days; the casements stood ajar admitting the nearly smokeless morning air. On the sill beyond, sparrows chattered. With all England a built-over mass of concrete and steel these creatures, most unattractive of birds, had managed to survive.

At the windows, arms folded and frowning faintly, stood a girl. She was tall and delicately proportioned, with the rare swaying curve to the back that gives a woman's body litheness. She wore a short belted robe of white towelling; her yellow-brown hair, still tousled from sleep, hung across her eyes. The eyes were long tailed, and combined with the sleek angle of the jaw to produce that facial type sometimes described by the fanciful as catlike. The girl was still enough not to disturb the birds; if their noise penetrated her consciousness, she gave no sign of it.

Her attention seemed totally drawn to the sunbather. As she watched the figure on the roof it sat up, waved an arm at the distant window of the flat. She acknowledged the gesture with the tiniest inclination of her head then turned away, still frowning slightly, face otherwise expressionless. She started, silently, to fix her bed. As she moved her feet whispered against concrete, raising faint moth-sounds from its bareness.

The flat was unusual in other respects apart from its lack of furnishing. No pictures relieved the walls, the little tridee epics that had recently become the rage in Town; and there was no calorie box, the omnipresent chute through which CentSup and their subsidiaries delivered packaged meals to half the country. The lack of eating arrangements was in fact complete; not even an ancient infrared grill was in evidence, and the wall cupboards lining the kitchenette alcove were empty of glass and plasticware.

The girl swung the coverlet across the bed and folded the top sheet back against the starkness of the pillow. She crossed the room to the shower, shrugged off the housecoat and bathed, soaping herself vigorously. Hot air hoses, sliding from the ceiling, dried her; she stepped out, dressed carefully in a white *cheongsam* and sat at a wall mirror to work some tidiness into her hair. By the time she was finished the sparrows had done with their squabbling and flown, and traffic sounds were floating up to the room from the sprawling city below.

She palmed a switch. The first of the day's news bulletins began to unroll itself, the letters of the announcements standing out in startling colour from the wall trivvyscreen. The girl watched a time impassively; then the switch was flicked again, the images vanished in a quick electronic popping. She pulled from under the bed a plastic grip; rummaging inside, she produced an old book. Very old it must have been, for its binding was of leather. She opened it to a mark, tucked the bookmark inside the cover, and began to read.

When her wrist chrono gave her a quarter of ten she stood up, flicking at the slight creases in her dress. The book was restored to its place of concealment; she picked up handbag and gloves, stared a last time round the apartment. She walked across and closed the windows then stepped through the door, hearing the lock wards shuffle to a fresh configuration behind her. At the end of the corridor was a vaclift. She entered it and was whirled down in a matter of seconds to the level of the street.

She touched her wrist to call a cab. The vehicle waited bumbling and fizzing, tapping its antennae impatiently while she eased herself into the passenger cubicle. She spoke her destination to the intercom, leaned back to let the seat cushioning take the acceleration.

The car picked up the control rails buried in the road surface, U-turned, and swooped for the first intersect a couple of hundred yards ahead.

The journey through London's confusion of traffic took some time. The cab finally slowed to a stop and she got out, feeding a token absently to the extruded box of the Auto-conductor. She stood in bright sunlight, looking round slowly. In front of her was a plaza. In its centre, beside the darkened swaths of the cabways, fountains played; around them a considerable crowd had already collected. Over the people rose a huge pale block of building, more than classically severe in design, with square windows set in geometric rows. On its forehead the place wore like a caste-mark a colossal statue, a triumph of the rediscovered Cubist movement; Justice, holding aloft a golden sword and scales, proclaimed the New Bailey, greatest criminal court in the land. The girl's destination was nearer, on her side of the square. Similarly vast and white, but unornamented; the Supreme Court of Judicature, hub of the country's administration of civil law. She squared her shoulders, a tiny reflexive gesture, and began to walk towards it, heels tinkling on the bright hardness of the pathway.

For a moment she was unobserved; then the people saw her. Shouting began; cameras were lifted, splashing back on their users her image in cubes of coloured gel; she saw a trivvyrig airborne and swooping, blunt nose aimed at her head. The crowd broke, beginning to run. State Troopers reached her first, formed round her a phalanx that butted its way through the jostling of the mob. There was much noise. More Troopers, arms linked in the old fashion, made a path for her to the entrance of the building; she stepped through the doors into a further tumult. Reporters boiled about, shouting questions and waving microphones; trivvyrigs darted from every side. She closed her mind to the uproar; her guards hurried her across the entrance hall and into a lift that spun her up into the high precincts of the place.

She sat in a small room, grey-painted, plain except for the grille of an airvent placed behind the solitary desk. At the desk, a woman regarded her sharply before consulting the lit panel in front of her and a sheaf of forms.

'Name?'

'Megan Wingrove.' The girl's voice was soft, with a trace of huskiness.

The other tapped a stylus irritably on a plastic sheet. 'Identification, please.'

'I'm sorry. M.E.G. one nine, stroke zero two.'

All this was formality. 'Tag?'

Megan searched quickly in her handbag, lifted the little metallic disc and held it forward. The other sniffed. 'Put it on please. You know the rules.'

'I'm sorry,' said the girl again. She slipped the dogtag on to her wrist, tightening the thong.

'Your place of manufacture?'

'Birmingham.'

'Year?'

'Two one seven two.'

'Thank you.' The stylus pointed. 'Wait in the next room, will you? You'll be told when your case opens.'

'Thank you . . .' Megan rose self-consciously, hips swaying a trifle, walked through the white-painted door. Beyond was a line of chairs; she sat down, fingers playing with the lace at her wrist, eyes on the ceiling indicator as she waited her turn.

The case of Davenport *v.* Davenport would have raised enough dust to satisfy even the trivvy magnates without the astounding disclosure by Mrs. Ira Amanda Davenport of the nature of the offence allegedly committed by her husband. For a famous painter, a delineator of the crowned and uncrowned heads of royalty, a master of egg tempera and chocolate boxes, to be involved in divorce proceedings was spectacular stuff; for the other woman to be named openly was better; but—and the full impact only hit an astounded newsworld after urgent consultations with the staff of the reconstituted Somerset House—for the Party Cited, Megan Wingrove, M.E.G. 19/02, to be a *Synth* . . . why, that was past all belief. The Davenport mansion, a steel and chromium pile located not far from the Haymarket on Level Three, was besieged *instanter*; but nothing more was forthcoming. Ira of course had long since taken herself off to the home of understanding friends and Henry Aloysius Davenport, A.R.C.A., R.A., eschewed comment; or rather his lawyer eschewed comment, Mr. Davenport himself being unavailable to the public gaze. In lieu of hard news, the rumours grew, so fast and so far that Lord Chief Justice Hayward in his opening remarks for the case felt in duty bound to dispel some at least of the fog surrounding the affair.

'I think it only proper,' said the Judge, 'before beginning an investigation of the business before us, to present to the court several aspects of the matter which may in the somewhat unfortunate enthusiasm shown by the . . . ah . . . popular organs, have become distorted; and to disabuse the minds of all present of certain irrelevancies which would appear to have attached themselves to it.

'There is no question of the responsibility of the Synthetic, Megan Wingrove, in the eyes of the law. The charge preferred by plaintiff against her husband Mr. Henry Aloysius Davenport is of mental cruelty, and is acceptable under the appropriate section of the Divorce Amendment Act of 1992 and subsequent Acts. In so far as the compliance of the said Megan Wingrove is concerned, the court must decide during and pursuant to this hearing what proportion of blame is to be attached.

'These facts I expect to be firmly borne in mind by you all, and wish specifically to bring them to the attention of counsels for the plaintiff and for the defendant. Gentlemen, am I understood?'

Mr. Neville Martensson, for the plaintiff, and Mr. Richard Blakeney, K.C., for the defendant, bowed in unison.

'Very well,' said the Lord Chief Justice. 'Then I feel we may begin. . . .'

Megan, sitting unobtrusively to one side of the court, had let her attention wander. She'd seen the interior of the great hall often enough on the trivvyscreens, one channel was permanently reserved for its proceedings; but she had never before set foot in it, not even in the public galleries. She looked round at them now, at the long lines of faces, many of them turned towards her. Below, the floor of the court was dominated by the Judge's bench and the jury box; British justice still insisted on leaving the ultimate authority in the hands of amateurs. Facing each other across a floor of pale orange wood were the desks of the opposing counsels; beyond them was the railed-off body of the court where witnesses and the more favoured of the audience waited expectantly. Imitation sunlight, generated by lines of high-powered lamps, flooded through clerestory windows; the whole effect was bright, almost gay. It reminded Megan of a stage set rather than a place for the sober dispensing of justice. In a sense of course it was a set; the trivvyrigs were everywhere, whirring and humming, swooping on their near-invisible supports of telescoping rods. She could see their operators, intent behind a long glass panel set just beneath the roof.

She was recalled to the business in hand by Mr. Martensson

rising to open for the plaintiff. The counsel was a short, square man, inclined to dumpiness, with pale eyes and a small red vee of a mouth that he kept tightly pursed imparting to his face an oddly prim expression. He stated his case briskly; he had a habit while talking of rubbing his hands over and over in a faintly sinister way, as if washing with invisible soap. Megan watched him, fascinated.

The facts of the matter were relatively simple. For some time Henry Davenport had been proclaimed among the top social set at least as the country's leading portrait painter. Five years previously he had married Ira, *née* Stowey, in one of the season's biggest weddings. Eighteen months later and several million dollars richer he had ordered from the Birmingham branch of InterNatMech (Great Britain) a Synthetic for general duties in the house as servant, maid-of-all-work and companion to his wife during his frequent and lengthy lecture tours abroad. The early evidence was rapidly dealt with; an official of InterNatMech confirmed the sale and delivery, while various other interested parties testified to the life of amity hitherto led by the Davenports. Martensson made his points quickly, wasting no words, and there were no interruptions from the defence.

Some months after the arrival of the Synth the first signs of friction had begun to appear. Henry it seemed had started to spend more and more time with his synthetic servant, preferring Meg's company to that of his lawful spouse. Many nights the two passed companionably by the romantic light of a fire, sitting chatting and reading poetry. The remonstrances of the unhappy Mrs. Davenport had fallen on deaf ears; then had come the evening of July 14, just three months ago now, and the great Incident. At this point counsel for the plaintiff called Mrs. Davenport to the stand; and the Lord Chief Justice, with a fine sense of timing, adjourned the court for lunch.

'Mrs. Davenport,' said Martensson, resuming his case in an air of hushed expectancy, 'perhaps you would like to tell me in your own words exactly what happened on that occasion?'

Ira, a rather overweight blonde from whom the best efforts of prosthetic makeup technicians had been unable to remove a faintly overblown air, sniffed and touched her nostrils with a balled-up handkerchief. 'It was . . . very terrible,' she said in a low voice. 'I . . . I shall never forget it, not to my dying day. . . .'

'Yes. Do please go on.'

'I . . . knew there was something wrong. As soon as I entered the house. I'd been staying with friends, I'd returned unexpectedly. The . . . atmosphere, I've always been most sensitive to atmosphere. Acutely sensitive. The . . . house was silent. Quiet as a g-grave. I . . . I was concerned, I didn't put on any lights. You see I knew something was terribly wrong . . . I went to my husband's room. He was not there. I . . . didn't know what to do . . .'

'Did you think of calling the police?'

'I . . . the scandal, the outrage. . . . We . . . had a position, Mr. Martensson. You understand . . .'

'Quite, quite,' said the counsel sympathetically. 'What did you in fact do, Mrs. Davenport?'

Henry Davenport, dapper, bearded, and clad in one of his famous cherry-coloured suits, began to exhibit strong signs of distress. He fidgeted in his seat, casting anxious glances at his counsel. The symptoms were not overlooked; a trivvyrig glided to him quietly, transfixing the artist with the cold eye of its lens. Richard Blakeney seemed blissfully unaware of the byplay; he persisted in his attempts to balance a stylus on the tip of one finger.

'I . . . waited,' said Ira. 'I daren't even . . . call out. I was having a terrible thought. I don't know what put it into my head. I . . . went to . . . that creature's room.' She indicated Megan with a flick of one varnished nail. 'I . . . I opened the door. Quietly, so as not to disturb . . . it. If it was sleeping . . .'

'And was it sleeping, Mrs. Davenport?'

'It was not. It was . . . lying on the bed. *With my husband.* . . .'

Excited hubbub from the court. The Judge rapped peremptorily for order.

'And what did you do then?'

'I . . . I screamed. I think I screamed. The shock, the outrage . . . frankly I can't remember. . . .'

Richard gave up his operations with the stylus and narrowed his eyes at the witness. Across the court Megan sat watching quietly, hands lying in her lap.

Martensson prompted smoothly. 'What happened then, Mrs. Davenport? Try to tell the court.'

'The . . . thing, the Synth . . . sat up. Its blouse was unbuttoned down the front, I saw that clearly. And my husband . . .' Ira put a hand to her forehead. 'The rest's gone. Just a blank. I'm sorry.'

'That's quite all right,' said Mr. Martensson. 'As the court appreciates, the whole affair was a great shock to you. I don't think I have any more questions for the moment.'

Richard Blakeney jackknifed himself to his feet. 'Permission to examine the witness, M'Lord?'

'Granted.'

The counsel approached the stand, leaned against it while he contemplated the ceiling of the courtroom. In physical appearance he was Martensson's complete opposite. He was tall and thin, inclined almost to droopiness; his face, with the wide mouth and long, half-veiled eyes, was that of a ballet dancer. His opponent, outwardly cocksure, watched him speculatively. The brain behind that sleepy mask had cost more cases than Martensson cared to remember.

Richard's eyes, roving quietly, stopped at Megan. He smiled, while she stared back uncertainly. He scratched an ear, harrumphed a couple of times, and turned at last to the witness. 'Er . . . good afternoon, Mrs. Davenport. . . .'

Titters of amusement. Judge Hayward rapped for order. Ira stared at the K.C., truculent and a little tear stained.

'Er . . . yes,' said Richard. 'Mrs. Davenport, have you ever been in a court of law before?'

'Objection!' Martensson bounced to his feet. 'The question is irrelevant. Counsel is trying to intimidate the witness.'

The Lord Chief Justice raised enquiring eyebrows at Blakeney. Richard looked vaguely troubled. 'On the contrary, M'Lord,' he said. 'The question was designed to assist Mrs. Davenport. I was about to remark that witness need have no cause for concern as long as she answers clearly and concisely what is asked her.'

Judge Hayward looked annoyed. 'Well, Mr. Martensson?'

'Objection withdrawn. . . .' Martensson sat back sulkily. Richard clucked at him faintly; he always liked to score a quick first point off his opponent. He turned back to the witness. 'Mrs. Davenport, on the night you described, the night of July fourteen, you claim to have been thrown into a state of shock by the discovery of your husband and Miss Wingrove together. Yet you noticed one apparently minor detail with great clarity: the unbuttoned blouse of Miss Wingrove. Is this not remarkable?'

'I . . . no. The little things, the d-details . . . they stand in one's mind. They're often the only things one does remember. . . .'

'Yes,' said Richard. 'Quite, quite. . . . Now the blouse you say was dishevelled. To what extent, Mrs. Davenport?'

'I . . . I told you. It was undone. . . .'

'Were the girl's breasts uncovered?'

'I . . . don't know.'

'Come, Mrs. Davenport, you saw this with great clarity. It was the one detail that burned itself, as it were, on your mind. Were her breasts exposed?'

'I . . .'

'*Were they*, Mrs. Davenport?'

'No,' said the woman sullenly. 'They were covered when she got up. But they hadn't been, they hadn't been. . . .'

'That, Mrs. Davenport, is an assumption that I think is unwarrantable. Are you in a position to prove your assertion?'

'Well . . . use your imagination. It was *obvious* what had been going on. . . .'

'With your imagination already working at capacity,' said Richard sweetly, 'any attempts on my part would I feel be superfluous.'

'Objection! Counsel is intimidating the witness. His last remark constitutes an open accusation of false testimony.'

'That, M'Lord,' said Richard, 'was nothing of the sort. I merely wished to establish the degree of dishevelment noticed by the witness, and to point out that what had happened prior to her entering the room can scarcely be known to her now. Or maybe it can. You claim you are a Sensitive, Mrs. Davenport. Do you perhaps possess second sight as well?'

'*Objection! . . .*'

'Question withdrawn,' said the counsel, hearing ripples of laughter in the audience. 'Now to proceed, Mrs. Davenport. Did you on entering your maid's room notice any other signs of disorder? Apart from the blouse which we seem to have established was only slightly disarranged?'

'She was lying in an abandoned attitude,' snarled the witness. 'Her thighs were exposed. . . .'

'Her thighs were exposed,' said Richard pensively. He stared round at a vista of thighs, all bared in accordance with the dictates of fashion. Mrs. Davenport, dressed herself in the season's highest mode, reddened and twitched her skirt across her knees. Richard smiled. 'Is it your opinion then,' he asked pleasantly, 'that bared legs are an infallible sign of depravity?'

'*Objection! . . .*'

'To ease the mind of my learned colleague,' said Blakeney, 'I will not press the witness to answer that question. Now Mrs. Davenport, before we leave this apparently delicate subject, were

there any other signs of dishevelment noted by you? So far we have I
think one slightly untidy blouse. Hardly conclusive proof of adultery, you must admit. . . .'

'His hair,' said Ira, groping. 'My husband's hair. It was all
. . . disarranged. All over his face. . . .'

'To what cause do you ascribe that?'

'She . . . it . . . had been stroking it. Running its f-fingers
through it. A *machine*! . . .' She shuddered, chewing at her lip.

Richard smiled again benignly. 'Mrs. Davenport,' he said, 'not a
hundred yards from this building is an establishment, often fre-
quented by myself, where the payment of a small sum secures
certain services. A machine will wash and shave me; it will sham-
poo my hair; and to my shame be it admitted, *it will massage my
scalp*. Twice a week I return to my Gomorrah; I luxuriate in
blackest sin, shoulder to shoulder frequently with highly placed and
respected officers of this city, while a machine strokes my hair. . . .'
He walked off quietly. Half way to his seat he shook his head
sorrowfully. 'She stroked his hair,' he said, as if to himself.
'*Stroked his hair*. . . .'

He reached his desk and turned, waiting for the amusement to die
down. 'On a point of information, Mrs. Davenport,' he said, 'far
from losing coherence, you would appear on the occasion under
discussion to have been remarkably . . . er . . . fluent.' He drew
from his pocket a slip of paper, squinted at it painfully. 'Did you not
call your husband . . . "a lecher, a louse, a two-bit for-
nicator" . . . You also said, unless my information is incorrect,
"You crafty little bastard, I'll get a hundred thousand a year for this.
. . ." The rest is written down, M'Lord. I'd like to pass it to you for
perusal. . . .'

Laughter broke in a wave.

Before releasing his victim Richard asked permission to recall
Mrs. Davenport during his defence. The matter was protested
vigorously by Martensson; but the counsel for the plaintiff was
overruled by the Lord Chief Justice. Blakeney sat down reasonably
satisfied.

Other evidence followed; the testimony of the State Troopers
called to the house by the distracted Mrs. Davenport, statements
from a doctor and a psychiatrist and from the officer in charge of the
Sector Station where Megan had temporarily been lodged. Martensson had a solid case, and he made the most of it; Richard, sitting
dreamily toying with the stylus, watched the black clouds gather.

'And there can be little doubt,' said the counsel for the plaintiff, winding up his attack on the second day, 'that Henry Davenport did in fact inflict the severest mental pain on his wife. By introducing into his hitherto happy establishment the person of the Synthetic Megan Wingrove he deliberately instituted a situation intolerable to his partner; its culmination, and his disgraceful and abnormal conduct, you have already heard described. I can only ask you, ladies and gentlemen of the jury, to recommend the strongest measures in dealing with this affair; an affair that has already cost an innocent woman more than money can repay in terms of suffering and very real grief.'

He turned triumphantly to the bench. 'M'Lord,' he said, 'the case for the plaintiff rests. . . .'

Court was adjourned for the remainder of the day.

On the third morning Blakeney opened for the defendant.

'The court cannot fail to have noticed,' he said, 'that despite the injunctions given at the start of these proceedings learned counsel for the plaintiff has seen fit to base his case totally on the affair of Megan Wingrove; he has sought to prove, unsuccessfully I might add, that an illicit relationship did exist and that adultery did in fact take place. The defence feels compelled to answer and finally demolish these charges. We shall show beyond reasonable doubt that such a state of affairs did not and could not exist; and we shall prove beyond all question that the accusations that have brought us here are at best the imaginings of an overwrought and highly strung woman, and at worst deliberate machinations dictated by vindictiveness and avarice. M'Lord, have I your permission to proceed?'

Judge Hayward nodded after a moment's consideration. 'Yes, Mr. Blakeney, you have.'

'Thank you, M'Lord,' said Richard easily. 'Then for my first witness I wish to call Mr. Pieter van Mechelren, President of InterNatMech, Amsterdam.'

A buzz of speculation. The parent company of InterNatMech was world-famous; it held exclusive rights of all processes connected with the production of Synths, and was one of the wealthiest business houses in Europe. To get their President on the case in person Blakeney had evidently been pulling some very powerful strings.

The man who took the stand was burly and dark haired; his eyes were big and brown in a plump, smooth-skinned face. He looked like a moderately successful market gardener. Richard knew better.

The counsel opened smartly. 'Your name is Pieter van Mechelren?'

'It is.' The voice was deep, with a faint guttural trace of accent.

'And you are the President of InterNatMech of Holland?'

'Yes.'

'Would you describe yourself as qualified to give opinions on the characteristics and inherent capabilities of the beings known as Synthetics?'

Pieter grinned slowly. 'Jus' about, I reckon.'

Richard consulted his notes. 'I believe you do yourself an injustice,' he said. 'You hold degrees in biochemistry, physics, and physiology, you are an honorary member of the Royal Society and the Royal Institution, of the Dutch Society of Physiomechanics and of the American Institute of Bioengineering. You hold a chair in Cybernetics at the University of Gröningen; and you are generally accepted to be the world's leading authority on all phases of the construction and operation of Synths. Am I not correct?'

Van Mechelren wagged his hands deprecatingly. 'There are maybe some diff'rent opinions on that.'

Richard smiled. 'I think yours, Mr. van Mechelren, will satisfy this court.' He indicated Megan, sitting a few yards from him. 'Tell me, did your firm market the figure you see here?'

'Yes, indirectly. She was produced under licence about three years back by InterNatMech Great Britain, at their installation in Birmingham.'

'I see. Now Mr. van Mechelren, you've heard the evidence already given in court. What is your professional opinion of it with regard to your product?'

'Wi' regard to our product?' Pieter spread thick-fingered hands. 'A load of hossfeathers, ahm afraid.'

There were sniggers.

Richard nodded. 'I see. Now before coming down to detail, perhaps you'd give the court a brief outline of the nature of Synthetic humans. A short history of their development if you like. I want everybody here to be fully conversant with the subject.'

Pieter shrugged. 'Would tak' a bit of time. Is a big subject.'

'Briefly then.'

'Briefly? Well, I try. . . . ' The Dutchman frowned thoughtfully. 'Th' idea of a Synth is mebbe ver' old. After all the Cretans had a guy called Talos, used to frighten the hell out of 'em 'cause he was made of brass. There is no time in the history of the race when we've bin without a robot of some kind. Something . . . automatic, something ticking, turning, singing. . . .' He rocked his hands, miming the actions of machinery. 'Engines that could go where we could not, because we were too big or too small; taste fire that was too warm for us, ice that was too cold; think faster, move faster, fly in the air, burrow through the sea. . . . Always machines, better an' better, more and more perfect robots for us to use. Only robot isn' a good name for the li'l girl here. Name comes from two hundred years back, an old Czech play. Robot, mechanical worker She isn' mechanical. She's a Synth. . . .'

'How long have Synths themselves been in existence?'

Van Mechelren shrugged his broad shoulders. 'Long, long time. Sometimes a' like to think, ever' machine we ever made, that was a part of them. Hundreds o' years they took, bein' born. A' could give names, you know; Holstein, Rigby, Capotek; but they don' mean nothing. Is no . . . date, no time you can set down and say *dere*, th' first Synth. They jus' came along, was a continuous process. Of . . . growth, development; a li'l bit here, another there. . . . Go back two centuries, there were computers. These were some of the' ancestors. . . .'

Richard nodded. 'But computers were, and occasionally still are, bulky affairs. How did they develop into the figure we see in front of us?'

'By simplification,' said the Dutchman. 'By the transistor supplanting the valve, being supplanted in its turn; always simpler, easier, quicker. That way we always grow up, we get smart. Like the petrol engine. Was a hell of a thing. Wit' diesel, easier. Turbines; nothin' to 'em. One day, who can say? Antigrav; nothin' to that at-all. Li'l guy wit' moons an' stars on his hat wave a wand, *presto* . . . right back to de start for us.'

He held up a sleeve. 'Look. Once was glass an' metal. To make' a computer then, a brain, needed all steel an' wire. Now see, I tak' two threads. From my jacket will do fine. So, I treat dem, so. . . . Now I pass through a current. In the threads, a change. Their resistance alters. To a further current, it will be greater. This is the start. This is memory.

'The li'l girl there, she has a head of cottonwool. Or what you call the stuff, candyfloss. . . . But ver' special candyfloss. The Wolfenden cerebral matrix, developed in this country fifty years ago. Intelligence; memory, extrapolation, decision, you know what it is? A function of number of cells, hookups between 'em. Nothin' difficult. So you spin a wire, ver' fine, put him in a resistant jacket. Then a thousand, just alike. A million. Ten million. Hook 'em up sideways, crossways, ever' way. You put a microscope on a Wolfenden matrix, you got chicken wire. Thousands, thousands o' layers, all balled together. There's your brain. It gets easy, it gets small. You mak' the body the same way; legs, arms, the muscles there, all easy, all small. It tak's years; but you keep tryin', you get there. You make a figure, a woman. You got a Synth. . . .'

'Well, it still sounds a very complicated process to me.'

'To understand is simple,' said the Dutchman, wagging his head. 'But to make . . . in truth, it is not easy. Not easy at all.'

'Now this girl,' said Richard, 'with her rather pretty candyfloss brain. What drives her, what makes her move?'

'Same as makes you an' me move,' said van Mechelren. 'She's a mass o' muscle, tendon, all packed in. Only she don' eat for energy, she gets her push-an'-pull another way. She synthesizes, from sunlight.'

'Like a plant, in other words?'

'Yah, so. But better'n a plant. A plant's imperfect, needs th' soil. A plant *converts*, she *collects*. A walkin' solar battery, she is. The skin, the hair. . . . She loves the sun, she'll bathe there all day long. She don' need no food. She don' stick her feet in de earth for salt.'

'So Synthetic figures are in fact dependent on the sun for their energy.'

'Ah, you see. Ideally, yes. But you shut one in a box she'll get sleepy soon, curl up. Go dormant. In a room, a city, is the same. So she can recharge other ways, if she needs. Sometimes at night, when she sleeps.'

'Tell us about this business of a sleeping period, Mr. van Mechelren. Is it important it coincides so closely with the human cycle?'

'No, not at all. Same way it don' matter she got two arms, two legs, or ten. We could build 'em any way we like. But people jus' prefer having things around that act like them, look like them. Nest o' wires an' eyes sits up an' says Daddy, they get worried. Is crazy but is true. So . . . things like dat.' He waved his hand at Megan, a queer, sharp little gesture that attracted her eyes instantly, and grinned. 'We prefer 'em that way too. . . .'

'How many Synths are produced in the course of a year?'

Van Mechelren frowned. 'Oh . . . two, three dozen at th' out-side. No more.'

'Then the population of these people is in fact quite small.'

'Ver' small. After all, they come a bit expensive.'

'Of course. I think the popular idea is of some sort of assembly line. This is incorrect.'

'*Ya*. . . .' Pieter scowled. 'Popular idea, I seen that. Here an assembly line, there another. De hands go on, plonk . . . de heads, bonk . . . like makin' automobiles. Is not like that at all. Is like a . . . hospital, more. A' wish you could see. Jus' one we work on, at a time. And careful, so careful. . . . This mus' be right, an' that; no flaws, not anywhere. Otherwise she jus' don' go. . . . Even the skin, the flesh. Grown so carefully. . . . Is a ver' long job.'

'*Grown*, you say?'

'*Ya*. Grown.' The Dutchman's eyes glittered with amusement. 'Is a hydrocarbon base, long-chain molecules. It grows. . . .'

'I see. Well, you make these people sound very human. *Are* they human, Mr. van Mechelren?'

'Ach, no. Never. Wit' humans . . . they get sick, they die sometime. They get mean, hell, sometimes they have a war. They have laws for each other, an' courts to try mak' 'em work.' He glanced round humorously. 'Wit' these people, never. They don' need no laws. They don' get mad, cut each other up. They know only one thing. Obey a human, when he talks. That's what we teach 'em, right from the start. Is a machine that drips it into 'em, ever' fibre of the brain, till they can't forget, not ever. They're not human, for damn sure. Not robot either. They're Synths. . . .'

'Thank you,' said Richard. 'Now you've heard already, in the course of these proceedings, various allegations levelled at the . . . ah . . . Synthetic, Megan Wingrove. How do you rate them, technically and professionally?'

'Like a' said. Hossfeathers.' Pieter started to grin. 'Why don' they sue de sideboard for sittin' there? Or arrest the trivvybox for attempted rape? Man, I never heard one thing the half as crazy. . . .'

'It is impossible then for a Synth to behave in such a way as to bring mental suffering to a human? Or to connive at such behaviour?'

'Is crazy. The human suffers, the fault is in dem. Maybe it hurts 'em to see the sun come up, they want the world to be dark. Is not the fault of de sun. . . . You know sometimes a' think,' said van Mechelren, 'a' like to get hold of a few of these humans. We put 'em through the mill, tie 'em on our squeakbox a couple of days, they better for it. One hell of a sight.'

'Yes, quite. Now returning to details, we've heard an accusation of immorality levelled against Megan Wingrove. How do you react to this?'

Van Mechelren reacted by rumbling with laughter. 'Man,' he said, 'how's she goin' to be immoral? What wit'?'

'I'm asking you that, sir.'

'There is no way,' said the Dutchman quietly. 'No way at all.'

'In fact you are unable to take the charge seriously.'

'I tak' it serious all right,' said Pieter darkly. 'But not like that. I think somewhere . . . is a bad smell of fish.'

At this point counsel for the plaintiff ejaculated something angrily. The doubts as to what Mr. Martensson actually said were never finally resolved; but a reporter sitting close behind his desk claimed, possibly with more optimism then accuracy, that the remark terminated with the phrase *Venus aversa*. It was enough to send a generation of newshounds scurrying for Sir Richard Burton and the *Kama Sutra*; the results of their investigations were spectacular to say the least.

The Dutchman's evidence closed the session for the morning and Blakeney promptly requested, and was granted, a recess till the following day. As soon as he was released from the stand van Mechelren walked over to where Megan was sitting by herself. He hooked a chair from beside the wall and squatted across it, arms on the backrest, chin on his hands. 'Hey magnificent,' he said, grinning. 'How's ever' li'l spurwheel?'

She looked at him startled, then began to grin back. It was the first time she'd smiled in court. A moment later Mr. Martensson, clearing the papers from his desk, glanced up and scowled. Richard, van Mechelren, and the Synth were in earnest consultation; he saw Megan lift a slim leg, tapping the knee and rotating the ankle as she made some little complaint about the joint.

'Hey, look,' said the Dutchman, still grinning, 'a' tell you what. If you can stand to watch a fat man eat, I tak' you both to lunch. O.K.?' They left with the girl shortly afterwards, van Mechelren with one hand dropped protectingly on her shoulder.

'And I wish it to be clearly understood,' said the Lord Chief Justice acidly when opening the fourth day's hearing, 'that in the event of a further outbursting of such offensive speculation, I shall order the court cleared and complete these investigations *in camera*. I trust the public, and those members of the press most guilty of this gross breach of privilege, will take due and solemn warning. Now Mr. Blakeney, are you ready to resume your case?'

For the moment Richard had no more questions for van Mechelren; the Dutchman was handed over to Mr. Martensson for cross-examination.

'I'm sure,' said the counsel for the plaintiff, opening sweetly, 'we all appreciated Mr. van Mechelren's exposition of yesterday, enlivened as it was with what I believe our Transatlantic cousins were once disposed to term crackerbarrel philosophy.'

A ripple of laughter. Martensson rode above it. 'There are, however, one or two points that I think could be elucidated. Mr. van Mechelren'—he hooked his thumbs in his lapels, a timeworn gesture—'you mentioned . . . ah . . . recharging as a process sometimes necessary to the Synths produced by your company. Will you elaborate on the system?'

'Certainly.' The Dutchman steepled his fingers. 'The charging is carried out from a standard wall socket an' supplements the main photosynthetic system of chemical energy storage. Reaction between ionised cells of the deep dermal layers an'——'

'A wall *socket*, you say?' Counsel interrupted, rotating sharply on his heel. 'I take it, then, that some form of . . . ah . . . socket exists on the body of the Synthetic?'

Van Mechelren began to smile. 'That is so. Normally, th' orifice is kept shut by a sphincter, a . . . ring muscle, I think you say.' He clenched his fist. 'See, so. Lowering of th' energy level in the lumbar cortex allows relaxation of the sphincter prior to insertion of the coupling. So. . . .' His fingers parted, forming a circle.

'I see.' Counsel appeared to be biting his words into fragments, and spitting them at the witness like small explosive bullets. 'And where, Mr. van Mechelren, is this . . . orifice, and its attendant muscular configuration, situated?'

The Dutchman wagged expressive shoulders. 'Wherever's convenient. Could be practic'lly anywhere; could be in the groin or hip, or the side of the thoracic cage. Sometimes in th' throat, the knee . . .'

'In the case of the Synthetic under discussion, where is the apparatus sited?'

A moment of intense silence in the court. Van Mechelren's grin became fractionally broader. 'In the right ankle,' he said, and added under his breath. '*you dirty li'l man.* . . .'

A sudden gusting of laughter from the public benches, quelled angrily by the Lord Chief Justice.

Martensson, rattled, wouldn't relinquish his bone. 'Mr. van Mechelren, would you describe to the court the exact steps by which recharging is carried out?'

The grin didn't leave the Dutchman's face, but his eyes became pure frost. 'No,' he said, with ominous gentleness. 'A' would not.'

'But I'm afraid I must insist that you do.'

'Mr. Martensson,' said van Mechelren easily, 'how exac'ly does your wife shave the hair from beneath her arms?'

Uproar, silenced loudly from the bench. 'The witness,' said Judge Hayward severely, 'will refrain from insolence towards the officers of the court. And he will confine himself to answering the questions put by counsel.'

Van Mechelren inclined his head gravely.

'Objection!'

Richard was on his feet, staring angrily at Martensson. 'M'Lord, the defence expresses its concern at the direction and tone of counsel's questioning. So far his remarks have contained nothing but pointless and embarrassing innuendo.'

The Lord Chief Justice peered over his spectacles to where Megan watched back wide eyed. 'The matter of embarrassment,' he observed, 'seems to me to be infinitely debatable. As to the direction of questioning, the court agrees that little profitable result is to be expected. Can counsel justify his mode of approach?'

Martensson smiled nastily. 'It is not our wish, M'Lord, unduly to . . . ah . . . embarrass counsel's witnesses. I am prepared therefore to withdraw my last question.'

The Judge nodded. 'Very well. Proceed.'

The mouth of the counsel for the plaintiff was compressed into a vicious little vee. 'Mr. van Mechelren, before you step down I would like confirmation of one further point. You gave it as your opinion that . . . ah . . . biological gratification of a human male by a Synthetic is an impossibility.'

'A' did.'

'And that was in fact, and remains, your considered opinion? On that you are prepared publicly to stake your professional reputation?'

Van Mechelren's eyebrows contracted to a wary scowl. 'In de present circumstances,' he said after a moment's pause, 'yes.'

Martensson pounced. 'I did not ask you to devise circumstances, Mr. van Mechelren, I asked a general question and require a general answer.'

'Wit' one of our li'l people,' said Pieter steadily, 'it would be out of the question.'

'Then the matter is after all an impossibility. You stand by your previous remark.'

'You'd have to build a special figure,' said the Dutchman thoughtfully. 'Ver' special. . . .'

'But InterNatMech never have?'

'No.'

'Then I repeat and I stress, Mr. van Mechelren, the thing is an impossibility. You seem well versed in prevarication, sir, but we must have you stand by something. Will you stand by that?'

'Nothin's impossible,' admitted van Mechelren. Then suddenly the grin was back. 'But hell, man,' he said. 'We never bin asked. . . .'

Martensson turned savagely to the bench. 'M'Lord, I ask the court to note that despite Mr. van Mechelren's evident technological prowess his bias in this matter is such as to make him a hostile witness.'

Judge Hayward regarded the counsel for the plaintiff mildly. 'The fact is noted, Mr. Martensson,' he said. 'I would have thought that it was self-evident. . . .'

There were titters of amusement.

Richard returned from the lunchtime recess with a long face. Certain enquiries he'd instituted had produced depressing answers. He arrived back at court early, tracked down an elusive Pieter van Mechelren with whom truth to tell he'd spent a good proportion of the previous evening in moody drinking. He ran the Dutchman to earth in a side room where Megan, refreshed after her first good night's sleep in weeks, was vainly trying to satisfy van Mechelren's curiosity.

'Loadings now,' Pieter was saying as he entered. 'Humeral max?'

'Nine five kilos. Dextral emphasis sixty-forty.'

Van Mechelren tapped a stylus against his teeth. 'Good, good girl . . . femoral?'

'Two fifty by two.'

'Main sphincters?'

'A hundred kilos rated max.'

'Pieter,' said Richard, leaning over him. 'You and I have troubles.'

The Dutchman flicked a sheet of his notes. 'You look after de humans, my son, tak' all your time. I got my problems here. . . .' He mumbled. 'Lumbar configuration twelve by twelve, ah-hah. . . . Ganglia dee-fourteen-nines, lymphatics low-pressure. . . . Reaction to prim'ry stimulus . . . one over fifty, tolerance zero zero five. . . .' Still tapping, he contrived to grin. 'She's a tough li'l girl, Richard. A' tell you what, a' tak' care an' never argue wit' her.'

Megan smiled at him.

The counsel lit a cigarette, sourly. He sat on the desk edge and crossed his long legs. 'She'll be a dead li'l girl if we don't watch points. You scared to die, Meg?'

'No.'

'But you do want to live?'

'Yes,' said the Synth. 'Yes.'

Van Mechelren exploded suddenly. 'What's this bloody rot, my son?'

Richard blew smoke. 'Second we lose this case the opposition'll take out an injunction against her. Destruct or modify.'

'*What?*'

'You heard,' said Richard. Then, insultingly, '*My son*. . . .'

Pieter swore, hugely. 'You can' modify a stable brain matrix, you know that bloody well. Go back to first principles——'

'I know. They know.'

'Then what in hell——'

'Destruct. There's a precedent. Limber *v.* Cassidy, Manhattan '63. Synth flipped its lid, chucked a couple of guys through an apartment window. Turned out it was a tall apartment. They got a destruct order and blew it apart on the spot. Owner tried for costs. He lost out.'

'Well damme, that's pleasant.' The Dutchman smacked angrily at the table. 'The thing got knocked off skentre. It had a clout, something. I was on dat case.'

'Yes, but they'll still get an order on the strength of it. Claim felonious conduct. Citizens' Protection Act, World Legislative

Council '65. I checked it through. The Limber Synth blew a pretty big scare, they wrapped it up but good. Meg could get a one-way ticket for spitting on the sidewalk. If she could spit. We lose this one and Ira D's got her cold.'

'That bloody woman,' brooded Pieter, 'could well use a kick up th' ass. Who tol' you this?'

'Little legal sparrow.'

The President of InterNatMech glowered at his protégée, then at Richard. 'So why you worryin', my friend? Meg ain't paying you.'

Richard slapped his cigarette on the desk and leaned forward. 'Listen,' he said, 'it so happens I'm still trying to get Henry Aloysius off the hook. The fact that my revered client is a creepy little bastard has nothing to do with the deal. If Meg loses, he loses. Only Henry merely gets bled white paying alimony. Megan . . . *kkkkssss*.' He drew a finger across his throat and leered.

Van Mechelren grunted. 'You think we lose?'

'It's tied up with cast-iron string. Martensson's got the case; so far all I've done's make pretty patterns round the edges. Somebody has to crack. Nobody has. If nobody does . . .' He shrugged, and left the rest unsaid.

'There be bloody good row first,' said the Dutchman ominously.

'So. There be bloody good row. Meg still loses.' He turned to the Synth. 'Megan, I'm going to try and get you in the hotbox this afternoon. I may be rough. If I'm not, our friends will be rougher. O.K.?'

She nodded gravely. He squeezed her knee, trying to remember she wasn't human. 'Keep the flag waving then. I think you're taking old Hayward's fancy.'

Pieter's eyes were narrowed thoughtfully. 'You reckon he let you get away with this, Rich?'

'I can try it. He's a crusty old devil but there's a chance I can swing him.'

The Dutchman shrugged largely. 'Better you than me, son. . . .'

'That's O.K.' Richard smiled like a wolf. 'That's what Davenport's paying me for. . . .'

The bell rang for the opening of the session. Pieter, his equanimity restored, rose and stowed the notebook in his voluminous jacket. He followed the others into the corridor. As he walked, he whistled pensively. The ancient tune had once had a title: *Tulips from Amsterdam*. The Dutchman was nothing if not a patriot.

'M'Lord,' said Richard carefully. 'I would like to call the Synth, Megan Wingrove, to the stand. . . .'

A minor hubbub from the public gallery, and an instantaneous objection from Martensson. Judge Hayward rapped irritably. 'Mr. Blakeney,' he said, 'you are as aware as the rest of this court that legal precedents preclude the evidence of a Synthetic. Your request is disallowed.'

An interruption from the foreman of the jury. 'On a point of information, M'Lord. . . .'

'Yes?'

The man shuffled uncomfortably. 'For many years evidence by trivvy, film, wire, tape, any mechanical means, has been permitted. Would you explain the distinction in the . . . er . . . present case?'

'The distinction,' said the Lord Chief Justice cuttingly, 'seems to me to be self-explanatory. The employment of a method of mechanical reproduction in no way signifies that the evidence of the machine is accepted as is the evidence of a witness. The machine does not originate the evidence; it is the means of its production, and as such is in itself irrelevant. A machine cannot take an oath; neither, for the same reasons, may a Synthetic. Unsworn evidence is of little positive value.'

Richard waited. 'M'Lord,' he said finally. 'May I then be allowed to interrogate an exhibit?'

'What exhibit is that, Mr. Blakeney?'

'The Synth, Megan Wingrove.'

Extraordinarily, the Lord Chief Justice smiled. 'I see no objection, counsel. You may proceed. . . .'

When Megan was installed in the witness box the Judge unexpectedly intervened. 'In many respects,' he said to the court in general, 'this hearing has already proved itself unique; and the present circumstance is certainly without precedent.' He peered at Megan. 'Before counsel starts his examination,' he said gently, 'I'm sure the court would like to hear in your own words some account of your . . . ah . . . manufacture, and subsequent experiences. Have you an objection, Mr. Blakeney?'

'Naturally not, M'Lord,' said Richard uneasily. The Synth, undirected, could hang herself higher than the walls.

Megan smiled apologetically. 'I'm afraid you'll be a little disappointed, My Lord,' she said. 'I can't remember much more of my . . . manufacture than a human remembers of her birth.'

'That,' said the Judge, 'is understood. Simply tell us what you can.'

Megan closed her eyes, thinking deeply. For a time there was silence. Then she looked up again. 'I was born,' she said, 'I'm sorry My Lord, but among ourselves we think of our . . . making as a birth. . . . I was born three years ago, in Birmingham. I don't remember much of the actual . . . process at all.' She paused again. 'There was a . . . darkness,' she said slowly. 'And a . . . coldness and hotness combined, the first Sensation. I can't adequately describe it. It seemed I was . . . floating, in some void, while round me a world was created. It was as if . . . things, objects, the warmth and coldness at first, came into being round me. As if I had always been there. If you can understand what I mean. . . .

'There were . . . voices in the void. They went on and on, saying over strings of figures, readings, pressures. . . . Only I didn't know, then, that they were readings. I didn't know they were voices. Sound was like warmth and cold to me, something . . . not-void. That's the only way I can describe it. Sometimes the voices were very distant. At others they were loud. When they came too close they turned to a sort of roaring that stopped, and then there was the void again. Nothingness. And it would start all over. I was being tested, of course. I realised that later when I . . . understood.

'Then I could see. But there was nothing at first except a sort of greyness. Like a fog. The . . . things, the objects, seemed to make themselves from it, and float back into it again. They had no meaning for me; sometimes they were like a . . . trivvy picture out of tune, they turned to lapping patterns of colour that had no . . . sense, no "up" and "down". In between them the voices were still threading about like other colours. There was no feeling of scale. I might have been a million miles tall or smaller than an electron. I still had no . . . understanding.

'I don't know when I started to be taught. Until then I could have no existence. I was the total of no experience, a sort of sum of zeroes. But I . . . remember first lying on a bed. There was a . . . room. It was small and white, and there was a noise. A humming. I could see; and I knew "up" was above me, and "down" was beneath. I think . . . yes, I could move my head. Because I turned it, and beside me was a machine. It was very big, and grey. Lights shone across it, in lines across its facias. Blue lights, and red, and green. It was very big, it seemed to tower over the bed. There were little discs turning and spools, and the whole thing was singing. That was the noise I could hear.

'I was joined to the machine by a thick loom of cable. It went into my neck just below the jaw. I could have reached up and pulled it away, but I didn't. I didn't move my hands. I didn't know I had "hands".

'I lay watching the lights, and seeing the discs turn; and it seemed the machine spoke to me. I could understand "speak" now, and "silence". "You are awake," it said. "I am a machine." That was all, for a very long time. "You are awake. I am a machine." . . .

'After that I found . . . things beside the bed. There was always something new there. I could pick the things up and handle them. The machine would tell me what they were. "These are flowers," it would say. "This is a book. This is a shoe." . . . Sometimes I didn't understand; then the discs would stop, and the lights would wobble and change, and something would happen inside me and the machine would start again. "This is a book. This is a shoe." It was very . . . patient.

'It told me other things too, when I was ready for them. "Beyond you is a window. Through the window is the sky. The sky is blue."

' "This is a city." . . .

' "It's name is Birmingham." . . .

' "You are a Synth." . . .

' "*This is a man*." . . .'

'How long,' asked Judge Hayward, 'did you remain linked to your machine?'

'The . . . indoctrination lasted two months. The other machine, the one they called a man, would disconnect the wires in little batches, carefully. By then I could speak. "Man," I'd say, "Man." . . . It sounded right to me—I knew "right" by then—but he'd laugh at me, and say "Man . . . *Man*." . . . I got it right in the end; but it took a long time.

'I was sorry when they took the machine away. They said I was finished with it then, they needed it for another like me. They taught me to walk. I was taught . . . properly, by a human. She gave me crutches to use and put me in a sort of tripod thing till I understood about balance. It held me round the waist and if I slipped the legs shot out to stop me falling. I couldn't understand why I had to walk. I just did as I was told.

'They taught me to wear clothes and wash and comb my hair . . . oh, hundreds of things. And of course each day I was going to school. That was easy. There was another machine. I could . . . connect myself to it, there were flexes and they'd left a little socket under my jaw. InSems, they called the lessons. Inducted Seminars. . . . I could choose, after a time, what I wanted to learn. If a . . . fact didn't fit in an established matrix I could research it, get a cross-reference. If the machine couldn't answer I could ask a human tutor. But that didn't happen very often.

'Sometimes they let me see the new figure they were making. She looked very pretty lying on her bed watching the machine, the little discs spinning and turning and the lights. She was coloured, they'd made her a sort of coffee brown. I remember I used to joke with them and say I wanted to be coloured too and I was jealous, but they wouldn't change me. I went back to my Seminaries. They said I had to be smarter than the rest, my owner would be a very particular man.'

'And that owner,' said the Judge, 'was Mr. Davenport?'

'Yes, sir. I met him the first time a few weeks before I was due for release. I remember he was very pleased with me. He made me turn round and stand up and walk. Then he said, "Get her some shoes. Heels. Show her height off. Otherwise, great." . . .' Megan smiled. 'So I had to learn to walk in high heels. It was the one thing they hadn't taught me.

'A short while after that I went out for the first time. Out of the Institute. It was strictly before I was allowed to. There was some trouble over it; Mr. Maskell the Director was very annoyed.'

'Because you left without permission?'

'Yes. I was trying something out, sir. Something I'd been studying. I wanted to see how well I could pass for a human.'

'And was the experiment successful?'

'Oh, yes.' Megan smiled again at a memory. 'I found a shopping level. I **bought** myself a hat and a dress and a pair of shoes. With heels. I wanted to please Mr. Davenport. . . . I was certain I'd be found out but I wasn't. It made me feel . . . good. An assistant wrapped the things and another—a human—held the door for me. I was very proud of myself.'

'How did you . . . ah . . . come by the money for this spree?'

'I stole it,' said Megan winningly. 'I calculated with the profit they were making on me they could afford that at least. In any case the clothes could be refunded. But they let me keep them. I think they were pleased too.'

Van Mechelren, sitting in the body of the court, smiled to himself, leaned back, and clasped his hands.

'A little while after that, after my final Seminars, Mr. Davenport came again. That time he brought his wife. She finally chose my name from a shortlist. It had to be an "M", I was in an *M* batch.'

'How was your second name determined?' asked Judge Hayward.

'By Random Selection apparatus,' said the Synth. 'It has no significance.'

'And after that, you were taken to Mr. Davenport's home?'

'I delivered myself. I was given the address, and an advance on my first month's salary.'

'I see. And . . . ah . . . if I may ask; what was the cost of your manufacture, Miss Wingrove?'

Megan smiled. 'Just over two million dollars.'

'Thank you,' said the Judge. 'And thank you for a most interesting . . . ah . . . exposition. Mr. Blakeney, if you would like to carry on. . . .'

'Thank you, M'Lord.' Richard walked forward to the box. 'Megan, will you tell us, once more in your own way, what happened after you joined the Davenport household?'

'Of course. For some time, some months, I was shown off to everybody. Mr. Davenport used to give a lot of parties. Some of them went on all night. All his friends wanted to see me, and I suppose he was naturally rather proud of me. He bought me a lot of things, clothes and dresses. Oh, and I learned to dance. That was very easy.'

'I see. So things ran smoothly for a time.'

'Yes.'

'What did Mrs. Davenport think of your arrival?'

'She was very pleased. It meant a lot to her, the . . . social distinction and all that. She told me once I was a walking, talking stat-symbol that beat all her friends down flat.'

An angry sound from the opposition desk. Martensson looked momentarily like interrupting, and thought better of it. In the court, van Mechelren grinned broadly.

'But after that,' said Richard, 'things took a turn for the worse?'

Martensson made his objection, noisily. 'Counsel is leading the w——' He stopped, realising the trap into which he'd fallen. Judge Hayward regarded him clinically. 'You wish to register an objection, Mr. Martensson?'

'No,' said the counsel for the plaintiff huffily. 'Not at this time. . . .'

'You'd better sit down then. Proceed, Mr. Blakeney.'

'Thank you, M'Lord.' Richard turned back to Megan. 'After that?' he prompted.

'Mrs. Davenport became . . . difficult. There were scenes. She said Mr. Davenport had no right setting me up to . . . make a laughing stock of her. It was over the dresses he'd bought, she didn't want me to have them. She said he didn't understand her and he didn't care about her. She wanted to send me back. He said I'd cost him two million, and he was going to get his use from me.'

'And after that?'

'She got . . . vindictive. She used to keep me up working till all hours. She tried to get me to do things that would damage me. Once she made me use a cleaning fluid that burned my hands. I had to go back to the Institute for grafting.'

'A charming preoccupation,' said Richard. 'But things didn't stay like that, did they?'

'No. They became much worse.'

'In what way?'

Megan hesitated. 'The . . . scenes became more violent. Once Mr. Davenport said he was sorry he'd ever married her. He said he'd sooner . . . sooner be married to a Synth, any day of the week, than a human. I think that was what first put the idea in his mind.'

'What idea?'

'Of teaching me poetry. He'd . . . take me driving, up on Top Level. There were birds and flowers and trees. . . . It was very beautiful. He'd take me to . . . cafeterias, and sit and talk. Nobody ever knew I wasn't . . . real.'

'And why do you think he was doing all this?'

'To get away from his wife. He told me once if it wasn't for me he'd . . . shoot himself.'

'Did he often become depressed? Speak of taking his life?'

'Yes. He was very . . . sensitive about his work. He used to say whenever he sold a portrait, it was one more nail in the coffin of Art. He wanted to . . . paint as he felt, not what the sitters expected to see. He painted me once.'

'Clothed?'

'Yes.'

'Did Mrs. Davenport see the portrait?'

'Yes. She wasn't supposed to. There was another row.'

'And what happened?'

'She had it burned.'

'I see. Who destroyed it?'

'She made me do it.'

'Was it a good portrait?'

'Yes,' said Megan gently. 'It was the best work he'd done.'

Richard let a few seconds elapse. Then, 'And all this time you were learning poetry? At the request of Mr. Davenport?'

'Not just poetry. I was reading a great deal. Mostly from the Old Masters.'

'Was this also at Mr. Davenport's instigation?'

'Partly. Partly for my own interest.' Megan smiled. 'I have a programmed bias to independent research.'

'Did Mrs. Davenport ever read?'

'Yes.'

'What type of material?'

'The fashion glossies.'

'Nothing else?'

'No.'

'Did she ever discuss Mr. Davenport's work with him?'

'She used to complain his prices weren't high enough.'

'Was that her sole interest in his calling?'

'Yes.'

'I can understand his preoccupation with suicide,' said Richard. 'Now can we move forward to the night of July fourteenth, when the incident we've heard described is alleged to have taken place?'

Megan waited.

'Describe it, please, in your own words.'

'Mr. Davenport had been . . . drinking heavily. His wife was away. He'd taken to drinking quite a lot. He called me several times through the day and talked. Once he asked me to go out and fetch him some more Scotch. He'd just about run through what was in the house.'

'What happened then?'

'He . . . drank it,' said the Synth unsteadily. 'Most all of it anyway. I asked him if he needed anything else. He said no. I was to go to bed. He said I was a . . . good girl, nobody else understood him.'

'And then?'

'I did as I was told. While I was . . . undressing, he came to the door. I let him in. He said there was . . . something he'd missed out on. He said he believed a man could fall in love with me.'

'And?'

'He kissed me,' said Megan quietly.

The court was silent; in the stillness the purring of the trivvyrigs was clearly audible. Van Mechelren, eyes narrowed, was watching like a hawk.

'What happened then?'

'He made me unbutton my blouse and lie on the bed with him. He . . . kissed my breasts, and said I was a goddess, and had ichor in my veins instead of blood. He said I was . . . warm, and lovely, and it was the first time he'd ever been happy. He started to cry.'

'And then?'

'He went to sleep.' Megan paused fractionally. 'He was very drunk. . . .'

From somewhere, a titter. Judge Hayward rapped angrily.

'I see. And that was all that took place between you?'

'Yes.'

'Tell me. . . .' The counsel leaned on the box. 'During this time, when Mr. Davenport lay asleep in your arms, were you conscious of doing wrong?'

The Synth frowned. 'I was conscious,' she said finally, 'of an unhappy situation. But I was not a free agent.'

'In what respect were you not free?'

'I was programmed to obey Mr. Davenport. He was my owner.'

'Thank you,' said Richard. 'Thank you very much.' He turned to the court. 'A great deal has been inferred,' he said, 'about the events that took place in the Davenport home prior to the separation which is the cause of our present proceedings. You have now heard, from an incontrovertible source, the truth of the affair; and a very innocent truth it seems to be. Mrs. Davenport lived for many months in a withdrawn and vicious world of her own, a prey to jealousy and insecurity, a drain on her husband's patience and emotions. That she and not the defendant instituted a campaign of mental torture is surely in no doubt. Ladies and gentlemen, a man of the calibre of Mr. Davenport needs understanding above all else. That understanding, that reassurance, was deliberately withheld. And Mr. Davenport, hungry for some comfort, resorted to the only person he knew who would exercise a compassion, a *humanity* towards him. That that person was a synthetic product, a thing not of flesh and

blood but of plastic and steel, is a sad reflection on ourselves. But
resort he did; and innocently, like a child afraid of the dark. For this,
he has surely been punished enough already.'

He smiled at Megan. 'Thank you, Miss Wingrove. I have no
more questions for you.'

'One moment. . . .'

Judge Hayward inclined his head. 'Mr. Martensson?'

'Permission to cross-examine, M'Lord?'

Richard shrugged mentally. If he'd thought Martensson would
miss out on this one, the hope had been wild and wilful.

The counsel for the plaintiff took his time about approaching the
box. When he finally addressed Megan, his first question was
explosive. 'Miss Wingrove,' he said quietly. '*Were you in love with
your owner?*'

'Objection!' Richard bobbed agitatedly. 'The question is seman-
tically confusing. The phrase doesn't allow of a precise definition;
Miss Wingrove is therefore unequipped to answer.'

'None the less,' said Judge Hayward after a pause, 'I feel in the
interests of fairness an answer should be attempted.'

'*Objection!*'

The Lord Chief Justice looked, and was, annoyed. 'Mr.
Blakeney?'

'Is Your Lordship aware,' said Richard quickly, 'that a finding
for the plaintiff would in all probability result in the destruction of
the Synthetic personage known as Megan Wingrove?'

A ripple of interest. Van Mechelren, watching carefully, pursed
his lips and elevated his eyebrows.

'Mr. Blakeney,' said Judge Hayward with some asperity, 'the
court is not unsympathetic to the problems involved here. But I must
stress that such a supposition can hardly be our concern at the
present time. It must certainly not be allowed to influence these
proceedings.'

'M'Lord,' said Richard, 'Miss Wingrove must not be compelled
to make a statement inherently damaging to herself.'

'You do appreciate,' said the Judge, 'that the . . . ah . . . witness
is not under oath?'

'I do, M'Lord. My objection stands.'

Judge Hayward considered long and carefully. Then, 'Upheld,'
he said. 'Mr. Martensson, will you rephrase your question?'

'M'Lord.' The counsel turned back to Megan. 'In your previous
testimony you referred on several occasions to your private feel-

ings. Of pride, pleasure, unhappiness, etcetera. What feelings did you have towards Mr. Davenport?'

Silence, while Megan considered.

'Were your feelings towards him friendly, or otherwise?'

'Friendly, I think. I . . . find it difficult to answer.'

'Why?'

'I was programmed to obey him,' said Megan simply. 'He was my owner. . . .'

Martensson was too old a hand to force an inconclusive issue. He bowed briefly to the bench. 'No more questions, M'Lord.'

Richard rose quietly. 'Permission to re-examine, M'Lord?'

'Granted.'

Counsel studied the jury carefully. 'Megan Wingrove, by her own testimony, is incapable of abetting even indirectly the infliction of mental pain. Her purpose, her only purpose, is to serve the race that conceived her and gave her birth. *She is a machine*. . . .'

He paused, significantly. 'No further proof should be needed of the absurdity of any allegation of misconduct. Yet my colleague appears unconvinced. If there exists in the mind of anyone here present the least shadow of doubt, it is my duty to dispel it. The Synth, Megan Wingrove, lay down with her owner. Because he ordered her to. That we make no attempt to deny. But she also burned the flesh from her hands by dipping them into a caustic cleaning fluid. *Because she was ordered to*. Because that is her function and her purpose. *To obey*. Now, Megan . . .'

The Synth raised her head.

'You obeyed your owner,' said Richard. 'And your owner's wife. Will you obey any human-originated order not damaging to another human?'

Meg nodded slowly. 'That is the purpose for which I was designed.'

'Will you obey me?'

A pause. Then, 'Yes. . . .'

From his pocket the counsel took a knife. A touch on the handle and the blade slid into place with an audible hard snap. He walked across the court to lay the weapon on the edge of the witness box, and returned to his place. 'Megan,' he said, 'in front of you is a knife. It's very sharp. Pick it up, please.'

The Synth hesitantly did as she was told.

Richard took a deep breath. 'Now,' he said, 'listen carefully. I want you to cut off your left hand, at the wrist. Do you understand?'

Megan stared blankly, lips parted. Van Mechelren leaned forward again intently. There was total silence.

Richard's voice crackled suddenly. 'You heard me, Megan. *Sever your wrist.* . . .'

The Synth started slightly, then lifted an arm to the edge of the witness box. Above her a trivvyrig swooped, predatory and sudden. The knifeblade touched flesh, trembled, started to saw. A trickle of some lubricant splashed her dress, ran golden across one knee; tendons showed, pinpoints of brightness.

'*Stop!*'

Richard walked forward, fingers clasped behind him. 'You will not cut off your hand,' he said, 'Instead, you will behead yourself.'

The knife moved in an uncertain arc to the girl's jaw.

'*Stop!*'

This time the interruption came from the Lord Chief Justice himself. 'Mr. Blakeney,' he said acidly, 'must the court endure this unpleasant and pointless exhibition?'

The counsel bowed. 'The point, M'Lord,' he said, 'has I believe been made; and the exhibition is finished.' Then to Megan, 'You may put the knife down now. I shall not ask you to destroy yourself.'

She relinquished the blade, trembling with reaction. Van Mechelren sat back, giving a flicker of a smile. The thing had been nicely timed; another few seconds and Meg's inbuilt defence systems would have pulled the plug, throwing her into stasis. InterNat-Mech Synths were all conditioned against self-immolation, for obvious commercial reasons.

A quick glance at the faces of the jury showed Richard a mingling of pity with disgust. 'Ladies and gentlemen,' he said quietly. 'I put this to you as intelligent and responsible people. Could that creature'—he raised an arm at the Synth—'that thing devoid of will, of fear, insensible to pain, passionless . . . a machine, that could have been destroyed at any time by a gesture, a word . . . could *that* have broken a home, shattered lives? Is *that* the reason, the sole reason, why we are here in this court?

'I suggest most strongly that that is not the case. The reasons of this affair, the passions that culminated here, are no concern of the thing you see in front of you. I propose to show you, ladies and gentlemen, something of those passions. For that purpose, I recall Mrs. Ira Davenport to the stand. Thank you, Miss Wingrove, you may get down——'

'M'Lord. . . .' Martensson, on his feet, was smiling nastily. 'With the permission of the bench, I would like to re-cross . . .'

Judge Hayward looked enquiringly at Richard. The counsel bowed and sat down, hoping for the best and fearing the worst.

'We have heard,' said Martensson deliberately, 'the account of a machine. We have heard what it did, and said, and saw. We have seen, in this court, something of the nature of that machine; and we admit readily that the exhibition staged by my learned friend was both . . . ah . . . gory and convincing.'

He smiled at Richard. The counsel for the defendant scowled back.

Martensson took a pace up the courtroom and turned. 'Yet,' he said, 'surely there still remains some doubt. A machine . . .' He stared Megan up and down. 'A machine of great loveliness. A thing of incredibly delicate construction, a poised, balanced, almost dare we say a *living* entity? . . . Machine? The doubt, ladies and gentlemen, must remain.

'We have heard the testimony of one of the world's leading experts on Synthetic humans. Yet there too a doubt remains; for Mr. van Mechelren himself'—he stressed the 'Mr.' nastily—'when pressed, owned himself not totally sure of his ground. Machine? One wonders. . . .'

He took from his pocket a folded sheet of paper, turned to Megan with it in his hand. 'My dear,' he said. 'I propose to test a further aspect of your . . . ah . . . remarkable talents. It has been given in evidence that Mr. Davenport is extremely fond of poetry. Did he perhaps inculcate into your . . . ah . . . *circuits* some such similar feeling? Could a *machine* speak the words of poetry, which so often are the words of love?'

Richard, sitting impassively, suppressed a desire to bury his face in his hands. The pit yawned; it was black and it was deep, and its bottom was hideously spiked.

'Six hundred years ago,' said the prosecutor, 'William Shakespeare penned what has since come to be accepted as one of the ultimate expressions of human love. I refer of course to *Romeo and Juliet*. You are acquainted with the play? It did I trust figure in your . . . ah . . . self-imposed course of studies?'

Quietly. 'Yes, sir.'

'Will you quote from it briefly, Miss Wingrove? Act Three, scene two, line . . . nineteen, I think will serve. . . .'

Megan's lips moved. Her voice gained volume.

> *'Come, night! Come, Romeo! Come, thou day in night!*
> *For thou wilt lie upon the wings of night,*
> *Whiter than new snow on a raven's back.*
> *Come, gentle night; come, loving, black-brow'd night,*
> *Give me my Romeo; and when he shall die,*
> *Take him and cut him out in little stars,*
> *And he will make the face of heaven so fine*
> *That all the world will be in love with night,*
> *And pay no worship to the garish sun. . . .'*

'Thank you,' said the counsel for the plaintiff. 'Now did you also by any chance run across the twentieth-century playwright Dylan Thomas?'

The fierce, erotic beauty of the *Winter's Tale*; the bawdy lustiness of *Under Milk Wood*. The Synth's voice, husking and limping, seemed to have some spell to quieten the court and the long public galleries. Martensson conducted her neatly, through Shelley and Keats to Tennyson, Byron; John Donne completed the lot. The counsel silenced her finally, waving his hands for quiet. 'Beautiful words,' he said slowly, into the hush that remained. 'Beautiful, immortal words of passion and love; and beautifully spoken. *By a machine!* . . .'

He slammed his way to his desk, and sat down. Richard, rising to conclude his case, remembered an ancient gag. The punch line was, *Wait till you nod your head. . . .*

'Mrs. Davenport,' said Blakeney, 'I would like you, if you would, to tell the court a little about your early life.'

Ira opened her mouth uncertainly, and closed it again.

'You were born,' said Richard, consulting a sheaf of notes, 'on May the eighth, twenty-one thirty-seven, in Montreal, Canada. The youngest of four children. Am I correct?'

'Yes. . . .'

'Tell me about your early life.'

Again a silence.

'Come now,' said Richard encouragingly. 'Anything you remember.'

'Yes. My . . . father died when I was eight, and after that we came back to England. When I was——'

'One moment.' Richard held up his hand. 'What was your father's profession, Mrs. Davenport?'

'Objection!' Martensson glared at his adversary. 'I fail to see how an investigation into the past of the plaintiff can assist in any way.'

The Lord Chief Justice looked quizzically at Richard.

'M'Lord,' said the counsel for the defendant, 'my purpose is to uncover and explain the motivation behind the charge levelled at Henry Davenport. Such motivation can only be understood in the light of a closer analysis of the past experiences of the plaintiff.'

'Objection overruled,' said the Judge. 'Proceed. . . .' Martensson sat down, red faced with annoyance.

Richard returned to the attack. 'Your father's profession, Mrs. Davenport?'

'He was a . . . steel erector. He worked on m-most of the big developments about that time. The tiering of Vancouver, Toronto . . . here and there, all over. . . .'

Richard nodded amiably. 'Steel erecting's a tough job I guess, Mrs. Davenport. Tough on the nerves, tough on the man. Wouldn't you agree?'

No answer.

'A lot of men just can't take it,' went on the counsel easily. 'The nerves go, after a time. But they still have to keep their families, don't they? They have to go on. . . .'

'I——'

'And your father was one of them, wasn't he, Mrs. Davenport? One of the guys that couldn't take it?'

'He was a . . . a good man,' she said. 'A good man, I won't hear bad talk about him. He was good to us, Pop was. Good to all the kids. He kept right on going, right to the end. He didn't give up——'

'Mrs. Davenport,' interrupted the counsel, 'your father died, at the early age of forty-nine, from alcoholic poisoning. Is this not correct?'

'*Objection!*'

'Mr. Martensson?'

'Counsel is needlessly maligning the witness.'

'The facts are on public record, M'Lord,' said Richard. 'That's where I got 'em from.'

'I must warn you,' said the Lord Chief Justice, 'the court does not approve of this method of approach. We deal in facts; in this instance the facts concerning and relating to the marriage of Mrs.

Davenport to her husband. You must justify the relevance of your questions.'

Richard's best acts were frequently impromptu. He walked to the middle of the court; standing there, he tore the notes he carried into fragments and scattered them slowly and impressively round his feet. 'M'Lord,' he said, 'greater issues depend on this case than the alimony awarded, or not awarded, against a man called Henry Davenport. The bench is aware that a finding for the plaintiff would imply the destruction of Megan Wingrove——'

'We've been through all that before,' snapped Judge Hayward. 'The matter is totally irrelevant to the case in hand. I am not accustomed, sir,' he added bitingly, 'to repeating my rulings during an action.'

Richard felt on the point of explosion. The Muse was definitely with him. 'Once, M'Lord,' he said, 'many centuries ago in a little town called Athens, a woman was condemned to death. She was reprieved; because counsel tore her shift, and asked the people there, "*Can we kill this?* . . ."' He turned to Megan; at a gesture, she stood up quietly. 'I wish,' he said, 'I could tear, not the shift, but the veil over a brain. A wonderful thing of gold and glass and steel, perhaps the most vital of its kind in the world. Beside this, against the fear I, all of us feel here for this . . . strange machine, anything is relevant. . . .'

The Lord Chief Justice coughed dryly. 'I find your reasoning obscure,' he said, 'and based on assumptions suspect in the extreme.' A pause. Then, 'You may continue, Mr. Blakeney. But carefully, carefully. . . .'

'Thank you, M'Lord. . . .' Richard turned back to Ira. 'After the death of your father your family fell on hard times. Money was scarce, jobs few and hard to get, none of the children really old enough to earn. So your mother supported her family'—he paused, significantly—'in the only way she was able. The only way she knew——'

'Objection! . . .'

'Mr. Martensson?'

'Pointless innuendo,' snarled counsel for the plaintiff. 'If my colleague intends to descend to mud-hurling . . .'

The first slip. Richard flung himself at his opponent. 'M'Lord, I am unable to understand the remarks of learned counsel. Mrs. Davenport's mother supported her family in the only way known to her; by continued hard work. Of course if counsel is in possession of facts unknown to me his reticence is understandable——'

'*My Lord!* . . .'

'Be quiet,' said the Judge. 'Both of you, you're wrangling like a pair of cats in an alley. Mr. Martensson, do you intend to press your objection?'

The counsel for the plaintiff looked as if he was swallowing cyanide. 'Objection withdrawn,' he said finally. 'Withdrawn. . . .'

Richard surveyed the court. 'In the only way known to her,' he said deliberately. Ira's old woman had been a whore all right; that made the point. He consolidated his triumph quickly. 'Mrs. Davenport, how many times in all have you been married?'

A long wait.

'Since you do not reply,' said Richard, 'I must acquaint the court myself. This is your third marriage, is it not?'

No answer.

'You do not deny that? Good. You were first married at the age of nineteen to a Mr. Aaron Shapeira of Maine, New England, a company director and a manufacturer of aqualung equipment and diving apparatus for the United States Department of Defense. An able, ambitious man whose luck unfortunately was not as good as it might have been. Shortly after your marriage Mr. Shapeira, encouraged possibly by you, began to expand his business. All went well for two years; then the loss of a major contract, the supplying of diving gear to the then-new Atlantic Project, America's first seabed town, left Mr. Shapeira as our friends across the water say ''out on a limb''. With the collapse of the company you obtained a divorce——'

'Objection——'

'Public record,' said Richard tiredly.

'Now don't start that again,' snapped the Lord Chief Justice. 'I have already warned you once, Mr. Blakeney. You must not draw unsubstantiated inferences.'

'I draw no inference, M'Lord, I merely allow the facts to speak for themselves.'

'*Hmmpph*. Proceed. . . .'

'Your reasons then as now were mental cruelty,' said Richard, 'coupled with a charge of adulterous conduct by Mr. Shapeira with a Puerto Rican woman; a charge which in fact was never substantiated. You next marriage was to a Monsieur Lefevre, a French businessman trading in England and associated with the CentSup distribution service. That lasted considerably longer; then finally there was unpleasantness. Condemned meat somehow got tangled with CentSup's supply; there were some minor outbreaks of food poisoning, a death or two—'

'That wasn't my f-fault! He was a . . . crook, a con-man. . . . How was I to know? . . .' Ira started to sniff, wadding a handkerchief in her fingers.

'Exactly, Mrs. Davenport: for once you yourself were taken for a ride. However, while your husband's case was pending you managed to meet in London one Henry Aloysius Davenport, an up-and-coming artist. A man of taste and distinction, a man with a future. . . .'

'He was good to me,' exploded Ira. 'I . . . didn't know what to do, where to t-turn. . . . I wanted to . . . kill myself. . . .'

'But you were saved your painful decision,' snarled Richard, 'by the timely intervention of your current husband, who one night in a Paris flat put into his mouth the muzzle of a point-three-eight automatic and succeeded in depressing the trigger. Just what sort of hell did you administer, Mrs. Davenport, to drive him to that?'

'*Objection!*'

'Question withdrawn,' said Richard instantly. He turned back to the witness. 'Mrs. Davenport, I suggest that many years ago a girl of poor family, ashamed of her background, of her father, of everything connected with her home, made a vow. That she would never again know loneliness, or hunger, or need. That she would move one day in the top circles of the land. That she would wear furs, Mrs. Davenport, and gold, and jewels. And I submit from that time on she dedicated herself, cold-bloodedly, to the realisation of her dream. But she found that as she grasped at them happiness and security eluded her, destroyed by the very things she had thought would secure them. Money, and influence, and social position. So that always she had to grasp higher and higher, reach for more and more. I suggest the history of that girl, your history, Mrs. Davenport, is a record of shameless and soulless social climbing. I suggest you discarded husbands one after the other, as they ceased to serve their purpose——'

'It wasn't like that! They didn't understand me, nobody understood me——'

'Until finally,' stormed Richard, 'you got what you wanted. What you thought was rightfully yours. A man of sensitivity, and culture, and wealth. And what happened, Mrs. Davenport? You found you couldn't keep him. Because you weren't his equal, madam, and you never will be. Not in a thousand years. You couldn't talk to him, Mrs. Davenport, you couldn't make him a home. You couldn't back him because you couldn't understand him. Maybe you never even tried. And you found in the end a machine was ousting you from his attentions; a thing not difficult to do, because for your husband you had nothing to offer. That was the final blow for you, wasn't it? That you lost out to a machine, that you were lower and less account than the Synth called Megan Wingrove. And you made another vow, didn't you? That the machine must be destroyed. Regardless of misery, regardless of cost. A cheap revenge, Mrs. Davenport, but one that suits you very well. Because you are cheap, madam. You started from the gutter; *and at heart you never left it———*'

'*Objection!*'

'Mr. Blakeney . . .' The voice of the Lord Chief Justice cut through the noise from the public gallery. 'You have repeatedly been warned against the maligning of the present witness. I shall warn you no more. I instruct that your last remark be removed from the record of these proceedings; and I will have you understand, further and finally, that if you persist in your approach I shall hold you in contempt of court.'

Richard revolved slowly to survey his victim. 'Thank you, M'Lord,' he said finally. 'I have no more questions for the . . . witness.' He turned his back deliberately while Ira, snivelling well, was removed from the stand.

He stayed quiet so long, head down and brooding, that His Lordship was compelled to address him. 'Mr. Blakeney,' said Judge Hayward testily, 'are we to take it you have concluded the case for the defence?'

Richard looked up and smiled. 'Not quite, M'Lord,' he said. 'I wish to call Henry Aloysius Davenport.'

A rustle of curiosity as the artist took the stand. Richard let the interest build before he turned to address him. Even then he took his time. 'Mr. Davenport,' he said finally. 'I had intended to question you, draw from you the last fragments of truth concerning this unhappy affair. But this I find myself unable to do. You stand condemned, sir; you must realise, as I realise, that this case is lost. . . .'

Uproar in the court; a fluttering of consternation on the opposition desk. Martensson's jaw sagged with shock; his eyebrows retreated towards his hair. Henry Aloysius himself looked to be on the point of collapse. He stared at Richard dazedly as the counsel approached the box.

Blakeney had evidently taken complete leave of his senses. 'Mr. Davenport,' he said, as soon as he could make himself heard, 'believe me when I say I speak now not as counsel or as an officer of this court, but as a friend. And in that capacity I tell you, there is only one course for you to follow.' He turned back to the court. 'Through all the untold years that men have fought and dreamed and died on this planet we call Earth the thinkers among them, the philosophers and poets, the artists, have sought for one ideal. One illusion. The perfect woman, selfless, beautiful, ageless, her soul untainted by the evils of the flesh, unmarked by lust or greed. The ideal, the dream, shone from a million pairs of starry eyes: Circe and Venus Anadyomene, Helen of Troy, Bathsheba, Cleopatra . . . chimeras all, they beckoned, they promised, they lured. But the search, like the grim cause of Art itself, was doomed as is any striving for beauty, for truth. For the hands of woman are red with blood, her heart drowned in rapacity, her face padded on a laughing skull. You, Mr. Davenport, and all your breed of dreamers, will find no solace in the minds of your fellows: for there is none to be had. No solace and no comfort. *Comfort yourself,* as a poet once remarked; *what comfort is in me?*'

Henry's world seemed to be collapsing in a crashing tumult of bells. His eyes began to bulge, his face changed from white to a deepening crimson. He gripped the edge of the box, still unable to believe the evidence of his ears.

Richard's voice rose triumphantly. 'But after all that, the long ages of groping and needing and dying unfulfilled, an answer was made. Yes, made, Mr. Davenport, and made by men; by scientists and engineers.'

He pointed dramatically at Megan. 'There, after so many empty years, lies your salvation, your perfection. Your Venus, uncorrupted and incorruptible, the timeless Virgin, your *alter ego*, your *döppelgänger*. There is your solace; the only solace to be had in an indifferent and brutalised world, a place chained and bound forever by the sins of the Parents of men. Mr. Davenport, ignore censure. Be damned to consequence, close your ears to the lowing of the herd. Take your salvation and be happy again; as you once were, all too briefly, before——'

A week of strain had left Henry's always precarious control in fragments. He whooped for breath, and it seemed suddenly the noise in his ears turned to laughter. Laughter that might spread across a country, across the world. He cracked; for a moment it looked as if he might begin to weep or just faint quietly away, then a more basic instinct gained the upper hand. He aimed at his persecutor's head a mighty blow; Richard prudently dropped flat, and instantly the court was a chaos of noise. Judge Hayward rose, glasses in hand and mouth ajar; Troopers, riotsticks swinging, scurried forward; Henry, pinned by spotlights and encircled by trivvyrigs, glared round wildly. His voice pierced the uproar in snatches, pitched on a thin high note of rage.

'*Don't laugh*. . . .' He took another ineffectual swipe at a trivvyrig that surged back out of reach. He gripped his aching head, pulled at his hair. 'Venus,' he babbled. 'Helen of Troy. . . .' His glazed glance caught Megan, standing shocked and still. He was out of the witness box with startling speed and scurrying across the floor. Blakeney, well placed to intercept him, made no move. 'What do you think you are?' squalled the artist. 'Did you think I wanted you? Were you laughing too? Nobody want's you. *Machine!* . . .' A Trooper grappled with him; Henry reeled under the outstretched arms. He slapped at Megan, bringing her hair out of its grips. She rocked, making no attempt to avoid the blows. 'Did you think I couldn't do any better?' panted Henry. 'Was that it? Did you think I wanted you? I'll show you what you are. Where's your cogs, your gears? . . . Why don't you . . . blow apart, spill 'em out across the floor? . . . Machine . . . *machine, machine, machine*. . . .'

Her blouse was ripped; trivvyrigs, swirling eagerly, obscured the details of the battle. Troopers grabbed the artist finally and pinned him, hauled him, legs kicking, from his victim. Megan squirmed from the fracas and ran, hands to her head. Twenty yards away she staggered. In her brain, inside the meshings of gold, the swirl and buzz of electrons, a breaker snapped apart. She dropped into stasis.

Van Mechelren, moving for all his bulk like well-greased lightning, caught her before she hit the floor.

On the opposition desk an anxious conference was taking place; Ira insistent, pounding on the grained wood with her fist, Martensson shaking his head and waving his arms. As order was restored he approached the bench of the Lord Chief Justice, talked agitatedly. Richard waited, leaning on his desk. A sharp question from Judge Hayward, an agonised nodding from the counsel for the plaintiff, and the Judge cleared his throat. 'I am given to understand,' he said frostily, 'that the plaintiff wishes to withdraw her case. *Is this correct?*'

Dead silence.

'Yes,' said Ira, exultantly. 'Yes. . . .'

Blakeney released pent-up breath in a long whistle of relief. It had had to work. Ira had seen her husband crawl, and the machine that had plagued her was dead. She wouldn't risk the Little Nell act again now, not if she could avoid it; she was getting just a little too long in the tooth. . . . Richard sat down to take the strain off his quivering knees. He grinned weakly, and caught a look from Martensson that was purest vitriol.

'My feelings,' said the Lord Chief Justice, 'at the wasting of the time of this court and its officers, in the prosecution of what I am compelled to describe as a personal vendetta, are probably best left unrecorded. However, under the circumstances forced on me I have no alternative but to assent.' He rapped sharply on the bench. '*Case dismissed.* . . .'

The court went wild again.

Counsel for the defendant overtook his client in the turmoil of the emptying public seats. Ira was hanging on to Henry's arm, crowing and posing for the trivvyrigs. The artist bared his teeth.

'Hank,' said Richard a little desperately, 'Hank, I'm sorry but . . . you wanted out, you're OUT. Look, Hank, I don't lose cases. Nobody'd crack, it just had to be you. . . .'

Henry Aloysius swore blisteringly. 'Send me your bill,' he said, 'then keep out of my sight. I'll come to your funeral. Don't let it be too long. . . .' The mob, swirling, bore him and his wife away.

Van Mechelren paced slowly, down and back across the little room, one arm round Megan, her hand gripping his shoulder. His fingers, low on her hip, felt the electric trembling as she tried for control. 'Make it work, sweetie,' he said. 'Make it work . . . You ever come out the clips before?'

'No, I . . . I don't think so . . .'

'Make it work,' he said. 'There, is good . . . Gimme spherical volume formula now, quick . . .'

'Sphere equals . . . sphere equals four over three times, times phi, by radius cubed . . .'

'Value of phi?'

'Just a . . . a minute . . .'

'No. While you walk, please . . .'

'Like . . . patting my head and rubbing my stomach,' she said foggily. 'Phi is . . . oh hell . . . three point one five . . . no, one four . . . one four, one five nine . . . approximations twenty-two over seven, three five five over . . . over one one three . . .'

'Ach, good,' he said. '*Good*. You're O.K. You be all right.'

'Pieter,' she said. 'I was in love with him. God, *I was in love with him* . . .'

'I know,' he said. 'Here, you sit now.' He steered her to a chair, stood in front of her, hands on knees, frowning and shaking his head. 'How you do it?' he asked. 'You bloody mess o' plastic an' glass, how you make it happen?'

She shook her head dazedly. 'I don't know. I just wanted him . . .'

'Play it quiet,' said van Mechelren. 'You're off the hook now, tak' it quiet.'

He scratched an ear, pensively. 'In Amsterdam,' he said, 'is boats still, an' trees. Oh, pretty . . . not like this dump. It's nice, you like it there. But Christ, we got a lot to do. You first of a kind, you know that? We gotta see just how you tick. We gotta have a lot more tickin', just like you . . .' He put a finger under her chin and turned her face. 'O.K.?'

'Yes,' she said. 'Yes, O.K. . . .'

She 'felt' his hand on her shoulder.

Manscarer

By dawn most of the spectators are in their places in the stands and already making a din that is causing Roley Stratford to rage and fume. This the plebs will never understand; that the true introduction to the coming spectacle is Silence. One cannot play Silence, the primordial entity; so there is nothing to which to listen, and the people are not quiet.

Roley has dressed for the occasion as a British admiral of the early nineteenth century; his white breeches are soiled with grass stains where he has helped one of the working parties make last-minute adjustments to the great shanks of *Manscarer* lying along the clifftop. Jed Burrows, A.D.C. for the day, fusses behind his temporary chief, carrying the bottle of rum Roley has declared indispensable to the period flavour. He also started out with a brass telescope and an astrolabe, but the latter was left behind as too unwieldy. The telescope he still carries, tucked in the crook of his blue-uniformed arm.

The dawn wind is cool; Jed shivers a little, stepping from one foot to the other as the shade of Nelson harangues the Leader of the Orchestra. A minor difficulty has arisen; the contract clearly specifies a thirty-minute overture before the *Pomp and Circumstance* extracts that will herald the Assembly, but only part of the band awnings has arrived in time. A harassed group of City engineers is still at work erecting the rest, manhandling the awkward lengths of billowing preformed plastic. Leader, Strings and Woodwind are prepared to play in the open air; the Brass Section, keen Union men one and all, are not. The boys claim it will chap their lips. Somewhat obscurely, Percussion and Effects are backing the argument. Jed tires of the row and wanders off, leaving the rum placed on a conspicuous outcrop of rock. Part of the Book calls for volleys of Verey lights; he will have ample warning of the start.

Most of the Colony are scattered round the concrete pads on which *Manscarer* will take shape, by the grace of God and in spite of the force of gravity. The working teams lounge on the grass, still keeping roughly in position; here and there a bottle is raised in greeting to Jed as he paces solemnly the dural beams of the Crow. As he walks he rehearses again in his mind the complex stages of Assembly. The first members, once socketed into their pads, will serve as derricks for the raising of the greater beams, the weighted and counterbalanced shafts that will set the head of the sculpture in huge and complicated motion. The beak itself, the *corvus*, lies along the clifftop like an old-time ploughshare monstrously over-large. There could be trouble with the placing of the assembly; it is heavy, very heavy, and the triplefold tackles that will bear its weight are none too hefty for the job. The answer would have been a flying crane, but Roley refuses to countenance the use of such an apparatus. The machine would spoil the form of *Manscarer* at a critical moment, and its din would drown the orchestra.

Jed checks the donkey engine that will make the great pulls. Steam is already raised—steam and steam only has been deemed fit by Roley for his masterpiece—and Bil-Bil and Tam are fretting over their gauges. On the roof of the engine shed Reggy Glassbrook, nimble and hairy, sits grinning like an ape. He is the Colony's steeplejack; he will be first into the rigging today, handling the split-second alignments as the beams sail to their positions, sure-footed and quick as one of Meg's pet geckos. As far as Jed is concerned he will be welcome to the job; the A.D.C. has no head for heights, and from the feet of the *Scarer* to his main goosenecks will be all of ninety feet.

A hundred yards beyond the donkey shack a gully running to the cliff edge makes a shallow windbreak. Crouched in its lee, Bunny, Whore Nonpareil and the Witch of Endor eat alternate sandwiches of crab and caviare and serve passers-by with Hock from a Georgian coffeepot. At their feet a coffee machine heated by a small spirit lamp glugs and burbles to itself. 'What are we, girls?' shouts Jed. 'Artists or engineers?' The gag, in the new 'flat humour' favoured by the Colony, raises a chorus of unanswers, nods and headshakes and somewhat glazed morning-after grinnings. Jed looks up, visualising the great blue negative the sky will make round the whirling bars of *Manscarer*. Pushes his telescope more firmly under his arm, touches his hat and moves on.

Artists or engineers? As an artist Roley called for underpinnings to reach down unseen into the cliff, a hundred and fifty feet to sea level. Through them *Manscarer* would have grown from earth's roots, sweeping up, continuing the lines of stress inherent in the bulging stone, shackling the ground firmly to the sky; but the City engineers refused him more than twenty feet, just enough to hold the ponderous swirling of the tophammer. It will serve though; *Manscarer* will peck and thunder, nibbling perhaps at his own sinews and feet to fall one day in glorious dissolution into the water. Perhaps before that the Colony will hold a ritual destruction; there will be more stands and more admission charges and more selling of high-priced ice cream. And the South Sector Symphonic again, if it can be arranged.

Symphonic . . . Jed, a quarter of a mile from the podium, can still hear in the breaks of the wind the evidence of Roley's apoplexy. The Overture was timed to start as the sun's disc broke clear of the sea; but the daystar has lifted now his own diameter from the horizon, and not a brass bleat has been heard from the pack of them. The occasion is ruined before it begins. Jed mounts a hillock of grass to gain a view of the distant stands. The State Police are having a mite of trouble keeping order over there; he marks a dozen separate and complicated scuffles taking place on the grass in front of the awnings. Programmes are being fluttered and some sort of organised chanting has started. He sees a man running, another being belaboured by a mounted Cossack. He swears at the risk to the Colony's precious horses.

He looks along the coast. Symphonies are playing already, the mute works the plebs refuse to hear. The notes are of lilac and seething pale blue, touched with the thin glittering of sunlight. Far below at the feet of the cliffs are the crawling lace curtains of the tide. Jed turns away slightly giddy. The Assembly teams are standing now, chafing their hands and flapping their arms across and back against their shoulders. The jeans and reefer jackets of the men amount almost to a uniform, but no two girls are dressed alike. Jed sees a fine Firebird swirling in a mist of fluorescent nylon; nearer are a Pompadour, a Puck, a shivery paint job all black and white zebra stripes. Meg Tranter is dolled up in ancient half-burned newsprint, the textured leaves flapping round arms and knees. She

carries a placard with the legend *Zeitgeist 1960*. That too is 'flat'
humour; she is explaining to the plebs what they lack the mental
equipment ever to understand.

Between the Assembly site and the nearest of the terracings a
collection of Colony possessions has been set up on display.
Armoured and well-guarded cases hold stacks of old books; dogs
and beribboned goats are being paraded and Piggy and The Rat are
doing a brisk trade in genuine hand-executed Seascapes. There is a
constant coming and going from the ranks of sightseers. In the City,
Colony artifacts fetch quaint prices; through them Jed's folk are
self-supporting in theory at least. Jed wipes his face and looks
farther along the cliffs. Way off and blue with distance he can see
the City's impossible side, like the edge of a hundred-yard thick
carpet pulled across the land. The structure covers all England with
its grinding weight and sameness. In its catacombs, trapped in the
miles on honeycombed miles of chambers and passages, men can
live and die, if they are born poor enough, without seeing the sun.
The tiny open spaces round the coasts, full of the mad artifacts of the
Colonies, provide a relief from Sameness that the people come
trooping year after year to see. Without them, populations might run
shrieking mad themselves. Artists are a therapeutic force now,
recognised and protected by Government; the lunacy of the few
safeguards the sanity of the many.

A bang-crock; the report and its echo lift a paperchase of gulls
from beneath Jed's feet. He watches them soaring out under the
glowing ball of the signal. Shreds of music reach him; at long last,
the Overture has begun. He paces back methodically, lips pursed,
keeping in character as he walks the quarterdeck of the cliff. From
the tail of his eye he sees Reggy, stripped now to shorts and
sleeveless leather jerkin, springing and posturing on the roof of his
little shed. Someone runs to Jed and presents him with chipolatas on
sticks and a stuffed olive. He munches as he walks, savouring the
Surreal delicacy of the gesture, climbs the rostrum where Roley
dances in a furor of creativity and apprehension. A speaking trum-
pet is gripped in his hand; the fingers that hold it are white-knuckled
with strain.

The music climbs towards its first climax. 'Lifting teams,' bel-
lows Roley. 'Teams, *ha—ul*. . . .' A jet of steam rises from the
donkey-hut; oddly assorted groups of Colonists, drilled to perfection, scurry across the grass, taking up the slack in the controlling
tackles. The spars of the lowest Configuration rise with surprising

speed, waver and . . . *bang-bang* . . . thump down, dead on beat,
into their sockets. The thing is done, like a conjuring trick out on the
grass. *Fortissimo* from the huge gaggle of musicians, a half-heard
firework gasp from the crowd and then cheering while Roley waves
his arms again leaping up and down and damn-blasting the plebs,
lilac in the face with rage. The gestures are eloquent, even effective;
the little blue-dressed figure, capering mad as a clockwork monkey,
quietens the crowd. The occasion after all is a solemn one; the
plebs, who have fought for tickets, are duly impressed. They are
witnessing a demonstration of an artform in which Roley alone
excels; the erection, to music, of a supermobile. Uncomprehending, they still stand in stark awe of lunacy. That after all is what they
have paid good money to see.

The Interval. After an hour's work the main spars stand supported by their guys like the disfigured kingpoles of a Big Top.
Smaller secondary beams, feathered with bright lapping sheets of
metal, already spin and dip, humming in the wind; the goosenecks
that will take the great spars of the main assembly are in place, and
the lifting tackles. The donkey-hut becomes obscured by steam as
Tam blows pressure from his waiting boiler; on the roof, Reggy,
still sweating from his exertions and wrapped in a hand-woven
poncho, holds court before an admiring half-circle of Colonists.
Roley, squatting on the edge of his rostrum, waves brief encourage-
ment before readdressing himself to his bottle of Captain Cat (home
brewed in the Colony). Below him, musicians lounge on the grass;
mush-sellers circulate between them bearing aloft feathery *incubi*
of green and pink candyfloss. The machines of aerial observers,
newsmen and photographers, hang racketing round the struts of the
mobile, some dangerously close to the guys; people from the
ground teams are waving their arms, trying to shoo them back.

The sun is hotter now; Jed mops his face with a bright bandanna.
Beyond the half-completed *Manscarer* other mobiles loom; Jed,
watching, sees *Fandancer* bow herself, making for an instant with
her wobbling slats the outline of a hip, the big thrust of trochanter
and the muscled curve below, before collapsing into Motion. One
of Roley's most ingenious creations that, though maybe lacking a
little in overall strength. Bil-Bil and Tam approve of her, and that
isn't always a good sign. She was a bitch on the drawing board, and
a bitch to put together as well. Her Assembly was a near-fiasco; it
took weeks of patient adjusting and rebalancing before she condescended to shimmy in the airs of Heaven. Behind her are other

sculptures, more distant still; Jed sees the flash and swoop of
Halycon, Manscarer's forerunner, before his beams, flattening
freakishly, lose themselves beneath a swell of grass. He looks up
again lovingly at the new Structure, shielding his eyes against the
sun, watching the lazily turning plates of dark blue and deathly
iridescent violet. The mobile has already a drama that the others
lack.

Manscarer is a crow, or the bones of one; a vast ghost that once
complete will thunder and peck along the cliff-top, the bird at last
turned hunter and revenger of dead fields. Or so runs the Manifesto.
Jed doubts if one in a hundred of the gaping Cityfolk have taken
the trouble to read it; it would mean little enough to them if they
did.

Jed moves to the hourglass strapped on the side of the rostrum.
The last few grains of sand are funnelling down. He raises his arm,
palm flat, and there is a scramble as the orchestra runs for its
instruments. Reggy erupts from the poncho; Roley raises his baton,
and construction begins again with a quiet passage in which Reggy,
balanced and slowly revolving in the blue, delicately attaches the
featherings of the upper rings. While he works, the hundred-foot
linked shafts of the main assembly are cleared for lifting.

The secondary Configurations are nearly complete now; hawsers
run from them to anchor points in the grass. Others are ready for the
main beams. *Manscarer*, unshackled, would rampage across a
three-hundred-yard circle, tearing and clucking at the grass; before
the last of the ropes are slipped bandstand and engine house will be
evacuated. Jed leaves the podium, where Roley still conducts in a
berserk frenzy, runs to his prearranged position on the tackles.
Every pair of hands the Colony can muster will be needed for the
coming operation.

Hawsers snake upwards to humming tightness as Tam, the winch
control levers in his hands, leans from the window of his shack. The
music drives towards its great central theme; a shout, a heavier
thundering from the engine shed, and the *corvus* lifts clear of the
grass, twenty feet long, glinting with a vicious rose-and-black
shimmer. Reggy balances on the skull plates, sticky-footed. A
medley of orders bellowed through the music, wiry strumming as
the beams snub at their restraining tackles and on the beat the whole
assembly soars, weaving impatiently as the feathered tail plates feel
the breeze. Jed loops his downhaul round a bollard, leans back as
the creaking rope takes the strain. The beams swing higher, clang

against the central masts to drop with a crash, sockets trued over the projecting goosenecks; the *corvus* falls and rises, dipping as it tastes the wind.

Triumph, and disaster. Somewhere in the rigging a shackle parts with a hard snap. Tackles come down flailing. The beams swing, driven by the wind, shearing the remaining cables. *Manscarer* rotates, unpredictable now and weighing tons, the focus of a widening circle of unhappiness. Jed sees a block swinging in decapitating arcs, falls flat and rolls on his back to watch the huge overhead clicking of violet bones. A dozen people skid past, drawn by their rope, chirping out a birdcage panic; a Cavalier's hat bowls across the ground, on edge like a little feathered wheel. The wind gusts; the *corvus* casts out far across the sea, swings back to rake screeching flinders from the awnings of the bandstand, tangles massively with the roof of the engine shed. Steam explodes outwards, gusting across to where the orchestra, on hands and knees, scuttles for its collective life. The beak, checked by the obstruction of the donkey shed, wavers and dips again to strike at the main struts, down which Reggy is still scurrying from danger. Another peck, a fleshy concussion, a shrill falling scream; a surprised gob of blood splashes across Jed's wrist from where Reggy, suitably scared, sails overhead, filling the close sky with legs and arms. He bounces against the cliff edge to fall again to the blue and white impatience of the water, his plunging splash lost far below in the morning noise of the sea. After him a French Horn, disembodied from its master, bounds disconsolately like a Surreal yellow snail.

Jed crawls to the cliff edge in the sunlight, and thoughtfully adds his quota of moisture to the ocean.

The flooring of the house is of polished yellow wood, broken by platforms and steps into various levels. Sunlight lies across it in calm rectangles. Round the dark blue walls white alcoves, circular-topped, house ancient ship models and tropical shells; handrails of copper and mahogany echo the nautical flavour. The end wall of the building is of glass; through it, distantly, can be seen the ocean. To one side of the living space stands a bright red twentieth-century M.G., her nose butted into a recess in the floor; in the centre of the room is a table covered with a spotless linen cloth. A silver breakfast service adds a last note of elegance.

Above the carport in the wall the curtains of a sleeping alcove are drawn back to reveal a plain divan covered by a heap of bright-

coloured scatter cushions. From the alcove, close under the oddly
pitched roof, a thick white-painted beam spans the room. Jed stands
beneath it, feet with their buckled shoes in a patch of sunlight, hand
on the hilt of his sword. 'That's my beam,' he says crossly. 'Just
you get off it, this minute.'

The girl above him makes no movement, staring down with eyes
wide with fright as those of a tarsier. 'That's my beam,' says Jed
more carefully. 'Nobody can sit up there, except me.'

Silence.

'I'll run you through without mercy,' declares the admiral,
exposing six glittering inches of the swordblade.

There is no reaction.

'I'll do terrible things. I'll keelhaul you and flog you through the
fleet. I'll throw you to the fishes. . . .'

The girl grips the beam a little harder with her jean-clad legs,
twining her bare ankles beneath it.

Jed looks thoughtful, pushes the sword back into its scabbard,
walks to the table and wields a silver pot. Steam rises fragrantly. He
adds sugar and milk, stirs carefully and picks up the cup in its
saucer, turning as he does so to look back at the roof. 'If they made
coffee in Heaven,' he calls, 'and tea in Hell, I'd take my turn at the
stoking.' The hot drink soothes, steadying the shaking of his hands.
He sits down, studies the table and selects a round of toast. He
butters it and spoons a blob of marmalade on to his plate. 'After
breakfast,' he says to the silence, 'I'll stop being an admiral. Is that
what you want?'

A headshaking from the girl on the beam.

'Polly,' says the retiring Captain Hardy, 'if you won't come
down I really shall knock you off. I shall do it with a broom.'

There is no response except a tensing of the legs. Polly indicates
her determination to stay on the beam until killed. Jed fixes her
again with a contemplative eye. 'I was sick this morning,' he says.
'I did it in the sea. Were you there when Reggy was pecked?'

A nodding. A violent reaction for Polly.

Jed pauses, the toast halfway to his mouth. 'He was killed,' he
says, unnecessarily. 'Is that why you got up there?'

The nodding again.

'Were you frightened?'

Headshaking. No, no . . .

'I've decided,' says Jed. 'I won't knock you down after all.
Instead I shall just wait till you get tired and fall off.' He lifts the pot

again. 'Polly, you do make lovely tea.' He finishes the cup, lays down his toast and walks forward to grip the girl's dangling feet. On the ankles are faint brown watermarks. He pushes the toes under his chin, leans his forehead against the cool frontal curving of the shins. 'Poll,' he says, 'you've got mucky feet.' Then looking up, 'You are a funny girl . . .'

The Colony, cowed by death, keep to their separate homes; Roley to his bleak little sixteenth-century pub, Piggy and the Rat to their queer thatched tower room, darkly glowing with light from fishtanks and crystal globes, Meg and the Witch of Endor to their clifftop bunker full of juju dolls and scuttling lizards and the apparatus of magic. Visitors poke and pry, disappointed at the lack of activity and at missing the morning's disaster. They traipse through Polly's fragile house, empty now, leaving its doors ajar to gusts of sunlight; but nobody comes near Jed's home. He would almost welcome interference. He lounges against the rear wheel of the M.G., a cushion at his back, his legs stretched out along the planking of the floor. He is reading from an ancient copy of the *Ingoldsby Legends*; from time to time he glances up half-aggravatedly from the verse to the *succubus* still straddling the beam. A mile away *Manscarer* spins angrily, clashing and banging in the circle he has cleared. His noise fills the peninsula on which the Colony lies, penetrates bumblingly through the glazed wall of the room.

At lunchtime Jed leaves, to be away from Polly's eyes. He hunts out sketchbook and pastels on the way, and lets the outer door slam. It is only then the girl becomes active. She slides off the beam in frenzied haste, scurrying with the nervous violence of an ant as she clears the table, washes, cooks. When Jed returns she is back on her perch. He looks a little disappointed; he had hoped to find his house no longer haunted. But the dinner simmering in the oven is very good.

Jed eats the meal in silence, carries the dishes and plates to the kitchen alcove and washes them, stacking them carefully in their racks. He clears the rest of the table, shakes the cloth outside the back door and folds it. By the time he has finished Polly has at least changed her attitude, she is riding the beam sidesaddle. It is a hopeful sign; perhaps at last the strain is telling. Jed stands underneath her again, looking up. 'I could pull you off quite easily now,' he says. 'You wouldn't be able to hang on at all.' She bites her lip, knowing he will do no such thing.

He scratches his head, badly worried. 'You're Making a Protest, aren't you?'

The girl nods.

'What's it about?'

No answer.

'Something's upset you terribly,' says the erstwhile admiral. 'It was to do with Reggy, but it wasn't him being killed. I don't know what it is. Couldn't you write it down?'

Negative. A large tear escapes from the corner of Polly's eye and runs down her cheek. She ignores it till it reaches her lip; then she fields it with the pointed tip of her tongue.

Jed fetches the sketchbook from where he flung it down carelessly, and holds it up. He says a little helplessly, 'These are for you.' Polly grabs with surprising speed, like a monkey stealing a banana. The drawings are of *Manscarer*, his posturings and violent movements under the yellow searchlight-stabbings of sunlight. Polly clutches the book to her chest, rocking and crooning, burying her nose in the pages to catch the sweet scent of new fixative. She is still holding it when Jed leaves to drink five evening pints of beer at the Lobster Pot and tell Roly his beam has been invaded by a woman. A runner is instantly despatched to take Polly a little hat, a copy of the Rieu *Odyssey* and a picture book of sailing ships to look at if she gets bored. Meg wants to send a gecko as well but Jed says no. Polly is a little afraid of them, and it wouldn't be fair.

When he returns, the peninsula is blue with summer dusk and the last grasshoppers in the universe are making the night shrill with their churring. He decides he can't face supper; he undresses in the dark, lies down and feels the bed swaying slightly from side to side. As long as he doesn't roll over violently he will be all right. An hour later a sudden thump wakes him from a doze. Muffled sounds follow at intervals as Polly pads about doing God only knows what. Jed draws himself up against the wall, waiting. He feels his heart, accelerating, bump faintly against the insides of his ribs; quick prickling sensations move across his skin. It seems an age before Poll swings up the ladder to the alcove. She moves a little stiffly, still suffering from her day of abstinence.

She wriggles her jeans off before sliding on to the divan. To Jed she feels soft and cool, a life-size doll.

The two figures swim in a morning dazzle of sunlight, seeing the cliffs rise giddily in the troughs between the waves. Above them the head of *Manscarer* appears once, violet and sullen, withdraws itself instantly with the ease and quick grace of a snake. The creaking of the slats carries down to the water.

Jed hangs on to a rock, seeing the long fringes of weed wash and swirl on the tide, watching the tiny close sunburnings reflect from water and bursting foam. The situation is baffling. Polly has him completely in her grasp now; he owes her a breakfast, a dinner and a night in bed, and he wants them all again. The whole affair is difficult in the extreme.

Reggy, swilling palely while the sea gurgles in his ruined side, can do nothing but nod his head up and down in agreement.

Among the bushes scattered in the little gully lights play and flash, now here, now gone; wayward gleams follow the voices of Oberon and Puck. Farther up the cliff Bil-Bil and Tam, the engineers, sit at a console alive with whirling tapespools, setting the words of the Dream spinning and fluting through the sky. The Colony listens sleepy with poetry, clustered in the summer night. *Manscarer* swirls and clacks, gaunt and small on the skyline; but he is forgotten.

Polly, sitting crosslegged just behind Jed, pulls glassblades miserably, chewing them and spitting them away. By Act Three she can no longer control the tensions inside her. She puts her head back and shrieks, rendingly. Then again, and again. The *son et lumière* is disrupted, for ever.

The Colony panics. Dumb things that scream are bad; like the stuffed fox in the poem barking, the oak walking for love. Polly isn't a deaf-mute; it's just that two years ago she decided she had nothing else interesting to say and vowed never to speak again. But it's difficult to remember that now she's been quiet so long. A confused battle starts in the gully, figures tumbling over each other and hitting out in alarm while Polly eels about between them still making sounds like a steam carousel. The play shuts down; Bil-Bil and Tam squeak miserably, enveloped by tape. Piggy finally catches the culprit by the heel and pins her while The Rat, never far away from trouble, kisses her to make her stop. Polly is uncooperative. Meg yelps, kicked firmly in the crotch; The Rat claps his hands to an eye jabbed by a hard little elbow. The Witch of Endor joins battle decisively; she administers three sound thumps before

Jed, raging, starts to hit her back. The skirmishing subsides; there is a silence, broken by the sea noise far below and the unhappy grunting of The Rat.

Roley Stratford mounts a rock and windmills his long arms against the sky. 'It's hopeless,' he booms, furiously. 'We can't hear plays if people have to scream. Polly, will you be quiet? And not start any more fights?'

Polly, still struggling, shakes her head violently and gulps. Jed claps his hand across her mouth, terrified in case she starts being ghastly again. She instantly bites his thumb. He swears, and calls up to the rock. 'She says no. . . .'

The Witch of Endor mutters something about 'nasty little freemartin'. The words come out slightly thick; she is trying to cope with a split lip. Jed, one arm round Polly, raises his free fist. The Witch ducks prudently, wriggling back out of reach. Roley jumps up and down on his rock. 'Then it's a trial. . . .' He raises his arms dramatically, fists clenched. 'A *tri-al.* . . .'

The shout, taken up by the Colony, becomes a chant. Figures surge round Polly and Jed, hoisting them to their feet; The Witch is propelled after them up the incline of the gully. Bil-Bil and Tam desert their tangled console, infected by the general enthusiasm.

'*A trial* . . . it's a *trial.* . . .'

Heavy Dutch oil lamps hanging from the rafters light the bars of the Lobster Pot with a soft brilliance. Beneath them the Colony is present in full strength, banging its tankards on the white-scrubbed tables and yelling for proceedings to begin. Roley, the Chief Justice, hammers louder on the counter top in front of him with the scarred and knotted shillelagh that is his staff of office. The Court Peculiar is convened; mine host calls for witnesses.

The Witch of Endor is shoved forward, willowy in an ankle-length dress of scrubbed hessian. Finding herself the centre of attention she sticks out her chest importantly. 'I got smacked in the teeth. . . .' She waves a bright-splotched hankie. 'I'm a witness . . .'

'Polly didn't do that!'

'Shame!'

'She did!'

'She didn't. It was Jed. . . .'

'Well it was all her fault. . . .'

'It wasn't!'

'Was!'

'You always want to bully her!'

'I *don't*! She started it!'

'*Shame!*'

The shillelagh beats half-moons into the counter top. 'Polly,' says the Judge. '*Did* you start it? Whatever it was?'

Polly, sitting on Jed's knee, jiggled happily and nods.

'What did you do?'

'*Nothing*. . . .'

'She *did*. . . .'

'It was The Rat kissing her. She didn't like it. . . .'

'That wasn't the start . . .'

'Well that was when she hit him in the eye . . .'

Roley hammers again for order. 'Did you mind him kissing you, Polly?'

Polly shakes her head.

'It wasn't that then,' says the Judge decisively. 'Now, is there an Indictment?'

'Tam's got it. . . .' Tam is driven into the open, protesting. He stammers badly; his olive-skinned woman's face is suffused with embarrassment.

'That P-Polly did wilfully d-d-disrupt a performance of Sh-Shakespeare. And upset J-Jed getting his b-breakfast for him, and his d-d-dinner. . . .'

'And she went to bed with him. . . .'

'That doesn't matter. . . .'

'It does. It ought to be included anyway. . . .'

The Rat has hauled a chair into a window recess; enthroned on its temporary eminence he feels secure. His one serviceable eye leers horribly. '*She was a virgin too*. . . .'

'She wasn't. . . .'

'She *was*. . . .'

'She couldn't have been. . . .'

Roley whirls the shillelagh. 'This might be *very important*. . . . Were you a virgin, Polly?'

Polly blushes, and hides her face against Jed's shoulder. The Colony, impressed, makes a concerted 'aaahhhh' noise, like a crowd of plebs when a rocket explodes. The Rat hiccups inconsequentially. 'C-c'n I have s'more beer, somebody. . . .'

A jug is handed up to him. It gets well swigged-from on the way. He pours what is left into his pot, mumbling to himself. Roley clears his throat. 'The Indictment is very confused,' he says, 'but evidently the whole affair's to do with Jed. That's the first point. . . .'

'She just wants him to do something back. . . .'

'Well he won't. . . .'

'He will. He'll do anything now, look at his face. . . .'

The counter top suffers again. 'It's to do with Jed,' says Roley loudly. 'And it's also to do with Reggy, because it started when he was killed. It started with the beam in Jed's house, that should have been in the Indictment. Right?'

Polly, nodding, seems to be trying to shake her head off her shoulders.

'Then we're getting somewhere,' says the Judge, very satisfied. He swigs violently from a quart pewter mug. His neck muscles writhe in the lamplight as he swallows.

'We'd get on quicker if she'd *talk*,' says the Witch of Endor, glaring. 'I think it's just *stupid*. . . .'

'*It isn't!*'

'IT IS!'

Proceedings instantly threaten to degenerate into another brawl. Splinters fly from the counter top as the Judge calls the court to order. '*I* think,' says the Witch primly as soon as she can make herself heard, 'she should be *made* to talk.' She tosses her wild yellow hair. 'We should push spills under her fingernails and light them. It would be quite proper.'

Polly clenches her hands protectively and starts to shiver.

'It seems to me,' says Roley reprovingly, 'that all in all you've rather got it in for the defendant.'

'*I haven't*.' Then, sullenly, 'All right, I suppose I have. I think she's an ungrateful little beast.'

'Why?'

' 'Cos I sent her a picture book,' howls the witch, dancing with sudden temper. 'An' all I got back was a slosh in the chops. . . .'

'And I rule that *irrelevant*. . . .'

The Rat, very drunk, starts to interrupt, sees the shillelagh poised to hurl at his head and subsides.

'Irrelevant,' says Roley again, to clinch the matter. He glares round him. 'All right. We've got the Indictment, or most of it; we need a Defence. Polly can't tell us why she started to be difficult. That's annoying, but it just can't be helped. So does anybody else know?'

'Yes,' says Jed quietly. 'I do.'

A hush, in which the shrilling of the grasshoppers sounds very loud. Polly turns startled to peer into Jed's face. He puts her aside, carefully, and stands up. He's wishing belatedly he'd worn his uniform and turned the proceedings into a Court Martial. Lacking lapels, he hooks his thumbs in his belt. 'Mr. Chief Justice,' he says. 'Ladies and gentlemen. This, I believe, is what she means. No more mobiles should be built. Furthermore, the figures already erected should be knocked down as soon as possible. Further——'

A gale of disagreement. Jed, shouted down, starts to jump about and wave his arms, mouth popping shut and open uselessly. Polly, looking desperate, sees above her a heavy beam. She is on the table instantly, and jumping for it. Roley howls his alarm; the Witch, quicker off the mark than the rest, dives at her, wrapping her arms round Polly's knees. A swaying confusion; Jed, leaping to the rescue, skids and vanishes under a scuffling pile of bodies; beer is spilled noisily; The Rat, whirling his pot in his excitement, falls headlong from his perch. Order is finally restored, and Polly restrained; but not before Piggy has been knocked half silly by a brickbat, and Meg and the Witch have had their heads banged together for punching. Roley returns to his position of authority, breathing a little heavily.

'Now then,' he says, surveying the court. 'I built these mobiles.' As he speaks he bangs with the handle of the shillelagh, emphasising each word. 'I gave 'em the best years of me wanin' youth. *I* want to know why Jed says to scrap 'em; so the rest of you, *SHARRAP!*' The head of the club, whirling, inflicts a final wound on the counter; Roley bows with great gravity to Jed. 'Mr. Burrows, if you would proceed. . . .'

'It isn't only the mobiles,' says Jed quickly. He feels oddly certain of his words. 'It's everything we do. The horseriding and the archery and reading Shakespeare in the dark and holding seances, and building all those castles about the place and knocking 'em down again like the last time we had a Mediaeval War. Piggy and The Rat must stop painting their pictures and put all their fish back in the sea, and Meg must burn her jujus, and you must stop pretending to be a sort of man who doesn't exist any more, Roley, and so must I. We must destroy the Colony, we must burn it. That's what we must do.'

In the awed silence, the Judge turns to Polly. He asks gently, '*Is* that what you meant?'

She nods again slowly, tears glistening in her eyes.

Nobody else seems able to speak. Roley says carefully, 'Why, Poll? Just because Reggy was killed?'

'No.' Jed is still quite sure of himself. 'Reggy's to do with it, but he isn't the reason. He just brought things to a head. You see they'd never murdered any of us before.'

'Who?'

'The plebs. Oh, Christ, it's so obvious. . . .' He stares round at faces changing from anger to puzzlement. 'We've failed, can't anybody else see that except Polly? All of us, in all the Colonies. When they let us come out here and gave us land and money to spend, and people to help us do every crazy thing that came into our heads, when we took their terms, that was when we failed. We let ourselves down, we sold our birthright. *And theirs*. . . .

'We were too dangerous to them scattered about anywhere and everywhere all over the City. We couldn't be pushed about and led by the nose and hammered into the same shape as everybody else. When the trivvyscreens yelled at us we threw things at them, and when the plebs put us in jail for it we sat and laughed because we knew what they didn't, that we were the makers of dreams. The movers and shapers of the world, or something like that. There's a poem about it somewhere. But we took their terms; and now we aren't artists any more. We don't deserve the name.'

He waves a hand angrily at his surroundings; the stone, the warm wood, the pools of light from the old lamps. 'Polly is telling us, all this is acting and pointless make-believe. That our lives are more sterile than the lives of the people we're supposed to despise.' He raises a declamatory finger. 'We let them short circuit us. We let them put us where they could see us and count us, where they could come every day to laugh and know they were safe from us and all the nasty things that happen when people start to think. They made us into State-licenced buffoons; and we fell off the thin edge, the tightrope between creativity and dilettantism, between free thought and aimless posturing for applause. That's why we lost, and how; and that's why we've got to stop now, before we burn ourselves up any further. If we . . . etiolate right out of existence there's no hope left. Not for anybody.' He swings slightly, and returns Roley's bow. 'Sir,' he says, 'I believe I have done. . . .'

The Witch of Endor, sitting rather dazedly on the floor, dabs at her lip with the hankie and frowns at the fresh mark it leaves. 'Well, all right,' she says. 'All right. But you haven't said anything new, have you? I mean, we all felt like that. Sort of empty inside, pointless. Only we didn't talk about it. We knew we'd been had all right, all of us.' She looks at the faces behind her, then back to Jed. 'It didn't need saying. But what I want to know is this. Suppose we do what you want, set fire to everything and smash it all up. They'll only build it for us again tomorrow. It won't prove anything. It'll just give them some fresh kicks, won't it? And what else *can* we do?'

Everybody looks at Polly, including Jed. She brushes one eyelid with the back of a finger, and gulps. Jed frowns, pulls at his lip with his teeth. 'There's a lot more in this,' he says. 'But I don't rightly know how to get to it.' Polly's eyes lock on to his and the frown becomes deeper. 'I think,' he says, 'I *think* . . . we must leave the Colony. Go back into the City, where we came from.'

Silence intensifies. Only Meg can find a voice. It sounds scratchy and thin.

'*Why* . . .?'

'Because . . . I don't know. Because I think'—again watching Polly—'because they *need* us. The plebs. They don't know it; but in a funny sort of way the . . . uncertainty . . . matters to them. Not knowing where we are, where we shall pop up next, the crazy things we shall do. They need people who've made lunacy a profession; and that's us. Without us, they'll forget they're living in Hell; they'll just sludge down into a sort of great doughy mass, and forget how to think, and how to eat, and one day they'll forget how to breathe. I think we've got to help them . . . keeps things stirred. Like worms tunnelling through earth, letting the air in. Us. The subversives. The Unsavoury Elements, the won't-do-gooders and won't-stay-putters. And I think we've got to do this even if it hurts because it's important to them as well. Because we might not like it, and we might refuse to face it, but in the long term the plebs are what matters to us more than anything else. Once we all opted for the Humanities. Well, there they are. The proper study of mankind. The plebs. *Man*. . . .'

Polly's lips move, echoing the words; he catches her eye again and she nods, positively and sorrowfully.

The Witch says very quietly, 'What about the sea?'

'We shan't see it any more.'

'Birds?'

'Not for us. Soon there won't be any anyway. The City will
spread over the Colony holdings as soon as we go and that'll be the
end.'

'No houses of our own?' That from Meg, in a squeak.

Jed shakes his head. 'No houses. Just miniflats in the levels, the
same as everybody else.'

'Sculpting?'

'Mobiles?'

'None. There won't be any room.'

'The sky?'

'We shall see it when we get a Liftpass. Like all the others.'

'We shall go mad . . .'

Jed nods. 'Yes, I think some of us will. But properly mad.
Effectively mad. Not like this. This is just . . . keeping up
appearances.'

Slowly at first, the idea catches on. 'I've had a monkey on my
back for years,' says the Witch. 'Here's where I shuck him right the
hell off. . . .'

'Jujus,' says Meg, brightening. 'New ones of all the Controllers.
We shall be outlawed. Sent to jail again.'

'Shot at on sight!'

'Brainwashing!'

'Trepanning!'

'Leucotomy! Loads of fun!'

'But we shan't give up . . .'

'Menacing letters in the news sheets!'

'Secret societies!'

'Things ticking in ventshafts!'

'Reign of terror!'

'Popping out all over!'

'Everything breaking up!'

'Arson!'

'Murder!'

'Incest!'

'Rape!'

'Secret printing presses!'

'Forbidden plays!'

'Subversive novels!'

'Art galleries in all the sewer flats!'

'Passwords!'

'Cloaks and daggers!'

'*Orgies!*'

Roley jumps on to his mangled counter, brandishing a bottle.

'Illicit stills!'

'Moonshining!'

'The plebs can't do this to us!'

'We demand our rights!'

'Summary execution!'

'Imprisonment without trial!'

'Curtailment of free speech!'

'*We'll start tonight . . . !*'

The Colony, transformed on the instant to a mob, surges for the doors. Shouts rise outside; voices call for torches, levers, fire. There are smashings and bangings in the night.

Jed doesn't run with the others. He stands in the doorway of the little phoney pub, slightly staggered at the revolution he has started. Flames are already springing up from a dozen points in the blackness as homes and artifacts begin to burn. Meg runs past screaming, hair blowing in the wind, a blazing brand shedding a bright trail of sparks. Jed turns back, rubbing his face, and sees he isn't alone. He walks across to where Polly is waiting, puts an arm round her shoulders and gives her a little shake. She watches up at him steadily. He says, 'I didn't finish, did I? I still didn't go down all the way, to what you're really trying to do.'

She gives him no help.

'I'm still trying to think,' he says. He looks over her brown hair at the beams of the pub, the high nicotine-glazed ceiling. An extra-loud crash comes from outside; smoke begins to drift thin and acrid across the bar. 'They're all drunk now,' he says. 'They'll be sorry for this in the morning. When they see the houses burned down, and all the things destroyed.'

He swallows, and purses his lips. 'I think,' he says, 'I think . . . there was a painter once called Van Rijn. He was famous, and rich, and he had a wife and I suppose he loved her. Then everything went wrong. His wife died and he lost his house and his money and his patrons forgot about him. Everything he had was taken away. And so . . . he started painting again. He made a portrait, *The Man in the Golden Helmet*. And then more. And more. And more. . . .'

Polly watches mistily, lips slightly parted.

'I think,' says Jed, 'if there's a Thing you can call by the name of Art, if it isn't all just a delusion . . . then the roots of the Thing have to reach right down, into bitterness and darkness. Somehow it needs

them, it's like a . . . swelling, a wanting to live where there's
nothing but death, a needing the sky when there's no sky left to see.
It's a . . . longing, an anger. That's what you've let loose; because
after tonight, when there's nothing left but the City, there'll be Art
again. Something locked away and suffocated, growing, not seeing
the sun. Like a . . . great flower in a box, thrusting and pushing and
pushing till one day it bursts the seams . . . Is that what you really
wanted, Polly? Just for there to be Art again? Am I right now?'

Polly hugs him suddenly, kissing and nibbling at his neck.

He lifts her head, tugging gently at her hair. 'In the City,' he says.
'Will you talk?'

She shakes her head, slowly.

'Funnyface,' he says. 'Funnyface. . . .' He holds her against him,
tightly.

In the night are pink blossomings of fire. The explosions carve
out the cliff edges, altering land that is soon to vanish. In their light
the mobiles flail, fall with thunderings and scrapings and long-
drawn bell notes into the sea. Ploughshares and vanes, wings and
sinews and metal feathers clanking and toppling; *Goliath, Civil
War, Cutty Sark, Juliet, The Ant, Titania, Excalibur, Fandancer,
Halycon* . . . and *Manscarer*, hugest and last. The procession of
Colonists winds between the ruins, tired now, ragged and smoke-
blackened and feverish-eyed. Leading them as they turn towards the
distant loom of the City is a tiny red car. Its driver sports the sword
and froggings, the buckles and epaulettes, the full panoply of a
British admiral; beside him a slighter shadow topped by a bonnet of
gull feathers clutches a picture book of sailing ships. Behind, Meg
carries boxes of scuttling animals, the Witch of Endor leads pranc-
ing dogs and a goat. The cavalcade, improvised banners swirling,
fades in distance; and in time the last tarara-rat-tan of a drum is
gone.

The dawn wind comes up from the sea. But the wind is alone.

Coranda

There was a woman in the great cleft-city of Brershill who was passing fair.

At least so ran opinion in that segment of low-level society of which she was undisputed queen. Though there were others, oldsters for the most part, who resented her beauty, finding her very fame an affront to decent living. Custom died hard in Brershill, most conservative—or most backward—of the Eight Cities of the Plain, the great ice steep men had once called the Matto Grosso. And in truth Coranda had given some cause for offence. If she was beautiful she was also vain and cold, cold as the ice plains that girdled the world: in her vanity she had denied even that sacrifice most beloved of great Ice Mother, the firstblood that belonged to the goddess alone. Long past the time of puberty she was, and the ceremonies of womanhood; and still the Mother waited for her due. In the blizzards that scourged the cleft, in the long winds of winter, her complaint might be heard, chilling the blood with threats and promises. All men knew they lived by the Mother's mercy alone; that one day, very soon now, the world would end, mantled for eternity in her sparkling cloth. *Coranda*, ran the whisper. *Coranda*, holding their lives in the hollow of her hand. Coranda heard, and laughed; she was just twenty, slim and black haired and tall.

She lay on a couch of white fur, toying with a winecup, mocking the young men of the cities as they paid her court. To Arand, son of the richest merchant of Brershill, she confided her belief that she herself was of the Mother's Chosen and thus above the pettiness of sacrifice. 'For,' she said, smoothing her long hair, 'is not the Mother justly famed for beauty, for the perfection of skin that matches the fresh-laid snow? The darkness of her eyes, all-seeing, the slenderness of the hands that guard us all? And have I not'—she tossed her head—'have I not, among your good selves at least, some claim to prettiness? Though Eternal Mother forbid'— blushing, and modestly lowering her eyes—'that I should fall into the sin of pride.' Arand, more than a little drunk, straightway burbled her divinity, speaking heresy with the ease of long practice or stupidity till she swept from him indignantly, angry that he should speak lightly of the deity in her presence. 'Will not the Mother's rage,' she asked Maitran of Friesgalt appealingly, 'de- scend alike on his head and mine? Will you protect me from the lightnings that fly in storms, lightnings such words may bring?'

That was a cunning touch, worthy of Coranda; for the animosity with which most Friesgaltians regarded the folk of Brershill was well known. Maitran's knifeblade gleamed instantly, and would no doubt have brought the Mother a pleasing offering had not Brershil- lian stalwarts pinned and disarmed the combatants. Some blood was shed certainly, from thumped noses and mouths, while Coranda regarded the wriggling heap with interest. 'Now,' she said, 'I think I must call my father's men, to punish; for do I mean so little to you all that you come here to my house and brawl?' She ran to the gong placed beside the door of the chamber, and would certainly have summoned an irate guard had not earnest entreaty prevailed.

'Well,' she said, tossing her head again in disgust. 'It seems you all have too much spirit, and certainly too much energy, for my comfort and your own safety. I think we must devise a small occupation, something that will absorb your wildness and will no doubt bring a suitable reward.'

There was a quietness at that; for she had hinted before that marriage to some rich and worthy boy might at long last assuage the Mother's need. She brooded, suddenly thoughtful, stroked hands across her gown so the fabric showed momentarily the convexities of belly and thighs. Lowered her eyes, glided swaying to the couch. They made way for her, wary and puzzled. Rich they all were, certainly, or they would none of them have passed her father's ironbound doors; but worthy? Who could be worthy of Coranda, whose beauty was surely Ice Mother's own?

She clapped her hands; at the gesture a house servant, blue liveried, laid beside her a box. It was made from wood, rarest of substances, inlaid with strips of ivory and bone. She opened it languidly; inside, resting on a quilting of white nylon, was a slim harpoon. She lifted it, toying with the haft, fingers stroking the razor edges of the barbs. 'Who will prove himself?' she asked, seemingly to the air. 'Who will take the Mother's due, when Coranda of Brershill comes to marriage?'

Instantly, a babble of voices; Karl Stromberg and Mard Lipsill of Abersgalt shouted willingness. Frey Skalter the Keltshillian, half-barbaric in his jewelled furs, attempted to kiss her foot. She withdrew it smartly, equally sharply kicked him in the throat. Skalter overbalanced, swearing, spilling wine across the pale floor. There was laughter; she silenced it sharply, lifting the little harpoon again, watching them all from long lashed, kohl-painted eyes. She relaxed, still holding the weapon, staring at the ceiling in the fast blue flicker of the lamps. 'Once,' she said, 'long ago, in the far south of our land, a whaler was blown off course by storms. When the Ice Mother's anger was spent, and she sent sunlight again and birds, none could make out where her breath had driven them. There was ice, a great smooth plain, and mountains; some of them smoked, so they said, throwing cinders and hot winds into the air. A very queer place it was indeed, with furry barbarians and animals from a child's book of fancies, stranger than men could believe. There they hunted, spilling and killing till their holds were full and they turned north to their home. Then they came on the strangest wonder of all.'

In her quiet the buzzing of the eternal fluorescent tubes sounded loud. Skalter poured himself more wine, carefully, eyes on the girl's face. Arand and Maitran stopped their glaring; Stromberg thoughtfully wiped an errant red trickle from his nose.

'In the dark of dawn,' said Coranda dreamily, 'in the grey time when men and ships are nothing but shadows without weight and substance, they met the Fate sent by Ice Mother to punish them their crimes. It surrounded them, flickering and leaping, soundless as snow, weird as Death itself. All across the plain, round their boat as they sailed, were animals. They ran and moved, playing; whole herds and droves of them, bulls and calves and cows. Their bodies were grey they said, and sinuous as seals; their eyes were beautiful, and looked wisely at the ship. But without doubt they were spirits from the Mother's court, sent to warn and destroy; for as they turned and leaped they saw each had but one horn, long and spiralling, that caught and threw back the light.'

She waited, seeming indifferent to her audience. At length Lipsill broke the silence. 'Coranda . . . what of the boat?'

She shrugged delicately, still playing with the barbed tip of the spear. 'Two men returned, burned by the Mother's breath till their faces were black and marbled and their hands turned to scorched hooks. They lived long enough to tell the tale.'

They waited.

'A man who loved me,' she said, 'who wanted to feel me in his bed and know himself worthy, would go to that land of shadows on the rim of the world. He would bring me a present to mark his voyage.'

Abruptly her eyes flicked wide, scorning at them. 'A head,' she said softly. 'The head of the unicorn. . . .'

Another pause; and then a wild shouting. 'Ice Mother hear me,' bellowed Skalter. 'I'll fetch your toy for you . . .'

'And me. . . .'

'And me. . . .'

They clamoured for attention.

She beckoned Skalter. He came forward, dropping to one knee, leaning his craggy face over hers. She took his hand and raised it, closed the fingers gently round the tip of the harpoon. Stared at him, fixing him with her great eyes. 'You would go?' she said. 'Then there must be no softness, Frey Skalter, no fainting of the spirit. Hard as the ice you will be, and as merciless; for my sake alone.' She laid her hand over his, stroking the fingers, smiling her cat-smile. 'You will go for me?'

He nodded, not speaking; and she squeezed slowly, still smiling. He stiffened, breath hissing between his teeth; and blood ran back down his arm, splashed bright and sudden on the weapon's shaft. 'By this token,' she said, 'you are my man. So shall you all be; and Ice Mother, in her charity, will decide.'

Early day burned over the icefields. To the east the sun, rising across the white plain, threw red beams and the mile-long shadows of boats and men. Above, dawn still fought with darkness; the red flush faded to violet-grey, the grey to luminous blue. Across the blue ran high ripplings of cloud; the zenith gleamed like the skin of a turquoise fish. In the distance, dark-etched against the horizon, rose the spar-forest of the Brershill dock, where the schooners and merchantmen lay clustered in the lee of long moles built of blocks of ice. In the foreground, ragged against the glowing sky, were the yachts; Arand's *Chaser*, Maitran's sleek catamaran, Lipsill's big *Ice Ghost*. Karl Stromberg's *Snow Princess* snubbed at a mooring rope as the wind caught her curved side. Beyond her were two dour vessels from Djobhabn; and a Fyorsgeppian, iron beaked, that bore the blackly humorous name *Bloodbringer*. Beyond again was Skalter's *Easy Girl*, wild and splendid, decorated all over with hairtufts and scalps and ragged scraps of pelt. Her twin masts were bound with intricate strappings of nylon cord; on her gunnel skulls of animals gleamed, eyesockets threaded with bright and moving silks. Even her runners were carved, the long-runes that told, cryptically, the story of Ice Mother's meeting with Sky Father and the birth and death of the Son, he whose Name could not be mentioned. The Mother's grief had spawned the icefields; her anger would not finally be appeased till Earth ran cold and quiet for ever. Three times she had approached, three times the Fire Giants fought her back from their caverns under the ice; but she would not be denied. Soon now, all would be whiteness and peace; then the Son would rise, in rumblings and glory, and judge the souls of men.

The priest moved, shivering in a patterned shawl, touching the boats and blessing, smearing the bow of each with a little blood and milk. The wind soughed in the riggings, plucked at the robes of the muffled woman who stood staring, hair flicking round her throat. The headlamps swung on their poles, glowing against the patched hulls, throwing the priest's shadow vague and fleeting as the shadow of a bird. The yachts tugged at their lines, flapping their pennants, creaking their bone runners, full of the half-life of mechanical things. All preparations were made, provisions stored, blood and seed given in expiation to the ice. The hunters grunted and stamped, swinging their arms in the keen air, impatient and unsure; and to each it seemed the eyes of Coranda promised love, the body of Coranda blessings.

The ceremony ended, finally. The priest withdrew to his tasselled nylon tent, the polebearers lifted their burden and trudged back across the ice. The boats were turned, levered by muffled men with crows till the sharp bows pointed, questing, to the south. A shout; and Lipsill's craft first blossomed sail, the painted fabric flying and cracking round the mast. Then the catamaran. Skalter's deceptively clumsy squarerigger; quick thud of a mallet parting the sternline and Lipsill was away, runners crisping, throwing a thin white double plume from the snow that had drifted across the ice. Stromberg followed, swinging from the far end of the line, crossing his scored wake as Skalter surged across *Princess*'s bows. A bellowing and the Keltshillian crabbed away, narrowly missing disaster, raising a threatening fist. Karl laughed, fur glove muffling the universal gesture of derision; the boats faded in the dawn light, swerving and tacking as they jockeyed for the lead. If the display moved Coranda she gave no sign of it; she stood smiling, coldly amused at the outcome of a jest, till the hulls were veiled in the frost-smoke of the horizon and the shouts lost beneath the wind.

The yachts moved steadily through the day, heading due south under the bright, high sun, their shadows pacing them across the white smoothness of the Plains. With the wind astern the squarerigger made ground fast; by evening she was hull down, her sails a bright spark on the horizon. Stromberg crowded *Snow Princess*, racing in her wake; behind him, spread out now, came the others, lateens, bulging, runners hissing on the ice. The cold was bracing and intense; snow crystals, blowing on the wind, stung his cheeks to a glow, beaded the heavy collar of his jerkin. Lipsill forged alongside, *Ice Ghost* surging and bucking. Karl raised a hand, laughing at his friend; and instantly came the chilling thought that one day, for Coranda, he might kill Lipsill, or Lipsill him.

They camped together, by common consent; all but Skalter, still miles ahead. Here, away from the eternal warmth of the cleft-cities, they must husband their reserves of fuel; they huddled round the redly-glowing brazier, the reflection lighting their faces, glinting out across the ice. The worn hulls of the yachts, moored in a crescent, protected them from the worst of the wind. Outside, beyond the circle of light, a wolf howled high and quavering; within the camp was cheerfulness, songs and stories passing round the group till one by one they took a last swig from their spirit flasks, checked their lines and grapples and turned in. They were up early next dawn, again by unspoken agreement, hoping maybe to steal a march on *Easy Girl;* but keen as they were, Skalter was ahead of them. They passed his camp, an hour's sail away. *Ice Ghost* crushed the remains of the brazier fire, the turned-out remnants still smouldering on the ice; one runner spurned the embers, sent a long banner of ash trailing down the wind. They glimpsed his sails once before the wind, rising again, blocked visibility with a swirling curtain of snow.

They were now nearing the wide cleft of Fyorsgep, southernmost of the Cities of the Plain. The smooth ice was crossed by the tracks of many ships; they shortened sail cautiously, shouting each to the next along the line. Hung lanterns in the rigging, pushed on again by compass and torchlight, unwilling to moor and give away advantage. *Snow Princess* and *Ice Ghost* moved side by side, a bare length separating them.

It was Stromberg who first heard the faint booming from astern. He listened, cocking his head and frowning; then waved, pointing behind him with a bulky arm. The noise came again, a dull and ominous ringing; Lipsill laughed, edging his boat even closer. Karl stared back as behind them an apparition loomed, impossibly tall in the gloom and whirling flakes. He saw the heavy thrusting of bowsprit and jibboom, the cavernous eyes of the landwhale skulls that graced the vessel's stem. They held course defiantly as she closed, hearing now mixed with the fog gongs the long-drawn roar of her runners over the ice. Stromberg made out the carved characters on her bow; the *Sweet Lady*, whaler, out of Friesgalt, bound no doubt for the Southern Moorings and a night's carouse.

The jibboom was between the boats, thrusting at their rigging, before they were seen. An agonized howl from above, movement of lanterns and dark figures at the vessel's rail; she rumbled between the yachts as they parted at the last instant, the long shares of her ice anchors nearly scraping their booms. They saw the torchlit deck, fires burning in crow's-nest and rigging; and the curious feature of an iceboat, the long slots in the bilges in which moved the linkages of the paired anchors. Dull light gleamed through her as she passed, giving to her hull the appearance of a half-flensed whale; a last bellow reached them as she faded into the greyness ahead.

'*Abersgaltian bastards. . . .*'

The skipper then had seen the big insignia at the masthead. This *Lady* was anything but sweet.

The night's camp brought near-disaster. Maitran came in late and evil tempered, a runner stay cracked on the catamaran, bound with a jury-lashing of nylon rope. Some chance remark from Arand and he was on his feet, knifeblade glinting. He held the weapon tip-uppermost, circling and taunting his enemy. Arand rose white-faced, swathing a bearskin round one forearm. A quick feint and thrust, a leaping back; and Lipsill spoke easily, still seated by the fire.

'The prize, Friesgaltian, comes with the head of the unicorn. Our friend would doubtless look well enough, grinning from Coranda's wall; but your energy would be expended to no purpose.'

Maitran hissed between his teeth, not deigning to glance round.

'You risk in any case the anger of the Ice Mother,' the Abersgaltian went on, reaching behind him to his pack. 'For if our Lady is in fact her servant then this hunting is clearly her design, and should bring her glory. All else is vanity, an affront to her majesty.'

Hansan, the Fyorsgeppian, dark faced and black browed, nodded sombrely. 'This is true,' he said. 'Bloodspilling, if it be against the Mother's will, brings no honour.'

Maitran half turned at that, uncertainly; and Lipsill's arm flaired up and back. The harpoon head, flung with unerring force, opened his cheek; he went down in a flurry of legs and arms and Stromberg was on him instantly, pinning him. Lipsill turned to Arand, his own knife in his hand. 'Now, now Brershillian,' he said gently; for the other, roused, would no doubt have thrown himself on his prostrate enemy and extracted vengeance. 'No more, or you will answer to us all. . . .'

Arand sheathed his dagger, shakily, eyes not leaving the stained face of the Friesgaltian. Maitran was allowed to rise; and Lipsill faced him squarely. 'This was evil,' he said. 'Our fight is with the wind and wide ice, not each other. Take your boat, and stay apart from us.'

In Stromberg's mind rose the first stirring of a doubt.

They moved fast again next morning, hoping for some sign of Skalter's yacht; but the wind that had raged all night had cleaned his tracks, filling them with fresh snow. The ice lay scoured, white and gleaming to the horizon.

They were now past the farthest limit of civilization, on the great South Ice where the whale herds and their hunters roamed. Here and there were warm ponds, choked with brown and green weed; they saw animals, wolf and otter, once a herd of the shaggy white bison of the Plains; but no sign of the ghostly things they sought. The catamaran reached ahead of the rest, the Friesgaltian reckless and angry, crowding sail till the slim paired hulls were nearly obscured beneath a cloud of pale nylon. Stromberg, remembering the split strut, sent up a brief and silent prayer.

Maitran's luck held till midday; then the stay parted, suddenly and without warning. They all saw the boat surge off course, one keel dropping to glissade along the ice. For a moment it seemed she would come to rest without further harm, then the ivory braces between the hulls, overstressed, broke in their turn. She split into halves; one hull bounded end over end, shedding fragments and splinters of bone, the other spun, encumbered by the falling weight of mast and sail, flicked Maitran in a sharp arc across the ice. He was up instantly, seemingly unhurt, running and waving to head them off.

In Arand's slow brain hatred still burned. He knew, as they had all known, that in a fight he was no match for the Friesgaltian. Maitran would have bled him, cutting and opening till he lay down and gasped his life out on the ice. They had saved him, the night before, but he had lost his honour. Now the rage took him, guiding his hands till they seemed possessed of a life of their own. They swung the tiller, viciously; *Chaser* swerved, heading in toward the wreck. Maitran shouted as the yacht crisped toward him; at the last moment it seemed he realized she would not turn. He tried to run; a foot slipped and he went down on the ice. A thud, a bright spattering across the bows of *Chaser* and she was past the wreck, yawing as she dragged the body from one sharp ski. Fifty yards on it twirled clear. She limped to a halt, sails fluttering. From her runner led a faint and wavering trail; her deck was marked with the pink blood of the Friesgaltian.

They gathered round the thing on the ice, Stromberg and the Djobhabnians stunned, Arand pale and mumbling. There was no life; the great wound in the head, the oozing of blood and brain-matter, showed there was nothing to be done. They made the sign of the Ice Mother, silently; turned away, anxious to leave the sight, left the body for her servants, the birds.

They were cheered later that day by the gleam of Skalter's sail far to the south; but the camp was still a sombre affair. They moored apart, sat brooding each over his own fire. To Stromberg it seemed all his past life now counted for nothing; they were governed by the Rule of the Ice, the code that let men kill or be killed with equal indifference. He remembered his years of friendship with Lipsill, a friendship that seemed now to be ended. After what he had seen that morning he would not dare trust even Mard again. At night he tried, unavailingly, to summon the image of Coranda's warm body; pray though he might, the succubus would not visit him. Instead he fell into a fitful sleep, dreamed he saw the very caverns of the Fire Giants deep under the ice. But there were no gleaming gods and demons; only machines, black and vast, that hummed and sang of power. The vision disturbed him; he cut his arm, in the dull dawn light, left blood to appease the Mother. It seemed even she turned her back on him; the morning was grey and cold, comfortless. He drank to restore circulation to his limbs, tidied his ship, left sullenly in the wake of Lipsill as he led them on again across the Plain.

As they moved, the character of the land round them once more changed. The warm ponds were more numerous; over them now hung frequent banks of fog. Often *Snow Princess* slushed her way through water, runners raising glittering swathes to either side. At breakfast the Djobhabnians had seemed remote, standing apart and muttering; now their identical craft began to edge away, widening the gap between them and the rest till they were hull down, grey shadows on the ice. By early evening they were out of sight.

The four boats raced steadily through a curling sea of vapour. Long leads of clear water opened threatening to either side; they tacked and swerved, missing disaster time and again by the width of a runner. Stromberg lay to the right of the line, next to him the Fyorsgeppian. Then Lipsill; beyond *Ice Ghost* was the blighted vessel of Arand, half-seen now through the moving mist. None of the boats would give way, none fall back; Karl clung to the tiller, feeling the fast throb of the runners transmitted through the bone shaft, full of a hollow sense of impending doom.

As dusk fell a long runnel of open water showed ahead. He altered course, following it where it stretched diagonally across his bows. A movement to the left made him turn. *Bloodringer* had fallen back; her dark hull no longer blocked his vision, Mard still held course; and still *Chaser* ran abreast of him, drawing nearer and nearer the edge of the break. Stromberg at last understood Lipsill's purpose; he yelled, saw Arand turn despairingly. It was too late; behind him, a length away, jutted the Fyorsgeppian's iron ram. Boxed, the yacht spun on her heel in a last attempt to leap the obstacle. A grating of runners and spars, a frozen moment as she poised above the gulf, then she struck the water with a thunderous splash. She sank almost instantly, hull split by the concussion; for a moment her bilge showed rounded and pale then she was gone. In her place was a disturbed swirl, a bobbing of debris. Arand surfaced once, waving a desperate arm, before he too vanished.

The sun sank over the rim of the ice, flung shadows of the boats miles long like the predatory shapes of birds.

In the brief twilight they came up with *Easy Girl*. Skalter hung in her rigging, leisurely reeving a halliard, waving and jeering at them as they passed.

All three vessels turned, Stromberg and Lipsill tightly, Hansen in a wider circle that took him skimming across the Plain to halt, sails flapping, a hundred yards away. Grapples went down; they lashed and furled stoically, dropped to the ice and walked over to the Keltshillian.

He greeted them cheerfully, swinging down from the high mast of the boat. 'Well, you keen sailors; where are our friends?'

'Fraskall and Ulsenn turned back,' said Lipsill shortly. 'Maitran and Arand are dead. Maitran at Arand's hands, Arand in an ice-break.' He stared at Stromberg challengingly. 'It was the Mother's will, Karl. She could have buoyed him to the land. She did not choose to.'

Stromberg didn't answer.

'Well,' said Skalter easily, 'the Mother was ever firm with her followers. Let it be so.' He made the sign of benediction, carelessly, circling with his hands, drawing with one palm the flat emptiness of the ice. He ran his fingers through his wild blond hair and laughed. 'Tonight you will share my fire, Abersgaltians; and you too, Hansan of Fyorsgep. Tomorrow, who can tell? We reach the Mother's court perhaps, and sail in fairyland.'

They grouped round the fire, quietly, each occupied with his own thoughts, Skalter methodically honed the barbs of a harpoon, turning the weapon, testing the cutting edges against his thumb, his scarred face intent in the red light. He looked up finally, half frowning, half quizzical; his earrings swung and glinted as he moved his head. 'It seems to me,' he said, 'the Mother makes her choice known, in her special way. Arand and Maitran were both fools of a type, certainly unfitted for the bed of the Lady we serve, and the Djobhabnians fainthearted. Now we are four; who among us, one wonders, will win the bright prize?'

Stromberg made a noise, half smothered by his glove; Skalter regarded him keenly.

'You spoke, Abersgaltian?'

'He feels,' said Lipsill gruffly, 'we murdered Arand. After he in his turn killed Maitran.'

The Keltshillian laughed, high and wild. 'Since when,' he said, 'did pity figure in the scheme of things? Pity, or blame? Friends, we are bound to the Ice Eternal; to the cold that will increase and conquer, lay us all in our bones. Is not human effort vain, all life doomed to cease? I tell you, Coranda's blood, that mighty prize, and all her secret sweetness, this is a flake of snow in an eternal wind. I am the Mother's servant; through me she speaks. We'll have no more talk of guilt and softness, it turns my stomach to hear it.' The harpoon darted, sudden and savage, stood quivering between them in the ice. 'The ice is real,' shouted Skalter, rising. 'Ice, and blood. All else is delusion, toys for weak men and fools.'

He stamped away, earrings jangling, into the dark. The others separated soon afterward to their boats; and Stromberg for one lay tossing and uneasy till dawn shot pearly streamers above the Plain and the birds called, winging to the south.

On its southern rim the Great Plateau sloped gently. The yachts travelled fast, creaming over untold depths of translucent ice, runners hissing, sails filling in the breeze that still blew from nearly astern. There would be weary days of tacking ahead for those that returned. If any returned; Stromberg found himself increasingly beginning to doubt. It seemed a madness had gripped them all, drawing them deeper and deeper into the uncharted land. The place of warm ponds was left behind; ahead, under the pale sun, shadows grew against the sky. There were mountains, topped with fire as the story had foretold; strange crevasses and plateaux, jumbled and distant, glinting like crystal in the hard white light. Still Skalter led them, mastbells clanking, barbaric sails shaking and swelling. They held course stubbornly, shadows pacing them as they raced to the south.

At the foot of the vast slope they parted company with the Fyorsgeppian. He had reached ahead, favoured by some trick of the terrain, till *Bloodringer* was a hundred yards or more in front of the rest. They saw the hull of the boat jar and leap. The smooth slope ended, split by a series of yard-high ridges; Hansan's runners, hitting the first of them, were sheared completely from the hull. There was something tragically comic about the accident. The gunwhales split, the mast jarring loose to revolve against the sky like an oversized harpoon; the Fyorsgeppian, held by a shoulder harness, kept his place while the boat came apart round him like a child's toy. The remnants planed, spinning at great speed, jolted to a stop in a quick shower of ice. The survivors swerved, avoiding the broken ground, whispering by Hansan as he sat shaking his head, still half stunned. The wreckage dwindled to a speck that vanished, lost against the grey-green scarp of ice. There were provisions in the hull; the Fyorsgeppian would live or die as the Mother willed.

For the first time that night the skyline round their camp was broken by valleys and hills. Still icebound, the land had begun to roll; there were gullies, hidden cliffs, ravines from which came the splash and tinkle of water. It was an eerie country, dangerous and beautiful. They had seen strange animals; but no sign or spoor of barbarians, or the things they sought.

Stromberg spoke to Skalter again at dawn, while Lipsill fussed with the rigging of his boat. He seemed impelled by a sense of urgency; all things, mountains and sky, conspired to warn his blood. 'It has come to me,' he said quietly, 'that we should return.'

The Keltshillian stood thoughtfully, warming his hands at the brazier, casting glances at the low sky, sniffing the wind. He gave a short, coughing laugh but didn't turn.

Stromberg touched a skull on the high side of *Easy Girl*, stroking the wind-smoothed eyesockets, unsure how to go on. 'Last night I dreamed,' he said. 'It seemed as it has seemed before that the Giants were not gods but men, and we their children. That we are deceived, the Great Mother is dead. Such heresy must be a warning.'

Skalter laughed again and spat accurately at the coals, rubbed arms banded with wide copper torques. 'You dreamed of love,' he said. 'Wetting your furs with hot thoughts of Coranda. It's you who are deceived, Lipsgaltian. Counsel your fancies.'

'Skalter,' said Karl uncertainly, 'the price is high. Too high, for a woman.'

The other turned to face him for the first time, pale eyes brooding in the keen face.

Stromberg rushed on. 'All my life,' he said, 'it seemed to me that you were not as other men. Now I say, there is death here. Maybe for us all. Go back, Frey; the prize is beneath your worth.'

The other turned to look up at the hulking shape of the boat, stroking her gunwale with a calloused hand, feeling the smoothness of the ivory. 'The price of birth is death,' he said broodingly. 'That too is a heavy sum to pay.'

'What drives you, Skalter?' asked Stromberg softly. 'If the woman means so little? Why do you strive, if life is purposeless?'

'I do what is given,' said Skalter shortly. He flexed his hands on the side of the boat and sprang; the runners of *Easy Girl* creaked as he swung himself aboard. 'Rage drives me,' he said, looking down. 'Know this, Karl Stromberg of Abersgalt; that Skalter of Keltshill lusts for death. In dying, death dies with him.' He slapped the halliards against the after mast, bringing down a white shower of ice. 'I also dreamed,' he said. 'My dream was of life, sweet and rich. I follow the Mother; in her, I shall find my reward.' He would say no more but stalked forward, bent to recoil the long ropes on the deck.

That morning they sighted their prey.

At first Stromberg could not believe; he was forced, finally, to accept the evidence of his eyes. The unicorns played and danced, sunlight flashing from their sides, horns gleaming, seeming to throw off sparks of brightness. He might have followed all day, watching and bemused; but Skalter's high yell recalled him, the change of course as *Easy Girl* sped for the mutated narwhal. Already the Keltshillian was brandishing his long harpoon, shaking out the coils of line as the yacht, tiller locked, flew toward the herd.

It was as the story had told; the creatures surrounded the boats, running and leaping, watching with their beautiful calm eyes. On Karl's left Lipsill too seemed to be dazed. Skalter braced his feet on the deck, flexed muscles to drive the shaft hissing into the air. His aim was good; the harpoon struck a great grey bull, barbs sinking deep through the wrinkled pelt. Instantly all was confusion. The wounded beast reared and plunged, snorting; *Easy Girl* was spun off course by the violence, the Keltshillian hauling desperately at the line. Boat and animal collided in a flurry of snow. The narwhal leaped away again, towing the yacht; Karl saw bright plumes flying as her anchors fell, tips biting at the ice.

The herd had panicked, jerking and humping into the distance; *Snow Princess*, still moving fast, all but fouled the harpoon line as Stromberg clawed clear. He had a brief glimpse of Skalter on the ice, the flash of a cutlass as the creature plunged, thrusting at its tormentor with its one great horn. He swung the tiller again, hard across; *Princess* circled, runners squealing, fetched up fifty yards from the ice. *Ice Ghost* was already stopped, Lipsill running cutlass in hand; Karl heard Skalter scream, in triumph or in pain. He dropped his anchors, grabbing for his own sword. Ran across the ice toward *Easy Girl*, hearing now the enraged trumpeting of the bull.

The great beast had the Keltshillian pinned against the side of the boat. He saw the blunt head lunging, driving the horn through his flesh, the yacht rocked with the violence of the blows. The panting of the narwhal sounded loud; then the creature with a last convulsion had torn itself away, snorting and hooting after the vanished herd.

There was much blood, on the ice and the pale side of the boat. Skalter sat puffing, face suffused, hands gripped over his stomach. More blood pulsed between his fingers, ruby-bright in the sun; cords stood out in his thick neck; his white teeth grinned as he rolled his head in pain.

Lipsill reached him at the same instant. They tried, pointlessly, to draw the hands away; Skalter resisted them, eyes shut, breath hissing between his clenched teeth. 'I told you I dreamed,' he said. The words jerked out thick and agonized. 'I saw the Mother. She came in the night, cajoling; her limbs were white as snow, and hot as fire. It was an omen; but I couldn't read. . . .' His head dropped; he raised himself again, gasping with effort. They took his hands then, soapy with blood, squeezed, feeling the dying vice-grip, seeing the eyes roll white under their lids. Convulsions shook him; they thought he was dead, but he spoke again. 'Blood, and ice,' he said faintly. 'These are real. These are the words of the Mother. When the world is dark, then she will come to me. . . .' The body arced, straining; and Lipsill gripped the yellow hair, twisting it in his fingers. 'The Mother takes you, Skalter,' he said. 'She rewards her servant.'

They waited; but there was nothing more.

They moored their boats, silently, walked back to the place of killing. The blood had frozen, sparkling in pink crystals under the levelling sun. 'He was a great prince,' said Lipsill finally. 'The rest is smallness; it should not come between us.' Stromberg nodded, not answering with words; and they began to work. They broke *Easy Girl*, smashing bulwarks and runners, hacking at her bone and ivory spars, letting her spirit free to join the great spirit of Skalter that already roamed the Ice Eternal. Two days they laboured, raising a mound of ice above the wreck; Skalter they laid on the deck, feet to the north and the domain of the Mother. He would rise now, on that last cold dawn, spring up facing her, a worthy servant and warrior. When they had finished, and the wind skirled over the glistening *how*, they rested; on the third morning they drove south again.

There were no words now between them. They sailed apart, bitterly, watching the white horizon, the endless swirl and flurry of snow. Two days later they resighted their quarry.

The two boats separated further, bearing down; and again the strange creatures watched with their soft eyes. The shaft flew, glinting; Lipsill's tinkled on the ice, Stromberg's struck wide of its mark. It missed the bull at which it was aimed, plunged instead into the silver flank of a calf. The animal howled, convulsed in a flurry of pain. As before the herd bolted; *Snow Princess* slewed, hauled round by the tethered weight, fled across the plain as the terrified creature bucked and plunged.

Less than half the size of the adults, the calf was nearly as long as the boat; Stromberg clung to the tiller as *Princess* jolted and veered, determined not to make Skalter's mistake of jumping to the ice. A mile away the harpoon pulled clear but the animal was blown; a second shaft transfixed it as it stood head down and panting, started fresh and giant paroxysms that spattered the yacht with blood. *Princess* flew again, anchor blades ripping at the ice, drawing the thing gradually to a halt. It rolled then and screeched, trying with its half-flippers to scrape the torment from its back. Its efforts wound the line in round its body; it stood finally close to the boat, staring with a filmed, uncomprehending eye. Close enough for Stromberg to reach across, work the shaft into its torn side till the tip probed its life. A thin wailing, a nearly human noise of pain; and the thing collapsed, belching thunderously, coughing up masses of blood and weed. Sticky tears squeezed from its eyes ran slow across the great round face; and Karl, standing shaking and panting, knew there was no need of the sword.

The anchors of *Ice Ghost* raised a high screaming. She ploughed across the ice, throwing a white hail of chips to either side, speed barely diminished. She had speared a huge bull; animal and boat careered by the stalled *Princess*. Stromberg cut his line, heavily, left the carcass with the bright harpoon-silks still blowing above it. Steered in pursuit.

Sometimes in the half hour that followed it seemed he might overrun Lipsill; but always the other boat drew ahead. The narwhal left a thick trail of blood, but its energy seemed unabated. The line twanged thunderously, snagging on the racing ice. Ahead now the terrain was split and broken; fissures yawned, sunlight sparking from their deep green sides. *Princess* bucked heavily, runners crashing as she swerved between the hazards. The chase veered to the east, in a great half-circle; the wind, at first abeam, reached farther and farther ahead. Close-hauled, Stromberg fell behind; a half mile separated the boats as they entered a wide, bowl-shaped valley, a mile or more across, guarded on each side by needle shaped towers of ice.

Ahead, the glittering floor veered to a rounded lip; the horizon line was sharp-cut against the sky. *Ice Ghost*, still towed by her catch, took the slope with barely a slackening of pace. Stromberg howled his alarm, uselessly; Lipsill, frozen it seemed to the tiller, made no attempt to cut his line. The boat crested the rise, hung a moment silhouetted against brightness; and vanished, abrupt as a conjuring trick.

Princess's anchors threw snow plumes high as her masthead. She skated sickeningly, surged to a halt twenty yards below the lip of ice. Stromberg walked forward, carefully. As he topped the ridge the sight beyond took his breath.

He stood on the edge of the biggest crevasse he had ever seen. It curved back to right and left, horseshoe-shaped, enclosing the valley like a white tongue. A hundred yards away the opposite side glowed with sunlight; across it lay the ragged shadow of the nearer wall. He craned forward. Below him the ice-walls stretched sheer to vanish in a blue-green gloom. There was mist down there, and water-noise; he heard booming, long-drawn threads of echo, last sounds maybe of the fall of the whale. Far below, impaled on a black spike of ice, was the wreck of Lipsill's boat; Mard, still held by his harness, sprawled across the stern, face bright with blood. He moved slightly as Stromberg stared, seeming to raise himself, lift a hand. Karl turned away sickened.

Realizing he had won.

He walked back to *Snow Princess*, head down, feet scraping on the ice, swung himself aboard and opened the bow locker, dumping piles of junk and provisions on the deck. There were ropes, spare downhauls, and mooring lines. He selected the best and thickest, knotting methodically, tied off to the stern of the boat and walked back to the gulf. The line, lowered carefully, swayed a yard from Lipsell's head.

He returned to *Princess*. She was stopped at an angle, tilted sideways on the curling lip of the crevasse. There were crowbars in the locker; he pulled one clear and worked cautiously, prising at the starboard runner, inching the yacht round till her bow pointed back down the long slope. The wind, gusting and capricious, blew from the gulf. The slope would help her gather way; but would it be enough?

He brailed the sails up as far as he dared, stood back frowning and biting his lip. At each gust now the anchors groaned. Threatening to tear free, send the boat skittering back down the incline. He scrabbled in the locker again, grabbing up more line. Another line, a light line that must also reach the wreck.

There was just barely enough. He tied the last knot, dropped the second coil down. Working feverishly now, he transferred the heavy line from the stern to a cleat halfway along the port gunwhale and locked the tiller to starboard. The anchors were raised by pulleys set just above the deck; he carried lines from them to the little bow windlass, slipped the ratchet, turned the barrel till they were tight. The handle, fitted in its bone socket, stood upright, pointing slightly forward over the stem of the boat. He tied the light line off to the tip, tested the lashing on the improvised brake. It seemed secure; he backed toward the cliff edge, paying both ropes through his hands. Mard seemed now to understand what he was doing. He called croakingly, tried to move. The wreck groaned, slipped another foot toward the crevasse. Stromberg passed the heavy line between his thighs, round one calf, gripped it between sole and instep. Let himself down into the gulf.

The descent was eerie. As he moved the wind pressure seemed to increase, setting him swaying pendulum-fashion, banging his body at the ice. The sunlit edge above receded; he glanced below him and instantly the crevasse seemed to spin. The ice walls, sloping together, vanished in a blackish gloom; the wind called deep and baying, its icy breath chilled his cheek. He hung sweating till the dizziness passed, forced himself to move again. Minutes later his feet reached the last knot, groped below it into emptiness. He lowered himself by his arms, felt his heels touch the deck of the boat. He dropped as lightly as he could, lunging forward to catch at the tangle of rigging. A sickening time while the wreck surged and creaked; he felt sweat drop from him again as he willed the movement to stop. The deck steadied, with a final groan; he edged sideways cautiously, cutting more rope lengths, fashioning a bridle that he slipped under Lipsill's arms. The other helped as best he could, raising his body weakly; Stromberg tested the knots, lashed the harness to the line. Another minute's work and he too was secure. He took a shuddering breath, groping for the second rope. They were not clear yet; if *Ice Ghost* moved she could still take them with her, scrape them into the gulf. He gripped the line and pulled.

Nothing.

He jerked again, feeling the fresh rise of panic. If the trick failed he knew he lacked the strength ever to climb. A waiting; then a vibration, sensed through the rope. Another pause and he was being drawn smoothly up the cliff, swinging against the rock-hard ice as the pace increased. The sides of the cleft seemed to rush toward him; a last concussion, a bruising shock and he was being towed over level ice, sawing desperately at the line. He saw fibres parting; then he was lying still, blessedly motionless, Lipsill beside him bleeding into the snow. While *Princess*, freed of her one-sided burden, skated in a wide half-circle, came into irons, and stopped.

The crevasse of Brershill lay grey and silent in the early morning. Torches, flaring at intervals along the grassy sides, lit Level after Level with a wavering glare, gleamed on the walkways with their new powdering of snow. Stromberg trudged steadily, sometimes hauling his burden, sometimes skidding behind it as he eased the sledge down the sloping paths. A watchman called sleepily; he ignored him. On the Level above Coranda's home he stopped, levered the great thing from the sledge and across to the edge of the path. He straightened up, wiping his face, and yelled; his voice ran thin and shaking, echoing between the half-seen walls.

'*Maitran* . . .'

A bird flew squawking from the depths. The word flung itself back at him, Ice Mother answering with a thousand voices.

'*Arand* . . .'

Again the mocking choir, confusion of sound reflecting faint and mad from the cleft.

'*Hansan* . . .'

'*Skalter*. . . .'

Names of the dead, and lost; a fierce benediction, an answer to the ice.

He bent to the thing on the path. A final heave, a falling, a fleshy thud; the head of the unicorn bounced on the Level below, splashed a great star of blood across Coranda's door. He straightened, panting, half-hearing from somewhere the echo of a scream. Stood and stared a moment longer before starting to climb.

Giving thanks to Ice Mother, who had given him back his soul.

The Grain Kings

1

The pamphlet was glossy and well thumbed. Harrison leafed the pages indifferently, glancing up from time to time at the bulkhead clock.

> *The principle of the combine harvester,* he read, *dates back to the early years of our century. The first machines were crude and small, and were usually controlled and operated by one man (See illustration opposite).*
>
> *A UN combine has been likened to a small township on caterpillar tracks. Aboard each great machine a crew of up to a hundred must eat, sleep and work for weeks at a time. The superstructure houses construction and repair shops, generator and boiler rooms, a sick bay, laboratories, a gallery; and for off-duty relaxation a restaurant, television lounge, bars and a cinema. A modern combine is big. It has to be; it has a big job to do. In Alaska alone, upward of a hundred thousand square miles of wheat must be harvested in not much more than a month. Wheat that is needed, desperately, to feed the teeming millions of our overcrowded planet.*

The wallclock pinged. Harrison yawned, tossed the booklet down and rose. A belted topcoat hung behind the door. He shrugged himself into it and left the cabin.

The corridor beyond, dim and quiet when he had come aboard,

vibrated faintly. The lamps in their wellglasses glowed brightly; the combine had raised running voltage. He turned left and right, climbed a flight of spindly metal stairs. The companionway gave on to B deck and the observation lounge.

On deck he was assailed by an echoing clamour. He stood blinking vaguely, saw without surprise that the combine was in motion. Above and close, the big metal girders of the hangar bay slid past one behind the next; he stared up, seeing the yellow bowls of service lights glide by, watching the shifting, repeating perspectives. Ahead, the exit doors had already rumbled back. Daylight gleamed outside, faint as yet and grey. The opening looked like the slit of a pillbox. In a building so vast, perspectives tended to confuse the brain.

The tannoys in the roof were working again, gobbing out their words in big, bouncing chunks of sound. The lights gleamed on the combine's broad forward casings. On her stubby mast, red and turquoise identification lamps sequenced steadily, like the landing lights of an aircraft. Harrison found notebook and stilus, leaned against the deckrail. He wrote: *It doesn't fly, so it isn't a plane. It doesn't float, so it can't be a ship. It's something else, something different. Outside experience.* He sneered at the phrase, scored it through. Beneath it he scribbled: *Clearing hangar sheds. 07.30 hours, Loudspeakers working; difficult for the uninitiated to make out the words. They wouldn't mean much if they did. Big combining already has a language of its own.*

The observation deck was filling now. On the port wing O'Hara was angling his camera for a shot of the control-room windows. Alison Beckett had made her appearance, well muffled. Harrison flicked his fingers at her, walked over to the photographer. The combine was nearing the exit ramp. Red lamps sprang into brilliance round the edges of the great doors. He heard the main diesels catch and thunder. She'd been running on her auxiliaries then. The engine beats steadied to a pounding throb. He thought, 'We shall be living with that noise. For days.' He said to O'Hara, 'Don't forget the old man's hangar shots.'

O'Hara grinned. He said, 'The great sheds sink slowly in the west.'

Harrison said, 'You take the pictures. I'll write the copy.'

O'Hara rolled film, turned the Bronica, made an adjustment. He said, 'It's the pictures that matter, boyo.'

'Every one,' said Harrison, 'is worth a thousand words.' He turned away, hands dug into the pockets of his coat.

A combine is too big to be solid. Rather it humps its way across the land, like a jointed, gigantic steel carpet. Harrison watched the forward casings rise steadily, taking the slight slope of the exit ramp. As they nosed into daylight they changed colour from brown to orange-red. The pitch of the engines altered as the main bulk felt the incline.

Beside him stood a stubby, grey-haired man, an off-duty engineer. Harrison said, 'Why were the main diesels only started just now? I thought they'd need longer to warm up.'

The engineer glanced at him, took a pipe from his pocket, tamped the tobacco and struck a match. He seemed in no hurry to answer. Finally he said between his teeth, 'She doesn't run on her mains. They're running 'em up for start of cut. She goes anywhere on her crawlers.'

Harrison said, 'Thank you. I wasn't sure.'

The bulk of the machine was clear of the sheds now. The noise of the loudhailers faded abruptly. In the open air the thunder of the engines was less oppressive. Harrison stared round him. The sky was an indeterminate grey-blue. He saw, or thought he saw, the last spark of a star. The eastern horizon, flat, was slashed with searing yellow.

On the wing, O'Hara was lining up the hangar shots. He'd got Alison to pose against the rail. She was wearing a headscarf. One long strand of hair had come free, was moving in the wind. She put her glove up, tucked it aside. The bridge speakers clicked and said, 'Good morning.'

The voice said, 'I am Controller Cheskin. I welcome you on behalf of the United Nations Organization and the World Food Council. The machine on which you are travelling is an American-built Rolls-Toyota of the Dakota class. She develops a total horse-power of just over a hundred thousand, and harvests on a two-hundred-and-fifty-meter swath. Her codename to base is Combine Patsy. We are travelling east, fifteen degrees north at a speed of ten Kilometres an hour. At zero nine hundred hours we shall be turning on to cut.'

The speakers crackled slightly. They said, 'Breakfast is now being served in the C deck restaurant. May I wish you all a pleasant and interesting trip. Thank you.'

Alison came over. She said, 'God, I'm frozen. Aren't you cold?'

Harrison said, 'Not too bad.'

'Coming to breakfast?'

He said, 'I've got some notes to get down. I'll take second tables.'

She said, 'You're too devoted.'

He said, 'I work better first thing.'

He walked back to his cabin, closed the door and hung the coat up. He lay on the bunk, hands clasped behind his head. Now, with the main engines running, the dural walls thrummed faintly. He closed his eyes, feeling the pulse of the combine. He remembered, arbitrarily, how someone once told him he made love to her at dawn, though the fleshly Harrison was two hundred miles away. He shrugged. The borderline between fantasy and fact is vivid and hard. Whoever holds it to be otherwise is either a liar or a fool. Probably the former. He lay now alone, a hardish pillow under his head. The counterpane was striped in sage green and orange, the cabin furnishings looked vaguely Swedish. The air conditioner whistled slightly, the clock hands stood at 08.05. Nothing and nobody would alter these facts.

He had a bottle of whisky in the bedside locker. He sat up, poured himself two fingers, grimaced and added the third. He thought, 'I should kick this early-morning drinking.' He drank, lit a cigarette, laid in it the tray. He was thinking about the flight home. He'd travelled, among others, in the company of a well-known divorcee. Her legs had been superb and she raised hell about the lunch. She left the plane at Idlewild. He thought, 'I should be over the other thing by now. Nine months is a good gestation.'

He opened his eyes again at ten hundred hours. The Scotch still stood on the locker; the cigarette had burned itself out half through. He thought, 'I missed start of cut.' But he could make that bit up. He reached for the notebook, considered for a time and wrote.

The main power system of a combine is diesel-electric. Motors situated above each set of cutter blades. Access from motor gallery forward; maintenance staff permanently on duty. He thought for a moment. Could they withdraw blade sets, service while in motion? He presumed so; still, it was a point worth checking.

The light through the cabin port was bright now. He buzzed the steward, asked for some coffee. While he was waiting he shaved. The coffee when it came was very good. He smoked a cigarette, stubbed it and walked back to the observation deck.

Climate control made these exercises possible. As he emerged into sunlight the combine was flowing past a radiator. The tower stood on tall black struts. Clamped to one of the stilt legs was a board with the legend *Danger. 10KV.* Below it was stencilled another warning: *Do not activate relays without blue and green authorities.* He wondered how service engineers reached isolated towers. Not by helicopter; the downdraught would flatten the wheat.

He stared above him. The sky had a hard, steely brilliance. The decks of the combine stretched out like a scarlet plain; ahead and to either side, the wheat was an immense level sea. He thought, 'Indian summer of technology,' and dismissed the phrase.

The radiator was well astern now. Ahead was a reef signal. The red disc bore a black triangle, point uppermost. He waited for the combine to change course. She didn't appear to; but the signal passed well to port. Beyond it, the smoothness of the grain was unmarred. He wrote: *'Dural girders. Aluminium panels. Ground clearance zero. Patsy is a fragile giant.'*

He thought, 'Aren't we all?'

He watched the horizon, hazed with blue. Nothing to see; no way of marking progression. The combine was on cut; but from up here there was no way of telling. He listened, carefully. Maybe the engine rumble was a fraction deeper, there was a shade more vibration. The endless roaring he'd expected wasn't there. The machine moved majestically, a ship against a yellow ocean. He wondered again about the sea metaphor. As yet he had nothing on which to peg his story. No theme. He watched the cutter coamings a hundred yards away. They rose and fell steadily, rolling with the contours of the land. He imagined he could hear, above the diesels, the sibilance of the blades slicing wheat.

Two dolly-bird reporters came up from below. The taller looked Scandinavian. They glanced at him as they passed, leaned backs turned to him against the rail. They seemed to have a lot to chat about. He walked to the starboard wing, propped the notebook on his knee.

A combine works to a predetermined grid, he wrote. *Strictly, it's flying by wire. Control units, buried by the score, kick out a parcel of signal frequencies; underbelly sensors keep each machine on a true heading. Course and pattern of cut are predetermined at base; onboard computers see to the rest. The system's accurate;*

you can do a lot with a two hundred and fifty metre datum line.

He touched the tip of the stylus to his teeth. He wrote: *'Patsy's cutting on a two hundred kilometre grid. Two hundred up, two hundred down. When she gets back to start of cut she won't be running more than a yard from true.*

'She could cut on a five hundred kilometer grid, or a thousand, or ten. Distance is no object; all we need is a big enough planet.'

He thought, 'I'm not getting anywhere.' He walked back down the companionway to C deck bar.

The room was wide and long, panelled in satin-finish dural. He'd read some of the Russian combines used mahogany and brass. Windows looked out through the underpinnings of B deck, across the main coamings to the wheat. There were chairs and tables set round, Audubon prints in thin black frames. A coffee machine sang and glugged on the countertop.

O'Hara was playing the Bandit. As Harrison walked in it paid fifty. O'Hara grinned a pale, square grin and said, 'What do I do with these?'

Swissy said, 'Use 'em for washers. Good for de car.'

Harrison said, 'Pint of beer. No, the English.'

Swissy said, 'D'American is very good.'

'I'll stick with this.'

Swissy rubbed his hands. He said, 'A dollar. T'ank you.'

Somebody said, 'He gets a bigger mark-up on the American.'

Harrison leaned on the bar and lit a cigarette. Swissy said, 'Where's de li'l girl?'

O'Hara turned back from the machine. He said, 'She's developing.' He winked at Harrison. He said, 'No point keeping these. The crafty bastard won't change 'em.'

Swissy said, 'Give you two dollar for 'em. Haven't counted.'

O'Hara said, 'I'd rather put them back.'

Swissy said, 'Anyway, she's tuned. Pay for t'ree dollar.'

Harrison said, 'You put more than that in it last night.'

Swissy smirked. 'Was wit' syndicate,' he explained. 'Get t'irty per cent anyway. Can't lose if I play wit' four.'

O'Hara said, 'He doesn't understand his systems any more than anybody else.'

Harrison drank beer. He said, 'Got your pictures for today then, Mike?'

O'Hara considered. He said, 'I didn't see you when we turned on to cut, boyo.'

'Quite so. How was it?'

O'Hara said, 'Spectacular.'

Harrison drank another pint, which tasted good. The missed-breakfast feeling was starting to leave him. By the third he was feeling nearly human, which wasn't in all respects a good idea. He walked to C deck restaurant, ate *entrecôte* steak with a scampi starter. You could say this for combiners' food—it was reliable. He signed the bill for the company and walked back to the bar. He had a tour fixed for the afternoon; he'd arranged to meet an engineer called Bertie Pritchard.

Bertie was short, boyish, greying and relatively tired. He looked like an ex-Navy man. He spoke with an explosive punctuation that could turn readily to a stammer. They propped the bar up till three. Swissy was back on duty. He was talking about the last execution in Berne. 'Dey climb up de trees,' he said. 'All de boys, you know? So dey see into de prison yard. Christ, an' down dey come den. Like de blowty apples.'

Somebody laughed.

Bertie said, 'You never *saw* a bloody *execution*.'

Swissy grinned. 'My fader tell me,' he said. 'You know, a man get his head cutted off, he don't stop wit' de blinking?' He mimed, rapidly. He did in fact succeed in looking like a severed corpse. 'Blinkin' de eyes,' he said, 'An' de mout' go, so; and out de trees day come. Christ, like apples.'

Bertie said, 'Who are you *with*?'

'World Geographic.'

'Good outfit?'

Harrison said, 'Fair. Like the rest.'

Bertie said, 'Christ, listen to the basstard.'

Swissy was saying indignantly, 'Is true. In Zürich I was apprentice from my fader, to a butcher. I drink lot of blood, when dey killing de calf. Good it was, hot. Dey go *ksss* on de li'l calf an' we catch and drink in de glass. Good for you.'

Bertie said, 'You are a *repulsive* basstard.'

'No, is true,' said Swissy. 'Only tell de trut. Very good for you. Help wit' de girls.' He smirked, clenched his fist, made short-arming motions. 'Good, de blood,' he said. 'You try it sometimes, Bertie. Bet on well.'

Bertie said, 'If you've finished, we'll get out of here.'

Swissy said, 'Chow, bot'. See you next time.'

In the corridor Bertie said, 'Where do you want to go first?'

Harrison said, 'It's your tour.'

They walked forward. Over a bulkhead door was a stencilled sign, *Crew Members Only*. Bertie ducked through. He said, 'Mind your head.'

Down here, the quality of sound was changed. There was a heavy roaring; Harrison guessed they were close to the main diesels. Bertie turned right and right again. There was a short companionway. He took it at the trot. He said, 'Links. Don't get your feet tangled up.'

The corridor, articulated, flexed slightly, moving with the movements of the combine. From somewhere came a faint, persistent squealing. Already, Harrison felt lost. He said, 'How long does it take to find your way about?'

Bertie snorted. He said, 'They're crazy f-fucking objects. Pointless complexity. All the same.'

Harrison said, 'What do they cost?'

'Twenty million. Give or take. Everybody gets a nice slice of the pie. Watch your feet.'

There was a final hatchway. Harrison stepped through, and stared. They had emerged in the forward casings, directly above the cutter service gantry.

The noise hit him first. It seemed compounded of all frequencies; hum of motors, whirl and clank of chains, *whick-hiss, whick-hiss* of the blades, echoing rumble from the combine's tracks. To right and left, long glints of daylight reached under the coamings. The air was yellow, fog-thick; through it the cutters glittered dully, spinning silver drums. Beneath his feet flowed a jostling brown river; the conveyors, edging the grain tons a minute to the threshers in the great belly of the machine.

He watched the men on the gantry. They wore one-piece suits of something that looked like asbestos. Visors covered their faces; on his back, each carried a bulky pack. Tubes from the packs dived beneath the wearers' armpits. Harrison mouthed a question. Bertie shook his head. He said, 'Self-contained systems. Ocy-nitrogen. You can't filter that muck. It gets in everything.'

Harrison said, 'What do these boys earn?'

Bertie said, 'A hell of a lot.' He leaned back, hands in his trousers pockets. He said, 'It's all right while it lasts.'

Harrison said, 'Silicosis?'

'There's quicker than that. Heard of combiner's balls?'

Harrison said, 'No.'

Bertie said, 'It means you don't have any. No skin on the tops of the thighs. It gets up inside the suits. Can't bloody stop it.'

Harrison said, 'They're welcome.'

Bertie said, 'They're the toughest basstards in the world.'

Near at hand, a crew were swinging a blade unit down into operation. One man was beating at the motor housing with a gauntleted fist. Harrison saw him raise his arms, make wash-out motions. He stared down. The movement of the grain beneath his feet was giddying.

Bertie said, 'Seen enough? I can't stand this bloody stuff for long.'

Harrison nodded, stepped back through the hatch. The engineer dogged it shut. The noise diminished. Harrison said, 'Christ.'

Bertie clattered ahead of him, down a flight of steps. At their foot, the decking surged unexpectedly. Harrison grabbed for the rail. Bertie said, 'This is E deck catwalk. We're alongside the threshers. Nothing much to see. The process is totally enclosed.'

The catwalk was long, and dim. They glided, it seemed, at eye-level with the wheat. Down here you could really hear the whisper, the sibilance. Glass panels were rigged at head height along the gallery. Harrison leaned close, stared into the endless brown-grey aisles between the stalks. Bertie said, 'That's virgin, of course. Julie's coming up from the west. We're cutting east, towards the Russkie patch.'

Harrison said, 'It's a new viewpoint.'

Bertie banged the screen with his fist. He said, 'We had to fit these last trip. Had some stupid little bitch of a journalist. She put her hand out in it. Said it reminded her of punting.' He tittered, soundlessly. 'You should have seen it,' he said. 'A little blood goes a long way.'

Harrison turned away. He thought, 'It's graceful, and soft. Touch it, and it opens to the bone.'

Bertie walked ahead. He said, 'This *might* interest you.'

Harrison watched the complex assemblage of levers. The whole device seemed to stride. A rod was poised, plunged into a gap beside the main housings. A pause; and the forward travel of the combine brought the links upright. The rod lifted, gleaming; a dark earth sample was ejected, whirled away, before the corer dipped again. Harrison said, 'What's it taking?' He was still thinking about the wheat.

Bertie said, 'They're checking soil organisms. Bacteria count. It's called a Tom Thumb sampler.'

He opened a bulkhead door. Beyond, a link corridor led to a big darkened space. Heat gusted back, heavily. Harrison saw steel drums rotating behind protective panels of mesh. Lamps gleamed here and there, red-mauve. Bertie said, 'The intake is damped south of the conveyors. Here it's irradiated, and dried.' He gestured at the lamps. He said, 'Pig-rearing lights.'

They walked on. In the combine's belly, sound levels varied continually. Sometimes the clatter of an auxiliary room drowned speech, sometimes the roar of the tracks. They walked down a serviceway, its floor panels composed of thick steel mesh. There was a rich, earthy smell; inspection lamps showed stubble flowing a yard beneath. Bertie ducked through a hatch. He said, 'Main tracks.'

The combine jolted and heaved. He reached back, steadied Harrison's arm. He said, 'OK?'

Harrison said, 'Yes.'

Bertie said, 'Don't want to have to scrape you off a bloody bobbin. Not while I've signed for you.'

The tracks were also lit. Harrison watched the steel rollers on which they ran bounce and jump. The links, each plate the size of a dinner table, rose up smoothly, passed out of sight overhead. He said, 'How many tracks does she run on?' Bertie said, 'They're rigged on twenty-metre centres. You can do the sum yourself.'

In the main diesel room an engineer wearing padded earmuffs waved to Bertie from his gantry. Bertie waved back. Harrison looked at his watch. Already they'd been an hour on the trip. Bertie closed the door behind him. He said, 'We're now going aft. Crews quarters on the left, and sick bay. Laboratories to the right. Can't go there; not my patch.'

There was a door marked: *Latrine, male. Field use only.* A part of Harrison's mind recorded the words.

Bertie said, 'When are you seeing the old man?'

Harrison said, 'Tomorrow morning.'

Bertie said, 'He's a queer basstard. Why they let him get hold of this thing I shall never know.'

They passed another door. Bertie said, 'Galleys. Bakehouse.'

Harrison said, 'I shouldn't think there's any shortage of flour.'

Bertie said, 'Under UN regulations, we can't touch our output. They fly the f-flour up from base. Amazing, the workings of the Oriental mind.'

There was light ahead. Daylight. He pushed a door open. He said, 'The ass-end of the process.'

Harrison walked to the rail. They were on the stern of the combine. Behind and above, unfamiliar from this viewpoint, the control bridge jutted at the sky. Astern stretched the great swath of stubble; again like a wake he thought, the wake of some ponderous geometric ship. Below him, slipways disgorged the produce of the machine like vast parcelled eggs, each pallet the size of a truck. Flying cranes were busy in the middle distance, droning like heavy dragonflies. He saw one settle its hooks into a bale, rise with it and lumber off to the south. The sun, already levelling, lit the great dustcloud, turning the grains to gold. As they entered the brilliance, the service vehicles became shadows. It was blue, and red of coamings, and gold; everywhere, the blue and gold.

Bertie said, 'As far as I'm concerned, you've seen the lot. Anything you want to ask?'

Harrison said, 'Later on maybe. I'm still taking it in.'

Bertie looked at his wrist. He said, 'Can you find your own way back? Got to meet another party. We ran a bit late.'

Harrison said, 'Don't you have a duty watch?'

Bertie said, 'I'm just the bloody liaison man. Tell 'em why the wheels go round.'

Harrison said, 'Thanks for the trip. I shall be OK.'

Bertie said, 'See you in the Swiss Embassy.' He ducked through the doorway, and was gone.

There was a seat, to one side of the observation deck. Harrison slumped on it, pulled his notebook from his pocket, stared at it for a time and put it away. He closed his eyes; and for a moment he was on a ship. She had just this same easy motion; the thunder of her diesels was muted, as it was muted here; and she was coming into Oban, from Mull. The sea was millpond calm, big vees of ripples starting and starting and spreading for miles. He thought, 'How often you hear that phrase, how seldom you see what it means.' He shut his eyes again. It had been bad all day. He thought, 'We were going there together, only you couldn't quite make it. You weren't on that ship, you bitch, and you are not here.'

Aloud he said, 'That'll do you a lot of bloody good.'

He leaned back, lit a cigarette. He was remembering Cheltenham, and the caryatid figures in the Colonnade, and buying the big buckled lovely handbag for her and the flat she'd taken in the town. He inhaled, blew smoke. He remembered the first months after the break-up. Time had telescoped; he'd lost nearly a year of his life. He hadn't believed such a thing was possible. He thought about the place he'd found in London, and the absurdity of it all, the sheer absurdity. Once, years back, he'd had a really bad pain. He remembered laughing jerkily, in the middle of it; it seemed a ridiculous state of affairs that any one thing could hurt that much. He thought, 'You sleep, not wanting to wake. But you wake. You get up, you get to the office, you trail back to your pad. You eat and speak and shave and wash and write words. Sometimes you can remember what you've done through the day. Sometimes you can't.' He remembered drinking sessions, sessions that started because the office had shut and just went on anyway; and empty Sundays and empty weekends and trailing out West for drag, the go-go dollies. He thought, 'Is there anybody anywhere, for whom pleasure is real, existence meaningful? What happens, inside Bertie? Inside Swissy? Is it any different for them?'

He glanced at the last thing he'd written that morning. *Distance is no object,* he read. *All we need is a big enough planet.*

He thought, 'I'm riding Combine Patsy. And Patsy is cutting a two-hundred-and-fifty-metre swath; and Patsy is a Wonder of the Age.'

Aloud he said, 'I couldn't bloody well care less.'

He looked at his watch. He'd caught himself wondering when the bars would open.

The sun was dropping towards the horizon. The air was keener now; astern, the dust-pall gleamed with a reddish light. He got up, walked back the way he had come. Finding his way through the combine's guts was a harder task than he'd realized. He passed along gantries he hadn't seen. Once he was challenged, made to show his press card. He got to his cabin finally. The thrumming of the walls felt familiar. He thought, 'Nearly like home.'

He took the Olivetti from its case, transcribed what notes he'd made. He added: *It's the dust you become aware of. It's in the air, a grittiness on the lips. It creaks underfoot as you walk. Nothing's really clean. Put a saucer down for an hour and lift it and you see the yellow bloom, the mark of where it lay. And this is only start of cut.*

He looked at his watch again. This past few months he'd got into the habit of marking the progression of hours and days. It was as if some bright point, some node of light and warmth, receded steadily; there was a compulsion to mark the regression. There were little anniversaries to be noted, transient things, affairs of hours, months. One day he supposed they would total years.

Loudspeakers were clattering somewhere in the combine. The sound reached him faintly, mixed with the humming of the cabin walls. He wrote: *In twenty minutes, if my mathematics serve me, we shall end our first pass.* He rose, took his coat down, put it on. He walked down the corridor, turned left and right, climbed the companionway to B deck.

The sun was low, the western hemisphere a bowl of dusty pink light. He thought, 'Red sky at night, climatologist's delight.' The upper works and rigging of the combine were sharp-cut against the glow. Forward and below, the light seemed to permeate the coamings; the figures on the cutter housings were haloed with brilliance. The combine roared steadily, still forging to the north.

Alison was leaning on the rail. He joined her. She put her hair back, glanced up and half-smiled. She said, 'It's queer somehow. Oppressive.'

He said, 'Did you get your prints done?' She nodded, not answering. He leaned on the rail. He thought, 'O'Hara gets an assistant. Maybe he needs one. I shouldn't take it out in her.'

The masthead lights began sequencing. He wondered vaguely why. The reflections hit her cheek and hair, scarlet, turquoise, scarlet, turquoise. He said, 'Was the stuff okay?'

She had a knack of not looking at him when she answered. She said, 'There's one advantage to big negs.'

'How do you mean?'

She said, 'You can always cut the middle out. It doesn't really matter where you point the camera.'

He thought, 'Maybe she doesn't like O'Hara. But everybody likes O'Hara.'

The bridge speakers clicked and began to breathe. This time there was no formal announcement; it seemed they'd merely circuited on to Control. A voice said, 'Two minutes from end of cut.' He heard Cheskin acknowledge.

A helicopter moved up overhead. The downdraught battered from the metal deck. He thought, 'They have to fly grid patterns too. Always this business about flattening the crop.'

The speakers clicked again and roared. The chopper pilot was talking through a hamburger. He said, 'End of cut, Roger.' The machine surged back, fell away into the gloom astern. A Klaxon began sounding somewhere. Alison said, 'All this fuss, just for turning round.'

Harrison said, 'It's a big machine.'

She said, 'They're just afraid they'll get on to somebody else's patch.'

Cheskin said, 'Time me, please.'

Another voice answered. It said, 'Forty five seconds, and counting.'

The klaxon cut out. Cheskin said, 'Stand by all stations. Ready on mains.'

The speakers said, 'Cut end . . .'

'Cease cut.'

The trembling of the deck eased. The speakers said, 'Halfspeed on starboard auxiliaries. Phase differentials.'

Harrison heard the engine stations acknowledge. He turned away, becoming bored. Cheskin said, 'Reverse starboard auxiliaries. All ahead port.'

A couple of stars were visible. Harrison watched their sideways drift. The big cauldron to the west was moving too, swinging round behind the bridge. The combine was vibrating, straining. From below came a confused roar. The speakers said, 'Ninety degrees. One hunderd degrees. One hundred ten.'

'Quarter speed on starboard auxiliaries.'

The sunset light was beginning to creep in from the right of the bridge. The combine nosed, questing.

The speakers said, 'I have forty degrees. I have thirty degrees. I have twenty degrees. Line-up good.'

Harrison said, 'Have dinner with me tonight.'

She looked up at him. She said after a pause, 'Yes. All right.'

Something bumped in his chest. He thought, 'That's very odd.'

She said, 'Which restaurant?'

'C deck. They've got lobster thermidor. I don't know how old the lobsters are.'

She said, 'I'm a martyr to my stomach. I think I'm a compulsive eater.'

The speakers said, 'I have line-up.'

Cheskin said, 'All stations stand by. Confirm your line-up.'

The speakers said, 'Green board. I have line-up.'

Cheskin said, 'Outphase differentials. All ahead. Begin cut.

Controller to log. Commenced second pass. I have eighteen, repeat eighteen, oh nine hours.'

She made a face. She said, 'Imagine that. Nine minutes late.'

O'Hara was weaving towards them across the observation deck. Harrison said, 'Where shall we meet?'

'Where do you want?'

He said, 'Swissy's bar. Twenty hundred.'

She said, 'You have a date.'

He went back to his cabin. He lay on the bunk and thought, 'One in the eye for you, Michael.' He lit a cigarette, smoked for a while. Then he shook his head, sat up. He rang the steward for a sandwich, said *'Gracias, Manuelo'* when it arrived and plugged in his shaver. He bathed and changed; by that time the wallclock read nineteen hundred hours. He picked up lighter and cigarettes, clicked the ceiling light off and walked round to Swissy's bar.

It was empty. Swissy was leaning on the counter reading a paper. He looked up and smirked. He said, "Evening, Mr. Harrison.'

Harrison said, 'Pint please, Swissy. English, not American.'

Swissy said, 'D'American is very good.' He drew the pint, set it on the bartop. He said, 'Looks good. Like in de picture house. Advertisement.'

Harrison lit a cigarette. Swissy said, 'Seen de paper?'

'What's new?'

Swissy said, 'Not'ing. Same blowty ol' t'ing. It doesn't go for my head.'

'What's that?'

Swissy said, 'Dey make big t'ing. Big fuss. 'Bout de combine. Dey say, Russia, America; blowty big row.'

'Where?'

Swissy showed him. The leader read:

Difficulties were prophesied today concerning the Russian-American grain link-up. Russia has lodged protests concerning what she describes as British-American infringements and infiltration. President Sukharevsky, in a strong note to the West, threatened Russian withdrawal from the World Food Council's biggest experiment to date, the Alaskan Grain Development Area. Harold Jenkinson, British Premier, expressed in the Commons his total disagreement with the Soviet attitude.

'The Alaskan Development,' he said, 'represents the biggest step so far in the cause of world unity and peace. The government

*of this country views these latest developments with disappoint-
ment, and grave concern.'* Commentators feel the underlying
cause of friction is the refusal of the United Nations select
committee to accept Russia's demands for a controlling interest
in the project.

Harrison put the paper down. He said, 'Like you said, Swissy.
Nothing new.'

Swissy said, 'It be stupid. Blowty stupid.'

Harrison said, 'It doesn't go for my head.'

The dolly birds came in. They bought lager-and-lime and a
Bloody Mary. Swissy said, 'I like to have dat one.'

'Which one? The blonde?'

Swissy snorted. He said, 'Ach, she be no good. Norwegian. Say,
do dis, do dat . . . same like blowty German.'

Harrison said, 'Are you married, Swissy?'

Swissy shrugged. He said, 'Divorce. Only mistake I made.'

'How so?'

'Ach,' said Swissy impatiently, 'she be no good. English.' He
leaned on the bar and wagged a finger. He said, 'I tell you dis. She
ask me to marry her, or I never would do it. Use to be on de boats.
Go round de world, have a good time. Come back, to dis.'

Harrison said, 'Are you drinking?'

Swissy said, 'T'ank you. Have a half.'

Harrison paid. He said, 'Any children?'

'Ya, two,' said Swissy. 'Nice kids.' He produced a bulging,
worn-looking wallet. He said, 'Nice kids, no?'

The pictures showed a gap-toothed little boy, a rather chunky
looking girl. Both were blonde. Harrison said, 'Why were you
divorced?'

'Ach,' said Swissy, 'she be no blowty good. I was manager, big
hotel. She make me take pub. She don' like to work, dat one. Not
like German. I tell her, you work. You blowty work. Den she don'
like it. I tell her, no blowty good. Never was any good. Never make
English gentleman out of me.'

Harrison said, 'Was this in England?'

'Ya, at Cheltenham. You know it?'

Harrison said, 'I was there for a time.'

Swissy said, 'Have de children at school in England.' He waved
his hand at the bar. He said, 'I do dis for dem. Make more money.
Kids come first, all de time. Eh? Not so?'

Harrison said, 'I wouldn't know.'

Bertie came in. He said, 'Got it all written down?'

Harrison said, 'I'm working on it.'

Swissy said, 'Had a good day?'

Bertie said, 'Christ, no. Been trying to service an auxiliary since seventeen hundred. Wanted to pull it out of line, but that stupid basstard'—he gestured upstairs—'won't have it. Says he's dropping behind schedule. As if it mattered . . .' He picked the paper up. He said, 'What's new?'

Harrison said, 'Why're you educating the children in England?'

Swissy said, ''Cause it's best. She start dat. De ex-wife. Maybe later I send 'em to Switzerland. I don't know.' He grinned. 'Christ,' he said. 'Have trouble wit' de family.'

'Why so?'

'Ach,' said Swissy, 'dey be pheasants. No, how you say dat?'

'Peasants.'

'Ah. Peasants. Be blowty peasants.'

'How do you mean?'

'Ah,' said Swissy, 'is difficult. Dey not understand. Dey t'ink I give de kids away.'

'You what?'

'Ah, well,' said Swissy. 'In my country, Z is no boarding school. State school only. All go dere, whatever parent. If you go odder school, eider parents dead, or prostitute . . . dat sort of t'ing.'

Harrison said, 'Can't you explain?'

Swissy said, 'My brodder understand. He be lawyer. De rest . . . Christ, got two aunt won't speak wit' me. I tell 'em, I no get de kids in de first place, den dere be trouble.'

'Because of being Catholic?'

Swissy brooded. 'Ach, yes, de Cat'olic,' he said, 'Be blowty rubbish.'

Harrison ordered another beer. He sat and wondered about his notes. The combine throbbed; but already it seemed he was accustomed to the noise. Only when he brought his mind back to it could he hear it. He thought, 'I should go on deck. Get the feel of the thing at night.' He remembered the reef markers. He'd been meaning to ask. He said, 'Bertie, those reef warnings. Are they necessary?'

Bertie looked at him blearily. He said, 'If you hit a b-bugger, you'd find out.'

'Can't the radar pick them up?'

Bertie said, 'Not under ten or twelve feet. These things only run a yard off the deck, and they're built of silver paper.'

'Couldn't they be levelled?'

Bertie said, 'If you'd tried picking all the rocks out of ten thousand fucking miles, you wouldn't ask.'

The Norwegian girl came to the bar with a glass. She said, 'Fill it, please.'

Swissy grinned. He said, 'For you, anyt'ing.'

Harrison drained his beer, lined up another. The bar was very quiet. The clock hands stood at 20.15. A couple of Americans drifted in. It seemed they knew Bertie. They sprawled across the bar, started an engineers' convention. He heard Bertie say, 'Well, what did you expect? The bloody com ring was shot.'

He wondered how long she'd be. He finished the beer, started on whisky. She walked in at 20.25.

She was wearing a little black dress. Her legs were delicious. Her hair gleamed; the bar lights made it look very blonde. Swissy grinned and said, 'Christ. Be all right wit' dat one.'

She said, 'I heard that, Swissy. 'Lo, John.'

He said, 'You're looking very nice, love.'

She said, 'I've got a great big ugly face. Compliments don't work.'

He asked her what she was drinking. She said, 'Scotch.'

He asked for a double. He said, 'How were the pictures?'

She perched on the bar stool. She said, 'I thought I wasn't going to make it. Big Brother wanted another batch put through.'

He laughed. He said, 'I thought you two got on.'

She said, 'He's the answer to the maiden's prayer. Didn't you hear?'

He stubbed his cigarette. She said, 'Have one of these.'

He lit up for her. He found himself starting to like her a little. He said, 'Where's the great man now?'

'Got a date. Or so he told me. I wished him luck.'

Harrison said, 'Swissy, do we have to book for the restaurant?'

Swissy said, 'Better, if you want table. No good eat at de bar. Not romantic.' He leered. He said, 'I fix it for you. Ten per cent.'

Harrison said, 'I'll buy your next beer.' It seemed a trite remark, and was. He thought, 'Maybe I'm talking too much. Which is absurd. I'm dead; so I can't be nervous.'

Swissy used the phone. He said, 'Ya, two. Chow, Man'el.' He turned back. He said, 'Got you corner table. Gipsy orchestra.'

Harrison said, 'Have another drink.' While Swissy was pouring he said, 'I wish you'd accept compliments. It's very unnerving.'

She said, 'I'm funny. Somehow I can never believe in them.'

He said, 'You don't like yourself all that much.'

She said, 'Not much. Not often.'

The clock had moved round to twenty-one hundred. Harrison said, 'Let's go on.'

She stood up. She said, 'I'll see you round there.'

He said, faintly surprised, 'I'll wait.'

Bertie looked up and smirked.

Outside, Harrison said, 'That little man did nothing but stare at your legs.'

'Which little man?'

'Bertie. In the corner.'

She said vaguely, 'Oh, he's not too bad.'

Harrison said, 'It was a comment, not a condemnation.'

Walking beside her, he was conscious for the first time how tiny she was. It had never appealed to him before. He caught a waft of her scent. He thought, 'It suits her.'

The restaurant wasn't too busy; half a dozen couples were eating, a few more sitting at the bar. The lighting was soft; they had no orchestra but piped music was playing. The tune was 'Blue Moon' He wondered how old it was.

Manuelo showed them a corner table, held her chair. Harrison ordered Liebfraumilch. Manuelo offered him the glass. He sipped, knowing there would be nothing wrong. He said, 'OK, I'll pour.'

Manuelo said, 'Thank you,' and left them alone.

She said, 'Swissy said this means Mother's Milk.'

Harrison said, 'I suppose it does.' He thought, 'You're not like her. But you could be her. Face not your fortune, but the same big eyes.'

. Over the main course she said, 'I'm glad you asked me out.'

Harrison said, 'You can't really be "out" in a combine harvester.'

She shook her head. She said, 'O'Hara can be a pig. I was getting really tired of him.'

He said, 'There's an easy answer.'

She said, 'It's not easy for me.'

He said, 'It will sort itself out. How's the lobster?'

'Mmm. John . . .'

'What?'

She said, 'I am enjoying myself.'

He thought, 'This is one of those Rare Moments.' Later he said, 'We could dance. Only there's no floor. Only I don't dance.'

She smiled, and opened her cigarettes. He lit up for her. She said, 'Was Swissy telling you about his family?'

'Yes.'

She said, 'He's divorced, isn't he?'

'I think so. I can't work it out. He's Catholic.'

She said, 'If he married outside the Church he'd have been lapsed anyway. Technically, he was living in sin.'

He said, 'You know a lot about it.'

She smiled, and pushed her hair back. She said, 'I'm a Catholic. Or was. I lapsed about a year ago.'

Harrison said, 'Why?'

She lifted her chin. She said finally, 'I don't know. I just couldn't see it any more. It's no good just doing it.'

He said, 'How did the family take it?'

'They're still trying to get me back. It's quite difficult.'

He said, 'How old are you, Alison?'

She looked at him. She said, 'Twenty-five.'

He said, 'I'm sorry. That was rather personal.'

She blew smoke. She said, 'I'm queer. I was always the rebel. My brother's much more conventional. He went into the family business. I moved out. Came up to Town.'

He examined his cigarette. He said, 'I was trying to work this afternoon. It wouldn't come. I think the photographic section's doing better.' He watched the fall of her hair and thought, '*Get back behind me, you shadow, you bitch*.'

She said, 'It'll come. I wish I could do that sort of thing.'

He offered the last of the Liebfraumilch. She shook her head. She said, 'Thanks. Reached my limit.'

He drank, slowly. In the restaurant the roar of the combine was very loud. Beside him, the long windows were blue with night. He said, 'Shall we have coffee in the cabin? The steward will send it up.'

She watched him a moment. She said, 'If you like. Yes, nice.'

He said, 'This place thrums too much. It gets into one's head.'

She said, 'It is noisy, isn't it? I suppose you get used to it.'

She walked ahead of him. They turned right, and right again. At the door he reached past her to click the light switch. She said, 'Oo, this is nice. Good heavens.'

'What?'

She said, 'What's this?'

He took it from her, carefully. He said, 'Rule one. Or so I'm told. Never wave a gun about till you know it's safe to.'

She said, 'Is it safe?'

He broke the cylinder. He said, 'It is now.'

She said, 'What is it?'

He said, 'Smith and Wesson. Point four five five.'

'It's a revolver.'

He said, 'Yes.'

She said, 'I've never handled a gun before. It's a beauty. Can I close it?'

He buttoned the intercom. He said, 'Just push it shut.'

The steward answered. Harrison said, 'Gaelic, Irish or plain?'

She said, 'Just plain.'.

He walked to her. He said, 'Can I show you?' He broke the revolver again. He said, 'It's a very old one. It's what's called a fixed frame. With a hinged frame, the chambers open upwards.'

She said, 'It's not much fun waving an empty gun about.'

He opened the locker drawer. He said, 'Here.'

She said, 'Gosh. Can I do it?'

He thought, 'I don't know quite what's happening.' He said, 'Go carefully, it's rather dangerous. Do it by numbers.'

She frowned, pushing the big cartridges home. Her hair fell forward, cascading. She shook it back. She said, 'Would it shoot now?'

He said, 'When it's cocked. So.'

She said, 'Oh, I see. The cylinder turns round.' She smiled. She said, 'I've found out about revolvers.'

He said, 'Hold it very carefully. Keep it pointing at the floor, else it's bad manners.'

She said, 'If I pulled the trigger now, it would go off.'

He said, 'Yes. But that wouldn't be a good idea so we'll . . . eject. So. Out come the cartridge cases.'

She said, 'I don't understand. Wouldn't they have been fired?'

He said, 'This part is the bullet. The shiny nose. This is the case. There's a cap at the bottom. When the pin hits it, it explodes.'

She collected the rounds carefully, gave them back. She said, 'It's safe now. Can I play with it?'

Harrison said, 'Most girls aren't interested in guns.'

She said, 'I'm not most girls.'

The steward buzzed with the coffee. She rolled back on the bed. She said, 'I'd like a gun. I'd like this one.'

'Whatever for?'

She said, 'To keep the ghosts away.'

He poured coffee. He thought, 'You are a funny little rat.'

She said, 'You know a lot about guns.'

'Not really. I think they're interesting.'

'Where did you get this one?'

He said, 'One of the German riggers at base. I think he was broke.'

She said, 'It would kill a person, wouldn't it?'

He said, 'I rather think it would kill anything.' He smiled. He said, 'Including ghosts.'

'Why did you buy it?'

He handed her the coffee. He said, 'It interested me.' He thought, 'What was it Hans said? 'Your English law is stupid. Every man need a gun. For the one time.' 'He said, ''For the one time . . .'' '

'What?'

He said, 'Nothing. Just a thought.'

She drew her knees up, sighted the revolver. He said, 'You look like Pussy Galore.'

She said, 'I feel like Pussy Galore.'

He thought, 'And the dynamo's running, you little bitch. But that's not possible.'

She said, 'You like nice things, don't you?'

'How do you mean?'

She said, 'Like the gun.'

He thought, 'This is out of the question, absurd.' He said, 'Alison, would you mind if I seduced you?'

She looked at him carefully. Then she put the Smith and Wesson down. She said, 'Not in the slightest.'

Harrison said. 'All right then. Better finish your coffee.'

She drank. He gave her a cigarette. They smoked for a while. Then he said, 'Were you serious?'

She said, 'Perfectly. Weren't you?'

He said, 'It was rather a silly question. I'm not sure how one goes about it.'

'Haven't you done it before?'

He said, 'I've been seduced. That's rather different.'

She put the cigarette down. She said, 'I don't want this.' She rose, walked over to him, sat on his knee. She said gently, 'This will do for a start.'

He lay back. She moved with him, softly. She was lithe, and light. She said, 'I'm sorry. I'm all hair.'

He said, 'Don't I know it.' He kissed her. She didn't mind his tongue. He found the cabin lights, dimmed to sleep level. In the half-dark, the thunder of the combine sounded louder.

She nestled, and kissed again. He found her dress clasp. She whispered 'No,' and didn't stop him.

The wine spun in his head. He said, 'Now I can say all the silly things. Like lovely, desirable, sweet. Nice little girl.'

She said, muffled, 'Nice big man . . .'

He stroked her, ran his fingers along her bra strap. He said, 'I'm not much good at this. Fumbly old job.'

The strap parted. She said, 'That wasn't bad for a novice.'

He worked her dress down, feeling satin skin. He thought, 'I'm going to go crazy with this, because it's too good. These things don't happen.' Aloud he said, 'Move your arms.'

'Why?'

'They're in the way.'

She whispered, Please. No, please John . . .'

'What's the matter?'

She said, 'It's silly. I'm shy.'

He said, 'You can stop if you want. I don't want to spoil any friendships.'

She said, 'It won't. Honestly. This is nice. Please, John . . .'

She kissed him, wound her arms round his neck. He pulled at the dress, carefully. She sat up then, shivering. She said, 'Well, this is me. For what it's worth.' And he saw it was possible for a blush to spread, across the neck, down the shoulders and back.

He said, 'You're very lovely.' He bowed his head. She squeaked; and he knew he had to be gentle. Incredibly gentle. Her body was like a tight-strung wire; he could feel the responses start, little jumps deep inside her. She said, 'No, please. Not down there.'

He said, 'Yes . . .'

She caught his fingers. She said, 'I've got you now. You can't get away.'

He used a trick. She said, 'I shall fight you . . .'

He said, 'Alison, fight all night. That's what it's all about.'

He held her again, carefully. She lay back, head against the chair. She said, 'You are nice.'

He said, 'Alison, come to bed.'

'No!'

'I shall say please then.'

'John, *no!* It's no good, I just get stubborn. It's too early . . .'

'Then we'll go to bed later.'

She said, 'I'm not ready. Don't try to make me. I shan't do it.'

He said, 'Love, no one shall make you.' He stroked her back, gentling; and she relaxed again. He thought, 'It could be her. She doesn't look like her, she doesn't act like her. But it could be her. I made it happen again.'

Her skirt had ridden up. She said, 'Don't look at me. I shall be decorous.'

He said, 'I'm enjoying you. Don't you like it?'

She said, 'No. Yes. I don't know . . .'

He said, 'What spectacular panties.'

She said, 'I'm a pantie fetishist. They always match my shoes. That's something you know about me now.'

He said, 'I shall blackmail you. Alison, come to bed.'

'*No!*'

'It's all right.'

She said, 'John, no. Don't do that.'

He said, 'You want it and you shall have it.'

'I don't. I don't.'—

He said, 'Don't fib.' He thought, 'Three years. She told me it had done me good. That's why I left her. But she was right. I know it now, I know how to make it good.'

She started to struggle. He said, 'Aren't I doing it right?'

She said, 'You're doing it too damned well . . . John, don't make me . . .'

He said, 'Girlie, you're made . . .'she was moving against him, arcing her body. She pushed her head back, soundlessly; he thought, '*Contact contact, flaring bloody contact* . . .' And it was over; she relaxed against him with the longest, deepest sigh he had ever heard.

Later he said, 'Did I hurt you?'

She nuzzled and whispered, not opening her eyes. She said 'Only in the nicest possible way.'

He laughed, in the near-dark. He said, 'Your bottom's cold.'

She said, 'It's the only part of me that is.'

He watched the clock hands move, feeling her weight against

him, hearing the great thunder of the combine. Once she stirred. She said, 'It's been a long time. I was only eighteen . . .' He stroked her till she was quiet. Much later, she pushed away. She said, 'I'm going to be a nuisance. I want to go back to my cabin now.'

He said, 'Stay in this one.'

'I can't.'

'You'll be all right.'

She said, 'You don't know O'Hara.'

'This isn't to do with O'Hara.'

She said, 'He keeps asking me, everybody asks me. The boss asked me. If he found out . . .'

Harrison said, 'Even O'Hara couldn't be that big a bastard.'

She said, 'Care to bet? Please, John . . .'

He said, 'Nobody shall make you do anything, lovie. You know that. Here . . .'

She sat upright, tousled. She said, 'I'm all undressed.'

He said, 'I like you that way.'

Her eyes looked huge. She said, 'I didn't know there were men like you.' She kissed him again.

Afterwards, he eased her to her feet. She tidied herself. He said, 'Lights on?'

She said, 'Yes. Trying to . . . find my comb.'

He swirled brightness back into the little cabin. The walls were the same, the bulkhead clock and the bunk; yet it was all different. Alive.

She stumbled, trying for her shoes. He caught her. He'd known she would be giddy. He thought, 'I did it right. I did something right.' He said, 'You had a trip.'

Her eyes were very sleepy. She said, 'It was lovely. John, I must go.'

He walked her to her cabin. The corridor lights were dimming now, a part of Combine Patsy preparing for sleep. She opened her door, pulled him half inside, kissed him quickly with all her body. He said, 'My head will be rather full of you, of course. I shall want to see you. Is that proper?'

She smiled. She said, 'It's human. I never knew you were. Good night, John.'

He said, 'Good night.' He stayed till the door closed, softly; then he walked away.

In his cabin the bed was rumpled. He walked to the shower

cubicle, rinsed his face and hands, lit a cigarette. He stood staring a while. The revolver lay where she had put it. He set it on the locker, twitched the covers straight.

Sleep was far from him. He walked back to C deck restaurant. The lights were out now, the place deserted. A bulb gleamed dully over the bar. Manuelo was drying a glass. He said, 'Coffee, Manuelo?'

The little man grinned and shook his head, jerked his thumb at the wallclock.

Harrison laid a dollar on the counter. He said, '*Por favor.*'

Manuelo grinned again, and walked to the dispenser.

He took the tall mug back to his room, sat and sipped. After a while he frowned, sniffed his sleeve. Her scent clung, faint and delightful. He thought, 'I was trying to make her. To fill a hole in my life. But I didn't know what she was like. I didn't know what she was going to be like.'

He drank again. After a while he thought, 'She trusted me. And she was shy.' The shyness had hooked him through the lip. He thought, 'The other thing was never like that. It couldn't be.' A ghost had faded, seeming past return. He thought, 'It was time. I went looking, and I made it happen again. A new thing.'

He finished the coffee, set the mug down, stood up. At the door he thought, 'That wasn't her voice. Those weren't her eyes. It was all new. Like a flower, opening in the hand.' He wondered, 'Are they all like that? When they're loved?'

He climbed to B deck. The air was rushing, intensely cold. Above, the bridge superstructure slid against an incrustation of stars. Darkness seemed to enhance the sense of speed. He saw the combine now as a great entity; he knew her blades spun and roared, her dynamoes hummed, her sensors probed with their electric fingers. He felt the exultation grow, and let it well. He thought, 'I paid for tonight. It's mine.' He saw, with heightened vision, Combine Patsy and her sisters; Julie, Susannah, all the rest, strung like beads of light and warmth against the moving dark. He thought, 'I'd forgotten. I'd sunk into the pit, and didn't know my need; and her hands raised me, unbeknown.' He thought, 'It flies at sense and logic; it flies in the face of reason. But we love; and we rejoice, because it sets us apart from the beasts.'

In the east, already, a new dawn was making. The night air was reaching him; he stubbed his cigarette, and turned away. He thought, 'We reap, and we thresh; grain for half the world. We are the Grain Kings, raised of old; and I a new God. A giant God, who was dead.'

2

He lay for a while in a floating half-awareness before opening his eyes. Sunlight slanted into the cabin from the one square port. The patch vibrated slightly, moving with the movements of the dural wall. He turned his head. The Olivetti stood on the side table; on the locker was the Smith and Wesson. These things pleased him. He studied them a while, unmoving. His awareness, his sense of colour and form, seemed unnaturally sharp.

The wallclock read 09.15. The intercom buzzed; he reached for the cord, lazily, thumbed the switch. The speaker said, 'Good morning, Mr. Harrison. Asked me to call you.'

He said, 'Joe. *Gracias*.'

He rose, padded to the shower cubicle. The stinging needlepoints enlivened him. In the cubicle the hum of the combine sounded loud. A can of shaving foam clattered softly against a glass shelf. He towelled, shaved, got out clean shirt and shorts, dressed. He found himself humming, vaguely, the theme from Thomas Tallis. He thought, 'That's good music. English west country music.' He picked up his jacket, stooped to wriggle heels into shoes. He'd thought he would never go into the west again. Maybe now he would.

He let his thoughts drift round to her, by slow degrees. Before he'd kept her out of his head, deliciously. He looked round the cabin. He thought, 'She was here, and she was naked. Funny little rat.'

He walked to C deck restaurant, ordered coffee, cereals and toast. He ate slowly, smoked a cigarette. At eleven hundred hours he was due to meet Controller Cheskin. He walked to the observation deck. The combine had turned once more on to a northern pass. He thought, 'Three since start of cut.' The sky was bright steely blue, the red bridge coamings sharp-cut in sunlight. He watched rigging shadows move, thin dark stripes against scarlet paintwork.

The wind buzzed faintly in the mast struts. The morning was very fair.

He thought, 'Maybe she's sleeping it off.'

He walked back to C deck bar. The place smelled of polish and dust. Except for one of the American engineers, it was empty. Swissy grinned at him. He said, 'Here he come. De great lover.'

He was faintly startled. He said, 'What?'

Swissy said, 'How you get on wit' her? De li'l girl?'

Harrison said, 'We had a nice evening.' He settled himself on the bar stool. He said, 'Not beer, Swissy. Fruit juice.'

Swissy stopped, hand over the pump. He muttered, 'Got to keep up de strengt' . . .'

Harrison nodded vaguely. He was remembering the smoothness of her skin, dimly seen, the firm fullness under her scanties, later the bursting of soft dark down between her thighs. He thought, 'These are my memories. It happened. Nobody can take them away.' He sipped orange juice. He thought, 'I feel for her, rushingly. I didn't know how much I wanted her.' The images would revolve now quietly, hour on hour, till he saw her again; as she had lain quiet in his arms. He thought, 'The smell of her was like a drawer of linen. Clean, lavender-fresh.'

Swissy said, 'Been up top?'

He said, 'It's a great morning.'

Swissy leaned on the bar. He said morosely, 'All right for some. I gotta work.'

Harrison said, 'I'm working all the time, Swissy.'

Swissy said, 'Yeah. T'ink about de li'l girl.'

Harrison said, 'You've got a one-track mind.'

The American glanced at his watch, nodded and strolled out. Swissy said, 'I t'ink after all I go back to de boats. Had good time den, get plenty girls. Used to stop 'Frisco, Honolulu. Christ, was a place, dat. I t'ink I go Tasmania, or New Zealand. Lovely country.'

Harrison said, 'Why'd you leave home anyway, Swissy?'

Swissy said, 'Oh, some t'ings go wrong.'

'Family?'

'Ach, no. But some odder t'ing. Dey be pheasant anyway. I t'ink, fowk 'em. You know? See a bit of de world. Five years I was on de boats. Den I come ashore. After dat, go to England. Christ, was bad t'ing, dat.'

The wallclock pinged. Harrison said, 'Got to go. Seeing the old man. Keep my seat warm.'

Swissy said, 'Chow.'

At the bridge steps a guard with UN tabs on his shoulders scanned his press card. He said, 'Wait, please,' and walked away. Harrison stood idly, heard an intercom buzz. The guard came back. He said, 'Follow me, please.'

Here, higher in the combine, the endless sway and roll were more evident. Harrison glanced round him. Officers' country seemed no less spartan than the rest of the machine. He was high above the wheat; a port gave him a view of it, like a sparkling, brilliant-yellow plain.

The guard tapped a door, opened it. He said, 'Mr Harrison, sir.' Harrison stepped through.

The cabin was wide, and carpeted. To one side a wallfire glowed cheerfully; above it was an oil painting in a heavy, ornate frame. There were cupboards of china and glassware; shelves held a further display. Cheskin sat at a polished desk fronting the great range of windows. He rose as Harrison walked towards him, and held out his hand. He said, 'Mr Harrison, how pleasant. World Geographic, I believe.'

Harrison said, 'I'm delighted to meet you, sir.' His mind was far away; down maybe with the racing, rolling wheat.

Cheskin said, 'Be seated, please. A drink?'

Harrison said, 'Thank you. Thanks very much.'

Cheskin said, 'Whisky perhaps.' He tinkled liquid from a decanter. He said, 'Your British whisky is the finest in the world.' He handed the glass. He said, 'Through peat, and over granite. I believe these are the requirements.'

Harrison smiled. He said, 'I've been told so, sir.'

Cheskin nodded briskly. He said, 'You will excuse me for not joining you. For me, it is a little early.' He pushed a box of cigarettes across the desk. He said, 'I have visited Scotland. A most lovely country. Sometime I hope to return, for the salmon fishing. Do you fish, Mr Harrison?'

Harrison said, 'Last time I tried, I managed a pike.'

Cheskin said, 'Ah. Yes.' He leaned back. He said, 'Have you been well looked after?'

Harrison said, 'Excellently. Mr Pritchard has been most helpful.'

Cheskin said, 'Good.' He steepled his fingers. He said, 'First, a few facts about myself. I am, as you undoubtedly know, Russian by birth. America has been for many years my country of adoption. I am a biologist and agriculturalist; during the Moscow crisis I served in the Russian army. My rank was colonel.' He smiled, He said, 'And you?'

Harrison said, 'Rather an ordinary sort of background, sir. Agricultural degree, then jobbing journalism here and there. I'm afraid I haven't led too adventurous a life.'

Cheskin said, 'I see. It is better that we know just a little of each other.'

Harrison's eyes had wandered. Cheskin caught the direction of his glance and turned. He said, 'Ah, the painting. Are you knowledgeable about paintings, Mr Harrison?'

Harrison said, 'Not really. But I think that's very unusual.' He was in a mood to be pleased by anything. He said, 'It's rather lovely.'

Cheskin smiled again. He said, 'It's not lovely. Rather, it is ugly. This is why I keep it.' He rose, walked to the picture. Its colours were sombre: flat reds, and browns. A table was set with a candlelit meal; a shirt-sleeved man sprawled across a bed, holding a stick over which a fluffy white poodle leaped. Cheskin said, 'It is, of course, a facsimile. The original was painted shortly before his death by a great Russian artist, Pavel Fedotov. You have perhaps heard of him?'

Harrison said, 'I'm afraid not.'

Cheskin said, 'He is not known much outside Russia.' He turned back to the canvas. He said, 'At twenty-five, Fedotov was a brilliant young officer of the Finlandsky Regiment of the Royal Guard. At thirty-seven he was dead, a pauper. This he produced in the last year of his life.'

He reached to touch the carved gilt frame. He said, 'The officer is drunk. The surroundings are squalid, suburban. As the dog jumps the stick, so his master is driven by boredom. By ennui. He too is a victim of his circumstances.'

Harrison said, 'I don't think I quite follow you, sir.'

Cheskin said, 'Though Fedotov was great, his life was wasted. The canvas serves to remind me of this. Effort misdirected is wasted. We must see clearly, rejecting dreams and the fantastic, holding at all times to the realities we perceive. We must not become such a man; jumping sticks, though we think we hold them for others.'

Harrison said, 'You seem very . . . aware of your homeland, sir. Have you never wished to return?'

On the desk was a silver-mounted photograph. It showed a

blonde, plumpish woman with a dog. Cheskin frowned across at it. He said, 'While my wife lived, perhaps. Now it would be pointless.'

Harrison said, 'I'm sorry, sir. That was extremely personal.'

Cheskin shook his head. He said, 'This is a part of your profession.' He turned to the shelves. He said, 'Here is something that may interest you. It is very rare.'

Harrison rose, walked to him. The Controller lifted a glass drinking vessel, turned it in his thin fingers. He said, 'It is a joke, really, on the part of the glassblower. It was made sometime in the early eighteenth century. Above the goblet, you see, is a fabulous beast; you would call it a chimaera. To taste the wine, you must press your mouth to his. His body fills, as if with blood.'

Harrison took the piece, carefully.

Cheskin said, 'These are modern works, by Tatyana Navrina. The city in which she was born is now called Gorky. Its folkart is well known in Russia. Here you see a circular composition. Tatyana shows us the fox, the hare and the cockerel. Famous beasts in our folklore. They chase each other round and round, merrily. It is pointless and gay; yet also perhaps a little sad. Like a fairground entertainment.'

Harrison said, 'Do you have a large collection, sir?'

Cheskin said, 'I have a house in America. In New Jersey. Most of my pieces are there. These few, my favourites, travel with me.'

He walked back to the desk. He said, 'A little more whisky. Now, to your article. Have you collected all the information you will need?'

Harrison said slowly, 'I've collected a lot of information. I think the problem now is putting it together, making a shape. I was looking for something to peg the facts on, to get all this across. Maybe a theme.' He took the plunge, feeling good. He said, 'Yesterday I thought I'd got it.'

Cheskin said, 'Ah, this business of a theme. I find it most interesting. You had thought perhaps of a ship? Or an aeroplane?'

Harrison said, 'I suppose everybody does.'

'Yes,' said Cheskin. 'This is most important. Remember the painting. There are no themes; merely realities. This is a large combine harvester. With a model number, known characteristics. I can give you rates of cut and thresh, length of cut, passage time on cut, estimated return to Grid Base. Are these things not enough?'

Harrison said, 'I'm not sure.'

Cheskin said, 'You thought in higher terms? In terms of significance, of poetry?'

Harrison said, 'Don't you approve of poetry, sir?'

Cheskin smiled fleetingly. He said, 'There is perhaps a poetry. Unheard, unsung.' He brooded. He said, 'No. I have no objection to poetry. But it is necessary to apply the proper labels. We should know at all times with what we are dealing.'

Harrison said, 'I'm not quite with you, sir.'

Cheskin said, 'There is your English author. Kipling. You have surely studied his work. He might perhaps render such a theme. He understood much of machines.'

Harrison said, 'I'm afraid I'm no Kipling, sir.'

Cheskin said, 'Perhaps that is as well.' He turned the cigarette box thoughtfully in his fingers. He said, 'In Kipling's work the machines are made to speak. They cannot; but the poet is skilful, and so we believe. Soon too England speaks, as an old grey Mother. The sea speaks to the Danish women, declaring itself a rival for the affections of their men. The little banjo speaks; and what a harmless instrument! So the world, which is as it is, becomes repeopled; with mirages, and Gods. Soon for us, stones speak and trees; we feel the touch of phantom hands. Here is a paradox, Mr Harrison. We do not worship stones and trees; yet we listen to our poets.'

He rose, stood back and turned, staring down across the miles on miles of wheat. A buzzer sounded on the bridge; Harrison heard the vague pealing of an intercom. Cheskin said, 'For me, the Grain Development Areas represent new hope. Here for the first time our many peoples work together, truly together, for the universal good. Here perhaps, if you search, you may find your poetry. This too is why none of us must be blinded. We must see, very clearly, what we do. We must see it as a good thing, perhaps a great one; but we must find no mystery. Moon and sun do not tug our brains, as they tugged the brains of earlier men. We reap, and we thresh. We are neither Gods nor ants. Our machines are our machines. As in this, so in our lives. Our hands work, our will directs the hands. The rest, our conceits, our grand words, are luxuries. We cannot permit ourselves such luxuries, Mr Harrison, if we are to survive. Dreaming, we are unaware; from unawareness springs grief, disaster, despair. For our own sakes, we must not dream.'

Harrison said slowly, 'I'm sorry if my ideas annoyed you, sir.'

Cheskin turned, and smiled. He said, 'I am not here to approve or

disapprove of your ideas, Mr Harrison. I am not a censor. I merely
warn.'

He walked back to the desk. He said, 'And now, if you have
finished your drink, I will show you Control.'

At lunch, Harrison ran into O'Hara. He was sitting at a corner table
in C restaurant, forging his way through a steak. He waved a fork, a
chip impaled tastefully on the prongs. Harrison joined him, not
particularly wanting to. He said, 'Hello, Mike. Where's Alison?'

O'Hara watched him palely. He said, 'I'm keeping her busy. It's
good for her waistline.'

Harrison ordered Dover sole and a glass of wine. He steered the
conversation on to safer grounds. There had been times when he'd
felt a compulsion to belt O'Hara on the nose. Today, he might just
do it.

He made his escape as soon as he decently could, walked round to
C deck bar. Bertie was in evidence. He said, 'The wanderer returns.
Have a beer.'

Swissy pulled a pint. He said, 'Is paid for.'

Bertie said, 'How'd you get on with the old man?'

Harrison said, 'This is good Russian beer. From the banks of our
own Volga river.'

Bertie tittered. He said, 'I know the feeling.'

Harrison said thoughtfully, 'He's a strange bird though. I can't
make out whether he loves Russia or hates it.'

Swissy said, 'All Russians funny bastard. Why he is hating it?'

Harrison said, 'I don't know. I had the feeling they maybe got rid
of his wife.'

Swissy said promptly, 'Wish I could get rid of mine. Bitch still
cost me twenty dollar a week, and she ain't even got de kids.'

Bertie said, 'If you will *do* these things . . .'

Harrison said, 'Are you married, Bertie?'

Bertie said, 'Yes, worse bloody luck.'

Swissy said, 'It don't stop him none.'

Bertie drank beer. He said, 'We've got a treat coming up this
afternoon. We're meeting the Russians. Did he tell you?'

Harrison said, 'Yes. When will it be?'

Bertie said, 'Fifteen hundred hours. Or should be. We're getting
near the end of the patch. We swing round north tomorrow. Start cut
two.'

Harrison said, 'Are the Russian combines any different from ours?'

Bertie said, 'They cover the ground a bit quicker. Got a modified pickup system. They're bloody cagey about it too.' He drained his pint, and pushed it across for a refill. He said, 'You'll get a good enough view anyway. They should pass two swaths out.'

Swissy said, 'Funny bastard, dese Russian. Get on better wit' de German.'

Bertie said, 'You are a fucking German.'

Swissy said, 'I be Swiss German. You know dat.'

Bertie said, 'Oh Christ, don't start.'

Swissy said, 'I don't start not'ing. Is big difference. You go to Switzerland, you find out.'

Bertie said, 'You go to Switzerland. You're so bloody fond of it.'

Harrison looked at the clock. It read 14.30 hours. He wondered about Alison. He said, 'I'd better get on deck.'

Bertie said, 'That's what everybody will do. You'll get just as good a view from here.' He set his beer down, lit a cigarette. He said, 'What did the old man talk about?'

Harrison said, 'Mainly a painter called Fedotov.'

Bertie tittered again. He said, 'I expect you saw his glassware.'

'Yes,' said Harrison. 'I did.'

Folk began drifting into the bar in twos and threes. Harrison walked over to the windows. Bertie followed him. He said, 'Bring us a couple of beers, Swissy.'

Swissy said, 'You come fetch 'em. Odderwise, plenty more bars.'

Bertie said, 'What I really like about you is your unfailing civility.'

The wheat flowed past beyond the main coamings, silently. At 14.55 the intercom speakers crackled. They said briefly, 'Combine Valeri is in sight from Control, and will pass on schedule.'

Harrison wondered again about going up to B deck. He thought, 'Maybe she's there.' Then he remembered, if she was O'Hara would be with her. He decided to stay put.

Just before fifteen hundred somebody said, 'There she is.'

The combine was still well ahead, but coming up fast. Behind her, her dustcloud was a dark yellow funnel trailing on the land. She was big; God, she was big. She made Patsy, ungainly as she was, look elegant and low. On her side she wore the hammer and sickle of the Soviets, above it a big red star. The rest of her was grey; workmanlike, and blank.

Somebody said, 'Here comes bloody St Basil's.'

Bertie said, 'They were putting onion domes on 'em last year.'

Harrison said, 'Why did they stop?'

Bertie said, '*Track* weight became *excessive*.'

She passed abeam, trailing the long dustcloud. Somebody said, 'That's it then.' On Patsy's bridge a loudhailer was working faintly.

Bertie turned and shouldered his way out of the crowd. He said, 'That's damn funny.'

Harrison said, 'What's funny?'

Bertie said, 'She was cutting a swath too close.'

Swissy said, 'De blowty Russians never could steer. Not even de aeroplanes.'

Bertie said, 'I'm going to look into that. See you blighters later.'

Harrison walked to B deck, stood on the starboard wing. The combine had certainly passed a single cut away. He stared astern. The Russian was still visible, small with distance. The dustcloud smoked away across the stubble. Beyond, the land lay brown and bare to the horizon. He walked to the forward rail. The double swath remaining stretched like a golden road. Nothing to be seen; just the endless perspectives of the land, shimmering a little with heat haze. Patsy thundered steadily.

The bridge intercom had been left live. The speakers clicked and said. 'Mr Puustjärvi to Control, please. Mr Puustjärvi.'

He didn't feel like work. He walked down to D deck. They had a little gift shop there. It sold corn dollies, paperbacks, wooden Russian toys. He thought, 'Flowers were out, anyway. Right last time. Not this.'

A showcase held bracelets and some jewellery. He glanced across the display shelves and said, 'Good Lord.'

The stewardess smiled professionally. She said, 'Can I help you?'

He said, 'Does this shoot?'

She lifted the tiny revolver out. She said, 'They're bracelet charms. They fire blanks.'

He said, 'I shouldn't think they need a firearms certificate.'

She said, 'They didn't say anything when we bought them.'

He said, 'How much?'

'I think there's a ticket. Nine dollars fifty.'

He said, 'You've sold it.'

He walked back to his cabin, lay on the bunk, took the little pistol from its box. It had a hinge-frame action. He broke it and loaded carefully. The tiny thing made a very respectable crack. He thought, 'Good for the littlest ghosts anyway.'

He put the charm in the side locker, picked up his notebook. He made a rough draft of the conversation with Cheskin. At the end he wrote: *Strange to see the china cabinets. Impress of a personality that still isn't Western. After all these years.*

He pushed the papers aside, thought for a time. Then he reached for the intercom lead, pressed the button. He said, 'Joe, do something for me.'

'Certainly, sir.'

'Page E deck. Miss Alison Beckett.'

Joe said, 'It shall be done.'

The wallspeaker was covered by a plain grey grille. It clicked twice and buzzed. Then it said, 'Hello, John.' The voice had an unexpected huskiness.

He said, ''Lo, Alison. How's things?'

A pause. The speaker said, 'Fine.'

'Busy?'

She said, 'O'Hara took a lot of shots of the Russians. We're just starting on them.'

He said, 'Shall I see you this evening?'

'Mmm. Yes. Where?'

He said, 'Swissy's bar. About twenty hundred. We can go on a pub crawl.'

She said, 'Done. Sounds lovely. John, I have to go now.'

He said, ''Bye, Alison.'

The speaker said, 'See you later. 'Bye.' It clicked, and went dead.

He walked to C deck restaurant, ordered a coffee. He sat over it a while before going back. He spread the notes out, lit a cigarette and daydreamed. He wasn't seeing Cheskin's cabin. He thought, 'The hell with it. It's there to be enjoyed. Like the aftertaste of brandy.' He thought, 'I still can't believe it. But it happened.' Aloud he said, 'You never know what another person's like. Maybe a lot of chances get dropped that way.'

He started on a first draft of the article. It ran well. He read it back, made his corrections, started again. At eighteen hundred hours he bathed and shaved. He walked round to Swissy's bar. In the corridors, evening light lay flaring. Where sunlight hit the satin-finish panels they glowed with minute grins of gold. The noise of the combine was a steady muted rumble.

Bertie was there. He seemed a bit the worse for wear. Swissy had a copy of the *Swiss Observer*. He said, 'Dere. Tell you all about it dere.'

Bertie said, 'The one thing that's always struck me as curious is why nobody ever really understood the William Tell legend.'

Harrison said, 'What do you mean?'

'Well,' said Bertie, 'look at it this way. For the sake of a few bob a week, the basstard was prepared to risk nailing his son between the eyes with a bloody iron bolt. That's the Swiss for you. They haven't altered.'

Swissy said indignantly, 'He be blowty good bloke. I tell you.'

Bertie said, 'Why, you ass . . . oh, what's the use?' He drank his wine, grimaced, and pushed the glass across. He said, ' 'Nother glass of your exorbitant plonk. This time, try filling it.'

Swissy said, 'Don' like to do 'em too full. Too much not good for you.' He recorked the bottle, looking pained. He said, 'Anyway, what about ol' Winkelried?'

Harrison said, 'Never heard of him.'

'Ach,' said Swissy. 'All de schoolchildren, dey learned him. Was a battle sometimes, can't remember when. Against de Austrians. Austrians had de long spear, what you call it?'

Harrison said, 'Pikes.'

'Ach. . Pikes. Anyway, was no good. Swiss only have de ball wit' spikes. So dey have to make a gap. An' Winkelried say, ''Look after de wife an' kids.'' Den he take all de spear to himself to de chest. An' de odders run over him.'

Bertie said, 'I can see you doing that. Why don't you try?'

Swissy said, 'Christ, no. But was a good chap. He say just like dat, ''Look after de wife an' kids . . .'' '

Bertie said, 'You told it once.'

O'Hara walked in. He slapped Harrison on the shoulder. He said, 'Here's the man who chats up my assistants.'

Harrison thought, 'One day I'll kill you and slice you, you bastard, and eat the strips. And I shall enjoy them.' He said, 'Have a beer, Mike.'

O'Hara sat and swung his legs. He was looking well manicured. The love life must be prospering. He said, 'You'll not get anywhere with her, boyo.'

Harrison said, 'Maybe I'm not trying to.'

O'Hara said casually, 'She's damn near married anyway. Reck-on they'll get spliced next trip. Bloke out in Gloucestershire somewhere, breeds horses. Old man's got a packet. Didn't she tell you?'

Harrison looked at his shoes. He said, 'I don't really know much about her.'

A klaxon sounded overhead. Feet pattered on the decking. The bridge tannoys said, 'Duty officer to Control, please. Emergency stations.'

Bertie said, 'Christ.' He put his glass down and ran for the door.

Harrison swung off the stool. O'Hara got ahead of him. He turned right and left, following the Irishman. They collided on the companion steps. O'Hara said, 'No fucking camera.' He ran back the way he had come.

B deck was filling. Somebody pointed. they said, 'Right up. Up ahead.'

Bertie was back, with a pair of heavy prismatics. He trained them and swore. He said, 'The basstards shouldn't be there at all.' He handed the glasses across.

She was big, as big as the last. To Harrison she looked like a great lurching biscuit tin on tracks, grinding across the land. He lowered the glasses. She was easily visible now to the naked eye. He stared behind him, up at the bridge windows. There was a pale blur that could have been Cheskin's face. The light was fading fast, dying in long swaths and banners. The dustcloud ahead caught the last of the sunset, glowed orange against dull red. To right and left the stubble shone darkly, like landscape seen on Mars.

The bridge klaxons blasted, driving sound at Harrison's shoulders and back. The intercom speakers said, 'All stations stand by. Maintain revolutions.'

The loudhailer seemed to solidify the air of B deck. The words rolled into distance, a barrage of thunder. Harrison said, 'What's he saying?'

Bertie tittered. He said, 'He's telling 'em to f-fuck off.'

Harrison said, 'She's on the next swath. She'll pass us.'

Bertie said, 'She's too close in. She's not even on the *grid*.'

The loudhailer bawled again, fell silent. The Russian machine was closing fast now. The light gleamed on her bridge wings and coamings. In the sudden quiet, the roar of her engines sounded clear.

Bertie turned, stared up at the bridge. He said, 'The crazy basstard.'

Harrison said, 'Why doesn't he swing?'

Bertie said, 'Because he can't. He's too bloody late.'

The Russian was nearly alongside. A final flurry from the loudhailer; and Cheskin spoke suddenly and urgently in English. He said, '*Emergency. Collision drill. Clear all starboard catwalks. Clear starboard casings. Hurry, hurry.*'

Harrison saw figures run crouching along the cutter housings. The grey superstructure reared beyond the bridge wing. Identification letters slid by; vast, curling, Cyrillic.

Patsy jarred, and shook. There was a report like a cannon shot, and another. The crowd on B deck surged back. Harrison saw steel handrail rise into the air, loop jerkily. The catwalk sheered, thunderously, back towards the stern. Something hit the deck wing. A glass screen starred and shattered.

Alison was there, holding his arm. He pulled her back instinctively, swung her away. Wire thrummed overhead. Bertie yelled, 'She's clear. She's clear . . .' The superstructure was diminishing, sliding out of sight behind the bridge.

The deck wing was a mess of wire and glass insulators. Somebody said, 'We got her aerial array.' Bertie spoke feelingly, glaring up at the bridge. He said, 'I hope he broke all his fucking *pots*.'

The speakers said, 'Damage reports to Control, please. Reports to Control.'

A crewman was wrestling with the coils of thick wire. Another swore and turned, showed a wrist dribbling scarlet. Alison said, 'Oh, God . . .'

Swissy was there in his white jacket, stogie clamped between his teeth. He said, 'Blowty Russians.' He turned to Harrison, grinning. He said, 'Like blowty Brand 'Atch. . . .'

The speakers said, 'Controller Cheskin. There is no major damage. There is no emergency. I repeat, there is no emergency. Please return to your quarters. We are continuing on cut.'

Bertie said, 'There'll be bloody hell to pay for this.'

Harrison swallowed. He said, 'Are you all right?'

She said, 'Yes. Yes, I'm OK.'

He said, 'Better come and have your drink. I think we need it.'

She shook her head, pushed her hair back. She said, 'In a minute. Got to go somewhere.'

He said, 'Are you sure you're all right?'

She said, 'Honestly. Go on down. I'll come.'

The bar was packed already. The American engineers were making most of the noise. A red-necked man with cropped hair was saying, 'Sons of bitches Russians.'

Swissy alone seemed unruffled. He was saying, 'Blowty Brand 'Atch' again. The phrase seemed to have taken his fancy.

Bertie was scribbling on the back of an envelope. His shoulders were shaking. Harrison jostled his way to the counter, called for a beer. He said, 'Why didn't he turn?'

Bertie said, 'Because he's bloody *mad*.'

Harrison said, 'What's so damn funny?'

Bertie seemed to be having difficulty controlling himself. He said, 'The Russians cut to a complicated *pattern*. Two ahead, close, and a follower. Always groups of three.'

'And?'

Bertie said, 'Well, we've encountered and dealt with two . . .'

It dawned. Harrison said slowly. 'Then there's—'

Bertie nodded. He said, 'Another basstard somewhere dead ahead.'

Harrison said quietly, 'How long?'

Bertie said, 'You can't be sure, of course. O seven hundred tomorrow. Give or *take* . . .'

Alison was back. She said, 'O'Hara's gone temporarily insane.'

'What for?'

'He wanted to wire his pictures out. There's a clampdown. Official news agencies only.'

Harrison said, 'We're not a news team anyway.'

She said, 'That's what I told him.'

He said, 'So the pictures . . .'

She said firmly, 'Can wait till morning. I've had enough of friend O'Hara.'

Swissy leered at her. He said, 'Here dey are. De love birds.'

Harrison bought a whisky. He said, 'I tried to book a call to the old man. The booths were too crowded.'

She said, 'O'Hara did it for you. They'll page you when it comes.'

He said, 'That was extraordinarily good of him.'

The bar was getting fuller than ever. He was jostled, beer spilled on his sleeve. The red-necked man was saying, 'Shoot the bastards then. All the bastards.'

Somebody said, 'Anyway, why the hell'd they let Cheskin get Controller?'

The red-necked man said, 'Sucking the bastard British.'

Harrison said, 'Let's try D deck. We can still have our crawl.'

She said, 'It won't be much better.'

Harrison said, 'We can try. Chow, Swissy.'

Swissy said, 'Chow.'

D deck bar was quieter, to his surprise. She perched on a bar stool, looking fairly at home. He hadn't had a chance to see her properly before. She was wearing a fawn sweater, a tiny kilt with a big dress pin. She looked about eighteen. He watched how her hair moved against the woolly. The texture contrast pleased him. He said, 'You were terrific last night.'

She frowned. He said, 'Don't you want to talk about it?'

She said, 'It isn't that. You took me by surprise.'

He said, 'What?'

She turned her glass round on the counter. She said, 'I didn't know you thought of me like that. It never showed.'

'Like what?'

She said, 'Well, as a woman.'

He thought, 'I can't have come back, after all these years, to this same arid place.' But his mind had spun already, added and made a total. He thought, 'I can't believe. I won't believe. It's a joke that's gone bad, through too much laughing. Just a joke gone bad.'

He smiled and said the first thing that came to him.

'Manuelo wants to buy the gun.'

She grasped the subject-change eagerly. She said, 'It fascinated me. I've never handled one before. I'd love to fire it, just once.'

He said, 'You were very good with it. But I don't think you'd like it when it went off.'

She said, 'I wouldn't mind. Not if I was ready.'

'You'd flinch anyway.'

She said, 'Is that wrong?'

Harrison said, 'It makes you miss the target.'

He opened his cigarettes. She said, 'No. Have one of these.'

He lit up for her. She blew smoke. She said, 'We could have done it just now, if we'd known the collision was coming. Nobody would have heard.'

He thought, 'Stop being desperate; for your sake, if not for mine.' He said, 'It's already an international incident. It would really have loused things up if the Russkies found a forty-five slug stuck in the works.'

The intercom speaker said, 'Mr John Harrison, World Geographic. International call.'

He said, 'Excuse me.' There were booths outside in the corridor. He walked to the nearest, closed the door. They took a time establishing the connection. Finally London came through. He listened and said 'Yes' several times. Then he put the handset down, stood staring at it. He thought, 'The mouth moves, and the facial muscles. The words form, while the odds increase to the power of n. Then you walk away. They call it maturity.'

He went back to the lounge. He said, 'That's about it then.'

She said, 'What's happened?'

He said, 'I'm being recalled. They're sending a bigger gun.'

'Who?'

He said, 'Bill Goldie.'

She made a face. She said, 'When do you have to leave?'

He said, 'Day after tomorrow. They're flying him from Tokyo. I take the helicopter back.'

She said, 'I think we're stopping on.'

He said, 'I think so. From what they said.'

She looked at him blandly. She said, 'You're not getting all uptight about it, are you?'

He steered back. He thought, 'Just twenty-four hours, and I've learned you all over again. My ducky little ball of solid brass.' He said, 'No, I'm not getting all uptight.'

She said, 'I'm sorry about on deck. I was scared.'

He said, 'You had every right to be.'

'I didn't think Swissy would ever stop laughing.'

Harrison said, 'Normally he only laughs at earthquakes.' He stubbed his cigarette. He said, 'Would you like to eat?'

She said, 'Not tonight, honestly. I couldn't.'

His skull felt blocked; too much personal stuff going through. He remembered Bertie and his envelope. He wondered if he should tell her. He said, 'What do you want to do?'

'I don't know. I don't mind, really.'

'Shall we go back to Swissy's?'

She brightened. She said, 'I like him. Yes, all right.'

Outside he said, 'I'm afraid it wasn't much of a crawl.'

She said, 'I'm enjoying myself. I just don't show things much.'

The Americans had gone. Bertie still sat at the bar. He looked in a bad way; his eyes were starting to run. Swissy said, 'Ah, here she come. De untouchable one.'

Alison said, 'Supposition, Swissy. Mere supposition.'

Bertie brightened momentarily, and greyed back over.

Swissy said, 'I was just telling Bertie here, 'bout dis duel. Last duel dey ever have, in Switzerland.'

Bertie said cloudily, 'Another of his horrible bloody stories.'

'No, is true,' said Swissy. 'Interestin'.' He turned back to Harrison. 'Dey have de doctor dere,' he said, 'An' one man, he get de end of his nose cutted off.' He started to giggle. 'An' before dey can sticked it back on,' he said, 'is eaten by de Alsatian dog.'

Alison said, 'I still don't understand about bullets. About part stopping in the gun.'

Harrison started drawing on a beermat.

Later she said, 'I know the lot. Matchlock, wheelock, flintlock, percussion cap. Then bullets. The percussion cap's still a bit dodgy.'

Harrison said, 'They only get more complicated. Just remember all guns are really clockwork.'

She said, 'I like finding out about totally new things.'

Swissy said, ' 'Bout time you give me de bar back.'

The time had passed, as any time passes. Harrison stood up. He said, 'G'night, Swissy. Bertie.'

Swissy said, 'Chow.' Bertie hiccuped faintly.

Outside she said, 'Bertie always looks so unhappy. Like a singularly mournful puppy.'

Harrison said, 'Maybe he is unhappy.'

They'd reached his cabin without the question being raised. Which he supposed was another hurdle crossed. He thought, 'I'm not going to leap on you now every time I get the chance. But you're not to know that, of course,' He opened the door, thumbed the lights to full. He said, 'Coffee?'

She sat on the bed. She said, 'Please. I mustn't be long, though. I feel whacked.'

He murmured something like, 'I wouldn't wonder.' It didn't much matter what he said; he'd lost interest in the words.

She drank her coffee, when it came. Afterwards he held his hands out. She looked uncertain. He said, 'Nobody shall take your clothes off. I won't let them.'

She walked to him, sat across his knees, relaxed. The pressure was back, and the warmth. She looped her arms round his neck and said, ' 'Lo.'

He kissed her. Her mouth was very soft. He thought, 'Here we are again then.' He said, 'Were you very mad?'

She said, 'I'm never mad. I just don't react when I should. I think there must be something wrong with me.'

He thought, 'If I stayed surprised for two hours and twenty minutes, I should see a doctor.' He touched her knee.

She said, 'No, John, please. Not tonight.'

He said, 'Very decorous.'

She said, 'I just wanted body contact. It's comforting.'

They lay silent. He watched the wallclock and rubbed her behind. Finally she stirred. She said, 'I was so worried.'

'What about?'

'You. And us. Being friends.'

He said, 'As far as I know, nothing's altered that.'

She said, 'I just don't know about . . . being lovers. I've had so many.'

He said, 'Lovers?'

'No, boys. Well, men. I didn't want you hurt.'

He thought, 'You lying, two-timing bitch and mother of bitches to be, that is the bloody last straw.' Aloud he said, 'I wouldn't worry too much about me.'

She pushed against his shoulder. She said, 'I'm better at . . . well, talking. I'm a great free thinker. That's why it wouldn't be fair.'

'What wouldn't be fair?'

She frowned. She said, 'The physical attraction thing. It always goes. It's only once. Then . . .'

He said, 'It must be very frustrating for you.'

She said, 'I've lost a lot of friends that way.'

He thought, 'How much do you want? Just how much?'

She drew her finger across his lips. Then she put her mouth up. He evaded her. She punched his chest, chuckling. She said, 'Oh, you . . . man . . .'

The wallclock pinged. He thought she'd move but she didn't. After a while she said, 'I don't think I shall ever marry. I don't know. I'm too independent or something. It just isn't me.'

He said very gently, 'My dear, all I have done so far is remove your knickers. There are rather a lot of steps between that and publishing the banns.'

She stiffened, and relaxed. He thought, 'You put your hand out to the flower; because it's perfumed, and lovely, and you're human. And you feel the cold, bristling worm. At last, I know the Enemy.' He felt tireder than he had thought possible; he wanted her weight, that was just a weight, shucked off.

He massaged, gently, the firm swelling of her woolly. She half put his hand away. She said, 'Don't please.'

He said, 'This isn't sex. This is friends.'

She said, 'It's in between.'

He thought, 'And you're starting to tighten behind the nipple.' He said, 'Come on. I'm taking you home.'

She sat up carefully, smoothed her skirt. She said, 'I shall have to find my comb.'

They walked up to B deck. The diesels roared, in the night. Overside, lamps were slung. Riggers were working, swinging in belts over the moving stubble. Most of the rubbish had been stripped clear. The combine's side gaped for thirty yards or more, iron brackets showing like bones.

The sky was crusted with stars. Not the same stars. She looked up. She said, 'What a lovely night.'

He walked her to her cabin. She stepped forward, kissed him quickly. She said, 'Good night. And thank you.'

He thought, 'And that, God preserve us, was the Regretful Parting Peck.'

He said, 'Good night.'

He walked back to his pad, sat on the edge of the bunk. Then it hit him. He thought, 'Last fling of lonely middle-aged man.' He picked the revolver up, broke the cylinder, loaded five. He closed the piece and cocked, hearing the creak of oiled steel. He laid the gun to his face, felt coldness touch temple and cheek. He thought, 'I should have barrelled her across the ear and got stuck in while she was giddy. It would have come to the same thing.' He broke the gun, worked the ejector. The cartridges fell to the bedcover, lay fatly shining. He got up, opened the locker door. The whisky was two-thirds gone. He slid the big gun into his pocket, walked to C deck restaurant. Manuelo was closing up. He said, 'Manuelo. Bottle of whisky. On my bill.'

Manuelo grinned, made a note on a pad. Harrison took the bottle. He said, '*Gracias*. And Manuelo . . .'

'Mr. Harrison?'

He held the revolver out, butt foremost. He said, 'Here.'

The little man's face lit up. He said, 'Mr. Harrison. *Gracias, gracias.*'

Harrison said, 'Good night, Manuelo.'

He walked back. On the way he thought, 'To her, it's dirty. She couldn't step right out. They never do.' He opened his cabin door, sat on the bunk. He raised the bottle, squinted through it at the ceiling light. He thought, 'When she hooks her Mister Right, it'll still be dirty. Only there'll be children, for excuses.'

He finished the whisky, cracked the new bottle. He thought, 'There's two cold spaces now. Hers, and the gun's. Odd to become attached to a material object. Any object.'

The wallspeaker clicked, hummed a moment and faded. He thought, 'Odd, too, what a jump that should give the heart.' Later he decided he had imagined the sound. He thought, 'We could have worked. For a little while. Now all the rest comes back. Like rubble, cascading in the mind.' He said aloud, 'I wonder if he did break his bloody pots?' He remembered the Fedotov painting. He'd thought he'd been doing the taking. But he'd been giving again. So much more than he could afford. He said, 'Now, I jump the stick. It isn't even original.'

His lids felt warm and heavy. He lay on the bunk knowing he wouldn't sleep. The combine was a monstrous weight, useless tracks grinding, useless blades spinning, useless bolts and nuts and chains and levers and wheels. He thought, 'Cheskin knows as well as I.'

He palmed the ceiling light to dim. He didn't want any more whisky; and he wasn't drunk. He lit a cigarette. The first drag brought phlegm up into his throat. He finished the thing anyway, lay back. The cabin walls trembled and thrummed. He closed his eyes and remembered how her bare hip felt under her skirt. He said, 'Get out, please God. Get out, get out, get out of my skull.'

He fell asleep.

The cabin was grey, when he opened his eyes. He felt chilled to the bone. Maybe the air conditioning had failed. He swayed upright, glared at the clock. He thought, 'Another day, another dollar.'

The hands stood at 06.35. He said, 'In time for the show.' He walked to the shower cubicle. He looked as rough as he felt. He shaved, washed his face, changed his shirt. He thought, 'Last night little Alison bestrode the grain, and was a Queen. Her eyes were stars, her flesh the good brown earth, her hair the golden crop.' He slapped his pockets, located matches and cigarettes. He thought, 'I saw a goddess, from old time. She enjoyed the touch-up.'

The corridor vibrated faintly. He closed the cabin door, turned left and right. He thought, 'One thing, only, is dirty. And that she didn't do. She'll give herself clean, the bells will ring her clean. They call it morality.'

He said, 'And I let her get away with it.'

B deck was crowded. The figures stood muffled, not speaking, watching to the north. The light was growing, across the waste of stubble. He thought, 'Bertie wasn't the only one with an envelope and pencil.'

He stared ahead. There was nothing. The dawn-streaks in the sky were high, clear green. He thought, 'Maybe she isn't on track. Big anticlimax kick.'

Beside him stood the grizzled engineer he'd spoken to on the first day. He said, 'There's nothing there then.'

The man sucked his empty pipe. He turned, looking faintly surprised. He said, 'They've had radar contact for half an hour. She's there. Reciprocal course.'

High in the combine's rigging a red light started to blink. It lit the backs of the people on the deck. The engine beats stayed steady. He wondered about Alison. He thought, 'If she needs a pair of comforting arms, there's always O'Hara.'

The wind stung his eyes. He rubbed, peering. There was something, after all. A smudge, on the wide, smudged horizon. On Patsy's mast, the identification lights started to sequence. The smudge made no response.

He could see her clearer now. High and square, like her sisters. Bone-pale. Somebody said in a conversational voice, 'Vostok class. Combine Ilya.'

Harrison looked back at the bridge windows. There were faces, staring ahead. He heard the loudhailer circuit start to breathe. The engineer said, 'We're privileged. We're seeing the start of World War Three.'

The path, the swath of uncut wheat, stretched ahead. The gap was closing now with increasing speed. Harrison clenched his fingers on the deck rail. He thought, 'He understands; and I know him. They took his wife, they took his birthright. Now they take his grain.'

He could make out the long rectangles of the bridge windows. Below, the Russian's forward coamings looked higher than the deck on which he stood. He thought, 'Combine Ilya.' The words made no particular sense.

The bridge speakers said, 'Eight hundred metres, sir. Closing speed constant.'

The loudhailers rumbled briefly, and were quiet. The engineer said wonderingly, 'Right on our bloody track.'

The combine was towering now against the horizon. Seen head-on, her silhouette was oddly complex. The speakers said, 'Five hundred metres, sir. Closing constant.' The voice was starting to edge up in pitch.

Cheskin said, 'Main beams, please.'

Brilliance burst, above Patsy's cutter coamings. The Russian's bridge windows reflected back a dazzled glare. The speakers said, 'Three hundred metres, sir . . .'

Abruptly, the combine bucked. A rumbling; then a tearing, crashing shock. The deck rail hit Harrison in the chest. He clung, stupidly. Somebody yelled '*Reef* . . .' Round him people were tumbling stiffly, legs and arms thrust out. He saw the forward casings fly apart, plates hang in the air like petals of a red steel flower. Something black came ploughing and shrieking. The air was full of din. On C deck promenade the windows bowed and banged.

He saw the body fly out below him, plunge to the main coamings. It seemed they opened to receive it, snapped like a mouth. The victim poised a moment, impossibly. The eyes blinked rapidly; it was as if Swissy once more gave his impersonation of a severed head. Then he was gone, into the tracks.

The emergency beacons were glaring, orange-pink bowls of fire. The klaxon sounded, huge and harsh. The Russian was slowing, slowing. Her prow reared over the coamings like a grey-white cliff. Then she was halted; and the noise of her many motors was a roaring, confused and dim.

The bridge speakers said, 'Emergency procedure, all departments. Give me full dampdown, please.'

There was a deepening whine as Patsy's diesels died.

Harrison laid the suitcase on the bed. He sorted used shirts, shorts and socks, slipped them into a polythene wrapper. He folded handkerchiefs, and ties, packed a box of quarto and half a dozen books. He closed the case, slid it to one side. He sat at the table, sorted the transcript sheets into order and pinned their corners with a staple. Somebody tapped the door. He said, 'Come in.'

It was Bertie. He sat on the bunk for a time and puffed. He said, 'Christ almighty, what a bloody day.'

Harrison said, 'There's some whisky in the locker.'

Bertie poured two fingers. He said, 'I don't know where the other glasses are, you'll have to get your own.'

Harrison helped himself. He said, 'Cigarette?'

Bertie said, 'Not at the m-minute.' He drank Scotch, grimaced. He said, 'D-did you see old Swissy take a dive?'

Harrison said, 'Yes.' He looked at the papers, frowned and laid them aside. He said, 'Were there many other casualties?'

Bertie said, 'Six in the cutter casings. They're still picking the bits out.' He stared at the Scotch. He said, 'Christ, I needed that.'

Harrison thought, 'I wish there was something I could think of to say. But it doesn't get to me. Any of it.'

Bertie said, 'Swissy's a lucky basstard.'

Harrison turned. He said, 'That's one way to look at it.'

Bertie said, 'Quite seriously. The basstard got away with it. They got him out. I think he lost a foot.'

Harrison said, 'Good God.'

Bertie finished the whisky at a gulp and stood up. He said, 'I've got to get on. Just thought you'd like the news.'

Harrison said, 'How badly are we damaged?'

Bertie said, 'It just about took her guts out. H-hell to pay.' He shook his head, clucked sorrowfully and closed the door.

Harrison called sick bay. The speaker said impersonally, 'The patient is sleeping. His condition is satisfactory.'

Harrison said, 'Thank you,' and broke the link.

The wallclock pinged. He frowned at it. In thirty minutes Cheskin was due to make a statement. He wondered if there was anywhere he could get a beer.

C deck was a shambles of girders and wire. To his surprise, the bar door was ajar. Manuelo was behind the counter, shovelling glass into a bucket. He said forlornly, 'Not much on, Mr. Harrison. All bottles go smash.'

Harrison said, 'Christ, what a mess. Any beer?'

Manuelo said, 'American.'

Harrison said, 'That's fine.'

He walked to the windows. The glass had gone. Below, they had a heavy tackle rigged. Crewmen were lifting aside a buckled hatch cover. Ahead, the forward coamings were split as clean as an axe-cut.

He finished the beer, got another. A tired-looking party of men came in. They were blackened with oil, one had an arm bandaged. Manuelo said, 'Sorry, sirs. American beer only.'

Harrison lit a cigarette. Sun patterns were moving on the dural walls; the polished panels glistened. He took the glass back to the counter, walked up to the bridge.

A flying crane was hovering alongside the combine. The downdraught beat at his clothes. He showed his pass to the security man, stepped into the cabin. The crane moved away.

The place was hazed with cigarette smoke. He found a seat. The dolly birds were there; one flashed him a frozen sort of smile.

Cheskin was sitting behind the desk. He said, 'Mr Harrison. Now, I think we are all here.' He looked at a paper. He said, 'At oh seven fourteen hours this morning, the combine ran foul to a hitherto-unmarked reef. We have sustained heavy damage to engines and plant, and can no longer function as a field unit. I regret to inform you that nine lives were lost. Under the circumstances, other injuries were remarkably slight.'

Somebody said, 'Have the Russ—the Russians been helpful, sir?'

Cheskin said, 'A medical team from Combine Ilya is at present working with our own sickbay staff. The seriously injured are being flown to base hospital. We are in contact with combines Maya and Valeri. Both have offered assistance, which is not at present required.'

An American said, 'Can you define our present position more closely, sir?'

Cheskin said, 'Certainly. We are proceeding to base under our own auxiliary power. Tankers are withdrawing reserves of diesel fuel, which may not be jettisoned in this area. Civilian personnel will not be evacuated; there is no danger, and the situation is under control.'

Somebody said, 'Can you tell us anything as yet about the Russian encroachment?'

Cheskin turned. He said, 'It is by no means certain an encroachment has taken place. It is possible a computer error was responsible. At the moment this is my personal opinion, and is not for publication. A full-scale investigation will, of course, be held.'

The American came back to the attack. He said, 'This reef, sir. Was it not detectable by radar?'

Cheskin said, 'Under the circumstances, no. It was masked by the bulk of the approaching vehicle. Yes?'

The question was barbed. 'Under the circumstances, I'd say this machine was a write-off. Where do you put the blame?'

Cheskin glanced up tiredly. He said, 'An investigation will be held. Until its findings are known, I cannot answer you.' He paused. He said, 'I am Combine Controller. I will naturally assume such responsibility as may be necessary.'

There were other questions. They tended to pass Harrison by. Finally Cheskin looked at his watch. He said, 'I have to inform you full communications have been restored. You may cable your stories if you wish. Thank you, gentlemen. And ladies.'

There was a rush for the door. Harrison let himself be left behind. At the door he turned. He said, 'Controller.'

'Mr Harrison?'

Harrison said, 'Had the reef not intervened, would you have closed down?'

Cheskin rose, stood hands clasped behind him. He stared down for a time at the ruined deck. Finally he turned. He said, 'I find your question difficult to understand. There would, of course, have been no other choice.'

Harrison said, 'Thank you, sir.'

Cheskin nodded. He said, 'Goodbye, Mr Harrison.'

Harrison walked back to his cabin, stood staring. But the packing was finished. He thought, 'Once more, I'm killing time. It does seem a waste.' He got the Olivetti out, started reworking his notes. He thought, 'While I'm doing this, the thing's still alive.' Finally, he got himself a meal. He had to wait a goodish while; C deck restaurant was still suffering malfunction. Afterwards there was some whisky to finish. He sat and swilled the glass round and thought, 'So life goes on. Habit is a wonderful thing.'

The intercom buzzed. He thumbed the control, said, 'Harrison.'

The speaker said, 'Mr Harrison, this is Sick Bay. We have a Mr Hauser asking for you; are you available?'

He thought, 'I don't know a Mr Hauser.' Then he remembered. He said, 'I'll come at once.'

C deck looked tidier now, but D level was still a shambles. Repair crews were working with cutters; he stepped over a mess of cables, ducked through a bulkhead door.

He nearly ran into her. She said, 'Oh . . . hello, John.'

He smiled. He said, 'All right?'

She said, 'Just about. I got knocked down. I'm bruised all over.'

'How's O'Hara?'

She said, 'Developing. The scoop of the year.'

He said, 'I'm going to see Swissy.'

Her eyes widened. She said, 'I saw it. It was horrible. You mean he's not . . .?'

He said, 'Apparently, he's still kicking. With one foot.'

She said, 'I'll come too.'

Harrison said, 'I don't suppose they'll mind.'

Emergency beds had been set up in the corridors. There was a clanging and clattering of trolleys. A nurse met them, a striking girl, dark-haired and high-cheekboned. On her shoulder tabs were neat red stars.

Harrison said, 'A patient was asking for me. Mr Hauser.'

She said, 'Yes.' She smiled. She said, 'I'm sorry. Small English. With me, please.'

She walked ahead, opened a door. She said, 'Doctor say—very short.'

Harrison said, 'Thank you.'

The room was tiny, not much more than a cubicle. Swissy looked very sick. A cage had been rigged over his legs; beside the bed a blood drip was set up.

He said feebly, 'Ah. De love birds.'

Harrison said, 'How are you, Swissy?'

He said, 'Had a foot gone. Christ, when I go t'rough dat t'ing. I t'ink dat's it. No more take de piss out of Bertie.'

Alison said, 'I'm . . . terribly sorry, Swissy.'

He waved a hand. He said, 'I get over it. Same like de rest. Could lose worse t'ing.' He leered. He said, 'Be in blowty trouble den. Chrissake . . .'

Harrison said, 'Is there anything we can do?'

Swissy said, '*Ya.*' He fumbled beside the bed, held out an envelope. He said, 'Little t'ing. You don' mind?'

Harrison said, 'I don't mind.'

Swissy said, 'Dey fly me out tomorrow. Don' want de kids to know. Tell 'em myself, in a bit. But dey need money.'

Harrison said, 'I'll go and see them.'

Swissy said, 'No, don't matter to see 'em. But send it on. Is in dollar. OK?'

Harrison said, 'OK.'

Swissy said, 'Christ, dat li'l one . . . only twelve, but she know how to spend. Know what she want already.'

Harrison said, 'It'll be done. Get some rest, Swissy.'

Swissy said, 'Ain't got much blowty choice . . . 'Bye, Al'son. Don't do not'ing I wouldn't.'

She said, 'Chow, Swissy.' She walked through the door. Harrison closed it after her.

She leaned on the wall and rubbed her face. He said, 'Are you all right?'

She nodded. She said, 'I just don't like hospitals.'

They walked back the way they had come. He said, 'I'm flying out tomorrow.'

She said, 'Yes, I know.'

He said, 'Meet me for a drink tonight? End-of-term party?'

She said, 'I suppose so . . . Haven't you got a lot to do?'

'It's done. Goldie takes over, anyway.'

She said, 'Swissy's bar. if it's open. About twenty hundred.'

Harrison said, 'OK.'

She said thoughtfully, 'It won't seem the same.'

He said, 'No. It won't.'

He walked back up to B deck. He was surprised, vaguely, to see it was evening already. The combine was heading nearly due west across the miles of stubble. He turned away from the pouring redness. A hundred yards off, a massive recovery tractor paced the crippled machine. A helicopter swooped low, belly lamps winking. He leaned on the rail, watched the slow flowing of the ground. He missed now the thunder of the mains; Patsy seemed somehow less than half alive, a crawling red shadow in the dusk.

A tanker moved away, left behind a rich gust of fumes. As the light faded, the torches working on the ruined forward housings sprang into prominence. He watched the white glare shift and flicker, the sparks fall like hot coals. He stayed still a long time, smoking, till the land was wholly dark.

The wind was rising, keening in the rigging. He pushed his jacket sleeve back, looked at his watch. He walked to his cabin, used the dry shaver and washed. He went to the locker, slipped the little charm into his pocket. He thought, 'We must be ships, passing in the night; but elegantly, so elegantly. Nobody gets hurt.'

Halfway to C deck he thought, 'I hope she's stood me up. It's about time.' But he pushed the door open knowing she would be there.

She wasn't that kind of girl.

The White Boat

Becky had always lived in the cottage overlooking the bay.

The bay was black, because there a seam of rock that was nearly coal burst open to the water and the sea had nibbled in over the years, breaking up the fossil ridden shale to a fine dark grit, spreading it over the beach and the humped, tilted headlands. The grass had taken the colour of it and the little houses that stood mean-shouldered glaring at the water; the boats and jetties had taken it, and the brambles and gorse; even the rabbits that thumped across the cliff paths on summer evenings seemed to have something of the same dusky hue. Here the paths tilted, tumbling over to steepen and plunge at the sea; the whole land seemed ready to slide and splash, grumble into the ocean.

It was a summer evening when Becky first saw the White Boat. She had been sent, in the little skiff that was all her father owned, to clear the day's crop from the lobster pots strung out along the shore. She worked methodically, sculling along the bobbing line of buoys; the baskets in the bottom of the boat were full and bustling, the great crustaceans black and slate-grey as the cliffs, snapping and wriggling, waving wobbling, angry claws. Becky regarded them thoughtfully. A good catch; the family would feed well in the week to come.

She pulled up the last pot, feeling the drag and surge of it against the slow-flowing tide. It was empty, save for the grey-white rags of bait. She dropped the tarred basket back over the side, leaned to see the ghost-shape of it vanish in the cloudy green beneath the keel. She sat feeling the little aches spread in shoulders and arms, narrow

193

ing her eyes against the evening haze of sunlight; and saw the Boat.

Only she didn't know then that White Boat was her name.

She was coming in fast and quiet, bow parting the sea, raising a bright ridge of foam. Mainsail down and furled, tall jib filling in the slight breeze. The calling of the crew came clear and faint across the water; and instinct made the girl scurry from her, pushing at the oars, scudding the little craft back to the shelter of the land. She grounded on the Ledges, the natural moles of stone that reached out into the sea, skipped ashore all torn frock and thin brown legs, wetted herself to the middle in her haste to drag the boat up and tie off.

Strange boats seldom came into the bay. Fishing boats were common enough, the stubby-bowed, round-bilged craft of the coast; this boat was different. Becky watched back at her cautiously, riding at anchor now in the ruffled pale shield of the sea. She was slim and long, flush decked, a racer; her tall mast with the spreading outriggers rolled slowly, a pencil against the greying sky. As she watched, a dingy was launched; she saw a man climb down to rig the outboard. She scrambled farther up the cliff, crouched wild as a rabbit in a stand of gorse, staring down with huge brown eyes. She saw lights come on in the cabin of the yacht; they reflected in the water in wobbling yellow spears. The afterglow flared and faded as she lay.

This was a wild, mournful place. An eternal brooding seemed to hang over the bulging cliffs; a brooding, and worse. An enigma, a shadow of old sin. For here once a great mad priest had come, and called the waves and wind and water to witness his craziness. Becky had heard the tale often enough at her mother's knee; how he had taken a boat, and ridden out to his death; and how the village had hummed with soldiers and priests come to exorcize and complain and quiz the locals for their part in armed rebellion. They got little satisfaction; and the place had quietened by degrees, as the gales went and came, as the boats were hauled out and tarred and launched again. The waves were indifferent, and the wind; and the rocks neither knew nor cared who owned them, Christ's Vicar or an English king.

Becky was late home that evening; her father grumbled and swore, threatening her with beating, accusing her of outlandish crimes. She loved to sit out on the Ledges, none knew that better than he; sit and touch the fossils that showed like coiled springs in the rock, feel the breeze and watch the lap and splash of water and lose the sense of time. And that with babies to be fed and meals to stew and a house to clean, and him with an ailing, coughing wife. The girl was useless, idle to her bones. Giving herself airs and graces, lazing her time away; fine for the rich folk in Londinium maybe, but he had a living to earn.

Becky was not beaten. Neither did she speak of the Boat.

She lay awake that night, tired but unable to sleep, hearing her mother cough, watching between the drawn blinds the thin turquoise wedge of night sky; she saw it pale with the dawn, a single planet burn like a spark before being swallowed by the rising sun. From the house could be heard a faint susurration, soft nearly as the sound the blood makes in the ears. A slow, miles-long heave and roll, a breathing; the dim, immemorial noise of the sea.

If the Boat stayed in the bay, no sound came from her; and in the morning she was gone. Becky walked to the sea late in the day, trod barefoot among the tumbled blocks of stone that lined the foreshore; smelling the old harsh smell of salt, hearing the water slap and chuckle while from high above came the endless sinister trickling of the cliffs. Into her consciousness stole, maybe for the first time, the sense of loneliness; an oppression born of the gentle miles of summer water, the tall blackness of the headlands, the fingers of the stone ledges pushing out into the sea. She saw how the Ledges curved, in obedience it seemed to some cosmic plan, became ridges of stone that climbed the dark beach, curled away through the dipping strata of the cliffs. Full of the signs and ghosts of other life, the ammonites she collected as a child till Father Anthony had scolded and warned, asked her once and for all time, if God created the rocks in seven days could He not have created those markings too? She was close to heresy, the things were best forgotten. She brooded, scrinching her toes in the water, feeling the sharp grit move and suck. She was fourteen, slight and dark, her breasts beginning to push at her dress.

It was months before she saw the Boat again. A winter had come and gone, noisy and grey; the wind plucked at the cliffs, yanking out the amber teeth of stone, sending them crashing and bumbling to the beach. Becky walked the bay in the short, glaring days, scrounging for driftwood, planks, broken pieces of boats, sea-coal to burn. Now and again she would watch the water, thin brown face and brilliant eyes staring, searching for something she couldn't understand out over the waste of sea. With the spring, White Boat returned.

It was an April evening, nearly May. Something made Becky
linger over her work, hauling in the great black pots, scooping the
clicking life into the baskets she kept prepared, while White Boat
came sidling in from the dusk, driven by a puttering engine, growing from the vastness of the water.

'*Boat ahoy . . .*'

Becky stood in the coracle and stared. Behind her the headland
cliffs, heaving slowly with the movement of the sea; in front of her
the Boat, tall now and menacing with closeness, white prow cutting
the water, raising a thin vee of foam that chuckled away to lose itself
in the dark. She was aware, nearly painfully, of the boards beneath
her feet, the flapping of the soiled dress round her knees. The Boat
edged forward, ragged silhouette of a man in her bows clinging
one-handed to the forestay while he waved and called.

'Boat ahoy . . .'

Becky saw the mainsail stowed and neat-wrapped on its boom,
the complication of cabin coamings and hatches and rigging; up
close she was nearly surprised to see the paint of White Boat could
have weathered, the long jib-sheets frayed. As if the Boat had
been nothing but a vision or a dream, lacking weight and substance.

The coracle ground, dipping, against the hull; Becky lurched,
caught at the high deck. Hands gripped and steadied; the great mast
rolled above her, daunting, as White Boat drifted slow, moved in by
the tide.

'Easy there . . .' Then, 'What're ye selling, girl?'

From somewhere, a ripple of laughter. Becky swallowed, still
staring up. Men crowded the rail, dark shapes against the evening
light.

'Lobsters, sir. Fine lobsters . . .'

Her father would be pleased. What, sell fish afore landing 'em,
and the price good too? No haggling with Master Smythe up in the
village, no waiting for the hauliers to fetch the stuff away. They paid
her well, dropping real gold coins into the boat, laughing as she
dived and scrabbled for them; swung her clear, laughing again,
called to her as she sculled back into the bay. She carried with her a
memory of their voices, wild and rough and keen. Never it seemed
had the land loomed so fast, the coracle been easier to beach. She
scuttled for home, carrying what was left of her catch, money
clutched hot in her hand; turned as White Boat turned below her in
the dusk, heard the splash and rattle as her anchor dropped down to
catch the bottom of the sea. There were lights aboard already, sharp

pinpoints that gleamed like a cluster of eyes; above them the rigging of the Boat was dark, a filigree against the silver-grey crawling of the water.

Her father swore at her for selling the catch. She stared back wide-eyed.

'*The Bermudan* . . .' He spat, hulking across the kitchen to slam dirty plates down in the sink, crank at the handle of the tall old pump. 'You keep away from en . . .'

'But f—'

He turned back, dark-faced with rage. 'Keep *away* from en. Doan't want no more tellin' . . .'

Already her face had the ability to freeze, turn into the likeness of a dark, sculpted cat. She veiled her eyes, watching down at her plate. Above in the bedroom she heard her mother's racking cough. There would be spatters of pink on the sheets come morning, that she knew. She tucked one foot behind the other, stroking with her toes the contour of a grimy shin, and thought carefully of nothing at all.

The exchange, inconclusive as it was, served to rivet Becky's attention; over the weeks, the strange yacht began to obsess her. She saw White Boat in dreams; in her fantasies she seemed to fly, riffling through the wind like the great gulls that haunted the beach and headlands. In the mornings the cliffs resounded with their noise; in Becky's ears, still ringing with sleep, the bird-shouts echoed like the creaking of ropes, the ratchetclatter of sheet winches. Sometimes then the headlines would seem to sway gently and roll like the sea, dizzying. She would squat and rub her arms and shiver, wait for the spells to pass and worry about death; till queer rhythms and passions reached culminations, she stepped on a knife blade, upturned in the boat, and slicing shock and redness turned her instantly into a woman. She cleaned herself, whimpering. Nobody saw; the secret she hugged to herself, to her thin body, as she hugged all secrets, thought, and dreams.

There was a wedding once, in the little black village, in the little black church. At that time Becky became aware, obscurely, that the people too had taken the colour of the place; an airborne, invisible smut had changed them all. The fantasies took new and more sinister shapes; once she dreamed she saw the villagers, her parents, all the people she knew, melt chaotically into the landscape till the cliffs were bodies and bones and old beseeching hands, teeth and eyes and crumbling ancient foreheads. Sometimes now she was afraid of the bay; but always it drew her with its own magnetism.

She could not be said to think, sitting there alone and brooding; she felt, vividly, things not readily understandable.

She cut her black hair, sitting puzzled in front of a cracked and spotted mirror, turning her head, snipping and shortening till she looked nearly like a boy, one of the wild fisherboys of the coast. She stroked and teased the result, while the liquid huge eyes watched back uncertainly from the glass. She seemed to sense round her a trap, its bars thick and black as the bars of the lobster pots she used. Her world was landlocked, encompassed by the headlands of the bay, by the voice of the priest and her father's tread. Only White Boat was free; and free she would come, gliding and shimmering in her head, unsettling. In the critical events of adolescence, after the fear, her pride in the shedding of her blood, the Boat seemed to have taken a part. Almost as if from under the bright mysterious horizon she had seen, and could somehow understand.

Becky kept her tryst with the yacht, time and again, watching from the tangles of bramble above the bay.

The sea itself drew her now. Nights or early iron-grey mornings she would slide her frock over her head among the piled slabs of rock, ease into the burning ice of the water, lie and let the waves lift her and move and slap. At such times it seemed the bay came in on her with an agoraphobic crowding, the rolling heights of headlands grey under the vast spaces of air; it was as if her nakedness brought her somehow in power of the place, as if it could then tumble round her quickly, trap and enfold. She would scuttle from the water, thresh into her dress. The awkwardness of her damp body under the cloth was a huge comfort; the cliffs receded, gained their proper aloofness and perspective. Were once more safe.

As a by-product, she was learning to swim.

That in itself was a Mystery; she felt instinctively her father and the Church would not approve. She avoided Father Antony; but the eyes of icons and the great Christos over the altar would still single her out in services to watch and accuse. By swimming she gave her body, obscurely, to assault; entered into a mystic relationship with White Boat, who also swam. She needed fulfilment, the shadowy fulfilment of the sea. She experienced a curious confusion, a sense of sin too formless to be categorized and as such more terrifying and in its turn alluring. The Confessional was closed to her; she walked alone, carefully, in a world of shadows and brittle glass. She avoided now the touches, the pressures, the accidental gratifications of her body that came nearly naturally with walking and moving and working. She wished in an unformed way to proscribe at least a vague area of evil, reduce the menace she herself had sought and that now in its turn sought her.

The idea came it seemed of its own, unlooked for and unwanted. Slowly there grew in her, watching the yacht swing at her mooring out in the darkening mystery of the water, the knowledge that White Boat alone might save her from herself. Only the Boat could fly, out from the twin iron headlands to a broader world. Where did she come from? Why did she vanish so mysteriously, and why return?

The priest spoke words over her mother's grave, God looked down from the sky; but Becky knew the earth had taken her to squeeze and squeeze, make her into more black shale.

The Boat came back.

She was frightened now and unsure. Before, with the less cluttered faith of childhood, she had not questioned. The Boat had gone away, the Boat would return. Now she knew, that all things change, and change is for ever. One day, the Boat would not return.

She had passed from knowledge of evil to indifference; for that, she felt herself already damned.

The thing she had rehearsed and dreamed of blended so with reality that she lived another dream. She rose silently in the black house, hearing the squabbling cough of a child. Her hands shook as she dressed; in her body was a fast, violent quivering, as if some electric force had control of her and drove her without volition. The sensation, and the mad thumping of her heart, seemed partially to cut her off from earthly contact; shapes of familiar things, chairbacks, dressertop, doorlatch, seemed to her fingertips muffled and vague. She slid the catch back carefully, not breathing, listening and staring in the dark. It was as if she moved now from point to point with an even pace that could not falter or check. She knew she would go to the bay, watch the Boat up-anchor and drift away; her mind, complicated, reserved beneath the image others that would be presented in their turn, in sequence to an unimagined end.

The village was black, lightless and dead; the air moved raw on her face and arms, a drifting of wet vapour that was nearly rain. The sky above her seemed to press solidly, dark as pitch except where to the east one depthless iron-grey streak showed where in the upper air there was dawn. Against it the tower of the church stood tall and remote, held out stiffly its ragged gargoyle ears.

In the centre of the bay a shallow ravine conducted to the beach a rill dribbling from the far-off Luckford Ponds. A plank bridge with a single handrail spanned the brook; the steps that led down to it were slimy with the damp. Once Becky slipped on a rounded stone, once felt beneath her pad the quick recoil of a worm. She crossed the bridge, hearing the chuckle of water; a scramble over wet rock and the bay opened out ahead, barely visible, a dull-grey vastness. On it, floating in a half-seen mirror, the darker grey ghost of the Boat. She crossed the beach, toes sinking in grit, feeling with her feet among the planes of tumbled stone. The water rose to calves and knees, half noticed; before her was a faint calling, the hard *tonk-tonk-tonk* of a winch.

Rain spattered on the dawn wind, wetting her hair. She moved on, still with the same mindless steadiness. The stone ledge, the mole, sloped slowly, water slapping and creaming where it nosed under the sea. She floundered beside it, waist deep, feet in furry tangles of weed. Soon she was swimming into the broad cold madness of the water. As the land receded she fell into a rhythm of movement, half hypnotic; it seemed she would follow White Boat tirelessly, to the far end of the world. The aches increasing in shoulders and arms were unnoticed, unimportant. Ahead, between the slapping dark troughs of waves, the shadow of the Boat had altered, foreshortening, as she turned to face the sea; above the hull had grown a taller shade that was the raising of the gently flapping jib.

To Becky it seemed an accident that she was here, and that the sea was deep and the cliffs tall and the Boat too far off to reach. She nuzzled at the water, drowsily; but the first bayonet stab in her lungs startled something that was nearly an orgasm. She retched, and kicked; felt coldness close instantly over her head, screamed and fought for air.

And there were voices ahead, a confusion of sounds and orders; the shape of the Boat changing again as she turned back into the wind.

There were hands on her shoulders and arms; something grabbed in her dress, the fabric tore, she went under again gulping at the sea. She wallowed, centred in a confusion of grey and black, white of foam, glaring red. Was hauled out thrashing, landed on a sloping deck, lay feeling beneath her opened mouth the smoothness of wood. The voices surged round her, seeming like the lap and splash of the sea to retreat and advance.

'*That one* . . .'

'Bloody fishergirl . . .'

The words roared quite unnecessarily in her ear, receded in their turn. She stayed still, panting; water ran from her; she sensed, six feet beneath, the grey sliding of the sea. She lay numbly, knowing she had done a terrible thing.

They fetched her blankets, muffled her in them. She sat up and coughed more water, hearing ropes creak, the slide and slap of waves. Her mind seemed still dissociated from her body, a cool grey thing that had watched the other Becky spit and drown. She was aware vaguely of questions; she clutched the rough cloth across her throat and shook her head, angry now with herself and the people round her. The movement started a spinning sickness; she was aware of being lifted, caught a last glimpse of the black land-streak miles off as the boat heeled to the wind. One foot caught the side of the hatch as they lowered her; the pain jarred to her brain, ebbed. She was aware of a maze of images, disconnected; white planking above her head, hands working at the blankets and her dress. She frowned and mumbled, trying to collect her thoughts; but the impressions faded, one by one, into silence.

She lay quiet, cocooned in blankets, unwilling to open her eyes. Soon she would have to move, go down and rake the stove to life, set the pots of gruel simmering and bubbling for breakfast. The house rolled faintly and incongruously, shivering like a live thing; across beneath the eaves ran the chuckling slap of water. The dream-image persisted, stubbornly refusing to fade. She moved her head on the pillow, rubbing and grumbling, fought a hand free to touch hair still sticky with salt. The fingers moved back down, discovering nakedness. That in itself was a sin, to tumble into bed unclothed. She grunted and snuggled, defeating the dream with sleep.

The water made a thousand noises in the cabin. Rippling and laughing, strumming, smacking against the side of White Boat. Becky's eyes popped open again, in sudden alarm. With waking came remembrance, and a clawing panic. She shot upright; her head thumped against the decking two feet above. She rubbed dazedly, seeing the sun reflections play across the low roof, the bursts and tinkles and momentary skeins of light. The cabin was in subtle motion, leaning; she saw a bright yellow oilskin sway gently, at an angle from the upright on which it hung. Perspectives seemed wrong; she was pressed against a six-inch wooden board that served to stop her rolling from the bunk.

The boy was watching her, holding easily to a stanchion. The eyes above the tangle of beard were bright and keen, and he was laughing. 'Get your things on,' he said. 'Skipper wants to see you. Come up on deck. You all right now?'

She stared at him wild-eyed.

'You'll be all right,' he said. 'Just get dressed. It'll be all right.'

She knew then the dream or nightmare was true.

Tiny things confused her. The latches that held the bunkboard, she had to grope and push and still they wouldn't come undone. She swung her legs experimentally. Air rushed at her body: she scrabbled at the blankets, came out with a thump, took a fall, lost the blankets again. There were clothes left for her, jeans and an old sweater. She grabbed for them, panting. Her fingers refused to obey her, slipping and trembling; it seemed an age before she could force her legs into the trews.

The companionway twitched aside to land her among pots and pans. She clung to the steps, countering the great lean of the boat, pulled herself up to be dazed by sunlight.

And there was no land. Just a smudge, impossibly far off across the racing green of the sea. She winced, screwing her eyes; the boy who had spoken to her helped her again.

The skipper sat immobile, carved it seemed from buttercup-yellow oilskin, thin face and grey eyes watching past her along the deck of the Boat. Above him was the huge steady curving of the sails; behind the crew, clinging in the stern, watching her bold-eyed. She saw bearded mouths grinning and dropped her eyes, twisted her fingers in her lap.

Before these people she was nearly dumb. She sat still, watching her hands twine and move, conscious of the nearness of the water, the huge speed of the boat. The conversation was unsatisfactory, Skipper watching down at the compass, one arm curled easy along the tiller, listening it seemed with only the smallest part of his mind. The faces grinned, sea-lit and uncaring. She had jammed herself into their lives; they should have hated her for it but they were laughing. She wanted to be dead.

She was crying.

Somebody had an arm round her shoulders. She noticed she was shivering; they fetched her an oilskin, wrestled her into it. She felt the hard collar push her hair, scratch at her ears. She must go with them, they couldn't turn back; that much she understood. That was what she had wanted most, a lifetime ago. Now she wanted her father's kitchen, her own room again. Shipbound, caught in their tightly male and ordered world, she was useless. Their indifference stung; their kindness brought the welling, angry tears. She tried to help, in the little galley, but even the meals they made were strange; there were complications, nuances, relishes she had never seen, White Boat defeated her.

She crawled forward finally, away from the rest, clung to the root of the mast with one arm round the metal hearing the tall halliards slap and bang, seeing the bows fall and rise and punch at the sea. Diamond-hard spray flew back; her feet, bare on the deck, chilled almost at once. The cold reached through the oilskin; soon she was shivering as each cloud shadow eclipsed the boat, darkened the milk green of the sea. The dream was gone, blown away by the wind; White Boat was a hard thing, brutal and huge, smashing at the water. She could work her father's little cockleshell through the tides and currents of the coast; here she was awkward and in the way. A dozen times she moved desperately as the crew ran to handle the complication of ropes. The calls reached her dimly, *'Stand by to go about,' 'Let the sheets fly,'* then the thundering of the jib, scuffle of feet on planking as White Boat surged on to each new tack, changed the angle of her decking and the flying sun and cloud shadows, the stinging attack of the spray. The horizon became a new hill, slanting away and up; Becky looked into racing water where before she had seen the sky.

They sent her food but she refused it, setting her mouth. She was sulking; and worse, she felt ill. She needed cottage and bay now with a new urgency, an almost ecstatic longing for solidness, for things that didn't roll and move. But these things were lost for all time; there was only the hurtling green of the water, fading now to deeper and deeper grey as the clouds grew up across the sun; the endless slap and tinkle of ropes, the misery at the churning pit of her stomach.

They offered her the helm, in the late afternoon. She refused. White Boat had been a dream; reality was killing it.

There was a little sea toilet, in a place too low to stand. She closed the lid and pumped, saw the contents flash past through the curving glass tube. The sea opened her stomach, brought up first food, then chyme, then glistening transparent sticky stuff that bearded her chin. She wiped and spat and worked the pump and sicked over again till the sides of her chest were a dull pain and her head throbbed in time it seemed with the thumping of the waves. The voices through the bulkhead door she remembered later, in fragments, like the recalled pieces of a dream.

'Then we'll do that, Skipper. Hitch a few pounds of chain to her feet, and gently over the side . . .'

The voice she knew. That was the boy who had helped her. The angry rising inflection she didn't know; that was the voice of Wales.

Something unheard.

'How can she talk, man, what does she bloody know? Just bloody dumb kid, see . . .'

'Make up the log,' said the skipper bitterly.

'Don't you see, man?'

'Make up the log . . .'

Becky leaned her head on her arms, and groaned.

She couldn't reach the bunk. She arced her body awkwardly, tried again. The blankets were delicious heaven. She huddled into them, too empty to worry about the after-scent of vomit on her clothes. She fell into a sleep shot through with vivid dreams; the face of the Christos, Father Antony like an old dried animal, mouth champing as he scolded and blessed; the church tower in the predawn glow, the gargoyle ears. Then flowers dusty in a cottage garden, her mum bawling and grumbling before she died, icy feel of water round her groin, shape of White Boat fading into mist. All faint things and worries and griefs, scuttling lobsters, tar and pebbles, feel of the night sea wind, the Great Catechism torn and snatched. She moved finally into a deeper dream where it seemed the Boat herself talked to her. Her voice was rushing and immense yet chuckling and lisping and somehow coloured, blue and roaring green. She spoke about the little people on her back and her duties, her rushing and scurrying and fighting with the wind; she told great truths that were lost as soon as uttered, blown away and buried in the dark. Becky clenched her fists, writhing; woke to hear still the bang and slap of the sea, slept again.

She came round to someone gently shaking her shoulder. Again she was disoriented. The motion of the boat was stopped; lamps burned in the cabin; through the ports other lights gleamed, making rippling reflections that reached to within inches of the glass. From outside came a sound she knew; the fast rap and flutter of halliards against masts, night-noise of a harbour of boats. She swung her legs down blearily; rubbed her face, not knowing where she was. Not daring to ask.

A meal was laid in the cabin, great kidgerees of rice and shellfish pieces, mushrooms and eggs. Surprisingly, she was hungry; she sat shoulder to shoulder with the boy who had spoken for her, had, she realized, argued for her life in the bright afternoon. She ate mechanically and quickly, eyes not leaving her plate; round her the talk flowed unheeding. She crouched small, glad to be forgotten.

They took her with them when they went ashore. In the dinghy she felt more at ease. They sat in a waterfront bar, in France, drank bottle on bottle of wine till her head spun again and voices and noise seemed blended in a warm roaring. She snuggled, on the Welshman's knees, feeling safe again and wanted. She tried to talk then, about the fossils on the rocks and her father and the Church and swimming and nearly being drowned; they scuffed her hair, laughing, not understanding. The wine ran down her neck inside the sweater; she laughed back and watched the lamps spin, head drooping, lids half closed on dark-lashed hazel eyes.

'Ahoy, White Boat . . .'

She stood shivering, seeing the lamps drive spindled images into the water, hearing men reel along the quay, hearing the shouts, feeling still the tingling surprise of foreignness. While White Boat answered faint from the mass of vessels, the tender crept splashing out of the night.

She was still barefoot; she felt the water tart against her ankles as she scuttled down to catch the dinghy's bow.

'Here,' said David. 'Not puttin' you to bed twice in a bloody day . . .'

She felt her head hit the rolled blankets that served as a pillow; muttered and grinned, pushed blearily at the waistband of her jeans, gave up, collapsed in sleep.

The miles of water slid past, chuckling in a dream.

She woke quickly to darkness, knowing once more she had been fooled. They had slipped out of harbour, in the night; that heave and roll, chuckling and bowstring sense of tightness, was the feel of the open sea.

White Boat, and these people, never slept.

There were voices again. And lights gleaming, rattle of descending sails, scrape of something rolling against the hull. Scufflings then, and thuds. She lay curled in the bunk, face turned away from the cabin.

'No, she's asleep . . .'

'Easy with that now, man . . .'

She chuckled, silently. The clink of bottles, thump of secret bales, amused her. There was nothing more to fear; these people were smugglers.

She woke heavy and irritable. The source of irritation was for a time mysterious. She attempted, unwillingly, to analyse her feelings; for her, an unusual exercise. The wildest, most romantic notions of White Boat were true; yet she was cheated. This she knew instinctively. She saw the village street then, the little black clustering houses, the church. The priest mouthing silently, condemning; her father, black faced, unfastening his broad, buckled belt. To this she would return, irrevocably; the dream was finished.

That was it; the point of pain, the taste and very essence of it. That she didn't belong aboard White Boat. She never would. Abruptly she found herself hating the crew for the knowledge they had given so freely. They should have beaten her, loved her till she bled, tied her feet, slammed her into the deep green sea. They had done nothing, because to them she was worth nothing. Not even death.

She refused food, for the second time. She thought the skipper looked at her with worried eyes. She ignored him; she took up her old position, gripping the friendly thickness of the mast. The day was sunny and bright; the boat moved fast, under the great spread whiteness of a Genoa, dipping lee scuppers under, jouncing through the sea. Almost she wished for the sickness of the day before, the hour when she'd wanted so urgently to die. As White Boat raised, slowly, the coast of England.

Her mind seemed split now in halves, one part wanting the voyage indefinitely prolonged, the other needing to rush on disaster, have it over and done. The day faded slowly to dusk, dusk to deep night. In the dark she saw the cressets of a signal tower, flaring, moving pinpoints; and another answering it, and another far beyond. They would be signalling for her, without a doubt; calling across the moors, through all the long bays. She curled her lip. She had discovered cynicism.

The wind blew chill across the sea.

Forward of the mast, a hatch gave access to the sail locker. She lowered herself into it, curled atop the big sausage shapes of canvas. The bulkhead door, ajar and creaking, showed shifting gleams of yellow from the cabin lamps. Here the water noise was intensified; she listened sullenly to the chuckle and seethe, half-wanting in her bitterness the boat to strike some reef and drown. While the light moved, forward and back across the sloping painted walls. She began picking half-unconsciously at the paint, crumbling little brittle flakes in her palm.

The loose boards interested her.

By the lamplight she saw part of the wooden side move slightly, out of time with the upright that supported it. She edged across, pulled experimentally. There was a hatch, behind it a space into which she could reach her arm. She groped tentatively, drew out a slim oilcloth packet. Then another. There were many of them, crowded away in the double hull; little things, not much bigger than the boxes of lucifers she bought sometimes in the village shop.

On impulse she pushed one of them into the waistband of her trews. She scurried the rest out of sight again, closed the trap, sat frowning. She sat rubbing the little packet, feeling it warm slowly against her flesh, determined for the first time in her life to steal; wanting some part of White Boat maybe, something to hold at night and remember. Something precious.

Somebody had been very careless.

There was a voice above her, a moving of feet on the deck. She scrambled guiltily, climbed back through the hatch. But they weren't interested in her. Ahead the coastline showed solid, velvet-black. She saw the loom of twin headlands, faintest gleam of waves round long stone moles, and realized with a shock and thrill of coldness that she was home.

She saw other things too, heresies that stopped her breath. Machines, uncovered now, whirred and ticked in the cabin. Bands of light flickered pink, moved against a scale of figures; she heard the chanting as they edged into the bay, seven fathoms five, four. As the devil-boat came in, with nobody at the lead . . .

The dinghy swung from its place atop the cabin, thumped into the sea. She scrambled down, clutching her parcelled dress. Another bundle was lowered, heavier, chinking musically. For her father, she was told; and to say, 'twas from the Boat. A bribe of silence that, or a double bluff, confession of a little crime to hide one monstrously worse. They called to her, low voiced; she waved mechanically, seeing as she turned away the last descending flutter of the jib. The dinghy headed in slow, the Welsh boy at the tiller.

She knelt upright on the bottom boards till the boat bumped the mole, grated and rolled. She was out then quickly, scuttling away. He called her as she reached the bottom of the path. She turned waiting, a frail shadow in the night.

He seemed unsure how to go on. 'You must understand, see,' he said unhappily. 'You must never do this again. Do you understand, Becky?'

'Yes,' she said. 'Goodbye.' She turned and ran again up the path to the stream, over the bridge to home.

There was a window they always left open, over the washhouse roof. She left the bundles in the outhouse; the door hinge creaked as she closed it but nothing stirred. She climbed cautiously, padded through the dark to her room. She lay on the bed, feeling the faint rocking that meant mystically she was still in communion with the great boat down there in the bay. A last conscious thought made her pull the package from her waist, tuck it beneath the layers of mattress.

Her father seemed in the dawn light a stranger. There was no explanation she cared to give, nothing to say. She was still drugged with sleep; she felt with indifference the unbuckling of her trews, heard him draw the belt slow through his hands. Dazed, she imagined the beating would have no power to hurt; she was wrong. The pain exploded forward and back through her body, stabbing in red flashes behind her eyes. She squeezed the bedrail, needing to die again, knowing disjointedly there was no help in words. Her body had sprung from rock and shale, the gloomy vastness of the fields; the strap fell not on her but on the headlands, the rocks, the sea. Exorcizing the loneliness of the place, the misery and hopelessness and pain. He finished finally, turned away groping to barge through the door. Downstairs in the little house a child wailed, sensing hatred and fear; she moved her head slightly on the pillow, hearing it seemed from far off the breathing wash of the sea.

Her fingers moved down to coil on the packet in the bed. Slowly, with indifference, she began picking at the fastenings. Scratching the knots, pulling and teasing till the wrapping came away. It was her pleasure to imagine herself blind, condemned to touch and feel. The fingers, oversensitive, strayed and tapped, turning the little thing, feeling variations of texture, shapes of warmth and coldness, exploring bleakly the tiny map of heresy. A tear, her first, rolled an inch from one eye, left a shining track against the brownness of the skin.

She had the heart of White Boat, gripped in her hand.

The priest came, tramping heavy on the stairs. Her father pushed ahead of him, covered her roughly. Her hand stayed by her side unseen as Father Antony talked. She lay quiet, face down, lashes brushing her cheek, knowing immobility and patience were her best defence. The light from the window faded as he sat; when he left, it was nearly night.

In the gloom she lifted the stolen thing, touched it to her face. The heretical smell of it, of wax and bakelite and brass, assaulted her mind faintly. She stroked it again, lovingly; while she held it gripped it seemed she could call White Boat to her bidding, bring her in from her wanderings time and again.

The sun stayed hidden in the days that followed, while she lay on the cliffs and saw the yacht flit in and go. A greater barrier separated her now than the sea she had learned to cross; a barrier built not by others but by her own stupidity.

She killed a great blue lobster, slowly and with pain, driving nails through the membraned cracks of its armour while it threshed and writhed. She cut it apart slowly, hating herself and all the world, dropped the pieces in the sea for a bitter, useless sacrifice. This and other things she did to ease the emptiness in her, fill the progression of iron-grey afternoons. There were vices to be learned, at night and out on the rocks, little gratifications of pleasure and pain. She indulged her body, contemptuously; because White Boat had come cajoling and free, thrown her back laughing, indifferent to hurt. Life stretched before her now like an endless cage, where, she asked herself, was the Change once promised, the great things the priest John had seen? The Golden Age that would bring other White Boats, other days and hope; the wild waves of the very air made to talk and sing? . . .

She fondled the tiny heart of the Boat, in the black dark, felt the wires and coils, the little tubes of valves.

The church was still and cold, the priest's breathing faint behind the little carved screen. She waited while he talked and murmured, unhearing; while her hands closed and opened on the thing she carried, the sweat sprang out on the palms.

And it was done, hopelessly and sullen. She pushed the little machine at the grille, waited greyly for the intake of breath, the panic-scrabble of feet from the other side.

The face of Father Antony was beyond description.

The village stirred, whispering and grumbling, people scurrying forward and back between the houses gaping at the soldiers in the street, the shouting horsemen and officers. Sappers, working desperately, rigged sheerlegs along the line of cliffs, swung tackles from the heavy beams. Garrisons stood at alert right back to Durnovaria; this land had rebelled before, the commanders were taking no chances. Signallers, ironic-faced, worked and flapped the arms of half a hundred semaphores; despatch riders galloped, raking their mounts bloody as the questions and instructions flew. A curfew was clapped on the village, the people driven to their homes; but nothing could stop the rumours, the whisperings and unease. Heresy walked like a spectre, blew in on the sea wind; till a man saw the old monk himself, grim faced and empty eyed, stalking the clifftops in his tattered gown. Detachments of cavalry quartered the downs, but there was nothing to be found. Through the night, and into the darkest time before the dawn, the one street of the village echoed to the marching tramp of men. Then there was a silent time of waiting. The breeze soughed up from the bay, moving the tangles of gorse, crying across the huddled roofs; while Becky, lying quiet, listened for the first whisper, the shout that would send soldiers to their posts, train the waiting guns.

She lay on her face, hair tangled on the pillow, hearing the night wind, clenching and slowly unclenching her hands. It seemed the shouting still echoed in her brain, the harangues, thumping of tables, red-faced noise of priests. She saw her father standing glowering and sullen while the cobalt-tunicked major questioned over and again, probing, insisting, till in misery questions became answers and answers made their own fresh confusion. The sea moved in her brain, dulling sense, while the cannon came trundling and peering behind the straining mules, crashing trails and limbers on the rough ground till the noise clapped forward and back between the houses and she put hands to ears and cried to stop, just to stop . . .

They wrung her dry, between them. She told things she had told to nobody, secrets of bay and beach and lapping waves, fears and dreams; everything they heard stony faced while the clerks scribbled, the semaphores clacked on the hills. They left her finally, in her house, in her room, soldiers guarding the door and her father swearing and drunk downstairs and the neighbours pecking and fluttering over the children, making as they spoke of her and hers the sign of the Cross. She lay an age while understanding came and grew, while her nails marked her palms and the tears squeezed hot and slow. The wind droned, soughing under the eaves; blowing strong and cool and steady, bringing White Boat in to death.

Never before had her union with the Boat seemed stronger. She saw her with the clarity of nightmare, moon washing the tilted deck, sails gleaming darkly against the loom of land. She tried in desperation to force her mind out over the sea; she prayed to turn, go back, fly away. White Boat heard, but made no answer; she came on steadily, angry and inexorable.

Becky sat up quietly, padded to the window. She saw the bright night, the moonglow in the little cluttered yard. In the street footsteps clicked, faded to quiet. A bird called, hunting, while cloud wisps groped for and extinguished the moon.

She shivered, easing at the sash. Once before she had known an alien steadiness, a coldness that made her movements smooth and calm. She placed a foot carefully on the outhouse tiles, ducked through the window, thumped into the deeper shadow of the house wall. She waited, listening to silence.

They were not stupid, these soldiers of the Pope. She sensed rather than saw the sentry at the bottom of the garden, slipped like a wraith through darkness till she was near enough almost to touch his cloak. She waited patient, eyes watching white and blind while the moon eased clear, was obscured again. In front of her the boy yawned, leaned his musket against the wall. He called something sleepily, sauntered a dozen paces up the road.

She was over the wall instantly, feet scuffling. Her skirt snagged, pulled clear. She ran, padding on the road, waiting for the shout, the flash and bang of a gun. The dream was undisturbed.

The bay lay silver and broad. She moved cautiously, parting bracken, wriggling to the edge of the cliff. Beneath her, twenty yards away, men clustered smoking and talking. The pipes they lit carefully, backs to the sea and shielded by their cloaks, unwilling to expose the slightest gleam of light. The tide was making, washing in across the ramps and up among the rocks; the moon stood now above the far headland, showing it stark against a milky haze.

In front of her were the guns.

She watched down at them, eyes wide, Six heavy pieces, humped and sullen, staring out across the sea. She saw the cunning behind the placement; that shot, ball or canister, fired nearly level with the water, would hurtle on spreading and rebounding. The Boat would have no chance. She would come in, on to the guns; and they would fire. There would be no warning, no offers of quarter; just the sudden orange thunder from the land, the shot coming tearing and smashing . . .

She strained her eyes. Far out on the dim verge of sky and sea was a smudge that danced as she watched and returned, insistent, dark grey against the greyness of the void. The tallness of a sail, heading in toward the coast.

She ran again, scrambling and jumping; slid into the stream, followed it where its chuckling could mask sounds of movement, crouched glaring on the edge of the beach. The soldiers had seen too; there was a stirring, a rustling surge of dark figures away from the cliff. Men ran to point and stare, train night glasses at the sea. Their backs were to the guns.

There was no time to think; none to do more than swallow, try to quiet the thunder of her heart. Then she was running desperately, feet spurning the grit, stumbling on boulders and buried stones. Behind her a shout, the rolling crash of a musket, cursing of an officer. The ball glanced from rock, threw splinters at her back and calves. She leaped and swerved, landed on her knees. She saw men running, the bright flash of a sword. Another report, distant and unassociated. She panted, rolled on her back beside the first of the guns.

It was unimportant that her body burned with fire. Her fingers gripped the lanyard, curled lovingly and pulled.

A hugeness of flame a roar; the flash lit the cliffs, sparkled out across the sea. The gun lurched back, angry and alive; while all down the line the pieces fired, random now and furious, the shot fizzing over the water. The cannonade echoed from the headlands, boomed across the village; woke a girl who mocked and squealed, in her bed, in her room, the noise vaunting up wild and high into the night.

While White Boat, turning, laughed at the guns.

And spurned the land.

The Passing of the Dragons

There's no real reason for an Epsilon Dragon to die. None the less, they do.

By 'real reasons' I don't, of course, include atmosphere, soil and plant pollution, direct and indirect blast effects and ultrasonic fracture of the inner ear. Most of the things that will do for a human being will do for a Dragon. They are, or were, more than humanly affected by high frequencies; the tympani were numerous and large, situated in a row down each side of the body an inch or so above the lateral line. Which you can see for yourself if you can get off your butt long enough to get down to the museum of the Institute of Alien Biology.

The other things that can kill a Dragon are more interesting, as I explained to Pilot (First Class) Scott-Braithwaite a few weeks after our arrival on (or coincidence with) Epsilon Cygnus VI. The specimen under consideration flowed and clattered into the clearing by the lab about thirteen hundred hours, Planetary Time. I was checking the daily meter readings, I didn't pay too much attention till I saw the three sets of whips a Dragon carries on its back flatten out and immobilize. It made the thing look like a little green and gold helicopter squatting there on the grass.

I picked up the stethoscope and the Röntgen viewer and walked outside. A Dragon has eight hearts, situated in two rows of four between the eighth and twelfth body segments. I attached the stethoscope sensors, studied the display. As I'd expected, the first cardiac pair had become inoperative. Pairs two and four seemed to be showing reduced activity; pair three, presumably, were sustaining residual body functions. Since breathing is by spiracles and trachaea, body function isn't all that easy to confirm. I used the viewer and stood up, leaned my hands on the knobbly back-armour. 'Well,' I said, 'our friend here is headed for the Happy Chewing Grounds. Or wherever they go.'

The Pilot (First Class) frowned. He said, 'How can you tell?'

I shrugged and walked round the Dragon. There was a slight injury in the soft membrane between two body segments; a little fluid had wept across the armour, but it didn't seem critical. If Dragons were arthopods, as their appearance suggests, collapse from a minor abrasion would be understandable; but the body is no fluidsac, they have a blood-vascular system as well defined as that of a mammal. On the other hand the possibility of infection couldn't be ruled out. I fetched a hypodermic from the lab, drew off a fluid sample. Later I'd take tissue cuttings. They'd be clean, of course. They always are.

I'd brought the surgical kit out with me. I rigged a pair of pacemakers, set the collars on the probes to the standard twenty-five-centimetre penetration. I measured a handspan from the median lines, pushed the needles down through the joint membrane, used the stethoscope again. The trace bounced around a bit, and steadied.

He leaned over me. I suppose one might say, 'keen face intent'. He said, 'Working?'

I shrugged, I said, 'Any fool can make a heart pump. It isn't much of a trick.'

He said, 'Then it'll be okay.'

I shook my head. I said, 'It'll die.'

He said, 'When?'

I lifted one of the whips, let it droop back. I said, 'In thirty hours, twenty-eight minutes Terrestrial.'

He raised his eyebrows.

I said kindly, 'Planetary revolution.'

I walked back to the lab. I'd decided to run a cardiograph. Not that it would tell us any more than the thousand or two already on file at IAB. But it's one of the things one does. It's called Making an Effort. Or showing the Flag.

He was still standing where I'd left him. He said, 'I can't understand these damn things.'

Most of his conversation was like that. Incisive. Really kept you on your toes.

I started attaching the sensors of the cardiogram. You should listen to a Dragon's heart sometimes. It's like the pulse of a star. Or maybe you're a fan of the Hottentots. They based their style on IAB recordings, so I'm told; so the Dragons, you see, have been of service to mankind.

He said, 'Why planetary revolution?'

I smiled at him. 'Do you know, Pilot, First Class,' I said, 'I have no idea.'

He frowned. He said, 'I thought you scientists had all the answers.'

His repartee certainly was a joy to the ear.

I said, 'I'm not a scientist. Just a Behaviorist,' I smiled again. 'Technician,' I said. 'Second class.'

He didn't answer that one. They don't encourage morbid self-analysis at Space School.

I walked back through the specimen lock. I'd had it rigged some time now. I'd been asked to take a living Dragon back to Earth. Not that it would survive phase-out. They never do. But that's what science is all about for most of us: a lot of little people doing what's been done before, and not succeeding either.

He followed me. He had that trick. He said, 'Can I help?'

I said, 'No, thanks.' I was thinking how difficult it must be for him, lumbered with a type like me. My teeth are less than pearly, my body is less than sylphlike; I don't play pelcta, I drink my ale by the pint and what I say sometimes has some relation to what I think. It must have been hell.

He lit a cigarette. At least he had one insanitary habit. Maybe there were more. You can never tell by appearances.

I switched the recorder on. The traces started zipping along the display. I turned the replay volume up. The sound thudded at us. He winced. He said, 'Do we have to have that?'

I said, 'It soothes me.' I gave the volume another notch. I said, 'You must have heard the Hottentots.'

He said, 'That's different.'

Man, was his conversation uptight. This was being a great tour.

I listened to the heartbeats. The rhythms phased in and out of each other like drums; or bells underground, ringing a change that was endless.

He said, 'And that thing's going to die?'

I didn't answer. I was thinking about the Dragon. Difficult to dissociate the notion of purpose from things that take exactly a day to die. Neither a second more nor less. But it's difficult to associate the notion of purpose from anything a Dragon does. Or did. For instance, they built cities. Or we thought they were cities. We were never too sure, one way or the other.

I ejected the sample into a centrifuge, locked the case and switched on. He watched me for a bit. Then he yawned. He said, 'I'm going to have a kip till contact time. Call me if you need me.'

I kept my back turned till the door had shut. With the din I'd set up he was going to be lucky. But some people can sleep through anything. Probably to do with leading a healthy life.

He started on the subject again at suppertime. He'd got a radio running; music was playing from the room next door. The room we call Earth. My Dragon's jazz was still thumping in the lab. I changed channels, got the Hottentots. It made an interesting counterpoint. He changed back. He said, 'How many of those things do you reckon there are out there?'

'What things? Pop groups?'

He said, 'Dragons.'

I let a can of soup preheat, picked it up, burned my fingers and opened it. I said, 'A hundred, hundred and fifty. That was at the last count. Probably halved by now.'

He frowned. He said, 'What's killing them?'

I did rather take that as a silly question. Epsilon Cygnus VI just happens to have a mineral-rich crust containing about everything Homo Sapiens has ever found a use for, from gold to lithium. My species had blown in ten years back; now the rest of the planet was an automated slagtip.

I started ticking points on my fingers. I said, 'Ecological imbalance triggered by waterborne effluent. Toxic concentration of broad-spectrum herbicides—'

He waved a hand, irritably. He said, 'They've got a whole damn subcontinent to live in. There's no mining here.'

I said, 'So they die from minor abrasions. Maybe they're making a gesture.'

He looked at me narrowly. He said, 'You've got some damn queer ideas.'

I said, 'I'm an observer. I'm not paid to have ideas.'

'But you said—'

'I pointed out psychological factors may exist. Or there again, they may not. Either way, we shall never know. Hence my engrossment.'

He frowned again. He said, 'I don't follow you.'

'There's not much to follow. I'm fascinated by failure. It runs in the family.'

He shook his head. I think he was grappling with a concept. He said, 'You mean—'

'I didn't mean anything. I was just making light conversation. As per handbook.'

He flushed. He said, 'You don't have to be so bloody rude about it.'

I slung the can at the disposal unit. For once, I hit it. I said, 'I'm sorry, Space Pilot.' I smiled. I said, 'Us civvies, you know. Nerves wear a bit thin. Don't have your cast-iron constitutions.'

I don't have the stoicism of the upper bourgeoisie either. If I cut my finger, I usually whimper.

He flashed me a white grin. That's the most offensive sentence I can think of, so I'll leave it in. It describes what he did so well. He said, 'Forget it, Researcher. I'm a bit on edge myself.'

Oh, those lines! I was starting to wonder whether he had an inexhaustible stockpile of them. There must be an end somewhere, even to aphorisms.

I walked to the blinds, lifted the slats. Night on Epsilon VI is greenish, like the days. Like a thick pea soup, with turquoise overtones. The heartbeat thudded in the next room.

I picked up a handlamp. I said, 'I'm going out to check the patient.' The comic-opera habit was evidently catching.

He said, 'I'll come with you.'

I think his nerves were getting bad. He had an automatic strapped to his hip; on the way through the lab he collected a rocket pistol as well. There are no dangerous fauna on Epsilon VI; in fact at the time of writing I'm predisposed to believe there are no fauna at all. There used to be some pretty big lepidoptera, though. I said, 'You should have brought a scattergun. They're difficult to hit with ball.'

He said, 'What?'

I said, 'The moths.'

He didn't deign to answer.

The Dragon squatted where we had left it. I turned the lamp on.

The halogen-quartz cut a white cone through the murk. Furry flying things blundered across the light. I swung the beam round. The jungle was empty.

He was standing with his hands on his hips, the holster flap tucked back. He said, 'What are you looking for?'

I said, 'The mourners should be arriving pretty soon.'

'The *what?*'

I said, 'Mourners. But again, I'm theorizing without data.'

'What do they do?'

I said, 'Nothing. Stand around. Generally they eat the corpse.'

He made a disgusted noise.

I said, '*Autre temps, autre mondes . . .*' I switched the light off. I said, 'I like these field jobs, you know. They broaden one.'

He walked back ahead of me to the lab. I closed the door and bolted it, for his peace of mind.

I don't sleep too well these days. Like the poet says, old bones are hard to please. I lay and read a while. Afterwards I drank whisky. The site storeroom had a cellar like nobody's business. It should have had; IAB observer teams had been stocking it surreptitiously for a decade. I poured myself another good slug. No point leaving the stuff to rot; there wouldn't be any more folk coming this way. They'd cleaned up all the easy deposits on Epislon VI; the archipelago on which we'd landed, a big curve of islands stretching into the southern ocean, was about the only land surface left unraped. It was also the last stronghold of the Dragons.

I put the glass down, sat staring at the dural wall. IAB had had assurance, of course, from Trade Control; but once assurances start arriving three times a year you know the end isn't far off. The principle of the thing's simple, as simple as all truly great ideas; while a single rumpled little Earthman with spiky yellow shoes can make a single rumpled little spiky yellow dollar, the killing goes on. Any killing. Next season they'd open-caste the islands; the Dragons had had their chance.

The Pilot (First Class) kept his light on well into the night. Maybe he was reading. I wandered vaguely whether he masturbated. I wasn't too concerned, one way or the other; but a Behaviourist gets into the way of collecting odd facts.

I'd turned the playback volume down but left it running. The Dragon's hearts thumped steadily through the thin metal wall. Toward the middle of the night the rhythm altered. I got up, pulled a jacket on and went outside.

There's no moon on Epsilon; but there is a massive aurora belt. The green sky flashed and flickered; it was like the brewing of a perpetual storm. The Dragon's whips vibrated faintly; the golden eye-clusters watched without interest. I used the stethoscope. The second and fourth heart pairs were dead. I applied a second and third set of pacemakers. Pair two picked up; pair four wouldn't kick over. I decided a stimulant couldn't do any harm. I went back to the lab, checked the chart, filled a syringe. I shot enough strychnine into the heart walls to kill a terrestrial horse. I saw the trace pick up and steady. Interesting. I thought vaguely I should have taken encephalographs as well.

The idea of stimulants was a good one. I went back, drank some more whisky. Then I dozed.

The mourners began to arrive at first light.

I heard the rustling and clattering and got up. I pulled on slacks and a shirt, stared through the lab port. The dawn was as green as the rest of the day; smoky emerald, fading to clear high lemon where Epsilon Cygnus struggled with the mist. A Dragon passed a yard or so away, jerking and lumbering like a thing at the bottom of an ocean. It was a big one, I judged a potential male. Dragons are parthenogenetic most of the time; over the years they sometimes develop sexual characteristics and mate conventionally. The analysis people had an idea it was to do with sunspot activity; but if there's a correlation we didn't give the computers enough hard facts to pinpoint it. The whole thing just made phylum classification a bit more entertaining.

The newcomer stopped a yard or more from the immobilized Dragon, and waved its whips. They were ten or twelve feet long, banded in green, orange and black. Ball and socket joints several inches across joined them to the body armour; round the base of each were tufts of stiff, iridescent hair.

The yellow eyes watched; the whips moved and stroked, touching the body of the dying creature from end to end. The head of the Dragon rotated, the jawparts clicked; then the thing reared its forepart into the air, lapsed into immobility. I'd seen the stance before. So had a lot of folk.

I opened the lab door, stepped outside. The morning air was cool and sweet. I walked up to the new arrival. The eye-clusters stared, like blank jewels. I wondered if it was seeing me.

I heard footsteps behind me. The Pilot (First Class) looked concerned. He said, 'Jupiter, is this the first?'

I nodded. I said, 'Good one, isn't he?'

He rubbed his face. He was wearing a white shirt, open to the waist. On his chest hung a heavy silver cross. Very fashionable.

There was a crackling in the jungle. Number two advanced slowly, through the moving coils of mist. It looked like a brilliant little armoured vehicle. The flowing of the clasper legs was invisible; you could have imagined readily enough that it was running on tracks.

It moved to the bunch of cables I'd stretched from the patient, and checked. The whips shook, stooped; rose again vertically above its back. It didn't seem to object to the cables overmuch; neither did it cross them. It turned, followed their line to the dying Dragon. The same ritual was observed. The whips rustled; then the creature arched itself, lapsed like its fellow into stillness.

The pilot (First Class) had his hand on the butt of the automatic. I shook my head. Dragons are harmless. Their mouthparts could take your arm off; but if you put your fingers between the mandibles they just stop working. I'd told him often enough, but it seemed he wasn't convinced.

He trailed after me back to the lab. He said, 'How many of these things do you expect to arrive?'

I said, 'Ten. Or a dozen.'

'What'll they do?'

I said, 'Like I told you. Stand around.'

He said, 'They're waiting for it to die.'

I set water on to boil. I said, 'Could be.'

He frowned. He said, 'They're obviously waiting.'

I laid out plates and cups. I said, 'It's by no means obvious. "Wait" as a concept depends on human-based time awareness. They may lack that awareness. In which case, they are not waiting.'

He said, 'It's a bit of a quibble though.'

I shook my head. 'Certainly not,' I said. 'Consider a proposition. "The rocks of the valley waited." That's more than a quibble. It's a howling pathetic fallacy.'

He glared at me. He said, 'If they're living, they have time awareness.'

I shrugged. I said, 'Try telling a tree.'

'I didn't mean that.'

'Then trees aren't living. Interesting.'

He said, 'You are the most argumentative bastard I ever met.'

I said, 'Hard words, Captain. In any case it's not true. For argumentative read definitive.'

He swallowed his temper, like a good skipper. My word, these boys have self-control. They're pretty fine male specimens, of course, all the way round.

By midmorning nine of the creatures had arrived. I set up the encephalogram, fixed the probes. A Dragon has a massive brain, situated behind and below the eyes. Capacity betters the human cranium by an average of twenty-five per cent. Nearly the same was once true of terrestrial dolphins. But they never learned to talk.

I watched the pens record. Something like an alpha rhythm was emerging. By thirteen hundred Planetary Time the wave forms were altering, developing greater valleys and peaks. The crisis was approaching; but it was nothing new. I lit a pipe, walked outside. The heartbeats thundered from the open lab door. At thirteen-forty the first pair shut down. Then pairs two and three. I counted the beats on pair four. Then the glade was silent. I said, 'That's it, then.' I logged the time; Earth Standard and Planetary, hours and minutes from sun-up. I pulled the probes out, disconnected them, started coiling the cables.

He stood staring. He said, 'Aren't you going to do anything?'

I said, 'Like what?'

He said, 'Try it with a shot. Something like that.'

I said, 'You can if you like. Speaking from my human-based awareness, I'd say it was a waste of time.'

Dead, the thing looked just as it had when living; but the gold was fading slowly from the eyes.

He sat on the metal step of the lab, and lit a cigarette. He looked shaken up.

The jade-green ring of Dragons made no move. They stood. poised through the afternoon, like so many cumbersome statues. Occasionally one or other of the pairs of whips would rise, tremble, sink again; but that was all. I cut tissue specimens for autopsy, stripped the pacemakers, autoclaved the probes. Then I scrubbed up and went through to the living quarters. He was sitting reading a glossy magazine somebody had left about. It had a full-frontal stereograph on the cover. She looked pretty good. I walked back to the lab, ran the tapes and started up. The heartbeat of the dead Dragon filled the air.

I heard him fling the book down. He stood in the doorway, staring. He said, 'Do we have to have that again?'

I said, 'We do. There might be a clue.'

'A *what?*'

I said, 'Think of it as a sort of Cosmic Code. It may help.'

We ate. The Dragons stayed in their circle. Afterwards he walked out. He didn't say where he was going, which is against the rules if you're going strictly by the book. There was a little vertol flier in one of the hangar sheds. I heard it start up, drone away towards the west.

I turned the replay volume up. The heartbeats thudded in the clearing. I got a heavy speaker housing from the lab, set it out on the grass, blasted the noise at the Dragons. It had been tried before, of course. They hadn't reacted then. They didn't react now. I dismantled the rig, put the gear away and shut down. The glade was very still, the veiled sun dropping towards the west.

I got my jacket, and a pair of prismatics. I walked due south, away from the lab. About a mile off, a rocky bluff thrust up through a mustard-green tide of trees. The front of the cliff, golden now in the slanting light, was riddled with holes. I used the glasses. A dozen were occupied; I could see the yellow masks staring down. The rest were empty and blank.

At the foot of the cliff was a roughly circular clearing. In it stood a dozen or more massive structures. The quartz chunks of which they were mainly composed flashed and glittered, throwing back the brilliant light. They formed columns, arcades, porticoes. At intervals openwork platforms pierced the towers; it made them look a little like gigantic rose trellises. Sprays of viridian creeper twined from level to level, enhancing the illusion. It was presumed the Dragons built them; though the proposition had never been proved. IAB had been interested in them for years, off and on. A docket went round whenever somebody had a bright idea. I'd seen nests, temples and free-form sculpture all put up as propositions. You paid your money, and you took your choice.

The city was the main reason for the siting of the lab. We'd put it a mile away initially in case the Dragons reacted to our presence. The hope had been wild and wilful; nobody had yet seen them react to anything.

I walked back to the lab. There was no sign of the Pilot (First Class). I set the coffee on again, picked up the girlie book, skimmed the pages. I was pleased to see they were letting a few white strippers back in on the act. Emancipation, like everything else, can go too far.

Towards nightfall I checked the port. The ring of Dragons had closed in; one of them was stretching its neck segments, nuzzling forward and back along the corpse like a cat skimming cream from a saucer. After a time the mouthparts settled to a steady motion. I logged the event.

The flier landed. A wait; and I heard the Pilot's footsteps in the clearing. He barged in through the lab door. He said, 'They're eating it. It's bloody horrible.'

I put the mag down. I said, 'The fact has been noted.'

He said, 'It's bloody horrible. And you reckoned those things were intelligent.'

'I can't remember reckoning anything. In any case it doesn't preclude the possibility.'

'You must be joking!'

I said, 'Perhaps it's a religious observance. Which would make it highly sophisticated.'

'A *what?*'

I remembered the cross round his neck. He was a neo-Catholic, of course. He had to be. I said, 'It has all the distinguishing characteristics.'

He sat down heavily, and lit a cigarette. He said, 'You're mad.'

'I wish I was. I'd get more fun out of life. Remember the Dream of the Rood?'

'No.'

I clucked at him. 'Dear me, And part of your course was the Humanities.'

He glowered. I smiled at him. I said, 'Teatime, Skipper. Your turn to undo the cans.'

He said, 'As a matter of fact, I'm not hungry.'

I said, 'Pity. I am. Force of habit, of course. But powerful. Rule One of the Behaviourist.' I got up, started banging pots and pans round in the galley. I said, 'Blood sacrifice. Eat, for this is my flesh. Also see Tennessee Williams. Mid-twentieth century. American.'

He stood. He said, 'I'm going to get cleaned up.'

I said, 'They probably have. It's a very old sofa.'

'*What?*'

'Nothing. Daddy has some timeslip trouble. Bear with an old man.'

He walked out. He'd started slamming doors.

I kicked the girlie stereo under the side table. Not so much from frustration as pique. One dislikes being constantly offered what isn't for sale.

He started singing in the shower. He always sang in the shower. His voice was very good. Light tenor. I expected he used a good aftershave too. I wondered just what the hell a Dragon would make of him anyway. Pink for skin, brown for hair, white for teeth. You could analyse the picture till it fragmented. Then you had a monster of your own.

The bath put him into a better humour. He emerged from his labours at seventeen hundred, Planetary. He was wearing a white uniform jacket, with the braids and brassard of his Order. He capered up to me, spun me round, slapped me on the back. Then he sat in a chair, legs asprawl, grinned and lit a cigarette. He said, 'Judy's coming through. On the Link.'

I said, 'I bet she's your fiancée.'

He looked hurt. He said, 'You know she is. You met her before lift-off. She's a model.'

I said, 'Ah, yes.' It was the Little Girl Look this year, Earthside. Which meant candid blue eyes, golden curls, tits like stoplights. I said, 'Thoughtless of me. I remember her well. A charming person, I thought.'

He looked at the chronometer on the lab bulkhead. He said, 'We're getting married. Straight after this tour.'

I said, 'I expect you are.'

He gave me a dirty look. He said, 'I suppose that fits a behaviour pattern too.'

I said, 'It very well might.'

He said viciously, 'Why don't you run a programme on it? You might come up with some new facts.'

I yawned. I said, 'Fortunately, I don't have to. I read tea leaves. Saves a lot of computer time.'

The buzzer sounded. He started the Richardsons. Earth Control exchanged the time of day; then Judy came on. She was as I remembered her. Love through the Loop; she had the sort of voice that can squeeze sex out of duralumin. He said, 'Hello, darling,' and she said, 'Hello, Drew.' Drew, yet . . . I tried the full effect. Drew Scott-Braithwaite. I got up, went looking for the whisky. I needed something to take the taste away.

She said, 'How are you?'

He said, 'Fine, love, just fine.'

I poured three fingers.

She said, 'How's the project?'

He said, 'Fine.'

I walked out to the lab, started labelling and packing the heart tapes. She said, 'Who's that with you? I can't see, he's not in camera.'

He said, 'Researcher Fredericks. You met him at lift-off.'

She said, 'Are you looking after him?'

He said, 'He's fine.'

The speaker said, 'Give him my love.'

Drew said, 'She sends you her love.'

I said, 'That's fine.'

The Richardson operator said, 'Epsilon, you are in overtime.'

Judy said, 'Gosh, your poor bank balance. Darling, I must go. See you soon.'

He said, ''Bye, bunny. Take care now.' I heard the crackle as the link broke. The generators cut, whined down to silence.

He walked to the lab door. He said, 'That was bloody uncivil.'

'What was uncivil?'

He said, 'Walking out like that.'

I said, 'It was your call, not mine.'

'As if that mattered!'

'It mattered to me. Anyway, I had some work to do.'

His face darkened. He said, 'You might as well know, I don't like your attitude.'

I said, 'The fact is noted.'

He took a step into the lab. He said, 'I'm also very well aware you don't like me.'

I said, 'On the contrary. I don't give a damn. Now, if you please. You do your thing, I'll do mine. OK?' I pushed past him, got myself another drink.

He stood and stared for a bit, breathing down his nose. He said, 'What would you do if I belted you between the eyes?'

I said, 'Lose consciousness. Later, in all probability, sue you.' I turned with a whisky in my hand. I said, 'For Christ's sake have a drink, man. And let it go.'

He took the glass, shakily. His moods were starting to switch about a bit. Too much for my taste. Anyway, he cooled down in time. Sat and told me about the place they were buying in the Rockies, his old man having weighed in with a few thousand dollars to help the mortgage; and the Chrysler automat he'd picked up on his last Earth furlough, and all the rest. He didn't quite get round to how many kids they were planning for, but sailed pretty close. He even gave me a standing invite to view the establishment after they got settled in; which would have been great if I could have afforded the fare. It was all great, life was great. I rejoiced for him. I couldn't help, though, having a momentary picture of the wedding night. You lie this way and I lie that, on sterilized polar sheets; while we devour, ritually, each other's bodies.

I walked out to the Dragons. Chitinous plates lay about; but the corpse had gone. The air was full of a sweet, heavy musk. One of the monsters was still in sight, moving away purposefully to the south.

Purposefully? I was getting as bad as Pilot (First Class) Scott-Braithwaite.

I walked the few yards to the landing vehicle. It stood canted on its fragile-looking legs, heat shields scorched by atmospheric entry. We still use conventional feeders, of course, even with the Richardson Loop; the Loop vehicle was parked somewhere out in orbit. We could probably slice it fine enough these days to make direct planetary landings; fact is, nobody's all that keen to be the guinea-pig. Get the Richardson axes a milli-degree or so out of true and your atoms could just get rammed cheek by jowl, so to speak, with the atoms of a mountaintop. Nobody's quite too sure whether that would represent a paradox or not. The consensus of opinion is that it would, and there'd be a bloody great bang.

Travelling by Loop isn't too bad; no worse, I suppose, than allowing yourself to be wheeled in for a major operation. But somebody still has to make planetfall the other end, which is a process as primitive as firing a thirty-eight. That's why even middle-aged IAB researchers need pilots; though it's true to say we need them more than they need us. Still, it's nice to have some Clean-Limbed Young Men about the place. Restores your faith in the world.

I woke with a thick head in the morning. I lay in the bunk for a while wondering whether a touch of whisky would scorch the taste out of my throat. I heard the Pilot moving around outside. He called me a couple of times. I swore eventually and answered. I dressed, walked blearily to the lab door. He said, 'We've got a visitor.'

He was squatting on his haunches a yard or two away in the clearing. Beside him was a Dragon. It was one of the smallest I'd seen. The whips, longer in proportion than the whips of an adult, were folded across its back. He was feeding it leaves off one of the palms; it was twisting its golden-eyed head and munching steadily. He looked up, grinning. He said, 'It's friendly.'

I said, 'It's eating.'

He frowned. He said, 'It's the same thing.'

I said, 'One statement is an observation. The other is a surmise.'

He said, 'Maybe it's thirsty. Does it want a drink?'

I said, 'They get all they need from vegetable fibres. You're wasting your time.'

He got a dish from the lab anyway, filled it with water and set it down under the thing's forelegs. He really thought he'd got some sort of green and gold, kingsize puppy dog there. The Dragon, of course, ignored it. He said, 'I've christened him. His name's Oscar. Do you know, I think he answers to it?' He crooned the name in a variety of voices, snapping his fingers and waving his arms. The Dragon twisted its head, keeping his hands in sight. He said, 'There, what about that?'

I said, 'Try throwing it a stick. Also, its ears aren't in its head. You'd be better off shouting at its arse.'

I put the coffee on to boil, and shaved. He played around with the thing half an hour or more longer. Finally he came inside. The Dragon stood where he had left it, motionless in the clearing. He watched it anxiously through the port while he was eating. He said, 'How old is he? I hope he stays around.'

I really think he was starting to get lonely.

We had a trip planned for the day. I strapped myself into the flier; he climbed in beside me, jetted up a couple of thousand feet and flew south. I sat with the instrument box on my knees and watched the treetops slide underneath. The sea became visible after a few minutes; a greenish shawl, fringed with an edging of paler lace. Farther out, a maroon stain spread across the horizon. A few biggish fish were floating belly-up. There were no other signs of life.

He turned west, following the coastline of the island. I waved to him to take the machine lower. Half a dozen clearings passed beneath, each with the curious towers of wood and stone. From above they looked vaguely Oriental, like outlandish pagodas. Nowhere was there movement; the sites lay open, and deserted.

We crossed the sea again, flew over the northerly islands. Half an hour later I touched his arm. I'd seen a clearing bigger than the rest, glimpsed something bronze-green moving in the jungle. I said, 'Set down.'

He said, 'Here? You must be joking.' He took the machine in, all the same, skimmed to a perfect landing between two of the glittering towers. He killed the motors. I sat while the miniature duststorm we had created subsided, then opened the cab door.

The air struck warm. A Dragon surveyed me indifferently from the edge of the jungle. Another, the one I had seen, was lumbering a hundred yards or so away. I walked towards it. It turned, whips waving, headed back into the trees. I let it go.

Clustering on the edge of the clearing were a series of curious six-sided structures, like pale green organ pipes a few sizes too large. The Pilot stood beside them, dusting his immaculate slacks. He said, 'What are these?'

I said, 'Were.'

'Well. What were they?'

I said, 'Nests. Moonstone termites. They were rather a pretty species. But they produced a formic acid variant that upset the chronometers at Transhipment Base. Earth lost a couple of freighters; they're still out somewhere in the Loop. So we cooked up a little systemic. It was pretty good; did the job in a couple of years.'

He fingered one of the mortared columns, and frowned.

I said, 'Never mind, old son. Can't stand in the way of Progress.'

Beyond the clearing a low earth bank was covered by sprays of dense viridian creeper. Regularly spaced holes showed blackly. All but one were deserted; in the nearest showed a familiar green and gold mask.

He said, 'Are these places where they live?'

'What?'

'The Dragons.'

I said carefully, 'These are where they are usually to be found.'

He nodded up at one of the quartz structures. 'They build those?'

I said, 'It seems probable. Nobody's seen them at it yet.'

He said, 'What the hell are they? What are they for?'

I said, 'We have no idea.'

He said, 'There's got to be a reason.'

'That's a comforting philosophy.'

He glared at me. I was starting to get under his skin again. For a Pilot (First Class) he was pretty touchy. He said, 'Everything has a reason.'

I said mildly, 'Most things have explanations. But if we could explain why these things were built it might not strike us as a reason.

Since we're hardly likely to explain them anyway, speculation is pointless.'

I walked forward. All the caves were tenanted; and all but a handful of the Dragons were dead. The bodies were flabby with decay, giving off the same sweet odour I'd smelled in the clearing. I counted forty-seven corpses. None of them showed any signs of damage. He frowned finally, pushed his cap back on his head. He said, 'Anyway, these weren't eaten.'

I said, 'Maybe there wasn't time. They all went together.'

'Do you think so?'

I said, 'It's possible.'

I sat on a rock and filled my pipe. He wandered off. A few minutes later I heard him call. I got up and walked in his direction.

There was a tower lower than the rest. On the timber staging were piled a dozen or more Dragons. I didn't care to approach too closely. The bodies were pretty far gone.

He said, 'That settles one thing anyway.'

'What?'

He gestured irritably. He said, 'They're burial platforms. It's obvious.'

I said, 'Or they climbed up there of their own accord. They were shuffling solemnly around, worshipping the sun, when they were struck with the same idea at precisely the same time.'

'What idea?'

I said, 'The idea our friend had in the clearing.'

'Which was?'

I said, 'You work it out.'

He said slowly, 'You think they're suiciding.'

I said, 'One possibility among many.'

He said angrily, 'It doesn't make sense.'

I said, 'Try not looking for the answers. You'll sleep easier.'

It was as if I'd challenged his Faith. He said, 'Everything makes sense.'

'Haciendas in the Rockies make sense. Laying women makes sense. Of a sort. Dragons don't.'

He shook his head. He said, 'I just don't understand you.'

'No,' I said. 'And we're the same species. Awe inspiring, isn't it?'

He walked back to the flier. I followed him. We searched the rest of the islands, landed a couple of times. We found nothing living. It seemed our local group of Dragons now represented the universal population.

We were back at the laboratory by nightfall. The little Dragon still squatted where we had left it. He seemed overjoyed to see it; started scurrying about pulling down armfuls of leaves. He sat while I brewed coffee, prodding them patiently at its jaws. I thought he might sling a blanket roll beside it to make sure it didn't stray.

There wasn't much to do round camp. He fed Oscar and tried to teach him to sit up and beg; I logged the meter readings, processed fluid and tissue samples, collected droppings for analysis. The Dragons sat in their caves and watched us; we watched the Dragons. Each day at seventeen hundred hours Planetary we reported to Earth Control, and they reported to us. We listened to Earth news via the Loop; and twice more the Pilot's fiancée spoke to him. The second time they had a considerable heart-to-heart. I left them to it, risking his wrath; there were a lot of tears flying about Earthside, the thing seemed pretty private. I repeated the experiment with the heartbeat recordings, beaming a ring of loudspeakers on to Oscar. He didn't respond, which was hardly surprising, though the Pilot pronounced himself delighted with his progress. If you tickled his foreleg joints with a stick for long enough, he'd sometimes rear. It didn't strike me as exactly a critical development.

We took the flier across to Continent Three. It wasn't much of a trip. I remembered the place as vivid green, furred with trees. Now drifts of puce and ochre dust stretched to the horizon. Heavy automats were working. They looked like magnified versions of the Dragons. The wind was blowing strongly, racing across the ruined land; you could see the trails of dust smoking along the ground, dragging their long shadows over the dunes.

We didn't land.

He was moody at supper. It transpired he wanted to get back to Earth. Something had gone a bit wrong with his scene, he wasn't too specific about it. 'It's all right for you,' he said bitterly. 'Nobody gives a damn how long you sit staring at bloody great insects, you've got nothing to get back to. If it lay with me, I'd just report the damn things extinct and clear out. Nobody's going to know the difference anyway.'

I sucked at my pipe. It was pulling sour again. 'Can't be done, my son,' I said. 'Impatience of the young, and all that. Can't brush science aside, y'know.'

'Science,' he said, 'Two men stuck here on a bloody dustball, watching a handful of incomprehensible objects die off for no good reason. You might be devoted to research . . .'

I chucked the pipe down, reached for the whisky. 'On the contrary,' I said, 'I couldn't care less.'

He stared at me. 'Then why're you here?'

'Because,' I said, 'I'm paid to be. Also, here's as good a place as the next.'

He shrugged. 'I'd say that was a pretty dismal outlook,' he said. 'It doesn't seem to me you've made much of your life. Anyway, that's your concern. I'm not going the same way, I can tell you.'

I said, 'Then you're a lucky man.' I filled a glass, shoved it across. He stared at me; then to my surprise picked it up and drained it at a gulp.

He called me next morning, early. I walked from the lab and stared. Oscar had immobilized; the whips thrust out at right angles from the body, producing that curious helicopter effect, and the eyes were lustreless. He was waggling greenstuff beneath the mandibles, but there was no response.

I set the meters up. It looked as if this might be one of the last chances we should get to gather data. The hearts failed, in their set pattern; I drove the probes, started the pacemakers, laid the syringes ready with the stimulants. The Pilot (First Class) took it hard. His pet was dying, certainly; there was no doubt of that. But the noise he made, you'd have thought he was losing a woman at the very least. He fumed and fretted, made trips out into the jungle to bring back this or that goody; he tried Oscar with tree leaves, bush branches, the pale green tubers that grew round the hangar sheds and landing pad. None of it, of course, made the slightest difference. The heart-pairs of the little Dragon faltered on through the night; the Planetary chronometers ran up their thirty hours; on cue, Oscar died.

The Pilot seemed broken up by the whole business. He vanished for a couple of hours or more; when I saw him again he was waving a whisky bottle. He took to his room, finally, in the afternoon. I presumed he was sleeping it off.

It was just as well. The funeral party arrived about fourteen hundred Planetary. They were commendably prompt. The ceremony didn't take long, the volume of the deceased being fairly small. They left the sherds of armour stacked neatly in the shadows of the lab; I heard the whips trail and rustle as they headed back south, toward the rock city and the quartzite towers. I labelled the new recordings, logged the time, took the routine call from Earth Control. I'd closed down the generators when I heard the lab door open and shut. I looked round, frowning. I'd no idea he'd managed to leave his room.

He didn't look too good. He had a bottle of rye in one hand and the rocket pistol in the other, which struck me as a bit unnecessary. Still, it was dramatic.

He flung the bottle down. It broke. He said, 'I was going to bury him. Those bloody murderers. With their bloody whips. Shaking their bloody whips . . .' He advanced, unsteadily. I suppose I should have told him to put that thing down before somebody got hurt. I didn't. It was the sort of line that would have come better from him.

He was fairly through his skull. I thought perhaps he didn't have too high a capacity; a lot of these clean-cut young men haven't. Also when they blow they really blow. He waved the pistol around a bit more and told me what was going to happen if I interfered within the next hour or so. I gathered a man had to do what a man had to do. Anyway when he finally staggered out I took him at his word. The girlie mag lay on the table; I got a bottle of whisky, poured myself a stiff one and started leafing through it. After all, there's nothing like curling up with a good book.

In time there was a hefty, rolling bang from the south, and another. Then some higher cracks that I took it were the automatic. I hoped he'd remembered to pack a few spare clips. After a bit the noise started up again, so it seemed he had.

I chucked the book down, lay back. I finished the bottle, sat watching the dawn brighten the green sky. It had been quiet a long time now; I wondered if he'd slipped on the bluff and broken his fool neck.

The lab door opened. He stood framed in the doorway, the gun still in his hand. His uniform was torn, his face haggard and dirty white. He said, 'I don't know what happened. I don't know what happened.'

I said, 'All?'

He said, 'It was their eyes. Staring. Their bloody eyes. They let me do it, they didn't move . . .' He rubbed a hand across his face. He said, 'If you waved at them, they didn't blink . . .'

I put the glass down, carefully. I said, 'One point, Space Pilot. Did you notice any signs of ritual behaviour among the survivors during the . . . er . . . event? If so, it should go on the report. You might have added to our store of Knowledge.'

He brought the gun round slowly. He said, '*You bastard. You bloody bastard* . . .'

I stayed where I was. I don't find life universally sweet, but that particular mode of exit has never appealed. I said as pleasantly as I could, 'I don't think that would be a good idea. I'm not worth it; you've still got Judy to think about.' The gun barrel wavered; and I smiled. 'If you've put all those rounds through that thing,' I said, 'it needs a clean. There's some water on next door; nip and sluice it through. I'll get some coffee going; you look as if you could use it.'

He stood a while longer, staring like a ghost; then it seemed it sank in. He turned silently, closed the door behind him.

'Next door' was my specimen lock. Amazing what autosuggestion can do. I clamped my foot on the floor switch, heard the bolts shoot home. He yelled something, started banging the wall; and I valved gas, a steady hissing, then a thump.

And blessed peace.

I bespoke Earth Control on the emergency frequency, explained the salient facts and got a clearance.

Lugging him to the shuttle wasn't the easiest part. I made it finally, strapped him in the couch, closed the hatches, ran through what countdown checks I could remember and gave myself back to Earth. Wire-flying through the Loop isn't a thing to be thought on too closely; but they made it. I transferred to the Richardson vehicle, tied myself down once more; and Earth pulled the tit, plastering our substance and the substance of the freighter thinly round the parameters of paradox.

When I regained coherence we were in stable Earth orbit, and the relief vessels were coming up to us. The Pilot (First Class) was awake, and saying quite a lot. He would probably have backed up speech with action in some unpleasant form or another, only I'd taken the precaution of tieing him down again. I listened for a while; eventually I got tired. I switched his voice circuit direct to Earth Control, and he had enough sense left to button his lip. I spent the time till docking thinking how interesting we are as a species. One and all, we build round ourselves little protective shells; but inside, when we're bottomed, we're really quite inhuman.

So IAB never got their Dragon. I was out of circulation for a time; when I got back I was told Trade Control had already issued authority for the automats to be programmed into the islands. Epsilon Development were losing money each day they didn't mine; they underwrote the cost of the station without too much complaint and endowed a research grant that will keep me in crusts for the next five years at least. I settled down to catalogue what had been learned of the humanoids on Proxime IX before Epsilon's power station ran supercritical; and the Dragons were forgotten.

Except that a few days later I had a visitor. I used the door sensors because only the week before there'd been a mugging a dozen floors below. But I hadn't got that sort of trouble this time. I opened the door and poured myself a whisky.

She was as pretty as her stereo. She'd been crying; and she was wearing the season's newest. I gave her a chair, but she wouldn't have a drink. She crossed her legs, tried them the other way. Didn't like that either. Finally she said, 'Remember me?'

I said, 'It's coming. Don't help me.'

She smiled. She said, 'I always expect Researchers to be much older men.'

I put the glass down gently, and sat at the desk.

She said, 'I've come from . . . from Drew. I wondered if you could . . . tell me a little more. He's so . . . reticent. You know.'

I said, 'There's a report going in tomorrow. It's irregular; but I can arrange for you to see a copy. If you so desire.'

She swallowed. She said, 'I . . . will have that drink, if you don't mind.'

I got it for her, sat down again.

She drank it, put the glass aside. She said, 'Researcher, the report . . . You know why I'm here. Don't you?'

I said, 'I'm always willing to be surprised.'

She stood up, without fuss. She laid her gloves down, unbuttoned her blouse and pulled it open. Then she just stood there, looking at me.

I shook my head and opened the desk drawer. I thumbed through the report and started to read.

'Until day fifty-seven, the life forms designated Epsilon VI brackets three stroke two showed no awareness of the presence of the observing party, and no animosity. Their attack was both sudden and unexpected. My companion, Space Pilot First Class Andrew Scott-Braithwaite, behaved with conspicuous gallantry. To him, certainly, I owe my life; and my final employment of GS 93 was at his instigation, though he himself was imperilled by the release of the gas. Our subsequent return was logged by Earth Control . . . etcetera.'

I tossed the papers over to her. I said, 'You read the rest. The style may be wanting here and there; but at least it's concise.'

She stared at the thing a moment, and burst into tears.

After she had gone Miss Braithwaite glided from the inner room. Miss Braithwaite is my secretary at IAB. She is also fat, fortyish and an optimist; but she cooks good suppers. Right now her eyes were misty with emotion; and she laid a hand shakily on my arm. 'Researcher,' she said, 'that's about the biggest thing I ever saw a person do.'

I patted her. 'That's all right,' I said, 'I'm like that.'

That's the sort of thing one has to live with.

They still have Pilot (First Class) Scott-Braithwaite down at the State Home for Bewildered Astronauts. But I did hear he'd being seconded for another tour of duty. Apparently that boy was one of the worst cases of Loop nerves they'd ever seen. Had I not plastered the cracks, he would certainly have been an ex-spacer by now; and Judy would have had to cast those honest wide blue eyes around fairly rapidly. Because Drew's disability pension would hardly have maintained her in the Manner to which. As things stand, I wonder which would have been the better turn to do him.

I wouldn't have thought he'd have blown like that; but you can never tell. After all, I once spent three years with a woman who closely approximated a Greek goddess. Appearances are deceptive; as a Behavourist, it's the first thing you learn.

The Lake of Tuonela

The dawn had been overcast, but by midmorning the weather had cleared. The small yellow sun of Xerxes burned in the planet's blue-green sky, waking shimmers and sparks from the little bow-wave the long boat drove ahead of it. The banks of the canal, lower here, were clothed with bushes and some stouter trees. Mathis, leaning his forearms on sun-warmed wood, felt their shadows stroke his cheek, touches of light and heat combined.

Here, in the bows of the vessel, the thud of her big single-cylinder engine was muted. He glanced back along the tented cargo space, turned once more to lean over the craft's side. The water was milky green; and some trick of light lent greater depth and perspective to the reflections than to the vegetation above. The tree leaves, small rounded sprays backlit to gold, passed smooth and silent fifty feet beneath the hull.

He studied the bow-wave, the fluctuating patterns within its stable form. The main crest curved from an inch or two before the vessel's blunt stem. Behind it the concave slope of water was glassy and clear. Some six inches ahead a smaller ripple began; the ends of this wavered, flicking forward and back in some pattern that seemed at the same time random and predetermined. Into it flowed the detailed images of branches; behind it the blue and gold melted into streaks that vanished in the deep green shadow of the hull.

He moved his shoulders, feeling the aches from the day before in back and arms. Thirty locks, in three flights of ten, had taxed his strength to the limit. The gates unused for years, were grass-grown, nearly too stiff to move; also leaks had started, round the heel plates and worn paddle gear. Chamber after chamber refused to fill; it had taken the weight of the boat, butting at the timbers, to force the gates back. Locking down, the problem would be aggravated; but he had no intention of turning back.

He glanced at the chronometer strapped to his wrist, stared ahead again. For two days the canal had paralleled the course of GEM tracks, raw swaths of earth curving through the scrub and marshland that comprised much of Xerxes' Northern Continent; but the last of these had long since swung away. There were no signs of civilization, either Terrestrial or Kalti, and no sounds save the sporadic piping of birds. The boat moved through a silence that the thudding of the engine only seemed to make the more complete.

He wondered, with something approaching interest, whether his absence had yet been noticed. A week had passed since leaving the lagoon that fringed Bran Gildo on the seaward side, climbing the vast lock flight that leads inland from the city. Mathis shrugged. If an alarm had been raised, it mattered little enough. Hidden for most of the time beneath the lapping tangle of branches, the boat would be invisible from a flyer; while the canals of the Southern Complex forked and meandered endlessly, joined by watercourse after watercourse, some natural, others artificial. The hamlets they had served, the mills and tiny manufactories, lay deserted now, the scrub growing up to and lapping across their walls; once lost in that complex, a spotter craft might search for a week and be no wiser at the end.

The air was humid beneath the trees. He wiped at his face and arms. On Earth, flies and midges would have made life burdensome; but the few flying insects of Xerxes, jewellike creatures resembling terrestrial dragonflies, had no interest in blood. He watched one now, darting and hovering beneath the miniature moss-grown cliff of the bank. The thing swooped, took something from the surface of the water, vanished with a bright blur of wings. The water, he noted, still flowed steadily. The current came via bypass sluices from the high Summit Level ahead. It was an encouraging sign.

In front of the boat a purple-flowered shrub hung low across the water. Her cabin passed beneath its branches with a scrape and rustle. A dozen times already she had been forced to a halt, while Mathis and his steersman used machetes to hack a way through the half-choked watercourse; but in the main the navigability of the canal after so many years disuse was a monument to the half-legendary Bar-Ab and his engineers.

Four Earth centuries ago, so ran the stories, Bar-Ab had been Prince of Bran Gildo, the palm-fringed city by the Salt Lagoon. He it was who in war after war had swept away the barbarous tribes of the interior, driving their remnants into reserves or into the sea; he also who had given to Xerxes the vast network of canals that, till Terran Contact, had remained the planet's major transportation system. From his line the Kalti, the Boatmen of Xerxes, claimed descent, when they troubled to claim anything at all. From the first, Mathis had been intrigued by them; the little dumpy men and the little dumpy women with their wide-brimmed, round-crowned hats and suits of Sunday black. Though the Kalti were a fast-vanishing race themselves. In every direction, through the swamps, across the uplands with their mile on mile of spindly forest, ran the broad trackways of the Ground Effect Machines; their windy rushing was the night-sound of Xerxes now, replacing the churring of frogs and hunting birds.

Mathis shrugged, and lit a cigarette. From the hundred or so he had brought with him, he allowed himself just two a day. He smoked carefully and slowly, thinking back to his interview with Jefferson, the Bran Gildo Controller. Just ten days ago, now.

He'd pushed his request as far as a Behaviourist (Grade 2A) reasonably could; and been mildly surprised at the result. A small but important circus had assembled to consider the proposition; Ramsden, head of Biology: an Engineer/Controller from the survey section; and Figgins from Liaison, complete with Earth-style secretary. It had been Figgins who opened the attack; Figgins fat, and Figgins bearded.

'John, I feel I must make one point at the outset. This sort of thing is hardly your Department's concern.'

The Terran Complex, an air-conditioned cube of dural and glass, overlooked the brick-red ruins of the Old Palace; the place where Bar-Ab once sat, planning the network of waterways that would span a continent. A boat was passing, on the broad green moat that fronted the ruins, gliding above its mirror image like a swan. A gay-striped awning covered it; on the foredeck lay a bare brown girl. Mathis shrugged. Difficult to keep his attention on the matter in hand. He said slowly, 'I never claimed my Department was involved. It's a personal project; and I've got a slab of leave come due.'

Figgins' secretary crossed her legs, looking bored. Ramsden, a neat, bald, compact man, ran his finger across an ornamental carafe—Kalti work—and frowned. The engineer doodled on a scratchpad. A little wait, while the Controller decided not to speak; and Figgins carried on.

'Speaking off the record,' he said, 'what would your object be in making a trip like this? What would you hope to prove?'

Mathis said, 'It's all in the report.'

Another wait. Nobody helped him.

The boat was nearly out of sight. He turned back from the window, unwillingly. The words sounded dry; meaningless with repetition. He said, 'We've been on Xerxes about one Earth generation. When we arrived we found a flourishing native culture. Backward on the sciences maybe but well up in the arts. We found a subculture, the Boatmen. They had a pictographic writing system like nothing we'd ever seen, and a religion we still haven't properly understood. One generation, and that culture is dying. I don't think we have that sort of privilege.'

Jefferson laid down the stylus he had been fingering. The click of metal on the rainbow-wood desk served to focus attention. Obscurely, Mathis wanted to smile.

The Controller said, 'I think we're rather wandering from the point. There are a lot of side effects to culture shock that none of us much like. But they're inevitable given the situation in which we find ourselves.'

He glanced at Mathis, eyes bright blue beneath shaggy brows. It was a standard mannerism; a look calculated to convey old-world kindliness combined with shrewdness. 'We might not have learned as much as we ought from three hundred planets,' he said. 'But this much we do know. The day we made contact with Xerxes, existing social patterns were doomed. Mr. Mathis, you mentioned privilege just now. Let's all be logical.' He turned briefly to the big coloured map that covered most of one wall. 'The hinterland of the Northern Continent is largely swamp,' he said. 'In time, that swamp will be drained and reclaimed. Better standards of living are going to bring a higher birthrate, more mouths to feed. We shall need that land. As of this moment . . . One Ground Effect Machine will traverse between Bran Gildo and Hy Antiel by any of half a dozen routes in a little under one day Planetary. It'll carry the payload of between five and six Kalti longboats, each of which would take a month on the trip. As I see it, our job isn't to resist a change that's already an accomplished fact. We're here to channel that change, help native cultures through a time of transition as smoothly and quickly as possible. In time, the Boatmen will learn new skills. Readapt. That's the way it has to be.'

Mathis said, 'In time, the Boatmen will cease to exist.'

The Controller nodded gravely. He said, 'That's also a possibility we must allow for.' He leafed through the docket on his desk. He said, 'You're asking for permission to take a Kalti boat through the Southern Complex by way of Hy Antiel Summit. And you still haven't answered Mr Figgins' question. What's your ultimate object?'

Mathis said, 'The word goes that that complex is no longer navigable. That isn't true; and I'm going to prove it. A tenth of what we spent last year on GEM terminals would restore it to full working use—and a hundredth of the labour. I want to see that happen; and I also want the matter of the Kalti culture raised at the next sitting of the Extraterrestrial Council. With your permission, I'm applying for a personal hearing. I want the Boatmen protected, and the entire Northern Continent declared a Planetary Reserve.'

The Controller raised his brows slightly. He said, 'Well, that's your privilege. Ramsden, what do you feel about all this?'

The biologist rubbed his chin. 'There's another factor, of course,' he said in his quiet, precise voice. 'Preservation equals stagnation; stagnation equals deterioration. This sort of thing has been tried enough before. In my experience, it's never worked.'

Figgins grunted. 'It seems to me,' he said, 'that you're starting from unsound premises anyway. These people, the Kalti, I haven't seen many of 'em clamouring for help. Could be they don't want the old way any more than we do. You preservationists are all alike, John. None of you can take the broad view.'

Mathis shook his head, still vaguely amused. How could he explain? If Figgins didn't understand, it was because he didn't want to. Study a Kalti pictograph, the swirls that were tenses, the shadings that were words, and the answer was plain enough. Through every design, like a great hyphen, slashed the *Bar-Ko*, the mark of the One who made water and earth, the green leaves and the sky. At the start of time, He decreed all things to be. If a man was to die, or a culture fail, then these facts were preordained; true a million years ago, and true for ever. This was all you needed; know it, and you knew the Boatmen.

But the Controller was speaking again. This time to the engineer. 'Mr. Sito, do you have anything to add?'

Sito shrugged. 'I'd say the whole thing was a pipedream. That cut hasn't been used in thirty years; even the Boatmen don't seem to know much about it any more. I shouldn't think you'd get through to Summit Level; and if you did, do you know the length of that tunnel?'

Mathis said, 'Not precisely, no.'

The other made a face. 'That's my point. Those blighters dug like beavers. There's a tunnel up in the Northern Marshes, Kel Santo, that measures out at the kilometres. We've had to put scaffolding through nearly a kilometre to hold the roof; and Kel Santos's never been out of maintenance. Take a boat into Hy Antiel and jam, and you'd not walk back out. It isn't a chance I'd take.'

The Controller nodded. 'Yes, Mr. Ramsden?'

The biologist said carefully, 'I have to point out it's not too healthy an area. Most of our cases of Xerxian fever have been brought in from the Antiel range. It's spread by a free-swimming amoeboid, gets into the smallest abrasion. Leave that untreated, and you're in trouble. I've seen some native cases; the medics call it the Shambles.'

The Controller said briskly, 'Right, I think that gives us all we need.' The stylus tapped the tabletop, again, with finality. 'I'm not unsympathetic,' he said to Mathis. 'Far from it. As far as appeals go, I'll forward your case with pleasure; we all know every frontiersman has that right. But for the rest, I have to think, first and foremost, of the safety of Base personnel. Both your own and the party we'd have to send out if you went missing. So . . . request refused. I'm sorry.' He shuffled the papers together, handed them across the desk and rose.

Ramsden caught up with Mathis in the other office. By mutual consent they took the elevator to the ground-floor bar. Earth interests on Xerxes were expanding steadily; they were brewing something on the planet now that tasted remarkably like whisky. The biologist called for doubles, drank, put the glass down and puffed a pipe alight. He said, 'Hm, sorry about that. Hardly expected anything else, though. Disappointed?'

Mathis smiled. He said slowly, 'Not particularly.'

The other glanced up sharply; and it occured to Mathis that alone of the committee, Nathan Ramsden had understood his real purpose. Better, perhaps, than he understood it himself. He'd known the biologist a long time. Once, a thousand years back on another planet, he'd been in trouble. He rang Ramsden; and Ramsden had listened till the bursting words were done. Then he said quietly, 'I see. Now, what's the first thing I can do to help?'

The older man took another sip of the pseudo-Scotch. He said, 'As you know, it's not my custom to offer unwanted advice. But I'm offering some now. Go home.'

Mathis stayed silent. He was seeing the canals; the endless shadings of green and gold, puttering of the long black hulls, interlacing of leaf and branch shadows in the brown-green mirror of the water. By pictograph, an answer might be made. The white and blue swirls formed themselves unasked, inside his head.

Ramsden set the glass down. He said, 'This'll be my last tour anyway. I'm looking forward to putting my feet up on an Honorary Chair somewhere. You're still young, John; you've got a year or two left yet.'

Mathis said vaguely, 'I suppose we're as young as we feel.'

The biologist said, 'Hmm . . .' He waited a moment longer; then rose. He said, 'Drink up. I've got an hour before my duty tour; I've got someone I'd like you to meet.'

The steersman called behind him; a high, sharp sound, like a yap. The Kalti waved and grinned, pointing to the bank; and Mathis smiled, nodding in return. Ahead rose a line of hills, outliers of the Hy Antiel massif. An arm of forest swept down to the canal; it enclosed a grassy clearing, quiet and golden with sunlight. The Boatman swung the painted shaft of the stern oar, nosing the big craft in towards the bank.

In the Lagoon, close under the old white city walls, the long vessels lay tied each to each; the sun winked from brass-trapped chimneys and round portglasses, gleamed on the painted coamings of cabins. On each stempost, knotted ropework was pipeclayed to whiteness; above each roof were the big running lamps with their filigree-work of brass; on each side, somewhere, was the mark of the God, the *Bar-Ko* with its sprays of leaves, gold and white and blue. Ramsden strolled beside the bright herd of boats, wiping his face and neck with a bandanna. He paused finally beside a craft tied up some distance from the rest, and called. 'Can't get my tongue round these Kalti names,' he said. 'I just call him Jack.'

The Boatman who bobbed from the diminutive bow cabin was

slimmer than most of his people. His bland face with the dark, slightly tilted eyes looked very young: to Mathis, he seemed little more than a boy. He grinned, ducking his head, showing a half-moon of brilliant teeth. Ramsden said, '*Hoki*, Jack. *Hoki, a-aie?*' The Kalti grinned again and nodded, waving a slender hand. The biologist stepped across to the raised prow, dropped, grunting, to the foredeck. Mathis followed him.

Hoki, the coffeelike beverage brewed by the Boatmen, had not at first been to Mathis's taste; but he had grown accustomed to its sharp, slightly bitter flavour. He squatted in the cramped cabin, the thin-shelled, brightly painted cup in his fingers, waited while Ramsden mopped his face again. 'He speaks a bit of Terran,' he said. 'Not much, but I think you'll get by. His parents are dead. He's twenty-five; usually their marriage contracts are settled before they're out of their teens but Jack's still working single-handed. Bit of an oddball, in many respects.'

The Boatman grinned again. He said, 'Too right,' in a clipped, slightly sing-song voice. He took Mathis's cup, poured more of the brownish fluid. The pot in which it was brewed, like all Kalti artifacts, was gaily decorated; the little discs of copper hanging round its circumference tinkled as he set it down.

Mathis looked round the cabin. It wasn't usual for Terrans to be invited aboard a Kalti boat. Nests of drawers and cupboards lined the walls. No inch of the tiny living space seemed wasted, there were earthenware bowls, copper measures and a dipper, a barrel for water storage, a minute stove. He wondered vaguely how Ramsden had come to know the Boatman. He seemed well enough at home.

The biologist lit his pipe again, staring through the open doors at the sparkling expanse of the Lagoon. 'This man will take you to Hy Antiel,' he said. 'By the old route, through the Antiel Range. He's a bit of a patriot in his own way too, is young Jack.'

Mathis narrowd his eyes. He said, 'Why're you doing this, Nathan?'

The older man shrugged and raised his brows. 'Because,' he said, 'if you intend to go, and I feel you do, I'd rather you have a good man with you. That way you stand a chance of coming back.' He prodded at the pipe bowl with a spent match. 'Just one thing,' he said, 'if they drag you out by the back hair, as they probably will, I shan't know a thing about it. I've got troubles of my own already. . . .'

He had one final memory: of sitting on the cabin roof of the great boat later that day, watching a vessel come in from planetary west. Through the glasses she seemed to make no progression, hanging shadowlike against the glowing shield of water. The figures that crowded her rocked, as she rocked, slowly from side to side. From them drifted a thread of sound—a single note, harsh and unnatural, taken up and sustained by voice after voice.

Mathis touched the young Kalti on the shoulder, pointed. 'Jack,' he said, 'what's that?'

'*Kaput*,' said the Boatman unexpectedly, 'all finish.'

Mathis said musingly, 'All the decks were dense with stately forms . . .' He glanced down sharply. He said, 'You mean it's a funeral.'

'All finish,' said Jack. Yes. Bloody bad luck.'

The canal shallowed towards the edges, banked with fine silt. He heard the slither and bump as the flat-bottomed craft grounded, and shrugged. A few minutes' work with the poles would shift her, at first light. For safety's sake he still carried a line ashore. The ground, unexpectedly soft, wouldn't hold a mooring spike. He tethered the boat instead to a sapling at the water's edge. He sat a while watching the shadows lengthen, the gold fade from the little space of grass. From the cabin at his back came shufflings, once a tinkle as the Kalti worked, preparing the mess of beans on which the Boatmen habitually lived. With the dusk a little breeze rose, blowing from the hills, heavy with the scent of some night flower.

The Kalti bobbed from the cabin slide. 'All done,' he said. 'Too quick.'

Mathis turned, stared up at the high line of hills losing themselves in the night. 'Jack,' he said, 'are we going to make it?'

The Boatman nodded vigorously. 'One time,' he said. 'No sweat. Too bloody quick.'

He had conned De Witt at Base into knocking him up a generator and headlamp to supplement the lighting of the Kalti boat. It rested now on the forward cabintop, an untidy arrangement of batteries and wires. He ran a hand across the motor casing as he smoked his final cigarette. The canal was restless; cheepings sounded and close plops, once a heavier crashing of branches followed by the *swack-swack-swack* of a bird taking off from water. The banks, and the shaggy bushes lining them, were mounded velvet; between them the water gleamed, depthless and pale. It seemed the canal itself gave off a scent; chill, and pervasive. The moon of Xerxes was rising as he sought his sleeping bag.

The morning was difficult. The channel, much overgrown here, had silted badly; time and again the boat grounded, sliding to a halt. The pole tip sank in the softness, raising blackish swirls that stained the clear green. The Kalti, patient and expressionless, worked engine and steering oar, using the boat's power now to drive her forward, now to draw back from an impassable shoal. The sun woke shimmers from the thread of water remaining, while Mathis sweated and heaved. By midday, he guessed they had covered little more than a mile. They rested a while, drawn beneath a tangle of bushes; and he heard the echoing whistle of a flyer, somewhere to the north. He waited, frowning. For a time the machine seemed to circle, the sound of its motors eddying on the wind. Then the noise faded. It did not return.

By midafternoon the condition of the waterway had improved. The boat resumed its steady pace, gliding still between high-mounded bushes. Some of the branches bore viciously sharp thorns; Mathis, standing in the bow, swung a machete, lopping a path clear for the steersman. That night he was glad of his rest.

Next morning they reached the foot of a long lock flight that climbed steadily into the hills. The chambers were well spaced, the pounds between them a mile or more in length. Over each pair of gates the *Bar-Ko* rusted in its bright iron frame, a valediction from the long-dead Prince. Viridian creepers had wound themselves into and through the scrollwork of the supports; their long tendrils brushed Mathis's face as the boat glided beneath. On the following day they entered the first of the cuttings.

For some time the ground to either side had been trending steadily upward; now the canal sides, still heightening, closed together, becoming near-vertical cliffs of dark purple rock. The strata of which they were composed were seamed and cracked; between the layers massive trees somehow found lodgement. The root bosses, gnarled and lichened, glistened with water that oozed its way steadily through the stone. Above, the higher trunks were festooned with the brilliant creeper. Some inclined at precarious angles, meshing their branches with those of their fellows on the opposite bank. From them the tendrils swayed, dropping masses of foliage to the water fifty or sixty feet beneath. Later the cutting, still immensely deep, opened out; here lianas, as thick as or thicker than

Mathis' arms, stretched pale and taut from the leaf canopy to the shelving rock. They did not, he saw, descend vertically but inclined on both sides at a slight angle to the water; so that driving between them was like passing through the forest-ribs of an enormous keel.

The cutting had one advantage; the height and density of the trees had thinned out secondary growth. The water still ran clear and green; the rock, though friable, seemed not to discolour it. Mathis sat in the damp warmth, hearing the magnified beat of the engine echo back from the high cliff to either side. In time he grew tired of staring up; then it seemed his sense of scale was altered. The bank beside which the boat slid, the foot or so of rock at the water's edge, became in itself a precipice, sheer and beetling. The sheets of lichen, the tiny mosslike plants clinging to the stone, were meadows and trees, above which the menacing shapes drifted like clouds. The tips of the great falls of creeper, touching the boat, discharged showers of drops that fell like storms of icy rain.

He thought vaguely of Ramsden, back at Base; the delight the biologist would take in the strange plant forms surrounding him. With the thought came another, less surely formed; a sense of loss, an aching regret at the necessity for actions. He knew himself better now; and understood more fully the nature of his journey. The notion, once admitted, remained with him, his mind returning to it with the insistence with which the tongue tip probes the wound of an extraction. This seemed to be the truth; that because nothing, no homecoming, waited beyond the hill range he was drawn forward, because of desolation and emptiness he had to go on. The trees stretched their ranks over the edge of rock above him; beyond he knew lay others and still more, mile on endless mile of forest haunted by rodents and owls. There were empty hamlets, empty villages, empty towns maybe, lapped by the rising green, wetted by rains, warmed by summer suns. He experienced a curious desire, transient yet powerful, to know that land; but know it in detail, hollow by hollow, as he knew the lines of his palm. He wondered at the state of mind, not wholly new to him; and wondered too at a curious notion Ramsden had once expressed that the Loop, in scrambling a man, never reassembled the same being twice. The oddity was allied to another, better known; that over seven years or so the elements of the body, the pints of water and pennorths of salt, are wholly changed so that physically and intimately one becomes a different being. Yet the thinking part, whichever that might be, goes on for ever; hurting, and giving pain.

A mile into the cutting the engine stalled with a thud.

He was amused, momentarily, at the flash of panic aroused in him. The mind, it seems, insists on clinging to patterns once known; maybe to the point of death. The long hull was swinging and losing way, pushed by the faint current from ahead; he fended with the pole, felt the bottom bump gently against mud. He climbed to the catwalk above the cargo space, walked steadily astern.

Round the rear of the vessel, immediately above the propeller, ran a narrow ledge. The Kalti was squatting on it, gripping onehanded, groping with the other arm beneath the water. For the journey, he had affected Terran garb; a sleeveless woollen jerkin, printed with Fair Isle patterns and plentifully daubed with oil, and a pair of frayed and faded jeans. His harsh, longish hair hung forward; between jeans and pullover showed a half-moon of olive skin. He straightened when Mathis spoke, grinning his inevitable grin; Mathis wondered suddenly if it was no more than a reflex of the nerves. 'All stuck up,' he said. 'Jolly bad luck.'

Mathis climbed down beside him. The tip of a nobbled branch protruded from the water; below, its cloudy shape was visible for a foot or more before vanishing in the greenness. He tugged at it. It felt immovable. His reach was longer than the Kalti's; he felt carefully for the propeller boss, traced his finger back along the battered edge of the blade. The log was jammed firmly between propeller and hull.

The Kalti pulled the sweater over his head, balancing with care. He folded the garment neatly and slid into the water. Mathis followed, feeling the buoyant chill.

From this viewpoint, the black hull seemed immense. The mud of the canal bottom sucked at his feet; he grabbed for breath, ducked, surfaced again. He ran fingers across the curving, crusted planks, carefully, remembering Ramsden's injunction. The Kalti heaved at the branch. It moved anticlockwise an inch or so, jammed again. Half-rotten, the wood was difficult to grip. Mathis clung to the step, exploring again with his free hand. The edge of the big prop had bitten deeply into the waterlogged fibres. He shook his head, made washout motions with his palm above the water.

He paddled to where he could once more swing himself aboard. The ironwood grating at the stern lifted readily enough. Beneath it the shaft gleamed dully, secured to the primitive gearbox by a flexible jawed coupling. He fingered the heavy hand-forged bolts. The Kalti nodded, and grinned again.

De Witt had made up a toolkit for the boat. None of the set spanners fitted; he used an adjustable, working carefully so as not to burr the edges of the nuts. As he worked, a light drizzle began, drifting in greyish veils from the heights above.

The nuts came clear, finally. He tapped the bolts back through the fibrous coupling plate, and gripped the shaft. It wouldn't budge.

He sorted the toolkit for the longest crowbar. A wooden wedge pressed against the gearbox end protected the coupling from damage. He leaned his weight carefully. The shaft stayed firm. He took a breath, jerked. The thing slid backward through the packing gland, with a faint creak. He reached behind him, pulled. The branch rolled clear and sank.

He eased the shaft forward, reconnected. He sat back, wiping his hands on a piece of fibrous husk. He said, 'Hoki, Jack?' The Kalti raised his thumbs. He said, 'Dear me, yes.' He scrambled forward, over the cargo space.

By midafternoon they were clear of the cutting. Beyond, the land fell away with startling speed to a steep and ragged valley. Across it strode an aqueduct, massive arches built of the same purplish rock. To one side, sluices discharged water from the canal lip with a sullen roar. The spray from the fall drifted back, obscuring the defile. Mathis, gripping the boat's rail, imagined the black hull, topped with the tilted brightwork of the cabins, sliding so high in the air. He saw the vessel from the viewpoint of an observer in the tangled valley bottom. Beyond the great structure the rock walls once more swooped together; and the Kalti moored for the night.

In the second cutting they were delayed again, this time by mud and weed. The weed, slimy strings of it twenty feet or more in length, wrapped itself persistently round the propeller, building a solid ball between blades and hull. As the obstructions formed the Boatman sliced them away patiently. Mathis poled dully, disinterested in time; later the machetes were once more brought into use. Finally the narrows were passed; the second cutting opened up ahead. The rock rose steeply, a hundred feet or more, clothed still for most of its height with living green. Through much of the day the far lip caught the sun; the feathery trees that lined it seemed to burn, haloed with pale gold. Later, clouds grew across the sky. The drizzle returned; and a thin mist, veiling the highest rock. In time the mist crept lower, rolling slowly, clinging in tongues to the water.

He was standing beside the steersman on the little stern grating.

The Kalti grunted, pulling his lips back from his teeth. Mathis shook his head; and the Boatman waved an arm. '*Mutta-a,*' he said to the surrounding heights. '*Mutta-a. Kaput.*'

Mutta-a. Mutti, Maman . . . The first sound any mammal's voice will make. Mathis said, 'You mean it's haunted.' Perhaps this was why the Kalti were disinclined to talk.

'*Mutta-a,*' said Jack, nodding vigorously. 'Rather silly.'

Mathis said, 'I can believe it.'

He walked forward. The mist, or cloud base, had thickened again; the tree limbs, some bleached, pushed through it, with curious effect. He was interested to find it was still possible to feel unease. He savoured the sensation with some care.

The huge walls angled to the left. The boat edged round the bend; and a black mouth showed ahead. The sloping hillside in which it was set climbed to unguessed height. Bushes clung to it; above were the trunks of the endless forest. The opening itself was horseshoe-shaped, its throat densely black. From fifty yards he smelled its breath, ancient, and chill. Mathis rubbed his face, then swung to the cabin top to start the generator.

This was the Tunnel of Hy Antiel.

He turned the handlamp. The ribbon of water ahead was tarry, nonreflecting. To either side the close brick walls were festooned with red and green slime; larger masses, leprous-white in the light, hung from the half-seen roof. As the boat brushed at them they broke with soft snaps. From the brickwork of the tunnel fell a steady chill rain.

He listened, turning his head. What he had not been prepared for was the din. The thudding of the boat's diesel echoed massively from the curved walls; but there were other sounds. A sighing rose to something like a roar, fled forward and back along the shaft. Maybe the boat had scraped the side, some sprag touched her hull; God only knew. The brick throat threw echoes back on themselves, lapping and distorting. At first the sounds had troubled him; but they had been travelling two hours or more, he had grown accustomed to the place.

He pitched the light farther ahead. For some time now a deeper roar had been growing in intensity. He saw its source finally; a curtain of clear water, sparkling as it fell from the roof. At its base the surface boiled and rippled, throwing up wavering banks of brownish foam.

This was the fourth airshaft he had seen. He ducked, tortoise fashion, into the little bow castle, heard the cannonade pass down the long tarpaulins of the cargo space to the stern. The big boat rocked; the sighing came again, mixed with the fading roar.

Here, in the encroaching dark, the swimming sense of motion was intensified. A memory returned to him, odd and unconnected; and he nearly smiled. It was of a journey back from London to his home, when he was a tiny child. On the trip down the monorail whispered and clattered, flashing through tunnel after tunnel beneath the great complexes of buildings; but now the darkness pressed uniform and baffling against the rounded panes of the carriage. He had asked, finally, when this tunnel would end; and his father, momentarily surprised, had dropped a hand to his shoulder and laughed. 'It isn't a tunnel, John,' he said. 'It's the night. . . .'

He leaned back, head against the bulky survival pack. He felt tired and a little dizzy. Maybe it was the fumes that hung in the shaft. He lit his daily cigarette, and closed his eyes. He saw with remarkable clarity the white walls and green palm clumps of Bran Gildo, the unused watchtowers pushing their dunce-cap roofs into the turquoise sky. It seemed he could smell the hot, spiced air, the fragrance of spike-leaved shrubs where the Terran girls walked with their pleated kilts and strapped native sandals and long bronzed limbs. From behind the Palace walls came the sounds of the city's traffic, cartbells mixed with the whine of the electric buggies that were a gift from an ever-benevolent Earth. He opened his lids, seeing the slime-hung walls. The two images, so disparate, were yet interlinked; pieces of an equation that one day must be solved.

Later, he must have slept; certainly he dozed, for when his eyes once more opened the engine of the boat was quiet. The cabin lamps were lit; Jack banged and clattered at the little stove.

He rose, awkward in the confined space. For a moment he was disoriented; and the child's confusion returned so that it seemed the boat must have passed the tunnel. Then he saw how the lamplight glowed in fans across wet brickwork; the air he drew into his lungs was chill and stale. He turned to the Boatman; and the Kalti grinned. 'Too far,' he said. 'Not much good.'

They were moored to what seemed to be the remains of a little wharf. Lines of rusting iron rings were let into the brickwork. He swung to the cabintop, started the generator. The lampbeam showed the black, unrippling water stretching ahead. To the right, joining the main line at a sharp angle, was a second shaft. The stonework of the curving groin where tunnels met looked new and fresh. He pointed to the shaft; but the Kalti shrugged, making washout motions with his hands. He said again, 'Not much good.'

With the boat motionless, the silence of the tunnel was complete. He lay a long time hearing the quietness hiss in his ears. Finally, sleep came; and, with it, dreams. They were untenanted, yet precisely detailed. They concerned ancient buildings, places seen once on Earth. A gatehouse, lost in a wood of tall Minster.

Finally it seemed he sat in an upper room of a very large house. The room, a study, looked out on wings of crumbling stone. Beyond were formal gardens, arbours framing leaden nymphs and gods. In the dream he knew with certainty that he would never leave the room, never rise from the chair; and that the light, the afternoon light, would never change.

The Kalti roused him. He was giddy and lightheaded; and his eyes seemed gummy, as though he had not slept. He ate the bean stew the boy set before him with little interest. Afterwards he walked to where the jetty, if jetty it was, narrowed, the stone fairing into the smooth brick of the shaft. His purpose satisfied, he stepped back to untie the ropes from the heavy rings. The Kalti swung up the engine; he poled the bow from the wharf, and the journey was resumed.

Twice in the hours that followed echoing roars from ahead warned of fresh ventshafts. Each discharged its torrent of water into the canal; but staring up as the boat approached, Mathis could detect no gleam of outside light. One shaft seemed partially choked; fibrous roots hung twisting in the downpour, their tips pale and rotted. At eleven hundred the boat passed a line of low flood arches. Water from the canal lip poured beneath them in steady greenish sheets. Mathis turned the lamp. At first it seemed a black void opened beyond; but this was a trick of light. The rock, covered with some dark, nonreflectant growth, was very close.

The workings in the tunnel were complex, like none he had seen. He wondered at their age. He asked the Kalti, shouting above the engine; but the Boatmen shook his head. '*Mutta-a*,' he said. He spread his fingers, and again. Many generations.

The tunnel was very old.

To his other questions there was no reply. The tunnel was very long.

Later in the day the brickwork ended.

The effect was odd. Beyond the shaft sides, a jet half-circle seemed to form and widen. He watched the spreading band a moment, puzzled; then the tunnel was falling away behind. The engine noise, that for so long had pounded in his ears, faded as the stern of the boat drew clear.

He swung the big lamp left and right, discovering no sign of walls; the gloom ahead was likewise unrelieved. At last the abundance of summit water was explained; they had entered an underground lake, of unknown size. He wondered fleetingly if Bar-Ab and his engineers had known. Had they plotted the extent of the cavern, tunnelled to its brink; or had the miners burst into the void, startled and unsuspecting. . . .

On impulse, he angled the light upward. Above, suspended it seemed from an infinite height, the *Bar-Ko*, dark red and dripping, marked the way. Beyond the great iron sign hung another; and another, dimly seen.

He nodded to himself. They had known.

The tunnel had been loud with noise. Running through the void, the opposite effect seemed to hold true. Silence, like the dark, pressed in on the boat; almost it seemed the cavern deadened sound, so that twice he scrambled to the cabin roof convinced the engine was no longer running. Each time he was reassured by the thumping ninety feet astern. Once he tried sounding, with the longest pole, but could touch no bottom. He turned his wrist in the beam of De Witt's spotlight, holding the chronometer close up to his face. He was surprised to see an hour had elapsed since quitting the shaft.

With time, the absence of sensation affected him strongly. The tunnel sounds returned, the whisperings and long sighs; but they were in his ears. Also it seemed that lights appeared, far across the water. It was as if a fairy army drove to meet him, yet for ever receded. He rubbed his face, knuckling at his eyes; and the lights were gone

Finally a fresher breeze blew from ahead. Also he saw, above the endless line of markers, a fold of stone that was the dipping of the cavern roof. Ghostings of grey appeared to either side; then, suddenly, the cavern walls began to close back in. The slime-hung brickwork returned; and he stared behind him at the velvet dark. He said, 'The Lake of Tuonela.'

Tuonela, where dead spirits walk.

In the outer world the time was thirteen hundred. The abstraction counted for little here. He wound the chronometer, staring up while the bow of the vessel bumped gently at what looked at first sight to be the gate of a stop lock. The journey was ended.

The tilted beam of light rolled slowly, illuminating a slope of wet, smooth rock. At its summit, the side of the second great caisson showed its panels of rusting iron. More iron, columns and tie rods, rose into the dark. Beyond was an engine house. The round-topped windows stared like dim sockets; above them the buttressed column that was the chimney grew up into the stone, thrusting for the open air. Mathis grinned, showing his teeth. He said softly, 'The crazy bastards.'

He sat on the cabin roof and lit a cigarette. He felt closer to Bar-Ab and his men than he would have thought possible. He rubbed the beard-stubble on his chin and asked himself, how could they have done it? How could they carve through twenty miles of rock, with pickaxes and plumb bobs, and keep their line and level? Those engineers in kilts and plumes? Like the Incas, their priests used the Rope of Thorns. Like the Victorians, they knew black powder and the barrow run. Like both, they vanished. They left . . . this.

They built an Inclined Plane, inside a bloody hill.

A sound at his elbow made him turn. The Kalti's face was a pale mark in the gloom. He waved an arm at the monstrousness; the caissons, the engine house, the rails with their great red bogies. He said, 'Make go.'

Mathis threw the half-smoked butt into the water. Sito would have given his back teeth for this. 'Yes, Jack,' he said. 'We must make it go . . .'

There was coal; great bunkers of it, growing here and there a rich skin of mould. Coal, but no kindling. For that they stripped the powdering frames from windows, boards from the enginehouse floor. Fuel oil from the boat's depleted tank would fire the furnace. The boiler they filled painfully, a bucket at a time. The top caisson already held water; the gate of the lower for a time refused to close. Mathis rigged a fourfold purchase from a mooring bollard, strained the thick iron partially shut; the boat herself, thundering in reverse, completed the job. Brown foam boiled; the big door closed, with protesting squeals. They lit the furnace then, sat an hour while pressure built to working head. Round the boiler were heavy riveted straps. In time the rivet heads began to sizzle and steam.

There was a bank of gauges, each set in a plate of foliated brass. The markings on the faces made no sense. It was guesswork, all the way.

Mathis edged the regulator forward. A rumbling; rust flew, in a thin rain. Below, the long chains stretched over the rock clanked to tautness. The boat slopped against the chamber side; the engine slowed as the ancient gearing felt the load. Steam roared from a union; and the boat was climbing, inching sideways up the Plane. The headlight, blazing, drew level with Mathis, began to pass. The Kalti heaved at the caisson side, adding his strength to the strength of the machine. He was happy. He had done what the strange Terr wanted: now others would come, with their engines that tore away rock and plucked down trees. And the long cuttings would once more fill. His head made pictures; he saw the blue and red stars that were the lamps of boats, sailing all night long from Bran Gildo to Hy Antiel.

A chain link parted, with a ringing crash. Mathis, sweating, wrenched at the emergency brake with blistered hands. The caisson, with its hundred-thousand-gallon load, lurched backward on the slope; and the Kalti's heels shot from under him.

'Oh dear,' said Jack. The bogies, gathering speed, severed his arm, ploughed crashing across his chest. The caisson took the water it had quitted with a thunderous splash. A tinkling; the headlight on the cabin roof swayed sideways and was extinguished.

The tunnel portal was set into a low, mounded hill. Beyond it the canal was fringed with low shrubs that blazed with smoky orange blossom. Above, saplings hung graceful and still, their sprays of rounded leaves catching the sunset light.

To an observer stationed at the tunnel mouth, the twin lamps of the Kalti vessel would have appeared at first like dim brown stars. For some time, such are the curious optics of tunnels, the stars would have appeared to grow no closer; then, suddenly it seemed, they swam forward. Between them the outlines of the boat became visible; the knotted headropes of the prow, the tilted cabin with its ornamented ports. Behind, sliding into the light, came the long tented cargo space; the engine house, hazed with blue; the stern deck with its grating, the *Bar-Ko* vaunting white and gold on the rounded black sides. The steersman, in once-white slacks and shirt, leaned wearily on the painted shaft of the oar. His face was fringed with a stubble of beard; from time to time he glanced down, frowning, at a bundle near his feet. In places the canvas of which it was composed was soaked and dark; and a runnel of fluid had escaped, staining the boat's dull side.

To Mathis, the transition from darkness to the light seemed

curiously unreal. He smelled the sweetness of the grass, heard the wind rustle in the tops of the trees and frowned again, shaking his head as if to clear it. His brain recorded, but sluggishly. Ahead and to the left, twin hills marked the position of Hy Antiel. This was the Summit Pound; five miles ahead the lock flight began that led to the city, stepping in green steps down a green and grassy hill. He'd walked beside it often enough, it seemed in some other life.

He squinted up at the high dusting of gold. To the right showed the pilings of a mooring place. Little bushes surrounded it, throwing their branch-shadows across the water. He turned the oar, unused as yet to the boat's response, glided the long vessel to the bank.

He was uncertain of the forms to be employed. He chose a spot finally; a grassy knoll beneath the branches of a broad, spreading tree. He had brought a spade and mattock from the boat; he wiped his forehead, and began to dig. Later he drove a stake into the grass at the head of the fresh-turned mound. To it he lashed a crosspiece for the *Bar-Ko* sign; then there was nothing more to do.

He searched the Kalti's few possessions. He found a breechcloth of silk, a scarf, a broad-brimmed, round-crowned hat; and a bolero crusted with pearly buttons, the sort of garment a Boatman would wear on a fest day in Bran Gildo. In a bag closed by a drawstring were two brooches set with semiprecious stones, a nugget of what looked to be iron pyrites and a lock-key charm in gold. There were also a prayer-roll sealed with the *Bar-Ko* mark, and a much-thumbed packet of postcards showing bare-breasted Terran girls. These last he returned to the bag before tucking it carefully away.

He didn't wish to eat. Instead he brewed up the Kalti coffee, drinking several cups. Slightly alcoholic, the drink had a heady effect. He smoked a cigarette, saw to his mooring stakes and spread his sleeping bag on the cabin roof. The spinning in his head was worse; he closed his eyes, and was quickly asleep.

He woke some time before the Xerxian dawn. To planetary east, the first faint flush of green heralded the sun. The canal was a silver mirror, set between velvet trees; and Barbara watched him from the bank, her chin in her hand. The light gleamed palely from her hair.

He pushed himself up on one elbow, and smiled. 'Hello,' he said. 'Are you coming on board?'

She considered, smiling in her turn, before she slowly shook her head. 'No, thanks,' she said. 'I think once was enough. I don't think I could go through it all again.'

He said, 'I can't say I blame you. You're better off where you are.'

She chuckled. 'My word,' she said, 'you've certainly changed.'

He said, 'I suppose we all do.' He rubbed his face. 'I wasn't expecting you,' he said. 'Not here. I thought I'd travelled much too far away.'

'Oh,' she said, 'you know me, John. I'm the little crab who always hangs on. Remember?'

'Yes,' he said. 'I do.'

She was quiet a moment, watching along the canal. She said, 'This is a lovely place.'

'It needed you,' he said. 'It was rather pointless before.'

'Where were you going?'

He said, 'Hy Antiel.' He gestured at the bank. 'There were two of us. But . . .'

She said, 'I know.' She shook her head. She said, 'You haven't altered all that much, after all.'

'What do you mean?'

'Poor John,' she said. 'You never could understand, could you? About other people.'

He said, 'I didn't want it to happen. I didn't want him to be hurt.'

She said, 'You never wanted anybody to be hurt. But you always forgot.'

He said, 'I'm sorry.'

She said, 'I know. It doesn't matter.'

A little silence. Then he said, 'Please come aboard.'

She laughed. She said, 'No, not now. But I will stay with you.'

He said, 'Thank you.'

She said softly, 'It's more than you deserve.'

He said, 'You were always more than I deserved.'

He let himself sink back. Later she too dozed, her head resting on her arm. For that he couldn't blame her. It had been a long way from Tuonela.

Sunlight lay in hazy patches on the water when he opened his eyes. He sat up slowly, pushing back the fabric of the bag, and saw how clever she had been. The light patch of her skirt was bright grass seen through a triangle of lapping boughs. The smooth root-stock of a shrub had made her ankle; and she had used a glistening branch for the sheen of hair. He moved, and she was gone. But there were many shadowed places on the canals, many quiet banks of grass; he found himself not without hope.

The shaking in his legs and arms was bad, but his head felt fractionally clearer. He started the engine, poled the boat from the bank. The canal was wider here and deep, curving gracefully beneath the overhanging bushes. The diesel chugged steadily; the wash ran slapping against earth banks studded with mossgrown holes. The *chikti* made them, the little burrowing mammals of the tropics.

Three miles before the flight a broad green arm of water opened to the left; the Coldstream branch, that once had served the villages to the south of Hy Antiel. He pushed the car, leaning his weight steadily, watching as the bow began to swing. He had understood a final thing; that pain is life, and death is when the pain has gone away.

Ahead, the lapping of blue and gold repeated itself into distance. Beyond, dimly glimpsed, were the low hills of the watershed through which the canal, broadening and meandering, lost itself once more in the marshlands of the south.

I Lose Medea

The first trouble was the ghosts. You wouldn't think a field of cloth of gold would get itself all that haunted but there they were all right, whole formations of them drifting round like smoke puffs and congregating above the hedgerows. I drove from the gate bumpety-bump, clank, bump, up across the swell of land to where you could see the barrows in the distance and the big stone circles crowning the downs, and the glower low down on the horizon that meant just there was the sea. Then Medea said, 'Stop, this is fine.' I don't know how she could always tell the exact place she wanted to be. I stopped the car and put the engine off and sat a minute thinking, 'We're here. We got here at last.'

But the light looked as if it was nearly ready to fade so I didn't fancy sitting around too long. I got out and unlocked the boot and pulled the lid up and Medea started throwing canvas out on the grass in rolls like big grey sausages. Then there was the holdall with the mallet and the spare hanks of nylon line and all the framing and stuff. Some of the framing was round and some was square, I could never remember at the start just how it all went except there were two big wishbone-shaped pieces that made the tent gables. I found the bits for them and fitted them together and laid them out along-side the rest.

Medea was looking good, she was wearing white stretch pants and a dark blue top and had a kerchief bound through her hair. When she squatted and started pulling the canvas into shape you could see a big half-moon of brown back. She got the tent laid out okay, then she changed her mind and said we were pitching wrong way on the

slope or something and started in again turning it all around. This
was the thing about Medea, she never had much of a sense of time.

The ground sloped down towards the back of the field and there
was a high tousled hedge with a gap in it and a stile, and a couple of
trash bins stuck at angles in the grass. I looked across and started
feeling a bit annoyed because the smoke puffs were separating
above the hedge and quite a few starting to drift our way. Medea got
the tent lined up and crawled inside with our the ridge-pole and one
of the uprights, you could see the canvas writhing round like a sack
with a good-looking ferret in it. I'd have nipped in after her, but I
was getting worried about the ghosts, one or two of them were
looking nasty. There was one big grey chap with horns. I could see
from his expression he was just looking forward to coming over our
way and dropping a hundredweight of fog on top of us which was all
we needed. I called to Medea to hurry up a bit and she said
something muffled inside the canvas, something about having got
the wrong pole. I couldn't see how that could be because she'd got
all the sections marked with bits of surgical tape with numbers on
them, and tied in bundles with lengths of the nylon cord.

The big chap was certainly extremely nasty but fortunately for us
he was none too well organized. He'd got himself caught up on the
briars and stuff in the hedge, he'd get one part free then something
else would catch and he'd roll over snapping and writhing like a
horizontal column of bonfire smoke. But I could see he was making
it by degrees and I was getting really mad with that slow old Medea.
Thing is, your own Field Spirits take over as soon as you've got
something up that looks vaguely like a roof and then you're okay,
but till then they're just plain disinterested. You can be anybody's
meat, whether you're on their patch or not.

Some of the nasties were fairly close. I broke up a couple of little
ones with one of the awning stays and swirled them round a bit on
the grass but there were some bigger jobs I didn't fancy tackling on
my own. I turned the car round to point at the hedge and put the
headlight on to main beam. The big chap flattened and streamed
down the other side out of sight, but I knew that wouldn't last for
long. I called to Medea to come out. I said, 'I'll get the thing up, you
do the other stuff. We're getting surrounded here.'

She crawled out with her jumper pulled half up her back and her
hair all tousled. She had a whole bundle of bits in the car, crucifixes,
lightning conductors, old cavalry sabres, that sort of thing. She
started walking round sticking them in the grass and muttering. She

set up an interesting crossfire of emanations, but I couldn't see the effect lasting much longer than the headlights, so I humped into the tent and started straightening things out. The tent was one of those with a built-in groundsheet which are fine when they're up but can be a nuisance if you don't know for sure what you're doing. I got the upright located and stood up and slipped the ridge-pole on top and called to Medea to put the end guy on and a couple of side lines, and after that it wasn't so hectic. With the second upright in place the tent ridge filled out nicely and the Field Spirits—there were a pair of them, husky-looking blighters as far as you could see—went thundering down past us cracking whips and such and the locals just shredded up and blew. The big chap went really amorphous, the last I saw of him he was streaming off into the valley like a snake of thick white mist. He was mad too, he kept looking back at us with his yellow eyes. Somebody was in for a bad night, but as it wasn't us I didn't worry too much.

I'd got pretty hot and sticky, pitching camp is not a thing I go for, though it's usually worth the effort afterwards. Also cloth of gold is great stuff but hell to get pegs into. I bent three all up and had to knock 'em straight again with the mallet, but eventually things got more organized. Medea had unloaded the rest of the stuff from the car, the twin-ring burner and the lamp and the big gas bottle and hanging larder and all that. I'd got the second ridge-pole up and guyed and the tent inner pegged down tight, all we had to do was rig the fly and the bell end and we were there. I lit a cigarette and sat back for a bit to cool off. There was a strip of light now along the top of the downs; the grass shone gold, nearly technicolored. There were a lot of people up there, you could see the priests in their white robes, very distant and sharp and clear. The stones looked good, the lintels dark against the glow, and the incense smoke threading straight up in the still air. Our field was very peaceful now with the ghosts gone, there was a smell of dog roses and hay.

We got started again and rigged the rest of the canvas and I went round and shifted a couple of pegs Medea had put in wrong. Then we got the stuff inside and lit the lamp and it all started looking more like home, beetles and moths blundering in knocking their fool heads against the light. I said, 'I'll get some water,' and Medea said, 'I'll come with you,' so we walked diagonally across the field to where there was a tap on a standpipe and an old enamel bath. There was a notice scrawled on a board saying not to empty detergents into the bath, I suppose because the cattle sometimes used it. The 'S' on the notice was printed the wrong way round, I'd never actually seen that done before. Medea had taken her shoes off, as she walked she kicked up little flurries of embers and dark sparks like jewels. Round the bath the ground was all muddy and churned up and she sloshed through that as well, mud never seemed to stick to her. Not for long, anyway.

While we were filling the water carriers I said, 'We shall have the place to ourselves,' which was a classic case of speaking too soon because a Land Rover came down the farm track nearly at once, towing a great long trailer. The car was full of young Danes, leastways I think they were Danes, they nearly all had fair hair. They all piled out laughing when they saw us and called to help unhitch the trailer because it was too long to swing in through the gate. But I wasn't having any of that. I said to Medea, 'Maybe if they can't get in they'll go off someplace else.' They had a maypole on the trailer, so it looked as if they wanted to be hectic. What with the war starting any minute it didn't seem there was going to be much rest and quiet.

The girls all had hip-length pants and little blouse tops in white and turquoise blue. They got the trailer unhooked and started shoving it about trying to angle it to get it through the gateway. It was a big trailer too, one of those lattice-sided things they used to call a Queen Mary. I took the water carriers from Medea and we walked back to the tent. She said she wanted to get the bed straight and hang our stuff up and get supper on, all of which things she was better at doing by herself. I walked over to see how the Danes were getting on. They were in the far corner of the field by the copse. They'd got the trailer in position and the maypole cleared for lifting. Up close you could see what sort of thing it was, I mean what it was all about. It was garlanded with flowers and green boughs and the tip all painted shiny ochre, lying there against the cloth of gold. They had some transistors stood about, one on the cab roof of the Land Rover, but fortunately the sound wasn't travelling very far.

I said we'd had some trouble with ghosts but they got shooed off and we didn't think they'd be back. They gave me some beer, they had cans and cans of it all strewn about. After I'd drunk it I decided I'd walk on up to the main road and see how the war was getting on.

The light was changing all the time now, which pleased me. The sky had turned a sort of pinky bronze, the sort of colour you get if you hold a candy wrapper up close to your eyes. There was a farmhouse on top of the hill, all little and twisted and built of stone like something in *Snow White*. It had very tall ornate chimney stacks, where the light caught them they burned orange like flames. Somebody had hooked a wire across the farm-track. It had a spring one end to keep it tight and a piece of white rag hung in the middle so you could see it was there. I hoped this meant no other people would come in because I had a proprietary feeling about that field of cloth of gold, having been there several times before. I stepped over the wire and walked on up the track. There was an old outhouse I hadn't really noticed before, it had a vintage Morris motor-car in it which pleased me a lot because I like old machinery. It was a pretty sad-looking Morris though, somebody had dumped a stack of old sacks on the roof and one tyre was flat. I wrote my name and Medea's name in the dust on the bonnet before moving on.

What made the campsite so secluded was the copse on the landward side, beech saplings I think they were. They weren't all that tall, but the lie of the land made it impossible to see much beyond. Once I got to the lane though the first of the castles came rearing back into sight, it wasn't really so far off. It was pretty huge; it always surprised you how big it was, it didn't matter how many times you saw it. There was a slip of moon behind it in the sky, in that light the stone didn't look any more substantial. The whole building looked sort of translucent, as if the light was really pouring through. Some of the windows flamed and reflected like diamonds, others were dark.

There were seven castles really, stretching away in a big curve into the distance, though only the first four were visible; the others were lost in the haze, or occulted one behind the next. The nearest, the big one, was silent though the next in line was working very hard. They had cranes rigged on the battlements and you could see loads of stuff going up and the empty slings swinging back down. That castle was really busy. I think it was prepared for trouble, which it was certainly going to get.

I couldn't see any guns from where I stood so I walked on up to the main road. There was a little wooden structure on the verge like a shop counter standing all on its own where you could buy jam and marmalade sometimes, and pots of cottage-made lemon curd. It was all sold out when I got there though, except for a bunch of flowers which looked pretty sad, and anyway I didn't want them. There was a blue Sellotape tin with some sixpences and florins and ten-shilling pieces in it, so it looked as if they'd had a busy day. I lit a cigarette and wondered where the batteries were, but after a while I saw them down below the road some couple of hundred yards away. There was a gate and nobody seemed to be worrying too much, so I opened it and walked on down. There were a lot of vehicles parked, and a steam traction engine with half-tracks. The guns were big things with angular shields in front of the breeches, I think they were eighteen-pounders. The crews all wore shabby peaked caps and khaki uniforms and queer-looking tightly strapped puttees. They had an officer with them, a captain. He looked harassed and red faced and kept making notes on a clipboard. There was a lot of running about and shouting; a fatigue party was filling sandbags from a big pile of sand dumped to one side of the emplacement, others were farther on down the valley hammering stakes into the ground and stringing coils of barbed wire between. It seemed too there was some trouble with the field telephone; a man with headphones on was cranking a handle and saying, 'Hello, HQ,' but nothing was coming through.

I watched them getting the guns lined up for a time. There were shells stacked about on the grass, big ones with shiny yellow cases. I wanted to see the crews open fire but they didn't seem anywhere near ready so I walked on to the next emplacement, which one of the gunners had said was called the Tudor Lines.

Of the two groups the Tudors seemed the better organized. One party was unloading tall wickerwork cylinders from a cart; another was arranging them as a breastwork in front of the guns, and filling them with earth. The guns were enormous things with ornate brass barrels, all rings and straps and curlicues. The gunners wore dusty brown leather costumes and shoes with big buckles and queer flat shiny leather caps. Behind the emplacement two men were mixing powder in a tub. They were using wooden spades so there wouldn't be a spark, but the whole operation still looked risky to me.

I'd expected some really heavy pieces to be brought to bear and so wasn't too surprised when I saw Mons Meg. A little farther on, though, they had the Dardanelles Gun, which struck me as a bit unnecessary. They had the breech and barrel shored up on stacks of timber and were trying to align them preparatory to screwing them home. They weren't having too much success, which considering the size of the piece wasn't surprising. The gun captain was standing up on top of the barrel trying to juggle it into line by stamping on it. I called up to him that what he needed was a jack, but he was too busy to listen, so I walked back to the twelve-pounder lines to see if I could borrow one. They didn't seem altogether keen. I got one eventually from one of the supply trucks, though I didn't really see why I should bother since it was my rest that was going to be disturbed. Anyway, I lugged it back across the grass and the Tudors were extremely pleased once they got the hang of it. They lifted the muzzle of the gun into line and a dozen started in with crowbars, ramming them into the sockets on the breech and twisting to get the thread started. But that didn't work too well either, as the thread was corroded through being left out in the weather so many years. I left them chipping away at the screw with cold chisels, and greasing it with butter and lard.

The RA captain was studying the nearest enemy position through a little pair of field glasses. He had longish fair hair that had strayed down outside his cap, and he was looking extremely annoyed. I said, 'What you need are some tanks,' but he just looked blank. Then I had another idea and said, 'I mean Land Ships,' but that didn't please him any better. He jumped down from where he was standing and started waving a revolver and shouting something about breaches of security. The revolver was a nasty-looking Webley .38, so I walked over to the nearest of the gun crews in case he started pointing it at me.

It seemed they'd got the land line working because shortly afterwards the order came through to fire. The first gun went off with a big crash and lurched back some distance from the breast-work of sandbags. One of the crew knocked the breech open; out came the shell case sizzling, in went another shell. This time I stood well back behind the line of flight. I found I could watch the shell in the air quite easily; for some reason it seemed to be making a lot of smoke. It was very accurately aimed; I thought it was going to hit the target dead centre, but at the last instant it veered like a side-winder missile and swerved behind the keep. I was expecting a fairly healthy bang over there, but instead the thing fizzled out nearly with a plop in midair. Or rather it didn't exactly fizzle out; it sort of dwindled to a dot and vanished, and the sky shut behind it. Wherever it had gone, it was obviously not going to do much good. I said to one of the gunners, 'At this rate you'll be here all week,' but he seemed very optimistic, he told me they just *hadn't* found the range. They set to at once loading the gun again and I walked back the way I had come as nothing else seemed likely to happen.

The Danes had got the maypole set up; they'd built a bonfire, which was against camp rules, and were making a lot of noise. Dusk was settling, but the flames lit their corner of the field cheerfully. On the crest of the downs the stones stood sharp and ragged like teeth, but nobody was moving up there, it all looked very grey and cold and far away.

Medea had cooked a paella, one of those dried, packeted things. She said, 'About time too,' when I stepped into the tent, and startled ladling the saffron-coloured rice on to a plate. She was wearing a big chunky sweater now, I thought how good she looked. I'd have shut the tent flap because it all looked bleak and miserable out there and it was worrying me, but I knew she'd want to see out so I let it be.

We'd got a bottle of wine, a Beaujolais; she'd put it by the cooker to warm and forgotten it, and it had really got hot. If you've ever tried drinking hot Beaujolais, it burns your throat right through. Also all we'd got was plastic cups, which didn't help the taste, and what with that and the barrage banging away over the wood I started getting annoyed again, though I'd nearly got over the business with the ghosts. I said, 'It's wrong to drink this with paella anyway, you should have got some white,' and she said, if I didn't like it I didn't have to drink it, then she had a big snuffly thing and I had to go over and comfort her though I didn't feel very much like it. However, I really enjoyed stroking her, she was really very nice, and afterwards she finished her paella and we had a cigarette and laughed about the Beaujolais being so hot. She sat a while with her head on my shoulder and watched the last of the light drain away over the downs, then she said, 'I want to go to bed, you shut the tent flap.'

I took the awning stays down and brought them inside and started lacing the canvas shut. She looked good getting undressed, with the greenish-yellow light from the lamp making big shadows on the canvas walls and the moths and bugs all zooming about. The barrage was still going on, I'd nearly got used to it; but just as I was putting the light out there was a big rolling crash louder than the rest, then another, then one you felt through the ground that made that old field of cloth of gold really shake and ripple. She said, 'What's that?' and I said, 'The Dardanelles Gun, they must have got it screwed together.' It didn't look as if we were in for a very peaceful night.

Anyway, the noise died down after a time and you could hear birds hunting and the crickets in the grass. I liked it lying there with her in the sleeping bag, feeling how smooth and firm her hips were. We made love several times, she was good to love, she was cool and she didn't get smelly and all that. Finally I got tired, so I rolled over on my side and went to sleep and she tucked in back of me with her arms round me, very comforting.

It didn't last all that long though, because the next thing I remember was her stepping on my ankle which woke me up very sharply. There was a lot of din going on that I couldn't at first place. I sat up and saw she'd lit the lamp and was trying to deal with all these cats, and boy there were some cats. We had cats like Bishop Hatto had rats. They were everywhere, six or eight were jumping up trying to claw the larder down, others were cleaning the bits off the plates we'd forgotten to wash, they were up to all sorts. It was raining too, the drops pattering and slashing on the canvas and the tent leaking all over, I suppose where Medea had touched it while she was trying to deal with the cats. I started yelling, 'Get rid of these cats, get rid of these damn cats.' I grabbed for a few myself, but it was no good, they just smoked off through your fingers worse than those old ghosts. Then I saw there were some three or four starting to drag the garbage bag out under the tent flap, so I shied something at them that turned out to be her handbag, bits and pieces flew all over. Then we really had a row. She had her arms full of cats but you could see she wasn't really trying to push them out, not all that hard. I said, 'They are your damn cats and you could get rid of them if you wanted.' Anyway, she started in crying again, really crying; then she started pulling the tent flap undone, she said she'd sleep in the car or outside someplace because I didn't want her either. Then the field guns let fly again over the hill and it was hell in there, I tell you. So I let her go which was a pity, she was only wearing a sweater and nothing below the waist and she looked really nice. I lay back and tried to get some rest in between the ground shaking. I remember thinking, 'She's got to be taught a lesson, she brought those damn cats on purpose.' I was still plenty mad.

I think I dozed for a time; anyway, when I sat up the lamp was still burning, hanging where she'd left it, and the rain was thudding down and the tent was empty. I felt really bad about her, I mean having sent her out in the rain and all. I got up and put some things on and started calling her, but there was no answer. Then I remembered she'd said she would go to the car. I ran out to fetch her but she wasn't there.

I really got upset then. I was mad with myself for going to sleep, it seemed most heartless under the circumstances. I ran down to the stile where the ghosts had been and called again, but there was nothing, only the wind. There were some big trees in the next field, really big, you could hear the wind boom in the branches. The flashes from the field guns kept lighting the sky, but they weren't bright enough to see by. Rain was trickling down my back and I was getting soaked. I looked back up the field and you could see the lamp on and the light glowing through the canvas, it all looked homely and warm, it was terrible she wasn't there.

I went back and put a blanket round my shoulders and sat shivering, listening to the rain. I must have got really confused then because I remember thinking I'd sent my cat out in the dark and it wasn't her fault at all, just me and my bit of bad temper. But there was nothing to be done, once a cat's gone it's gone in a big way, as I expect most of you know. I lay on my side after a bit. I kept thinking, 'Come back, Medea, it's all right,' and trying to set up a sort of mental beacon for her to home on if she couldn't see the light. I didn't think I'd sleep, but eventually I dozed off again.

I was warmer when I opened my eyes. I lay there for a bit feeling good, thinking about the breakfast we were going to have; cereals and marmalade and toast, and oatcakes and Scottish cheese. Then I remembered and sat up feeling terrible. I went out to the car, but there was no sign of Medea, the whole field was still and empty and the dew all grey on the grass and rough.

I put the kettle on and made some coffee, but I didn't want it, with her things all scattered about like that it just wasn't the same. I thought I'd better take the car and go and look for her, though really I had no idea where to start. I got in anyway and started the engine and I was just turning round when one of the Danish boys came over shouting and waving his arms. He said a girl had cut her throat in the night and would I come and see. I asked was it Medea, that was how bad I was feeling. He said no it wasn't, but I still had to see.

I looked across to the corner of the field. It was still shadowy there, the ground being low and beneath the spinney. The little tent in which it had happened, being soaking wet, had taken up some rather nasty colour from the groundsheet, which colour was staining upward in fans across the canvas. They had lit lamps inside, which made the whole effect somewhat worse, they should have known better. I said, 'I don't want to see a thing like that,' and drove away.

I'd forgotten the wire across the track till I drove into it, giving the car a scrape across the paintwork. Anyway, I didn't stop, I was too

concerned about Medea. There was no sign of her in the lane, so I
drove up to the main road. It was broad and white and empty. There
was a Shell filling station to one side, but it was shut. I drove the car
to the batteries, turned into the gateway and got out. I stood looking
over the gate. They'd had more success than I had expected. The
nearest castle was a ruin, great shells of wall pierced and fretted
with windows and high doorways, all still and vague in the early
light. The other castles were still fighting; I saw some nasty-looking
stuff drift over, like soft, dark flak.

The eighteen-pounder emplacement was a mess. The grass had
been churned into mud and the guns were filthy, all streaked with
black and big chunks of mud sticking to the wheels. There were
shell cases scattered everywhere and the crews were sitting about in
greatcoats looking huddled and miserable. A man with a bandage
round his head was cooking sausages over a stick fire, but they none
of them looked as if they wanted to eat.

The captain had got his Blighty one sometime during the night;
they had him on a stretcher, tucked round with bright red blankets,
and there were a couple of nurses. He was propped up with a
greatcoat for a pillow, he had a cigarette in his hand and was
shouting something about getting more sandbags, but I didn't like
his colour. His cap was off; I saw his hair was grey rather than
yellow. I asked him if he'd seen Medea and he said no, nobody had
come that way.

I went on to the Tudor Lines but nothing was moving there at all.
The fires were out, and the big cannon strewed anyways across the
hill. One was cocked up on its carriage pointing at the sky, and the
muzzle and barrel all smashed. Round it the grass was black and
trampled and there was a smell of burned powder, like fireworks.

They had some little gay-striped tents, each one topped with a
pennant, but I didn't feel much like looking inside. I walked back
the way I had come. As I passed the captain, he pushed himself up
on one elbow. He shouted, 'They were going to send us naval
support. They promised us naval support.' Then he started to cry,
big tears rolling down his face. I felt very sorry for him, but there
was nothing I could do.

I got back into the car and drove off. I thought, I don't know why,
that she'd probably gone down to the coast, to one of the bays.
Trouble was there were several bays, I had to look into them all. I
drove to four but they were all the same, there were stands of gorse

and bracken, drystone walls, little farmhouses and barns with tractors parked outside. The sea was pale silver, very cold looking, and it was still only halfway light.

The fifth bay was big, with cliffs of crumbling grey clay. I drove the car as near the edge as I dared, got out and looked over. I saw her at once, lying down there tiny as a moth. Beyond her the beach was a wide half-moon stretching to the sea. The sea was still, nearly unrippling. There were big mirror-streaks of swell moving in, lazy and calm; and out in the bay a ship of the line was practising at the great guns. The broadsides rolled out fleecy clouds of smoke; the noise of the barrage came in dim across the water, like thunder a long way off.

I started climbing down the cliff. There were gullies, crisscrossing, and the paths were very slippy. I reached the beach near where a little stream ran out under a plank bridge, soaked itself away across the pebbles. Beside the bridge was an old concrete pillbox. The beach was littered, there were sprags of wire, bits of old dried seaweed and half-bricks and broken bottles and big boulders that had tumbled down out of the cliffs. Nearer the water the sand was smoother, firm and grey. I kept wondering what Medea was doing there anyway because it was none too warm and she was wearing this little white cotton bikini, very small. I called her but she didn't answer.

I reached her, squatted down. She was lying on her side, back turned to the sea and her head on her arm. I touched her ankle. She was very light, I think she must have been hollow. When I touched her her whole figure moved, sand and bits of dark grey shale started trickling into the depression where her hip had been. I remembered the whole thing then, about snipping her out of a calendar page and pasting her down so carefully. I was really upset because it was all my fault, I'd just stopped thinking of her in the round and that had been enough. Though what with the war and all I suppose it was understandable.

Anyway, she was still three-dimensional, which was something. I started moving round her in a rather ungentlemanly way, being curious to see what she looked like from behind. Which was my second big mistake because I took my mind off her again just for a second and it gave her a chance to flatten right out. She was supported at the back by a framework of scantling, very neatly made. The wood was new, pinkish yellow, and two struts were pushed down into the sand to keep her firm. I started getting really depressed then because Medea hadn't been the sort of exercise you can do all that often; I mean, these days even good calendar pages aren't all that easy to come by.

The frigate seemed to be drifting in closer to the cliffs, I looked up and she was getting really vast. She was turning too, showing the black and amber stripes along her side and her row of gunports. It wasn't a good place to stop but I was still worried about Medea. I thought for a bit but I couldn't see how I was going to take her with me, she was too big to go in the car even with the hood down and naturally being a soft-top there was no roof-rack. It seemed I was just going to have to leave her there, which was a great pity on top of all that had happened. It was raining again, a thin, misty drizzle, I could see her buckling pretty soon and getting spoiled.

In the end I turned her round so at least she was facing the sea, and propped her with a couple of stones. I ran back the way I had come. As I got to the top of the path there was a boom and the whole cliff shook. I looked back and saw shingle and bits of rock fly up in the air. I was really sorry then, I felt I should have tried to take her with me instead of leaving her to get blown apart. I should have guessed they'd use her as a mark.

I sat in the car for a bit and thought things through. The first problem was the tent, which had of course been hers. Also there were her things, her clothes and all the rest. It seemed probable the whole lot would have vanished, leaving my gear just strewn about on the grass. I sincerely hoped so, as I wasn't relishing the prospect of burning the camp. Killing a pretty woman now and then is all very well but getting rid of her possessions afterwards is quite another thing. However, there was plainly only one answer, I had to go and find out. The drizzle had misted the windscreen so that I couldn't see, I started the wipers and drove that damn old car away up the hill.

Weihnachtsabend

1

The big car moved slowly, nosing its way along narrowing lanes. Here, beyond the little market town of Wilton, the snow lay thicker. Trees and bushes loomed in the headlights, coated with driven white. The tail of the Mercedes wagged slightly, steadied. Mainwaring heard the chauffeur swear under his breath. The link had been left live.

Dials let into the seatback recorded the vehicle's mechanical well-being: oil pressure, temperature, revs, k.p.h. Lights from the repeater glowed softly on his companion's face. She moved, restlessly; he saw the swing of yellow hair. He turned slightly. She was wearing a neat, brief kilt, heavy boots. Her legs were excellent.

He clicked the dial lights off. He said, 'Not much farther.'

He wondered if she was aware of the open link. He said, 'First time down?'

She nodded in the dark. She said, 'I was a bit overwhelmed.'

Wilton Great House sprawled across a hilltop five miles or more beyond the town. The car drove for some distance beside the wall that fringed the estate. The perimeter defences had been strengthened since Mainwaring's last visit. Watchtowers reared at intervals; the wall itself has been topped by multiple strands of wire.

The lodge gates were commanded by two new stone pillboxes. The Merc edged between them, stopped. On the road from London the snow had eased; now big flakes drifted again, lit by the headlights. Somewhere, orders were barked.

A man stepped forward, tapped at the window. Mainwaring

buttoned it open. He saw a GFP armband, a hip holster with the flap tucked back. He said, 'Good evening, Captain.'

'*Guten Abend, mein Herr. Ihre Ausweiskarte?*'

Cold air gusted against Mainwaring's cheek. He passed across his identity card and security clearance, He said, '*Richard Mainwaring. Die rechte Hand des Gesandten. Fräulein Hunter, von meiner Abteilung.*'

A torch flashed over the papers, dazzled into his eyes, moved to examine the girl. She sat stiffly, staring ahead. Beyond the security officer Mainwaring made out two steel-helmeted troopers, automatics slung. In front of him the wipers clicked steadily.

The GFP man stepped back. He said, '*Ihre Ausweis wird in einer Woche ablaufen. Erneuen Sie Ihre Karte.*'

Mainwaring said, '*Vielen Dank, Herr Haputmann. Frohe Weihnachten.*'

The man saluted stiffly, unclipped a walkie-talkie from his belt. A pause, and the gates swung back. The Merc creamed through. Mainwaring said, '*Bastard . . .*'

She said, 'Is it always like this?'

He said, 'They're tightening up all round.'

She pulled her coat round her shoulders. She said, 'Frankly, I find it a bit scary.'

He said, 'Just the Minister taking care of his guests.'

Wilton stood in open downland set with great trees. Hans negotiated a bend, carefully, drove beneath half-seen branches. The wind moaned, zipping round a quarterlight. It was as if the car butted into a black tunnel, full of swirling pale flakes. He thought he saw her shiver. He said, 'Soon be there.'

The headlamps lit a rolling expanse of snow. Posts, buried nearly to their tops, marked the drive. Another bend, and the house showed ahead. The car lights swept across a facade of mullioned windows, crenellated towers. Hard for the uninitiated to guess, staring at the skilfully weathered stone, that the shell of the place was of reinforced concrete. The car swung right with a crunching of unseen gravel, and stopped. The ignition repeater glowed on the seatback.

Mainwaring said, 'Thank you, Hans. Nice drive.'

Hans said, 'My pleasure, sir.'

She flicked her hair free, picked up her handbag. He held the door for her. He said, 'OK, Diane?'

She shrugged. She said, 'Yes. I'm a bit silly sometimes.' She squeezed his hand, briefly. She said, 'I'm glad you'll be here. Somebody to rely on.'

Mainwaring lay back on the bed and stared at the ceiling. Inside as well as out, Wilton was a triumph of art over nature. Here, in the Tudor wing where most of the guests were housed, walls and ceilings were of wavy plaster framed by heavy oak beams. He turned his head. The room was dominated by a fireplace of yellow Ham stone; on the overmantel, carved in bold relief, the *Hakenkreuz* was flanked by the lion and eagle emblems of the Two Empires. A fire burned in the wrought-iron basket; the logs glowed cheerfully, casting wavering warm reflections across the ceiling. Beside the bed a bookshelf offered required reading: the Fuehrer's official biography, Shirer's *Rise of the Third Reich*, Cummings' monumental *Churchill: the Trial of Decadence*. There were a nicely bound set of Buchan novels, some Kiplings, a Shakespeare, a complete Wilde. A side table carried a stack of current magazines: *Connoisseur, The Field, Der Spiegel, Paris Match*. There was a washstand, its rail hung with dark blue towels; in the corner of the room were the doors to the bathroom and wardrobe, in which a servant had already neatly disposed his clothes.

He stubbed his cigarette, lit another. He swung his legs off the bed, poured himself a whisky. From the grounds, faintly, came voices, snatches of laughter. He heard the crash of a pistol, the rattle of an automatic. He walked to the window, pushed the curtain aside. Snow was still falling, drifting silently from the black sky; but the firing pits beside the big house were brightly lit. He watched the figures move and bunch for a while, let the curtain fall. He sat by the fire, shoulders hunched, staring into the flames. He was remembering the trip through London; the flags hanging limp over Whitehall, slow, jerking movement of traffic, the light tanks drawn up outside St. James. The Kensington Road had been crowded, traffic edging and hooting; the vast frontage of Harrod's looked grim and Oriental against the louring sky. He frowned, remembering the call he had had before leaving the Ministry.

Kosowicz had been the name. From *Time International*; or so he had claimed. He'd refused twice to speak to him; but Kosowicz had been insistent. In the end, he'd asked his secretary to put him through.

Kosowicz had sounded very American. He said, 'Mr Mainwaring, I'd like to arrange a personal interview with your Minister.'

'I'm afraid that's out of the question. I must also point out that this communication is extremely irregular.'

Kosowicz said, 'What do I take that as, sir? A warning, or a threat?'

Mainwaring said carefully, 'It was neither. I merely observed that proper channels of approach do exist.'

Kosowicz said, 'Uh-huh. Mr. Mainwaring, what's the truth behind this rumour that Action Groups are being moved into Moscow?'

Mainwaring said, 'Deputy Fuehrer Hess has already issued a statement on the situation. I can see that you're supplied with a copy.'

The phone said, 'I have it before me. Mr. Mainwaring, what are you people trying to set up? Another Warsaw?'

Mainwaring said, 'I'm afraid I can't comment further, Mr. Kosowicz. The Deputy Fuehrer deplored the necessity of force. The *Einsatzgruppen* have been alerted; at this time, that is all. They will be used if necessary to disperse militants. As of this moment, the need has not arisen.'

Kosowicz shifted his ground. 'You mentioned the Deputy Fuehrer, sir. I hear there was another bomb attempt two nights ago, can you comment on this?'

Mainwaring tightened his knuckles on the handset. He said, 'I'm afraid you've been misinformed. We know nothing of any such incident.'

The phone was silent for a moment. Then he said, 'Can I take your denial as official?'

Mainwaring said, 'This is not an official conversation. I'm not empowered to issue statements in any respect.'

The phone said, 'Yeah, channels do exist. Mr. Mainwaring, thanks for your time.'

Mainwaring said, 'Goodbye,' He put the handset down, sat staring at it. After a while he lit a cigarette.

Outside the windows of the Ministry the snow still fell, a dark whirl and dance against the sky. His tea, when he came to drink it, was half cold.

The fire crackled and shifted. He poured himself another whisky, sat back. Before leaving for Wilton, he'd lunched with Winsby-Walker from Productivity. Winsby-Walker made it his business to know everything; but had known nothing of a correspondent called

Kosowicz. He thought, 'I should have checked with Security.' But then, Security would have checked with him.

He sat up, looked at his watch. The noise from the ranges had diminished. He turned his mind with a deliberate effort into another channel. The new thoughts brought no more comfort. Last Christmas he had spent with his mother; now, that couldn't happen again. He remembered other Christmases, back across the years. Once, to the child unknowing, they had been gay affairs of crackers and toys. He remembered the scent and texture of pine branches, closeness of candlelight; and books read by torchlight under the sheets, the hard angles of the filled pillowslip, heavy at the foot of the bed. Then, he had been complete; only later, slowly, had come the knowledge of failure. And with it, loneliness. He thought, 'She wanted to see me settled. It didn't seem much to ask.'

The Scotch was making him maudlin. He drained the glass, walked through to the bathroom. He stripped, and showered. Towelling himself, he thought, 'Richard Mainwaring, Personal Assistant to the British Minister of Liaison.' Aloud he said, 'One must remember the compensations.'

He dressed, lathered his face and began to shave. He thought, 'Thirty-five is the exact middle of one's life.' He was remembering another time with the girl Diane when just for a little while some magic had interposed. Now, the affair was never mentioned between them. Because of James. Always of course, there is a James.

He towelled his face, applied aftershave. Despite himself, his mind had drifted back to the phone call. One fact was certain: there had been a major security spillage. Somebody somewhere had supplied Kosowicz with closely guarded information. That same someone, presumably, had supplied a list of ex-directory lines. He frowned, grappling with the problem. One country, and one only, opposed the two empires with gigantic, latent strength. To that country had shifted the focus of Semitic nationalism. And Kosowicz had been an American.

He thought, 'Freedom, schmeedom. Democracy is Jew-shaped.' He frowned again, fingering his face. It didn't alter the salient fact. The tip-off had come from the Freedom Front; and he had been contacted, however obliquely. Now, he had become an accessory; the thought had been nagging at the back of his brain all day.

He wondered what they could want of him. There was a rumour—a nasty rumour—that you never found out. Not till the end, till you'd done whatever was required from you. They were untiring, deadly and subtle. He hadn't run squalling to Security at the first hint of danger; but that would have been allowed for. Every turn and twist would have been allowed for.

Every squirm on the hook.

He grunted, angry with himself. Fear was half their strength. He buttoned his shirt, remembering the guards at the gates, the wire and pillboxes. Here, of all places, nothing could reach him. For a few days he could forget the whole affair. He said aloud, 'Anyway, I don't even matter. I'm not important.' The thought cheered him, nearly.

He clicked the light off, walked through to his room, closed the door behind him. He crossed to the bed and stood quite still, staring at the bookshelf. Between Shirer and the Churchill tome there rested a third slim volume. He reached to touch the spine, delicately; read the author's name, Geissler, and the title, *Toward Humanity*. Below the title, like a topless Cross of Lorraine, were the twin linked 'F's' of the Freedom Front.

Ten minutes ago the book hadn't been there.

He walked to the door. The corridor beyond was deserted. From somewhere in the house, faintly, came music: *Till Eulenspiegel*. There were no nearer sounds. He closed the door again, locked it. Turned back and saw the wardrobe stood slightly ajar.

His case still lay on the side table. He crossed to it, took out the Lüger. The feel of the heavy pistol was comforting. He pushed the clip home, thumbed the safety forward, chambered a round. The breech closed with a hard snap. He walked to the wardrobe, shoved the door wide with his foot.

Nothing there.

He let his held breath escape with a little hiss. He pressed the clip release, ejected the cartridge, laid the gun on the bed. He stood again looking at the shelf. He thought, 'I must have been mistaken.'

He took the book down, carefully. Geissler had been banned since publication in every province of the two empires; Mainwaring himself had never even seen a copy. He squatted on the edge of the bed, opened it at random.

> *The doctrine of Aryan co-ancestry, seized on so eagerly by the English middle classes, had the superficial reasonableness of most theories ultimately traceable to Rosenberg. Churchill's answer in one sense, had already been made: but Chamberlain, and the country, turned to Hess. . . .*

The Cologne settlement, though seeming to offer hope of security to Jews already domiciled in Britain, in fact paved the way for campaigns of intimidation and extortion similar to those already undertaken in history, notably by King John. The comparison is not unapt; for the English bourgeoisie, *anxious to construct a rationale, discovered many unassailable precedents. A true Sign of the Times, almost certainly, was the resurgence of interest in the novels of Sir Walter Scott. By 1942 the lesson had been learned on both sides; and the Star of David was a common sight on the streets of most British cities.*

The wind rose momentarily in a long wail, shaking the window casement. Mainwaring glanced up, turned his attention back to the book. He leafed through several pages.

In 1940, her Expeditionary Force shattered, her allies quiescent or defeated, the island truly stood alone. Her proletariat, bedevilled by bad leadership, weakened by a gigantic depression, was effectively without a voice. Her aristocracy, like their Junker *counterparts, embraced coldly what could no longer be ignored; while after the Whitehall* Putsch *the Cabinet was reduced to the status of an Executive Council. . . .*

The knock at the door made him start, guiltily. He pushed the book away. He said, 'Who's that?'

She said, 'Me. Richard, aren't you ready?'

He said, 'Just a minute.' He stared at the book, then placed it back on the shelf. He thought, 'That at least wouldn't be expected.' He slipped the Lüger into his case and closed it. Then he went to the door.

She was wearing a lacy black dress. Her shoulders were bare; her hair, worn loose, had been brushed till it gleamed. He stared at her a moment, stupidly. Then he said, 'Please come in.'

She said, 'I was starting to wonder. . . . Are you all right?'

'Yes. Yes, of course.'

She said, 'You look as if you've seen a ghost.'

He smiled. He said, 'I expect I was taken aback. Those Aryan good looks.'

She grinned at him. She said, 'I'm half Irish, half English, half Scandinavian. If you have to know.'

'That doesn't add up.'

She said, 'Neither do I, most of the time.'

'Drink?'

'Just a little one. We shall be late.'

He said, 'It's not very formal tonight.' He turned away, fiddling with his tie.

She sipped her drink, pointed her foot, scuffed her toe on the carpet. She said, 'I expect you've been to a lot of house parties.'

He said, 'One or two.'

She said, 'Richard, are they . . . ?'

'Are they what?'

She said, 'I don't know. You can't help hearing things.'

He said, 'You'll be all right. One's very much like the next.'

She said, 'Are you honestly okay?'

'Sure.'

She said, 'You're all thumbs. Here, let me.' She reached up, knotted deftly. Her eyes searched his face for a moment, moving in little shifts and changes of direction. She said, 'There. I think you just need looking after.'

He said carefully, 'How's James?'

She stared a moment longer. She said, 'I don't know. He's in Nairobi. I haven't seen him for months.'

He said, 'I am a bit nervous, actually.'

'Why?'

He said, 'Escorting a rather lovely blonde.'

She tossed her head, and laughed. She said, 'You need a drink as well then.'

He poured whisky, said, 'Cheers.' The book, now, seemed to be burning into his shoulderblades.

She said, 'As a matter of fact, you're looking rather fetching yourself.'

He thought, 'This is the night when all things come together. There should be a word for it.' Then he remembered about *Till Eulenspiegel*.

She said, 'We'd honestly better go down.'

Lights gleamed in the Great Hall, reflecting from polished boards, dark linenfold panelling. At the nearer end of the chamber a huge fire burned. Beneath the minstrels' gallery long tables had been set. Informal or not, they shone with glass and silverware. Candles glowed amid wreaths of dark evergreen; beside each place was a rolled crimson napkin.

In the middle of the Hall, its tip brushing the coffered ceiling, stood a Christmas tree. Its branches were hung with apples, baskets of sweets, red paper roses; at its base were piled gifts in gay-striped wrappers. Round the tree folk stood in groups, chatting and laughing. Richard saw Müller, the Defence Minister, with a striking-looking blonde he took to be his wife; beside them was a tall, monocled man who was something or other in Security. There was a group of GSP officers in their dark, neat uniforms, beyond them half a dozen Liaison people. He saw Hans the chauffeur standing head bent, nodding intently, smiling at some remark; and thought as he had thought before, how he looked like a big, handsome ox.

Diane had paused in the doorway, and linked her arm through his. But the Minister had already seen them. He came weaving through the crowd, a glass in his hand. He was wearing tight black trews, a dark blue roll-neck shirt. He looked happy and relaxed. He said, 'Richard. And my dear Miss Hunter. We'd nearly given you up for lost. After all, Hans Trapp is about. Now, some drinks. And come, do come; please join my friends. Over here, where it is warm.'

She said, 'Who's Hans Trapp?'

Mainwaring said, 'You'll find out in a bit.'

A little later the Minister said, 'Ladies and gentlemen, I think we may be seated.'

The meal was superb, the wine abundant. By the time the brandy was served Richard found himself talking more easily, and the Geissler copy pushed nearly to the back of his mind. The traditional toasts—King and Fuehrer, the provinces, the Two Empires—were drunk; then the Minister clapped his hands for quiet. 'My friends,' he said, 'tonight, this special night when we can all mix so freely, is *Weihnachtsabend*. It means, I suppose, many things to the many of us here. But let us remember, first and foremost, that this is the night of the children. Your children, who have come with you to share part at least of this very special Christmas.'

He paused. 'Already,' he said, 'they have been called from their crèche; soon, they will be with us. Let me show them to you.' He nodded; at the gesture servants wheeled forward a heavy, ornate box. A drape was twitched aside, revealing the grey surface of a big TV screen. Simultaneously, the lamps that lit the Hall began to dim. Diane turned to Mainwaring, frowning; he touched her hand, gently, and shook his head.

Save for the firelight, the Hall was now nearly dark. The candles guttered in their wreaths, flames stirring in some draught; in the hush, the droning of the wind round the great facade of the place was once more audible. The lights would be out, now, all over the house.

'For some of you,' said the Minister, this is your first visit here, For you, I will explain.

'On *Weihnachtsabend* all ghosts and goblins walk. The demon Hans Trapp is abroad; his face is black and terrible, his clothing the skins of bears. Against him comes the Lightbringer, the Spirit of Christmas. Some call her Lucia Queen, some *Das Christkind*. See her now.'

The screen lit up.

She moved slowly, like a sleepwalker. She was slender, and robed in white. Her ashen hair tumbled round her shoulders; above her head glowed a diadem of burning tapers. Behind her trod the Star Boys with their wands and tinsel robes; behind again came a little group of children. They ranged in age from eight- and nine-year-olds to toddlers. They gripped each other's hands, apprehensively, setting feet in line like cats, darting terrified glances at the shadows to either side.

'They lie in darkness, waiting,' said the Minister softly. 'Their nurses have left them. If they cry out, there is none to hear. So they do not cry out. And one by one she has called them. They see her light pass beneath the door; and they must rise and follow. Here, where we sit, is warmth. Here is safety. Their gifts are waiting; to reach them they must run the gauntlet of the dark.'

The camera angle changed. Now they were watching the procession from above. The Lucia Queen stepped steadily; the shadows she cast leaped and flickered on panelled walls.

'They are in the Long Gallery now,' said the Minister, 'almost directly above us. They must not falter, they must not look back. Somewhere, Hans Trapp is hiding. From Hans, only *Das Christkind* can protect them. See how close they bunch behind her light!'

A howling began, like the crying of a wolf. In part it seemed to come from the screen, in part to echo through the Hall itself. The *Christkind* turned, raising her arms; the howling split into a many-voiced cadence, died to a mutter. In its place came a distant huge thudding, like the beating of a drum.

Diane said abruptly, 'I don't find this particularly funny.'

Mainwaring said, 'It isn't supposed to be. Shh.'

The Minister said evenly, 'The Aryan child must know, from earliest years, the darkness that surrounds him. He must learn to fear, and to overcome that fear. He must learn to be strong. The Two Empires were not built by weakness; weakness will not sustain them. There is no place for it. This in part your children already know. The house is big, and dark; but they will win through to the light. They fight as the Empires once fought. For their birthright.'

The shot changed again, showed a wide, sweeping staircase. The head of the little procession appeared, began to descend. 'Now, where is our friend Hans?' said the Minister. '*Ah* . . .'

Her grip tightened convulsively on Mainwaring's arm. A black-smeared face loomed at the screen. The bogey snarled, clawing at the camera; then turned, loped swiftly towards the staircase. The children shrieked, and bunched; instantly the air was wild with din. Grotesque figures capered and leaped; hands grabbed, clutching. The column was buffeted and swirled; Mainwaring saw a child bowled completely over. The screaming reached a high pitch of terror; and the *Christkind* turned, arms once more raised. The goblins and werethings backed away, growling, into shadow; the slow march was resumed.

The Minister said, 'They are nearly here. And they are good children, worthy of their race. Prepare the tree.'

Servants ran forward with tapers to light the many candles. The tree sprang from gloom, glinting, black-green; and Mainwaring thought for the first time what a dark thing it was, although it blazed with light.

The big doors at the end of the Hall were flung back; and the children came tumbling through. Tear-stained and sobbing they were, some bruised; but all, before they ran to the tree, stopped, made obeisance to the strange creature who had brought them through the dark. Then the crown was lifted, the tapers extinguished; and Lucia Queen became a child like the rest, a slim, barefooted girl in a gauzy white dress.

The Minister rose, laughing, 'Now,' he said, 'music, and some more wine. Hans Trapp is dead. My friends, one and all, and children; *frohe Weihnachten!*'

Diane said, 'Excuse me a moment.'

Mainwaring turned. He said, 'Are you all right?'

She said, 'I'm just going to get rid of a certain taste.'

He watched her go, concernedly; and the Minister had his arm, was talking. 'Excellent, Richard.' he said. 'It has gone excellently so far, don't you think?'

Richard said, 'Excellently, sir.'

'Good, good. Eh, Heidi, Erna . . . and Frederick, is it Frederick? What have you got there? Oh, very fine . . .' He steered Mainwaring away, still with his fingers tucked beneath his elbow. Squeals of joy sounded, somebody had discovered a sled, tucked away behind the tree. The Minister said, 'Look at them; how happy they are now. I would like children, Richard. Children of my own. Sometimes I think I have given too much. . . . Still, the opportunity remains. I am younger than you, do you realize that? This is the Age of Youth.'

Mainwaring said, 'I wish the Minister every happiness.'

'Richard, Richard, you must learn not to be so very correct at all times. Unbend a little, you are too aware of dignity. You are my friend. I trust you; above all others, I trust you. Do you realize this?'

Richard said, 'Thank you, sir. I do.'

The Minister seemed bubbling over with some inner pleasure. He said, 'Richard, come with me. Just for a moment. I have prepared a special gift for you. I won't keep you from the party very long.'

Mainwaring followed, drawn as ever by the curious dynamism of the man. The Minister ducked through an arched doorway, turned right and left, descended a narrow flight of stairs. At the bottom the way was barred by a door of plain grey steel. The Minister pressed his palm flat to a sensor plate; a click, the whine of some mechanism, and the door swung inward. Beyond was a further flight of concrete steps, lit by a single lamp in a heavy well-glass. Chilly air blew upward. Mainwaring realized, with something approaching a shock, they had entered part of the bunker system that honeycombed the ground beneath Wilson.

The Minister hurried ahead of him, palmed a further door. He said, 'Toys, Richard. All toys. But they amuse me.' Then, catching sight of Mainwaring's face. 'Come, man, come! You are more nervous than the children, frightened of poor old Hans!'

The door gave on to a darkened space. There was a heavy, sweetish smell that Mainwaring, for a whirling moment, couldn't place. His companion propelled him forward, gently. He resisted, pressing back; and the Minister's arm shot by him. A click, and the place was flooded with light. He saw a wide, low area, also concrete-built. To one side, already polished and gleaming, stood the Mercedes, next to it the Minister's private Porsche. There were a couple of Volkswagens, a Ford Executive; and in the farthest corner a vision in glinting white. A Lamborghini. They had emerged in the garage underneath the house.

The Minister said, 'My private short cut.' He walked forward to the Lamborghini, stood running his fingers across the low, broad bonnet. He said, 'Look at her, Richard. Here, sit in. Isn't she a beauty? Isn't she fine?'

Mainwaring said, 'She certainly is.'

'You like her?'

Mainwaring smiled. He said, 'Very much, sir. Who wouldn't?'

The Minister said, 'Good, I'm so pleased. Richard, I'm upgrading you. She's yours. Enjoy her.'

Mainwaring stared.

The Minister said, 'Here, man. Don't look like that, like a fish. Here, see. Logbook, your keys. All entered up, finished.' He gripped Mainwaring's shoulders, swung him round laughing. He said, 'You've worked well for me. The Two Empires don't forget their good friends, their servants.'

Mainwaring said, 'I'm deeply honoured, sir.'

'Don't be honoured. You're still being formal. Richard . . .'

'Sir?'

The Minister said, 'Stay by me. Stay by me. Up there . . . they don't understand. But we understand . . . eh? These are difficult times. We must be together, always together. Kingdom and Reich. Apart*. . . we could be destroyed.' He turned away, placed clenched hands on the roof of the car. He said, 'Here, all this. Jewry, the Americans . . . Capitalism. They must stay afraid. Nobody fears an Empire divided. It would fall!'

Mainwaring said, 'I'll do my best, sir. We all will.'

The Minister said, 'I know, I know. But, Richard, this afternoon. I was playing with swords. Silly little swords.'

Mainwaring thought, 'I know how he keeps me. I can see the mechanism. But I mustn't imagine I know the entire truth.'

The Minister turned back, as if in pain. He said, 'Strength is Right. It has to be. But Hess . . .'

Mainwaring said slowly, 'We've tried before, sir . . .'

The Minister slammed his fist on to metal. He said, 'Richard, don't you see? It wasn't us. Not this time. It was his own people. Baumann, von Thaden . . . I can't tell. He's an old man, he doesn't matter any more. It's an idea they want to kill, Hess is an idea. Do you understand? It's *Lebensraum*. Again. . . . Half the world isn't enough.'

He straightened. He said, 'The worm, in the apple. It gnaws,

gnaws. . . . But we are Liaison. We matter, so much. Richard, be my eyes. Be my ears.'

Mainwaring stayed silent, thinking about the book in his room; and the Minister once more took his arm. He said, 'The shadows, Richard. They were never closer. Well might we teach our children to fear the dark. But . . . not in our time. Eh? Not for us. There is life, and hope. So much we can do. . . .'

Mainwaring thought, 'Maybe it's the wine I drank. I'm being pressed too hard.' A dull, queer mood, almost of indifference, had fallen on him. He followed his Minister without complaint, back through the bunker complex, up to where the great fire, and the tapers on the tree burned low. He heard the singing mixed with the wind-voice, watched the children rock heavy-eyes, carolling sleep. The house seemed winding down, to rest; and she had gone, of course. He sat in a corner and drank wine and brooded, watched the Minister move from group to group until he too was gone, the Hall nearly empty and the servants clearing away.

He found his own self, his inner self, dozing at last as it dozed at each day's end. Tiredness, as ever, had come like a benison. He rose carefully, walked to the door. He thought, 'I shan't be missed here,' Shutters closed, in his head.

He found his key, unlocked his room. He thought, 'Now, she will be waiting. Like all the letters that never came, the phones that never rang.' He opened the door.

She said, 'What kept you?'

He closed the door behind him, quietly. The fire crackled in the little room, the curtains were drawn against the night. She sat by the hearth, barefooted, still in her party dress. Beside her on the carpet were glasses, an ashtray with half-smoked stubs. One lamp was burning; in the warm light her eyes were huge and dark.

He looked across to the bookshelf. The Geissler stood where he had left it. He said, 'How did you get in?'

She chuckled. She said, 'There was a spare key on the back of the door. Didn't you see me steal it?'

He walked toward her, stood looking down. He thought. 'Adding another fragment to the puzzle. Too much, too complicated.'

She said, 'Are you angry?'

He said, 'No.'

She patted the floor. She said gently, 'Please, Richard. Don't be cross.'

He sat, slowly, watching her.

She said, 'Drink?' He didn't answer. She poured one anyway. She said, 'What were you doing all this time? I thought you'd be up hours ago.'

He said, 'I was talking to the Minister.'

She traced a pattern on the rug with her forefinger. Her hair fell forward, golden and heavy, baring the nape of her neck. She said, 'I'm sorry about earlier on. I was stupid. I think I was a bit scared too.'

He drank, slowly. He felt like a run-down machine. Hell to have to start thinking again at this time of night. He said, 'What were you doing?'

She watched up at him. Her eyes were candid. She said, 'Sitting here. listening to the wind.'

He said, 'That couldn't have been much fun.'

She shook her head, slowly, eyes fixed on his face. She said softly. 'You don't know me at all.'

He was quiet again. She said, 'You don't believe in me, do you?'

He thought, 'You need understanding. You're different from the rest; and I'm selling myself short.' Aloud he said, 'No.'

She put the glass down, smiled, took his glass away. She hotched towards him across the rug, slid her arm round his neck. She said, 'I was thinking about you. Making my mind up.' She kissed him. He felt her tongue pushing, opened his lips. She said, '*Mmm . . .*' She sat back a little, smiling, She said, 'Do you mind?'

'No.'

She pressed a strand of hair across her mouth, parted her teeth, kissed again. He felt himself react, involuntarily; and felt her touch and squeeze.

She said, 'This is a silly dress. It gets in the way.' She reached behind her. The fabric parted; she pushed it down, to the waist. She said, 'Now, it's like last time.'

He said slowly, 'Nothing's ever like last time.'

She rolled across his lap, lay looking up. She whispered, 'I've put the clock back.'

Later in the dream she said, 'I was so silly.'

'What do you mean?'

She said, 'I was shy. That was all. You weren't really supposed to go away.'

He said, 'What about James?'

'He's got somebody else. I didn't know what I was missing.'

He let his hand stray over her; and present and immediate past became confused so that as he held her he still saw her kneeling, firelight dancing on her body. He reached for her and she was ready again; she fought, chuckling, taking it bareback, staying all the way.

Much later he said, 'The Minister gave me a Lamborghini.'

She rolled on to her belly, lay chin in hands watching under a tangle of hair. She said, 'And now you've got yourself a blonde. What are you going to do with us?'

He said, 'None of it's real.'

She said, '*Oh* . . .' She punched him. She said, 'Richard, you make me cross. It's happened, you idiot. That's all. It happens to everybody.' She scratched again with a finger on the carpet. She said, 'I hope you've made me pregnant. Then you'd have to marry me.'

He narrowed his eyes; and the wine began again, singing in his head.

She nuzzled him. She said, 'You asked me once. Say it again.'

'I don't remember.'

She said, 'Richard, please. . . .'

So he said, 'Diane, will you marry me?'

And she said, 'Yes, yes, yes.'

Then afterwards awareness came and though it wasn't possible he took her again and that time was finest of all, tight and sweet as honey. He'd fetched pillows from the bed and the counterpane. They curled close and he found himself talking, talking, how it wasn't the sex, it was shopping in Marlborough and having tea and seeing the sun set from White Horse Hill and being together, together; then she pressed fingers to his mouth and he fell with her in sleep past cold and loneliness and fear, past deserts and unlit places, down maybe to where spires reared gold and tree leaves moved and dazzled and white cars sang on roads and suns burned inwardly, lighting new worlds.

He woke, and the fire was low. He sat up, dazed. She was watching him. He stroked her hair a while, smiling; then she pushed away. She said, 'Richard I have to go now.'

'Not yet.'

'It's the middle of the night.'

He said, 'It doesn't matter.'

She said, 'It does. He mustn't know.'

'Who?'

She said, 'You know who. You know why I was asked here.'

He said, 'He's not like that. Honestly.'

She shivered. She said, 'Richard, please. Don't get me in trouble.' She smiled. She said, 'It's only till tomorrow. Only a little while.'

He stood, awkwardly, and held her, pressing her warmth close. Shoeless, she was tiny; her shoulder fitted beneath his armpit.

Halfway through dressing she stopped and laughed, leaned a hand against the wall. She said, 'I'm all woozy.'

Later he said, 'I'll see you to your room.'

She said, 'No, please. I'm all right. She was holding her handbag, and her hair was combed. She looked, again, as if she had been to a party.

At the door she turned. She said, 'I love you, Richard. Truly.' She kissed again, quickly; and was gone.

He closed the door, dropped the latch. He stood a while looking round the room. In the fire a burned-through log broke with a snap, sending up a little whirl of sparks. He walked to the washstand, bathed his face and hands. He shook the counterpane out on the bed, rearranged the pillows. Her scent still clung to him; he remembered how she had felt, and what she had said.

He crossed to the window, pushed it ajar. Outside, the snow lay in deep swaths and drifts. Starlight gleamed from it, ghost-white; and the whole great house was mute. He stood feeling the chill move against his skin; and in all the silence a voice drifted far-off and clear. It came maybe from the guardhouses, full of distance and peace.

> *'Stille Nacht, heilige Nacht,*
> *alles schläft, einsam wacht . . .'*

He walked to the bed, pulled back the covers. The sheets were crisp and spotless, fresh smelling. He smiled, and turned off the lamp.

> *'Nur das traute, hochheilige Paar.*
> *Holder Knabe mit lochigem Haar. . . .'*

In the wall of the room, an inch behind the plasterwork, a complex little machine hummed. A spool of delicate golden wire shook slightly; but the creak of the opening window had been the last thing to interest the recorder, the singing alone couldn't activate its relays. A micro-switch tripped, inaudibly; valve filaments faded, and died. Mainwaring lay back in the last of the fireight, and closed his eyes.

> *'Schlaf in himmlischer Ruh,*
> *'Schlaf in himmlischer Ruh. . . .'*

2

Beyond drawn curtains, brightness flicks on.

The sky is a hard, clear blue; icy, full of sunlight. The light dazzles back from the brilliant land. Far things—copses, hills, solitary trees—stand sharp-etched. Roofs and eaves carry hummocks of whiteness, twigs a three-inch crest. In the stillness, here and there, the snow cracks and falls, powdering.

The shadows of the riders jerk and undulate. The quiet is interrupted. Hooves ring on swept courtyards or stamp muffled, churning the snow. It seems the air itself has been rendered crystalline by cold; through it the voices break and shatter, brittle as glass.

'*Guten Morgen, Hans . . .*'

'*Verflucht Kalt!*'

'*Der Hundenmeister sagt, sehr gefahrlich!*'

'*Macht nichts! Wir erwischen es bevor dem Wald!*'

A rider plunges beneath an arch. The horse snorts and curvets.

'*Ich wette dir fünfzig amerikanische Dollar!*'

'*Einverstanden! Heute, habe ich Glück!*'

The noise, the jangling and stamping, rings back on itself. Cheeks flush, perception is heightened; for more than one of the riders, the early courtyard reels. Beside the house door trestles have been set up. A great bowl is carried, steaming. The cups are raised, the toasts given; the responses ring again, crashing.

'*The Two Empires . . .!*'

'*The Hunt . . .!*'

Now, time is like a tight-wound spring. The dogs plunge forward, six to a handler, leashes straining, choke links creaking and snapping. Behind them jostle the riders. The bobbing scarlet coats splash across the snow. In the house drive an officer salutes; another strikes gloved palms together, nods. The gates whine open.

he'd heard it vaguely, leaving and returning. He doubted if the affair would have held much appeal.

He strolled back to the TV lounge, watched for an hour or more. By lunchtime he was feeling vaguely piqued; and sensing too the rise of a curious unease. He went back to his room, wondering if by any chance she had gone there; but the miracle was not repeated. The room was empty.

The fire was burning, and the bed had been remade. He had forgotten the servants' passkeys. The Geissler copy still stood on the shelf. He took it down, stood weighing it in his hand and frowning. It was, in a sense, madness to leave it there.

He shrugged, put the thing back. He thought, 'So who reads bookshelves anyway?' The plot, if plot there had been, seemed absurd now in the clearer light of day. He stepped into the corridor, closed the door and locked it behind him. He tried as far as possible to put the book from his mind. It represented a problem; and problems, as yet, he wasn't prepared to cope with. Too much else was going on in his brain.

He lunched alone, now with a very definite pang; the process was disquietingly like that of other years. Once he thought he caught sight of her in the corridor. His heart thumped; but it was the other blonde, Müller's wife. The gestures, the fall of the hair, were similar; but this woman was taller.

He let himself drift into a reverie. Images of her, it seemed were engraved on his mind; each to be selected now, studied, placed lovingly aside. He saw the firelit texture of her hair and skin, her lashes brushing her cheek as she lay in his arms and slept. Other memories, sharper, more immediate still, throbbed like little shocks in the mind. She tossed her head, smiling; her hair swung, touched the point of a breast.

He pushed his cup away, rose. At fifteen hundred, patriotism required her presence in the TV lounge. As it required the presence of every other guest. Then, if not before, he would see her. He reflected, wryly, that he had waited half a lifetime for her; a little longer now would do no harm.

He took to prowling the house again: the Great Hall, the Long Gallery where the *Christkind* had walked. Below the windows that lined it was a snow-covered roof. The tart, reflected light struck upward, robbing the place of mystery. In the Great Hall they had already removed the tree. He watched household staff hanging draperies, carrying in stacks of gilded cane chairs. On the Minstrels' Gallery a pile of odd-shaped boxes proclaimed that the orchestra had arrived.

At fourteen hundred hours he walked back to the TV lounge. A quick glance assured him she wasn't there. The bar was open; Hans, looking as big and suave as ever, had been pressed into service to minister to the guests. He smiled at Mainwaring and said, 'Good afternoon, sir.' Mainwaring asked for a lager beer, took the glass to a corner seat. From here he could watch both the TV screen and the door.

The screen was showing the world-wide link-up that had become hallowed Christmas afternoon fare within the Two Empires. He saw, without particular interest, greetings flashed from the Leningrad and Moscow garrisons, a lightship, an Arctic weather station, a Mission in German East Africa. At fifteen hundred the Fuehrer was due to speak; this year, for the first time, Ziegler was preceding Edward VIII.

The room filled, slowly. She didn't come. Mainwaring finished the lager, walked to the bar, asked for another and a packet of cigarettes. The unease was sharpening now into something very like alarm. He thought for the first time that she might have been taken ill.

The time signal flashed, followed by the drumroll of the German anthem. He rose with the rest, stood stiffly till it had finished. The screen cleared, showed the familiar room in the Chancellery; the dark, high panels, the crimson drapes, the big *Hackenkreuz* emblem over the desk. The Fuehrer, as ever, spoke impeccably; but Mainwaring thought with a fragment of his mind how old he had begun to look.

The speech ended. He realized he hadn't heard a word that was said.

The drums crashed again. The King said, 'Once more, at Christmas, it is my . . . duty and pleasure . . . to speak to you.'

Something seemed to burst inside Mainwaring's head. He rose, walked quickly to the bar. He said, 'Hans, have you seen Miss Hunter?'

The other jerked round. He said, 'Sir *shh* . . . please . . .'

'*Have you seen her?*'

Hans stared at the screen, and back to Mainwaring. The King was saying. 'There have been . . . troubles, and difficulties. More perhaps lie ahead. But with . . . God's help, they will be overcome.'

The chauffeur licked his mouth. He said, 'I'm sorry, sir. I don't know what you mean.'

'Which was her room?'

The big man looked like something trapped. He said, 'Please, Mr. Mainwaring. You'll get me into trouble. . . .'

'*Which was her room?*'

Somebody turned and hissed, angrily. Hans said, 'I don't understand.'

'For God's sake, man, you carried her things upstairs. I saw you!'

Hans said, 'No, sir . . .'

Momentarily, the lounge seemed to spin.

There was a door behind the bar. The chauffeur stepped back. He said, 'Sir. Please . . .'

The place was a storeroom. There were wine bottles racked, a shelf with jars of olives, walnuts, eggs. Mainwaring closed the door behind him, tried to control the shaking. Hans said, 'Sir, you must not ask me these things. I don't know a Miss Hunter. I don't know what you mean.'

Mainwaring said, 'Which was her room? I demand that you answer.'

'I can't!'

'You drove me from London yesterday. Do you deny that?'

'No, sir.'

'You drove me with Miss Hunter.'

'No, sir!'

'*Damn your eyes, where is she?*'

The chauffeur was sweating. A long wait; then he said, 'Mr. Mainwaring, please. You must understand. I can't help you.' He swallowed, and drew himself up. He said, 'I drove you from London. I'm sorry. I drove you . . . *on your own.*'

The lounge door swung shut behind Mainwaring. He half-walked, half-ran to his room. He slammed the door behind him, leaned against it panting. In time the giddiness passed. He opened his eyes, slowly. The fire glowed; the Geissler stood on the bookshelf. Nothing was changed.

He set to work, methodically. He shifted furniture, peered behind it. He rolled the carpet back, tapped every foot of floor. He fetched a flashlight from his case and examined, minutely, the interior of the wardrobe. He ran his fingers lightly across the walls, section by section, tapping again. Finally he got a chair, dismantled the ceiling lighting fitting.

Nothing.

He began again. Halfway through the second search he froze, staring at the floorboards. He walked to his case, took the screwdriver from the pistol holster. A moment's work with the blade and he sat back, staring into his palm. He rubbed his face, placed his find carefully on the side table. A tiny ear-ring, one of the pair she had worn. He sat a while breathing heavily, his head in his hands.

The brief daylight had faded as he worked. He lit the standard lamp, wrenched the shade free, stood the naked bulb in the middle of the room. He worked round the walls again, peering, tapping, pressing. By the fireplace, finally, a foot-square section of plaster rang hollow.

He held the bulb close, examined the hairline crack. He inserted the screwdriver blade delicately, twisted. Then again. A click; and the section hinged open.

He reached inside the little space, shaking, lifted out the recorder. He stood silent a time, holding it; then raised his arms, brought the machine smashing down on the hearth. He stamped and kicked, panting, till the thing was reduced to fragments.

The droning rose to a roar, swept low over the house. The helicopter settled slowly, belly lamps glaring, downdraught raising a storm of snow. He walked to the window, stood staring. The children embarked, clutching scarves and gloves, suitcases, boxes with new toys. The steps were withdrawn, the hatch dogged shut. Snow swirled again; the machine lifted heavily, swung away in the direction of Wilton.

The Party was about to start.

Lights blaze, through the length and breadth of the house. Orange-lit windows throw long bars of brightness across the snow. Everywhere is an anxious coming and going, the pattering of feet, clink of silver and glassware, hurried commands. Waiters scuttle between the kitchens and the Green Room where dinner is laid. Dish after dish is borne in, paraded. Peacocks, roasted and gilded, vaunt their plumes in shadow and candleglow, spirit-soaked wicks blazing in their beaks. The Minister rises, laughing; toast after toast is drunk. To five thousand tanks, ten thousand fighting aeroplanes, a hundred thousand guns. The Two Empires feast their guests royally.

The climax approaches. The boar's head, garnished and smoking, is borne shoulder-high. His tusks gleam; clamped in his jaws is the golden sun-symbol, the orange. After him march the waifs and mummers, with their lanterns and begging-cups. The carol they chant is older by far than the Two Empires; older than the Reich, older than Great Britain.

'Alive he spoiled, where poor men toiled, which made kind Ceres sad . . .'

The din of voices rises. Coins are flung, glittering; wine is poured. And more wine, and more and more. Bowls of fruit are passed, and trays of sweets; spiced cakes, gingerbread, marzipans. Till at a signal the brandy is brought, and boxes of cigars.

The ladies rise to leave. They move flushed and chattering through the corridors of the house, uniformed link-boys grandly lighting their way. In the Great Hall their escorts are waiting. Each young man is tall, each blond, each impeccably uniformed. On the Minstrels' Gallery a baton is poised; across the lawns, distantly, floats the whirling excitement of a waltz.

In the Green Room, hazed now with smoke, the doors are once more flung wide. Servants scurry again, carrying in boxes, great gay-wrapped parcels topped with scarlet satin bows. The Minister rises, hammering on the table for quiet.

'My friends, good friends, friends of the Two Empires. For you, no expense is spared. For you, the choicest gifts. Tonight, nothing but the best is good enough; and nothing but the best is here. Friends, enjoy yourselves. Enjoy my house. *Frohe Weihnachten*. . . . !'

He walks quickly into shadow, and is gone. Behind him, silence falls. A waiting; and slowly, mysteriously, the great heap of gifts begins to stir. Paper splits, crackling. Here a hand emerges, here a foot. A breathless pause; and the first of the girls rises slowly, bare in flamelight, shakes her glinting hair.

The table roars again.

The sound reached Mainwaring dimly. He hesitated at the foot of the main staircase, moved on. He turned right and left, hurried down a flight of steps. He passed kitchens, and the servants' hall.

From the hall came the blare of a record player. He walked to the end of the corridor, unlatched a door. Night air blew keen against his face.

He crossed the courtyard, opened a further door. The space beyond was bright-lit; there was the faint, musty stink of animals. He paused, wiped his face. He was shirt-sleeved; but despite the cold he was sweating.

He walked forward again, steadily. To either side of the corridor were the fronts of cages. The dogs hurled themselves at the bars, thunderously. He ignored them.

The corridor opened into a square concrete chamber. To one side of the place was a ramp. At its foot was parked a windowless black van.

In the far wall a door showed a crack of light. He rapped sharply, and again.

'*Hundenmeister* . . .'

The door opened. The man who peered up at him was as wrinkled and pot-bellied as a Nast Santa Claus. At sight of his visitor's face he tried to duck back; but Mainwaring had him by the arm. He said, '*Herr Hundenmeister*, I must talk to you.'

'Who are you? I don't know you. What do you want? . . .'

Mainwaring showed his teeth. He said, 'The van. You drove the van this morning. What was in it?'

'I don't know what you mean . . .'

The heave sent him stumbling across the floor. He tried to bolt; but Mainwaring grabbed him again.

'What was in it . . .?'

'I won't talk to you! Go away!'

The blow exploded across his cheek. Mainwaring hit him again, backhanded, slammed him against the van.

'Open it . . . !'

The voice rang sharply in the confined space.

'*Wer ist da? Was ist passiert?*'

The little man whimpered, rubbing at his mouth.

Mainwaring straightened, breathing heavily. The GFP captain walked forward, staring, thumbs hooked in his belt.

'*Wer sind Sie?*'

Mainwaring said, 'You know damn well. And speak English, you bastard. You're as English as I am.'

The other glared. He said, 'You have no right to be here. I should arrest you. You have no right to accost *Herr Hundenmeister*.'

'What is in that van?'

'Have you gone mad? The van is not your concern. Leave now. At once.'

'Open it!'

The other hesitated, and shrugged. He stepped back. He said, 'Show him, *mein Herr.*'

The *Hundenmeister* fumbled with a bunch of keys. The van doors grated. Mainwaring walked forward, slowly.

The vehicle was empty.

The captain said, 'You have seen what you wished to see. You are satisfied. Now go.'

Mainwaring stared round. There was a further door, recessed deeply into the wall. Beside it controls like the controls of a bank vault.

'What is in that room?'

The GFP man said, 'You have gone too far. I order you to leave.'

'You have no authority over me!'

'Return to your quarters!'

Mainwaring said, 'I refuse.'

The other slapped the holster at his hip, He gut-held the Walther, wrist locked, feet apart. He said, 'Then you will be shot.'

Mainwaring walked past him, contemptuously. The baying of the dogs faded as he slammed the outer door.

It was among the middle classes that the seeds had first been sown; and it was among the middle classes that they flourished. Britain had been called often enough a nation of shopkeepers; now for a little while the tills were closed, the blinds left drawn. Overnight it seemed, an effete symbol of social and national disunity became the Einsatzgruppenfuehrer; *and the wire for the first detention camps was strung. . . .*

Mainwaring finished the page, tore it from the spine, crumpled it and dropped it on the fire. He went on reading. Beside him on the hearth stood a part-full bottle of whisky and a glass. He picked the glass up mechanically, drank. He lit a cigarette. A few minutes later a new page followed the last.

The clock ticked steadily. The burning paper made a little rustling. Reflections danced across the ceiling of the room. Once Mainwaring raised his head, listened; once put the ruined book down, rubbed his eyes. The room, and the corridor outside, stayed quiet.

Against immeasurable force, we must pit cunning; against immeasurable evil, faith and a high resolve. In the war we wage, the stakes are high: the dignity of man, the freedom of the spirit, the survival of humanity. Already in that war, many of us have died; many more, undoubtedly, will lay down their lives. But always, beyond them, there will be others; and still more. We shall go on, as we must go on; till this thing is wiped from the earth.

Meanwhile, we must take fresh heart. Every blow, now, is a blow for freedom. In France, Belgium, Finland, Poland, Russia, the forces of the Two Empires confront each other uneasily. Greed, jealousy, mutual distrust; these are the enemies, and they work from within. This, the Empires know full well. And, knowing, for the first time in their existence, fear. . . .

The last page crumpled, fell to ash. Mainwaring sat back, staring at nothing. Finally he stirred, looked up. It was zero three hundred; and they hadn't come for him yet.

The bottle was finished. He set it to one side, opened another. He swilled the liquid in the glass, hearing the magnified ticking of the clock.

He crossed the room, took the Lüger from the case. He found a cleaning rod, patches and oil. He sat a while dully, looking at the pistol. Then he slipped the magazine free, pulled back on the breech toggle, thumbed the latch, slid the barrel from the guides.

His mind, wearied, had begun to play aggravating tricks. It ranged and wandered, remembering scenes, episodes, details sometimes from years back; trivial, unconnected. Through and between the wanderings, time after time, ran the ancient, lugubrious words of the carol. He tried to shut them out, but it was impossible.

'*Living he spoiled where poor men toiled, which made kind Ceres sad . . .*'

He pushed the link pin clear, withdrew the breech block, stripped the firing pin. He laid the parts out, washed them with oil and water, dried and reoiled. He reassembled the pistol, working carefully; inverted the barrel, shook the link down in front of the hooks, closed the latch, checked the recoil spring engagement. He loaded a full clip, pushed it home, chambered a round, thumbed the safety to

Gesichert. He released the clip, reloaded.

He fetched his briefcase, laid the pistol inside carefully, grip uppermost. He filled a spare clip, added the extension butt and a fifty box of Parabellum. He closed the flap and locked it, set the case beside the bed. After that there was nothing more to do. He sat back in the chair, refilled his glass.

'*Toiling he boiled, where poor men spoiled . . .*'

The firelight faded, finally.

He woke, and the room was dark. He got up, felt the floor sway a little. He understood that he had a hangover. He groped for the light switch. The clock hands stood at zero eight hundred.

He felt vaguely guilty at having slept so long.

He walked to the bathroom. He stripped and showered, running the water as hot as he could bear. The process brought him round a little. He dried himself, staring down. He thought for the first time what curious things these bodies

He dressed and shaved. He had remembered what he was going to do; fastening his tie, he tried to remember why. He couldn't. His brain, it seemed, had gone dead.

There was an inch of whisky in the bottle. He poured it, grimaced and drank. Inside him was a fast, cold shaking. He thought, 'Like the first morning at a new school.'

He lit a cigarette. Instantly his throat filled. He walked to the bathroom and vomited. Then again. Finally there was nothing left to come.

His chest ached. He rinsed his mouth, washed his face again. He sat in the bedroom for a while, head back and eyes closed. In time the shaking went away. He lay unthinking, hearing the clock tick. Once his lips moved. He said, 'They're no better than us.'

At nine hundred hours he walked to the breakfast room. His stomach, he felt, would retain very little. He ate a slice of toast, carefully, drank some coffee. He asked for a pack of cigarettes, went back to his room. At ten hundred hours he was due to meet the Minister.

He checked the briefcase again, A thought made him add a pair of stringback motoring gloves. He sat again, stared at the ashes where he had burned the Geissler. A part of him was willing the clock hands not to move. At five to ten he picked the briefcase up, stepped into the corridor. He stood a moment staring round him. He thought, 'It hasn't happened yet. I'm still alive.' There was still the flat in Town to go back to, still his office; the tall windows, the telephones, the khaki utility desk.

He walked through sunlit corridors to the Minister's suite.

The room to which he was admitted was wide and long. A fire crackled in the hearth; beside it on a low table stood glasses and a decanter. Over the mantel, conventionally, hung the Fuehrer's portrait. Edward VIII faced him across the room. Tall windows framed a prospect of rolling parkland. In the distance, blue on the horizon, were the woods.

The Minister said, 'Good morning, Richard. Please sit down. I don't think I shall keep you long.'

He sat, placing the briefcase by his knee.

This morning everything seemed strange. He studied the Minister curiously, as if seeing him for the first time. He had that type of face once thought of as peculiarly English: shortnosed and slender, with high, finely shaped cheekbones. The hair, blond and cropped close to the scalp, made him look nearly boyish. The eyes were candid, flat, dark-fringed. He looked, Mainwaring decided, not so much Aryan as like some fierce nursery toy; a feral Teddy Bear.

The Minister riffled papers. He said, 'Several things have cropped up; among them, I'm afraid, more trouble in Glasgow. The fifty-first Panzer division is standing by; as yet, the news hasn't been released.'

Mainwaring wished his head felt less hollow. It made his own voice boom so unnecessarily. He said, 'Where is Miss Hunter?'

The Minister paused. The pale eyes stared; then he went on speaking.

'I'm afraid I may have to ask you to cut short your stay here. I shall be flying back to London for a meeting; possibly tomorrow, possibly the day after. I shall want you with me, of course.'

'Where is Miss Hunter?'

The Minister placed his hands flat on the desktop, studied the nails. He said, 'Richard, there are aspects of Two Empires culture that are neither mentioned nor discussed. You of all people should know this. I'm being patient with you; but there are limits to what I can overlook.'

'*Seldom he toiled, while Ceres rolled, which made poor kind men glad . . .*'

Mainwaring opened the flap of the case and stood up. He thumbed the safety forward and levelled the pistol.

There was silence for a time. The fire spat softly. Then the Minister smiled. He said, 'That's an interesting gun, Richard. Where did you get it?'

Mainwaring didn't answer.

The Minister moved his hands carefully to the arms of his chair, leaned back. He said, 'It's the Marine model, of course. It's also quite old. Does it by any chance carry the Erfurt stamp? Its value would be considerably increased.'

He smiled again. He said, 'If the barrel is good, I'll buy it. For my private collection.'

Mainwaring's arm began to shake. He steadied his wrist, gripping with his left hand.

The Minister sighed. He said, 'Richard, you can be so stubborn. It's a good quality; but you do carry it to excess.' He shook his head. He said, 'Did you imagine for one moment I didn't know you were coming here to kill me? My dear chap, you've been through a great deal. You're overwrought. Believe me, I know just how you feel.'

Mainwaring said, 'You murdered her.'

The Minister spread his hands. He said, 'What with? A gun? A knife? Do I honestly look such a shady character?'

The words made a cold pain, and a tightness in the chest. But they had to be said.

The Minister's brows rose. Then he started to laugh. Finally he said, 'At last I see. I understood, but I couldn't believe. So you bullied our poor little *Hundenmeister*, which wasn't very worthy; and seriously annoyed the *Herr Hauptmann*, which wasn't very wise. Because of this fantasy, stuck in your head. Do you really believe it, Richard? Perhaps you believe in *Struvwelpeter* too.' He sat forward. He said, 'The Hunt ran. And killed . . . a deer. She gave us an excellent chase. As for your little Huntress . . . Richard, she's gone. She never existed. She was a figment of your imagination. Best forgotten.'

Mainwaring said, 'We were in love.'

The Minister said, 'Richard, you really are becoming tiresome.' He shook his head again. He said, 'We're both adult. We both know what that word is worth. It's a straw, in the wind. A candle, on a night of gales. A phrase that is meaningless. *Lächerlich*.' He put his hands together, rubbed a palm. He said, 'When this is over, I want you to go away. For a month, six weeks maybe. With your new car. When you come back . . . well, we'll see. Buy yourself a girl friend, if you need a woman that much. *Einen Schatz*. I never dreamed; you're so remote, you should speak more of yourself. Richard, I understand; it isn't such a very terrible thing.'

Mainwaring stared.

The Minister said, 'We shall make an arrangement. You will have the use of an apartment, rather a nice apartment. So your lady will be close. When you tire of her . . . buy another. They're unsatisfactory for the most part, but reasonable. Now sit down like a good chap, and put your gun away. You look so silly, standing there scowling like that.'

It seemed he felt all life, all experience, as a grey weight pulling. He lowered the pistol, slowly. He thought, 'At the end, they were wrong. They picked the wrong man.' He said, 'I suppose now I use it on myself.'

The Minister said, 'No, no, no. You still don't understand.' He linked his knuckles, grinning. He said, 'Richard, the *Herr Hauptmann* would have arrested you last night. I wouldn't let him. This is between ourselves. Nobody else. I give you my word.'

Mainwaring felt his shoulders sag. The strength seemed drained from him; the pistol, now, weighed too heavy for his arm.

The Minister said, 'Richard, why so glum? It's a great occasion, man, You're found your courage. I'm delighted.'

He lowered his voice. He said, 'Don't you want to know why I let you come here with your machine? Aren't you even interested?'

Mainwaring stayed silent.

The Minister said, 'Look around you, Richard. See the world. I want men near me, serving me. Now more than ever. Real men, not afraid to die. Give me a dozen . . . but you know the rest. I could rule the world. But first . . . I must rule them. My men. Do you see now? Do you understand?'

Mainwaring thought, 'He's in control again. But he was always in control. He owns me.'

The study spun a little.

The voice went on, smoothly. 'As for this amusing little plot by the so-called Freedom Front; again, you did well. It was difficult for you. I was watching; believe me, with much sympathy. Now, you've burned your book. Of your own free will. That delighted me.'

Mainwaring looked up, sharply.

The Minister shook his head. He said, 'The real recorder is rather better hidden, you were too easily satisfied there. There's also a TV monitor. I'm sorry about it all, I apologize. It was necessary.'

A singing started inside Mainwaring's head.

The Minister sighed again. He said, 'Still unconvinced, Richard? Then I have some things I think you ought to see. Am I permitted to open my desk drawer?'

Mainwaring didn't speak. The other slid the drawer back slowly, reached in. He laid a telegram flimsy on the desk top. He said, 'The addressee is Miss D. J. Hunter. The message consists of one word. '*Activate*.'

The singing rose in pitch.

'This is well,' said the Minister. He held up a medallion on a thin gold chain. The little disc bore the linked motif of the Freedom Front. He said, 'Mere exhibitionism; or a deathwish. Either way, a most undesirable trait.'

He tossed the thing down. He said, 'She was here under surveillance, of course, we'd known about her for years. To them, you were a sleeper. Do you see the absurdity? They really thought you would be jealous enough to assassinate your Minister. This they mean in their silly little book, when they talk of subtlety. Richard, I could have fifty blonde women if I chose. A hundred. Why should I want yours?' He shut the drawer with a click, and rose. He said, 'Give me the gun now. You don't need it any more.' He extended his arm; then he was flung heavily backward. Glasses smashed on the side table. The decanter split; its contents poured dark across the wood.

Over the desk hung a faint haze of blue. Mainwaring walked forward, stood looking down. There were blood-flecks, and a little flesh. The eyes of the Teddy Bear still showed glints of white. Hydraulic shock had shattered the chest; the breath drew ragged, three times, and stopped. He thought, 'I didn't hear the report.'

The communicating door opened. Mainwaring turned. A secretary stared in, bolted at sight of him. The door slammed.

He pushed the briefcase under his arm, ran through the outer office. Feet clattered in the corridor. He opened the door, carefully.

Shouts sounded, somewhere below in the house.

Across the corridor hung a loop of crimson cord. He stopped over it, hurried up a flight of stairs. Then another. Beyond the private apartments the way was closed by a heavy metal grille. He ran to it, rattled. A rumbling sounded from below. He glared round. Somebody had operated the emergency shutters; the house was sealed.

Beside the door an iron ladder was spiked to the wall. He climbed it, panting. The trap in the ceiling was padlocked. He clung one-handed, awkward with the briefcase, held the pistol above his head.

Daylight showed through splintered wood. He put his shoulder to the trap, heaved. It creaked back. He pushed head and shoulders through, scrambled. Wind stung at him, and flakes of snow.

His shirt was wet under the arms. He lay face down, shaking. He thought, 'It wasn't an accident. None of it was an accident.' He had underrated them. They understood despair.

He pushed himself up, stared round. He was on the roof of Wilton. Beside him rose gigantic chimney stacks. There was a lattice radio mast. The wind hummed in its guy wires. To his right ran the balustrade that crowned the facade of the house. Behind it was a snow-choked gutter.

He wriggled across a sloping scree of roof, ran crouching. Shouts sounded from below. He dropped flat, rolled. An automatic clattered. He edged forward again, dragging the briefcase. Ahead, one of the corner towers rose dark against the sky. He crawled to it, crouched sheltered from the wind. He opened the case, pulled the gloves on. He clipped the stock to the pistol, laid the spare magazine beside him and the box of rounds.

The shots came again. He peered forward, through the balustrade. Running figures scattered across the lawn. He sighted on the nearest, squeezed. Commotion below. The automatic zipped; stone chips flew, whining. A voice called, 'Don't expose yourselves unnecessarily.' Another answered.

'*Die kommen mit den Hubschrauber . . .*'

He stared round him, at the yellow-grey horizon. He had forgotten the helicopter.

A snow flurry drove against his face. He huddled, flinching. He thought he heard, carried on the wind, a faint droning.

From where he crouched he could see the nearer trees of the park, beyond them the wall and gatehouses. Beyond again, the land rose to the circling woods.

The droning was back, louder than before. He screwed his eyes, made out the dark spot skimming above the trees. He shook his head. He said, 'We made a mistake. We all made a mistake.'

He settled the stock of the Lüger to his shoulder, and waited.

YOU'LL ENJOY THESE
SCIENCE FICTION FAVORITES
FROM BERKLEY

ALPHA 6
ed. by Robert Silverberg
(03048-2—$1.50)

BARNARD'S PLANET
by John Boyd
(03239-6—$1.25)

THE BEST FROM ORBIT 1-10
ed. by Damon Knight
(03161-6—$1.95)

THE CHALK GIANTS
by Keith Roberts
(03115-2—$1.25)

CLARION SF
ed. by Kate Wilhelm
(03293-0—$1.25)

COLOSSUS
by D.F. Jones
(03229-9—$1.25)

THE COMPUTER CONNECTION
by Alfred Bester
(03039-3—$1.50)

DAMNATION ALLEY
by Roger Zelazny
(03123-3—$1.25)

Send for a *free* list of all our books in print

These books are available at your local bookstore, or send
price indicated plus 30^e per copy to cover mailing costs to
Berkley Publishing Corporation
390 Murray Hill Parkway
East Rutherford, New Jersey 07073

MORE EXCITING S.F. FROM BERKLEY